ELFSLAYER

WHILE TRAVELLING TO Marienburg to fulfil his dying father's last request, Felix Jaeger and the Dwarf Trollslayer Gotrek run into their old acquaintance Max Schreiber and his beautiful travelling companion, the seeress Claudia Pallenberger. The two Imperial wizards have been sent to investigate disturbing portents off the north coast of the Empire and ask Gotrek and Felix to join them. Together the four companions set sail for the Sea of Claws, where they discover a terrifying plot that threatens the Empire and beyond.

Can Gotrek & Felix fight their way through a black ark swarming with dark elves in time to stop a coven of sorceresses from unleashing a spell that could pull the very world itself apart?

More Gotrek & Felix from the Black Library

GOTREK & FELIX: THE FIRST OMNIBUS
by William King
(Contains books 1-3: *Trollslayer, Skavenslayer & Daemonslayer*)

GOTREK & FELIX: THE SECOND OMNIBUS
by William King
(Contains books 4-6: *Dragonslayer, Beastslayer &
Vampireslayer*)

Book 7 – GIANTSLAYER
by William King

Book 8 – ORCSLAYER
by Nathan Long

Book 9 – MANSLAYER
by Nathan Long

More Nathan Long from the Black Library
BLACKHEARTS: THE OMNIBUS

(Contains the novels *Valnir's Bane, The Broken Lance &
Tainted Blood*)

A WARHAMMER NOVEL

Gotrek and Felix

ELFSLAYER

Nathan Long

For Channing, my dark elf nemesis. One day I will defeat you.
Thanks to Mike Lee and Rob Clark for the lore.

A BLACK LIBRARY PUBLICATION

First published in Great Britain in 2008 by
BL Publishing,
Games Workshop Ltd.,
Willow Road, Nottingham,
NG7 2WS, UK

10 9 8 7 6 5 4 3 2 1

Cover illustration by Geoff Taylor
Map by Nuala Kinrade.

A CIP record for this book is available from the British Library.

ISBN 13: 978 1 84416 575 9
ISBN 10: 1 84416 575 2

Distributed in the US by Simon & Schuster
1230 Avenue of the Americas, New York, NY 10020.

See the Black Library on the Internet at
www.blacklibrary.com

Find out more about Games Workshop
and the world of Warhammer at
www.games-workshop.com

Printed and bound in the US.

THIS IS A DARK age, a bloody age, an age of daemons
and of sorcery. It is an age of battle and death, and of the
world's ending. Amidst all of the fire, flame and fury
it is a time, too, of mighty heroes, of bold deeds
and great courage.

AT THE HEART of the Old World sprawls the Empire, the
largest and most powerful of the human realms. Known
for its engineers, sorcerers, traders and soldiers, it is
a land of great mountains, mighty rivers, dark forests
and vast cities. And from his throne in Altdorf reigns
the Emperor Karl-Franz, sacred descendant of the
founder of these lands, Sigmar, and wielder
of his magical warhammer.

BUT THESE ARE far from civilised times. Across the
length and breadth of the Old World, from the knightly
palaces of Bretonnia to ice-bound Kislev in the far north,
come rumblings of war. In the towering Worlds Edge
Mountains, the orc tribes are gathering for another assault.
Bandits and renegades harry the wild southern lands of
the Border Princes. There are rumours of rat-things, the
skaven, emerging from the sewers and swamps across the
land. And from the northern wildernesses there is the
ever-present threat of Chaos, of daemons and beastmen
corrupted by the foul powers of the Dark Gods.
As the time of battle draws ever nearer,
the Empire needs heroes
like never before.

'And so, for the first time since that long ago night when I made my vow to the Slayer, I returned to the city of my birth, to find neither the welcome I had hoped for, nor that which I had feared, but a reality more strange and terrible than either.

'Our failure to reach Middenheim in time to take part in its defence precipitated the Slayer into the most prolonged despondency of our acquaintance. Indeed, I feared for a time that he might never recover from it. But then a chance meeting with an old ally drew us into one of the maddest, most desperate adventures we ever shared, and the Slayer's spirits revived, though it seemed on many occasions during those days that we might pay for his recovery with our lives.'

– From *My Travels With Gotrek*, Vol VII,
by Herr Felix Jaeger (Altdorf Press, 2528)

ONE

Felix Jaeger looked at himself in the gilt-framed mirror in the grand entry hall of his father's Altdorf mansion as he smoothed his new grey doublet and fixed the collar of his shirt for the tenth time. The deep gash in his forehead that he had received when the *Spirit of Grungni* exploded was now just a curving pink scar above his left eyebrow. The other smaller cuts and scrapes were gone entirely. The physicians who were caring for him were astonished. Less than two months had passed since the crash, and he was fully recovered. The sprains in both ankles from hitting the ground while wearing Makaisson's 'reliable' no longer hurt. The headaches and the double vision had cleared up. Even the multitude of burns had left no marks, and the cultist's sword cut that had opened him to the ribs under his left arm was no more than a fading line.

He sighed. It was of course a very good thing to be fit and healthy again, but it also meant he'd had no more excuses not to visit his father.

There was a discreet cough from behind him. He turned. His father's butler stood on the marble stair that led to the upper floors.

'He'll see you now.'

Right, thought Felix, this is it. Can't be worse than facing down a daemon, can it?

He swallowed, then started up the stairs after the butler.

GUSTAV JAEGER WAS a shrivelled manikin drowning in a sea of white bedclothes. His withered hands lay still and pink on the top of an eiderdown quilt. A gaudy gold ring, set with sapphires surrounding the letter 'J' picked out in rubies, hung loose on one shrunken finger. His face sagged from his bones like wet laundry on a line. He looked like he was already dead. Felix barely recognised him as the man he still thought of as towering over him. Only his eyes were as he remembered – alive and angry, and capable of turning Felix's insides to water with a single steel-blue glance.

'Forty-two years,' came a voice like steam. 'Forty-two years and nothing to show for it. Pathetic.'

'I've travelled the world, Father,' said Felix. 'I've written books. I…'

'I've read 'em,' snapped his father. 'Or tried to. Rubbish. The lot of them. Didn't make a crown, I'll warrant.'

'Actually, Otto says…'

'Have you any savings? Any property? A wife? Children?'

'Uh…'

'I thought not. Thank the gods Otto's pupped. There'd be no one left to carry on the Jaeger name if I'd left it to you.' Gustav lifted his feeble head from the pillow and fixed Felix with an acid glare. 'I suppose you've come back to beg for your inheritance.'

Felix was offended. He hadn't come for money. He had come to make peace. 'No, Father. I…'

'Well, you will beg in vain,' the old man sneered. 'Wasting all the advantages I offered you – the education, the position in the family business, the money I earned by the sweat of my brow, all to become a *poet*.' He spat the word out like another man might say 'orc' or 'mutant'. 'Tell me when a poet has ever done anything useful in the world!'

'Well, the great Detlef…'

'*Don't* tell me, you idiot! You think I want to hear your milk-sop prattle?'

'Father, don't excite yourself,' said Felix, alarmed as he saw Gustav's pink face turning a blotchy red. 'You're not well. Shall I fetch your nurse?'

His father sank back onto his pillow, his breath coming in whistling wheezes. 'Keep that… fat poisoner… away from me.' He turned his head and looked at Felix again. His eyes looked clouded now – troubled. One of his claws beckoned Felix closer. 'Come here.'

Felix shifted forwards on his chair, heart thudding. 'Yes, Father?' Perhaps his father was finally going to soften. Perhaps they would heal the old wounds at last. Perhaps he was going to tell him that in his heart of hearts he had actually always loved him.

'There is… one way you may regain my favour and… your inheritance.'

'But, I don't want an inheritance. I only want your–'

'Don't interrupt, damn you! Did they teach you nothing at university?'

'Sorry, Father.'

Gustav lay back and looked up at the ceiling. He was silent and still for so long that Felix began to be afraid he had died then and there – and with his words of reconciliation unspoken and Felix to blame for interrupting.

'I...' said Gustav, his voice almost inaudible.

Felix leaned forwards eagerly. 'Yes, father?'

'I am in danger of losing Jaeger and Sons... to a villainous pirate by the name of Hans Euler.'

Felix blinked. Those were not the words he expected. 'Losing...? Who is this man? How did this happen?'

'His father Ulfgang was an old associate of mine, an honourable man of Marienburg who dealt in... er, tariff-free merchandise.'

'A smuggler.'

'Call him what you will – he always dealt fairly with me.' Gustav's face darkened. 'His son, however, is another matter. Ulfgang died last year, and Hans, the black-hearted little extortionist, has come into possession of a private letter I wrote to his father thirty years ago which he claims proves I imported contraband into the Empire and avoided Imperial tariffs. He says he will show the letter to the Emperor and the board of the Altdorf Merchants' Guild if I do not give him a controlling interest in Jaeger and Sons before the end of next month.'

Felix frowned. '*Did* you import contraband and avoid Imperial tariffs?'

'Eh? Of course I did. Everybody does. How do you think I paid for your wasted education, boy?'

'Ah.' Felix was quietly shocked. He had always known that his father was a ruthless man of business, but he hadn't realised he had actually broken the law. 'And what will happen if this Euler brings the letter to the authorities?'

Gustav began to turn red again. 'Are you a lawyer suddenly? Are you weighing the merits of my case? I'm your father, damn your eyes! It should be enough that I ask.'

'I was only…'

'The Guild will blackball me and the Imperial Fisc will seize my assets, is what will happen,' said Gustav. 'That corrupt old bitch Hochsvoll will take away my charter and give it to one of her cronies. It will mean prison for me, and no inheritance for Otto, or for you. Is that enough to move your pity?'

Felix flushed. 'I didn't mean…'

'Euler awaits my answer at his house in Marienburg,' continued the old man, lying back again. 'I want you to go there and recover the letter from him, by any means that you see fit. Bring it to me and you shall have your inheritance. Otherwise you can die in poverty as you deserve.'

Felix frowned. He wasn't sure what he had expected from this meeting, but this wasn't it. 'You want me to rob him?'

'I don't want to know how you do it! Just do it!'

'But…'

'What is the difficulty?' rasped Gustav. 'I read your books. You go about the world, killing all and sundry and taking their treasure. Will you baulk to do the same for your father?'

Felix hesitated to answer. Why should he do this? He didn't want his inheritance, he didn't care enough for his brother Otto to be concerned that he wouldn't get his, and he doubted that his father would live long enough to serve any time in prison. He certainly didn't feel he owed the old man anything. Gustav had cast him out without a pfennig twenty years ago and hadn't asked after him since, and he had been a harsh, uncaring father before that. There had been numerous times over the years when Felix had hoped that the old man would choke on his morning porridge and die, and yet...

And yet, hadn't Felix come here to put an end to the old anger? Hadn't he wanted to tell his father that he at last understood that, in his way, he had tried? Gustav might have scolded his sons unmercifully, and held them to impossibly high standards, but he had also given them a childhood free from want, paid for the best schools and tutors, spent untold amounts of money trying to buy them titles, and offered them positions in his thriving business. He might not have been able to express himself except with curses and slaps and insults, but he had wanted his sons to have good lives – and Felix had come to thank him for that, and to put the past behind them. How, then, could he refuse what might well be his father's last request?

He couldn't.

Felix sighed and lowered his head. 'Very well, Father. I will get the letter back.'

So ANXIOUS HAD Felix been before meeting his father that he had looked neither left nor right on the way to his house, but now, as he walked back towards the Griffon, clutching his cloak about him in the chill of a late autumn morning, his eyes roamed hither and thither and the crowded Altdorf streets became streets of memory.

There on the right, with the green wall of the Jade College looming behind them, were the apartments of Herr Klampfert, the tutor who had taught him his alphabet and his history and who had smelled strongly of rose-water. There was the house of Mara Gosthoff who, at the tender age of fourteen, had let him kiss her at a Sonnstill Day dance. Off to the west, as he turned and pushed south down the bustling Austauschstrasse, he could just see the towers of the University of Altdorf, where he had studied literature and poetry and had fallen in with the young rabble-rousers who had preached abolishment of the ruling classes and equality for all.

The further he walked, the faster the memories came, rushing towards the moment when his life had changed forever and there had been no going back. Just down that street was the courtyard where he had fought his duel with Krassner and killed him when he had only meant to wound. Now he was entering the Konigsplatz, where he and his fellow agitators had lit their bonfires and led the crowds in their grand protest against the injustice of the Window Tax. There was the statue of Emperor Wilhelm that Gotrek had dragged him behind when the Reiksguard cavalry had charged the protesters, slashing indiscriminately with their swords. Those were the cobbles on which half a dozen lancers had died by Gotrek's axe, their blood soaking into the filth and black ash of the bonfires. And here, just before the Reiksbruck bridge, was the tiny alley that led to the tavern where he and Gotrek had got blind drunk together, and where, in the wee hours of the morning, Felix had pledged to follow the Slayer and record in an epic poem his great quest to die in battle.

He stopped in the mouth of the alley, staring into its shadowed depths as a stew of conflicting emotions bubbled up inside him. Part of him wished he could walk down it and back into time to tap his younger self on the shoulder and tell him not to make the pledge. Another part of him imagined the life he would have had had he not made it – a life of marriage and property, and responsibility – and thought he should stay right where he was.

He shook himself and continued on. It was very strange to be back in Altdorf. It was full of ghosts.

* * *

FELIX PAUSED AND looked up as he reached the low-lintelled door of the Griffon, a faint scrabbling sound drawing his attention towards the roof, four storeys above. He saw nothing but closed shutters and birds' nests. Pigeons fighting under the eaves, no doubt. He went in.

A few late risers still lingered over their breakfasts in the inn's warm, flagstoned taproom. He nodded to Irmele, who was clearing away plates and cups, and saluted Rudgar, the landlord, who was rolling a fresh keg of Mootland ale into place behind the bar.

'Has he come down?' Felix asked.

Rudgar nodded towards the back of the room. 'He never went up. Kept Janse up all night, filling and refilling his stein. He was there when you left this morning. You didn't see him?'

Felix shook his head. He had been too preoccupied with his visit to his father to notice anything on his way out. Now he peered into the shadows at the far end of the taproom. Half hidden in a nook behind the inn's enormous fireplace was Gotrek, slumped unmoving in a low chair, his bearded chin on his chest and a stein of ale held loose in one massive hand. Felix shook his head. The Slayer looked terrible.

It wasn't Gotrek's wounds that gave Felix pause. For the most part they were gone – healing as they always did – cleanly and completely. Except for the bulky cast on his right arm, he was good as new. What concerned Felix was that the Slayer had stopped taking care of himself. The roots of his crest showed an inch of brown where he hadn't bothered to dye them. Patchy stubble furred his scalp, obscuring his faded blue tattoos, and his face looked bloated and slack. There was dried food in his beard and the once-white plaster of the cast was grimed with filth and stained with beer. His single eye stared half closed at the wall in front of him. Felix couldn't tell if he was awake or asleep. He grimaced. This was becoming an all too common occurrence.

'Has he paid you?'

'Oh aye,' said Rudgar. 'Gave us one of his gold bracelets. He's paid up 'til Sigmar comes back.'

Felix frowned. That was bad. Gotrek had no vault to carry the treasure he had amassed during their adventures, so he wore it on his wrists. The golden bracelets and bands that circled his powerful forearms were as precious to him as the hoard of any dwarf king. He parted with them only in the direst emergencies. Felix had known him to go hungry for weeks rather than use one to buy food. Now he had paid his drinks bill with one.

The Slayer would never have done that in the past. But these days the Slayer was as morose as Felix had ever seen him, and had been since they had come to Altdorf after the destruction of the *Spirit of Grungni* – since they had missed the siege of Middenheim.

IT HAD BEEN the strangest waking in a life of strange wakings, that day when Felix had opened his eyes after falling from the sky. At first he could see nothing but white, and he wondered if he was lying in a cloud, or had died and gone to some strange world of mist. Then a trio of Malakai's students had pulled the silk canopy of Malakai's 'air catcher' off him and crowded above him, their heads silhouetted against a crimson sunset sky as they checked him for broken bones.

Things remained strange when they sat him up, for he found that he was in the middle of some farmer's field with the massive shapes of the corrupted cannons that Magus Lichtmann had hoped to bring to Middenheim jutting up at odd angles from the furrows all around him, like the iron menhirs of some long-forgotten cult. In an adjacent field, the smoking remains of the gondola of the *Spirit of Grungni* lay half-buried, a shattered metal leviathan seemingly about to dive beneath a sea of earth.

Then, to his left, the strangest sight of all – Gotrek, high up in a tree, dangling from the silk cords of his air catcher as more of Malakai's students climbed the branches to cut him down.

Malakai himself was by a split-rail fence, trying to convince a group of pitchfork-wielding farmers that he and his companions weren't daemons or northmen or orcs, and not having much luck.

When all had been sorted out, the crew of the *Grungni* discovered that they had crashed in the heart of the Reikland, not far north of Altdorf. With no fit cannons or supplies to bring to the front, there was no more reason for them to continue on to Middenheim, and something had to be done with the tainted guns. The evil things couldn't be left where they were. Their influence would corrupt the land and the people for miles around. Malakai decided he must take them back to Nuln in order to find a way to dispose of them safely. He hired carts to take them back, and another to take Gotrek and Felix to Altdorf, as their wounds were too severe for them to make the long journey all the way back to Nuln.

Though Gotrek protested mightily that he would go on to Middenheim broken arm or no, in the end, even he admitted that he wouldn't be much use in a fight with a bone sticking out through his skin. So, two of Malakai's students escorted him and Felix to the capital and used Gunnery School funds to pay for their lodgings and for the care of proper physicians. Malakai had said it was the least the school could do for them after they had stopped the cursed cannons from reaching Middenheim and possibly bringing about the downfall of the Empire. 'And it would ha' been the school's fault, an' mine, had it happened,' the engineer had said morosely, 'Fer nae seeing that the puir wee things had been cursed in the first place. I'd ha' shaved my heid all over again.'

And so, for the last two months, Gotrek and Felix had stewed in Altdorf, waiting for their wounds to heal, with nothing to do but sit in the taproom of the Griffon. The enforced inaction wouldn't have been so bad except that, ten days after they arrived, news had come from the north that Archaon had retreated from Middenheim and the siege was lifted.

The war was over.

Gotrek hadn't stopped drinking since.

Felix couldn't blame him, really. From the moment they had arrived in Barak Varr that spring and learned of the invasion, the Slayer had had his heart set on facing a daemon on the field of battle, and once again his doom had been denied him. It had put him in a mood so bleak that Felix was concerned he might die from it.

Felix had seen Gotrek in the depths of despair before, but never like this. Always before, no matter how low he sank, anger or insult could rouse him. Now the jibes of peevish drunks and the threats of swaggering bullies didn't even raise his head. He just continued to stare straight ahead, as if there was nothing in the world except him and his ale stein.

It made Felix heartsick to see it. One couldn't say of a Slayer that he had lost his will to live, since his whole life was a search for death, but it was a sad thing indeed to see a Slayer who had lost his will to seek a good doom.

FELIX SAT DOWN across from Gotrek in the alcove behind the fireplace. The Slayer didn't seem to notice.

'Gotrek.'

Gotrek continued staring into the middle distance.

'Gotrek, are you awake?'

Gotrek didn't turn his head. 'What is it, manling?' he said at last. 'You're interrupting my drinking.' His voice sounded like someone grinding stones against each other in a tomb.

'I… I want to go to Marienburg.'

Gotrek contemplated this news for a long moment before answering. 'Taverns there are the same as here. Why bother?'

'I have something to do for my father there. You're welcome to stay here if you like, though a change of scenery might be refreshing. It should only take three weeks or so.'

Gotrek gave this some more thought, then at last shrugged his massive shoulders. 'One place is as good as another.' He raised his stein for another drink.

Felix was just trying to work out if that was a yes or a no, when something flashed past his nose and shattered Gotrek's stein, spilling beer all over the Slayer's beard and lap.

Gotrek looked up slowly as Felix turned in the direction from which the dart had come. Something long and narrow poked through a missing pane in a mullioned window. A dart flashed from it. Felix flung himself aside. Gotrek lifted his arm, and the dart stuck in the plaster of his cast. He glared with cold, one-eyed fury at the window as he reached down for his axe, which was propped against his chair.

'That was a waste of beer,' he said.

TWO

GOTREK AND FELIX ran out of the Griffon and thumped down the shadowed alley beside it, their weapons out. Gotrek swayed and stumbled as he ran, but considering he had been stone drunk for a solid month, his progress was remarkable.

Halfway around to the stable yard from which the dart had come, a flicker of movement above them caught Felix's eye. He looked up, still running. Something indistinct dropped past his eyes and hit his collarbone. He looked down. A slim grey rope lay across his chest. He reached for it.

It snapped tight, biting deep into his neck, and he jerked to a stop like a dog at the end of its chain, losing his sword and almost losing his footing. The cord pulled higher, forcing him onto tiptoes as he gagged and clawed at it. A slurred curse came from beside him, and he saw the Slayer staggering in a drunken circle with his cast raised over his head like he was waving it, a rope noose tight around his wrist, tugging it upwards violently.

'Cowards!' shouted Gotrek. 'Come down and fight!'

The Slayer aimed his axe at the rope, but before he could swing, a cobblestone hit him in the face. He snarled and turned, blood dripping from his forehead. Felix swung around, his vision darkening as he fought for air. Out of the shadows rushed a crowd of crouching men holding cudgels, nets and sacks. Gotrek lashed out at them with his axe, but a jerk on the rope that held his cast ruined his aim, and the men surged all around him, throwing ropes and nets at him.

A cudgel struck Felix a glancing blow on the back of the head as he scrabbled at his belt for his dagger. Another hit his shoulder. He kicked at his attackers but overbalanced and fell to one side, the rope around his neck taking all his weight. The pain and lack of air made black spots dance before his eyes. Fists and sticks pummelled him from all sides. The men's eyes were wild and wide, their lips black and wet with drool. There seemed to be scores of them.

Three men with an open sack were calling to some others. 'Lift him up! Hurry!'

Felix heard heavy thuds and cracks, and men flew back from Gotrek, bloody and maimed, but more closed around him, beating him and wrapping him up like a cocoon. His axe was pinned to his side.

'Loose me, you damned silkworms!' the Slayer roared, then threw both feet up and dropped right on his rump in the alley filth, knocking his tormentors back and pulling sharply on the rope holding his cast. There was a squeal from above and a black shape plummeted from the Griffon's top storey to land with a thud on a lower roof on the opposite side of the alley. The rope went slack.

The crowd of men closed in on Gotrek again as their companions lifted Felix towards the mouth of the sack, but the Slayer had a hand free now. The grimy cast flashed out, cracking men across the shins and knees. Gotrek surged up, struggling out of the entangling nets as they stumbled back.

They leapt at him again, trying to pin him before he got his axe free, but the razor-sharp rune blade tore through the last ropes and gutted the first man in. He fell back, his entrails spilling through his clutching hands, and crashed into the men lowering Felix into the sack.

The one holding Felix's left arm stumbled aside, letting go as he fought for balance. Felix took the opportunity and snatched his dagger from his belt. His captors flinched back and cried out, but they weren't his targets. Instead he swiped the blade over his head, severing the slim cord that choked him. The men dropped him as they took his full weight unexpectedly, and he slapped hard on the wet muck of the alley.

'I have him!' cried a man as he dived on Felix's dagger hand, trying to hold it down.

But Felix's other hand found his sword, half-submerged in alley sludge, and he hacked him with it. The man shrieked as the blade gashed his shoulder, and he rolled away, blood soaking his ragged clothes. The others swung their sticks and clubs at Felix, but he laid about him with Karaghul and they leapt back, bleeding from grievous wounds.

Felix staggered to his feet, his vision swimming and his balance gone. He waved the sword weakly in front of him as he dropped his dagger and clawed at the grey rope, which still bit deeply into his neck. It came free at last and he sucked in a beautiful, painful breath.

His vision cleared a little as blood pumped throbbingly back into his head. He looked around. Bloody corpses lay everywhere, some missing hands or arms. The remaining attackers were running for both ends of the alley. Gotrek was chasing the dozen or so heading for the inn yard, shouting at them to turn and fight. Felix stumbled after him, trying to make his legs obey his commands. They felt like they were made of custard.

Who were these men? And what did they want with them? It couldn't possibly be just some random attack. Were they cultists of the Cleansing Flame looking for revenge? Were they thralls of the Lahmian vampiresses who had sworn vengeance on them? If so, why had they tried to capture them and not kill them? Felix shivered as he imagined what those three harpies would do to him if they had him helpless. A bloody death in a back alley would be infinitely preferable.

Felix skidded into the Griffon's yard, a muddy dirt lot with the stables and privies on one side and an empty ale-cart on the other. Gotrek was just disappearing through the back gate into the alley behind, still trailing a length of rope from his cast.

Felix ran through the gate after him. Their mysterious attackers were fleeing around a corner ahead of him, into a narrower alley.

'Come back here, vermin!' roared Gotrek.

The men failed to obey.

'Do you know what this is about?' asked Felix as they charged into the alley after them. 'Who are they?'

'The ones who spilled my beer,' rasped Gotrek.

They chased their attackers through a maze of alleys – night-dark though it was almost noon, because the buildings that rose above them were so tall. Felix was surprised to find that, despite his shortness of breath and

Gotrek's short legs, they kept up with the men easily. They appeared in terrible shape – weak and confused, staggering and wailing and colliding with each other as they ran.

Unfortunately they were not the only danger. As Felix and Gotrek turned a further corner, another dart parted the Slayer's crest and glanced off the alley wall beside them. They looked up. A dark shape blurred from one roof to another and vanished behind a chimney. Visions of Ulrika dancing across the rooftops of Nuln echoed through Felix's mind. Was it her? Another of the Lahmians? They were the only foes he could think of who could leap like that.

Gotrek and Felix burst out of the narrow alley into a crowded market. Felix remembered the place from his youth, the Huhnmarkt, a poultry market where his father's cook had bought chickens and ducks for the larder. Their attackers were shoving through the press of shopping servants and shouting poultry-sellers, and leaving a trail of chaos in their wake. Cages of chickens and geese were overturned, and egg men and butchers were shaking fists and cleavers at them. Gotrek ploughed after the fleeing men, heedless – trampling fallen cages and shouldering more to the ground in his single-minded pursuit. Felix gritted his teeth and started after him, ears burning at the angry shouts that followed them.

'The watch!' shouted a woman. 'Someone call the watch!'

The cry echoed all around them.

Halfway across the square, the ragged men slowed, trapped between a wall of chicken cages and a cart that was unloading more. Before they could squeeze through, Gotrek was on them, burying his axe in the last one's back and grabbing the next. Cornered, they turned to fight, lashing out with their crude weapons and throwing anything they could get their hands on.

Mostly, this was chickens. Chickens in cages, chickens out of cages, dead chickens, live chickens and chickens that had been reduced to their component parts, all flew towards Gotrek and Felix in a squawking, flapping storm. Felix and the Slayer batted them aside with sword and axe and cast, smashing cages and butchering birds as they tried to close with their foes. Blood, feathers and splintering wood flew everywhere.

Felix ducked a cage of angry geese and impaled a man armed with a studded club, then hacked at another who had taken up a butcher's cleaver and flailed wildly with it. This was the first time since the noose had settled around his neck that he had been able to get a clear look at his attackers, and he found that they were very strange men indeed.

To a man they were as ragged and degenerate as any beggar Felix had ever encountered, with matted hair and beards, grimy skin and greasy, tattered clothes – but what truly alarmed him were their faces. Their eyes glittered with an unnatural excitement, and they drooled constantly – ropey black strands of spit that stained their lips and gums and spattered their clothes.

Though weak and spindle-thin, they fought with a feverish excitement and a twitchy quickness that made their attacks hard to predict. Was it a drug that made them this way? Zealotry for some god? Were they enslaved to some evil master? Felix might have felt pity for their miserable state except for the fact that they had nearly strangled him and were even now trying to beat him senseless. He cut the man with the cleaver across the knuckles. Though the wound went to the bone the man barely seemed to feel it, and swung again.

Felix blocked then thrust, stabbing deep into the man's shoulder. He screamed and fell aside. Felix looked to Gotrek. The Slayer was surrounded by bodies, and two more men were falling away from him, trailing streamers of blood from calamitous wounds. Three more madmen leapt at him from behind, wailing like the damned. Gotrek spun and split one from neck to nape, then caught a second by the belt and threw him over his shoulder into another. The men crashed through a butcher's stall, bringing down the canvas roof and landing upon sacks of plucked feathers as the butcher and his apprentices dived away. An explosion of feathers filled the air.

Two more men charged through the whirling cloud at Felix. He chopped easily through their clubs with his rune sword, then just as easily cut through their muscle and bone on his backswing. They fell screaming before him.

He looked around, wary, but the fight was over. In the middle of a ruined poultry stand, Gotrek was rising from decapitating the last of the men. He wiped his bloody forehead with the back of his bloody hand.

'Interrupt my drinking, will you?' he growled at a corpse.

The Slayer was covered from head to toe in blood, sweat and feathers. They clung to the gore that clotted his axe. They stuck to his face and shoulders and were matted in his beard, crest and eyebrows. Felix looked down at his hands and realised he must look the same. They were furred with patchy clumps of white and brown feathers. He had feathers in his mouth and up his nose. There were feathers stuck to his eyelashes.

'What's all this then?' came a voice behind him.

Felix and Gotrek turned. Stepping through the settling feathers was a patrol of the city watch, a tall, stringy captain at their head, looking around at the wreckage like a disapproving headmaster.

'Sigmar's blood!' he said, as he found the body of one of the strange men. 'There's been murder done! Who's responsible for this?'

Everyone in the square pointed at Gotrek and Felix.

'It was them!' cried a big woman in an apron and rolled sleeves. 'They chased them poor beggars in here and chopped 'em to pieces!'

'The villains smashed up my stand!' called a vendor.

'They killed my chickens!' complained another.

'All my eggs is broken!' wailed a third.

'Captain, I can explain,' said Felix, stepping forwards.

But the captain stepped back and signalled his men to go on guard. Suddenly Felix was facing a thicket of swords.

'You'll stay where you are, murderer,' the captain said. He shook his head. 'Nine, ten, eleven dead. By all the gods, what a massacre.'

'We were attacked,' said Felix. 'We defended ourselves.'

The captain didn't look as if he believed it. 'You can make your defence to Commander Halstig at the watch house. Now surrender your weapons and put your wrists behind your backs.'

Gotrek's head lowered menacingly. 'No man takes my axe.'

'Gotrek…' said Felix.

The captain sneered. 'Resistance will only make it harder on you, dwarf.' He motioned his troops forwards. 'Take it from him.'

Gotrek dropped into a fighting stance as the swordsmen edged forwards. 'Try and you die.'

'Gotrek,' said Felix, desperate, 'We can't fight the watch. They're not our enemies.'

'If they try to take my axe they are,' the Slayer growled.

Felix stepped between Gotrek and the watchmen, holding up his hands. 'Gentlemen, please. If you allow us to keep our weapons we will come peacefully, I promise you.'

'And what is the promise of a murderer worth?' asked the captain. 'Surrender your weapons immediately.'

Felix backed away as the watchmen advanced. He looked over his shoulder. 'Gotrek, please.'

'Step aside, manling.'

A young watchman raised his sword at Felix, his eyes nervous. 'Your sword. Now.'

Felix stepped back again. 'I... I cannot.'

The watchmen took another step, closing ranks.

'Don't be a fool...' said the young watchman, then gasped and clutched at his neck. A black dart sprouted from it, just above the collar of his breastplate. His eyes rolled up in his head and he dropped to the ground.

The other watchmen jumped back, shouting, unsure what had happened. Felix stepped back too, crouching and scanning the roofs around the square. Another dart flashed past him. Gotrek deflected it with his axe. It thudded against the canvas of the collapsed stall, its tip glistening, black and wet.

'What's happening?' shouted the captain.

'There!' said Felix, pointing to the roof of an exchange on the far side of the square.

The watchmen followed his gaze just in time to see a dark shape scurrying over the peak of the roof.

'And there!' said another watchman, pointing to the left.

A dart caught him on the cheek and he collapsed on top of his comrade. Another shadowy form ducked back behind the lip of a townhouse roof.

'Down!' shouted the captain.

His men dived for cover.

'Come on, manling,' said Gotrek, starting through the smashed stalls in the direction of the townhouse.

Felix shot a look at the watchmen, then followed, keeping low.

'Stop!' cried the captain. 'After them!' he called to his men.

They hesitated, wary eyes on the rooftops.

'Go!' the captain shouted.

The watchmen started after them, but slowly, keeping in cover. Gotrek turned and twisted through the maze of stalls, trailing feathers and leaving bloody footprints. His eye never left the roof of the townhouse.

'We'll never catch them,' said Felix, falling in with him.

Gotrek said nothing, walking through a stall full of complaining chickens and out the back as the owner cowered behind a chopping block. They were on the edge of the square now. The townhouse was to their left. Behind them Felix heard a babble of voices, as the watchmen trailed reluctantly after them.

A silhouetted head popped up on the townhouse roof. Gotrek swung his axe in an arc before him and knocked another dart to the ground.

'Cowards,' he rumbled.

'He's moving,' said Felix, pointing to where the silhouette had appeared briefly again at the top of the roof.

Gotrek ran into the alley between the townhouse and another building. The dark form blurred as it leapt from roof to roof further down the alley – an impossible jump – then disappeared over a gable.

Gotrek grunted and hurried on.

'Gotrek, it's useless!' called Felix. 'He's too fast.'

The Slayer ignored him.

* * *

SEVEN BLOCKS LATER, Gotrek stopped and glared around at the roofs above him. Felix caught his breath, relieved. He was hot and sticky, and the feathers he was covered with itched horribly.

They had seen no sign of the dart shooter for four blocks, and he was just going to suggest to Gotrek that they give up, when the Slayer grunted, disgusted, then turned and started shuffling slowly down a side street. Felix stared after him. One moment he had been angry and determined and nearly his old self, the next his eye had gone dull and far-away again, like it had been for the last month. It was like someone had pulled his spine out.

'Gotrek? Where are we going?' asked Felix, trailing after him.

'I need a drink.'

'At the Griffon? But, uh, the watch will ask around. They'll find us there.'

'Let them.'

Felix hemmed uneasily. 'Listen, Gotrek, I have no interest in fighting the watch. Nor do I wish to live the life of an outlaw again. Why don't we go to another inn? Say in Marienburg.'

Gotrek said nothing, only plodded on dully.

Just then, three watchmen ran out of an alley ahead of them. They saw Gotrek and Felix and skidded to a stop in surprise.

'Halt!' said the first, the oldest of the three, though no more than twenty at the most. The watch recruited young these days, with so many older men dead in the war.

The boys went on guard. Gotrek didn't slow, only lowered his head and readied his axe. Felix groaned. This was just what they needed.

'Gotrek, they're only doing their job,' he murmured.

'They're in my way.'

'Gotrek, please!'

'Hand over your weapons,' said the young watchman. His voice quavered, but he stood firm.

Still stumping forwards, Gotrek raised his head and looked the watchman in the face. Felix saw the boy's eyes widen with fear. Felix didn't blame him. He'd taken the full brunt of that piercing, one-eyed glare before. It had shrivelled his guts every time.

'Step aside,' the Slayer said calmly. 'Tell your captain you didn't find us.'

The watchmen shot nervous glances at each other, hesitating.

Gotrek kept coming. He raised his axe, still crusted with blood and feathers and filth. Felix held his breath, not wanting to look.

The young men fled.

Felix let out a sigh of relief.

Gotrek grunted and walked on. 'Marienburg,' he said, nodding. 'One place is as good as another.'

AN HOUR LATER, after a wash at a bathhouse of less than sterling repute, Felix slipped through the back door of the Griffon while Rudgar and Irmele were busy serving dinner, changed into his old clothes and his old red Sudenland cloak, collected his and Gotrek's few belongings, slipped back out again, and walked with the Slayer to the Reikside docks. He left a stack of coins on the dresser to pay for the room, and the bloodstained grey doublet as well, cursing the ruination of yet another set of good clothes. He decided that he would never again buy clothes of any quality for himself. He always managed to destroy them almost instantly.

At the docks he enquired about services to Marienburg and learned that the *Jilfte Bateau*, a Marienburg passenger boat, was leaving in two hours, so he and Gotrek settled into the Broken Anchor to wait. Though the Anchor was far from the Griffon and the Huhnmarkt, and there was little likelihood of the watch coming to look for them there, Felix still picked the table in the darkest corner of the room and looked up nervously every time someone walked through the door.

He spent the rest of the time looking to the diamond-paned windows, expecting drugged darts to come whistling from missing panes again at any moment. He still didn't know who their strange attackers had been. His money was on the Lahmians, but he couldn't rule out the Cleansing Flame either. Did they have any other enemies in the Empire? They had been away for so long, how could they? Whoever they were, would the men find them again? Would they follow them to Marienburg? From things Ulrika and the countess said, he had the impression that the Lahmians had agents everywhere. If it was them, he and Gotrek might never escape their reach.

Despite Felix's worry, their wait at the Anchor passed without incident and they made their way through the twilit Altdorf streets to the bustling docks just as the *Jilfte Bateau's* purser dropped the rope and waved the passengers aboard.

Gotrek grumbled and spat as he climbed the gangplank to the foredeck of the long low boat. 'Slopping about on the water in a leaky wooden bucket,' he muttered. 'Makes me sick. I'm going below.'

Felix smiled to himself. Every time they travelled by water Gotrek made the same complaints, but it never stopped him from boarding.

'You'll feel better if you stay above,' he said. 'Seeing the shore pass helps, I'm told.'

'Man wisdom,' said Gotrek contemptuously, and stumped for the door to the staterooms.

Felix shook his head, bemused, then turned to the rail. He wasn't going to share a cramped cabin with the Slayer when he was in such a foul mood. Better by far to watch his fellow passengers board the boat and enjoy the warmth of the late autumn sun.

The people making their way up the gangplank were a mixed lot: poor folk who had obviously paid their last coin for a berth in steerage, merchants in broadcloth on their way to trade in Bretonnia or Marienburg, their bullies carrying their baggage for them, a full company of Hochland handgunners under a bellowing captain, nobles and their retinues in silks and velvets being ushered aboard by fawning stewards, tanned and bearded sailors with packs on their backs, and fat merchant princes of Marienburg, dressed more gaudily than the nobles, returning home after signing trade agreements with wholesalers and distributors of the Empire.

It was all so normal and mundane that Felix felt an unaccustomed longing for a regular life. These people weren't attacked by strange, drooling madmen in taverns. These people weren't on a first-name basis with vampire countesses. These people didn't know anybody who had vowed to die a glorious death in battle. They'd never fought a troll. They most likely had never even seen a troll.

Maybe his father was right. Maybe he should have followed the path the old man had set out for him. Things certainly would have been more comfortable. But also more boring. Not that boredom was the worst fate that could happen to a man. It was certainly preferable to finding oneself covered in blood and chicken feathers and being hunted by the watch.

A richly appointed coach rolled up the dock and stopped near the gangplank. Though it had no insignia, it was obvious that someone important was inside. The coach was flanked by eight Reiksguard knights in steel breastplates and blue and red uniforms, and the purser ran out to meet it, bringing a low step and setting it before the door while stewards hurried to take the luggage handed down to them by the coachmen.

Felix watched with interest as the coach door opened, wondering who would emerge. First to step out was an older man in long, cream-coloured robes, over which he wore a darker travelling cloak, the voluminous hood pulled up to hide his features. Felix marked him for a wizard, not just because of his clothes and the long amber-tipped staff that he carried, but also for the fear and awe that he inspired in the purser and the stewards who waited upon him. The purser seemed torn between showing him every courtesy and bolting like a scared rabbit. The stewards handled his luggage as if it might explode at any moment.

The wizard turned back to the coach and offered a hand to its other occupant. Felix raised his head for a better look, for the woman who stepped delicately down to the dock was striking to say the least.

She was dressed in silk robes of a deep, rich blue, like a summer sky just after sunset, embroidered all over with sigils of the stars, planets and moons – a seeress of the Celestial College then – but no wizened crone, weighed down with the burden of foreknowledge that came from years of divination. This woman was young, hardly more than twenty by Felix's estimate, and as slim and graceful as a cat. Long straight hair the colour of honey fell down her back almost to her waist, and she carried her fine-featured head high, looking about her with alert interest, her lips quirked into a permanent half-smile, as if she knew a secret no one else did, which, considering her college, she undoubtedly did.

The older wizard walked her to the boat, his head bent to talk to her as they went, while the purser bowed and scraped before them and their Reiksguard escort marched on either side of them.

Felix's fellow passengers whispered and muttered amongst themselves as the pair started up the gangplank.

'Sigmar preserve us, they're not travelling with us?' asked an Altdorf matron.

'Oh, they're all right,' said her husband. 'They're from the colleges. Reikers wouldn't be travelling with 'em if they weren't.'

'Still warlocks all the same,' said another man. 'Can't trust 'em.'

'And even if they're good 'uns, what're they doing here? Nothing good happens around a wizard,' said a third man.

'Aye,' said the matron. 'I'm not travelling with 'em. Henrich, talk to the purser.'

'But, Hieke, my love. There isn't another boat for two days. And we must get to Carroburg by Aubentag.'

And on and on. Felix didn't blame them. Even the best of wizards made him nervous. Like any weapon in the Empire's arsenal they could be as dangerous to friend as to foe if something went wrong – powder could explode, cannons could crack, a sword could be turned against its owner, and wizards could go mad or bad, as he knew from recent personal experience.

He turned with the other passengers as the sorcerous pair reached the top of the gangplank and allowed themselves to be led towards the door to the staterooms. Felix gave the young seeress another look now that she was nearer. She was as beautiful close up as she had been far away, with high cheekbones, full lips and bright eyes that matched the deep blue of her robe.

She smiled at him as they passed, and the older wizard looked up to see who she was looking at.

Felix blinked in recognition as they made eye contact. There was a beard now where there once had been none, and grey hair where there had once been brown, but the eyes that looked at him from the lean, lined face were the same, as was the sad, slow smile that broke through the man's solemn expression.

'Felix Jaeger,' said Maximilian Schreiber. 'You haven't aged a day.'

THREE

IN A CHAMBER far beneath the deepest cellars of Altdorf, Grey Seer Thanquol hand-fed his personal rat ogre Boneripper, the thirteenth of that name. It was important with such beasts to make sure that their food – and their punishment – came only from their master. In that way was meek devotion and savage loyalty won. In that way were they his and his alone.

With some effort he lifted a fat man-leg from the basket of scraps his servants had brought and tossed into the corner where the massive rat ogre crouched, devouring another choice niblet. This incarnation of Boneripper was particularly impressive, for it was milk-white from its thick-clawed feet to its misshapen, blunt-horned head, and had the viscera-pink eyes of an albino. Thanquol had picked him from the litter Clan Moulder had offered him, particularly for his colour, which matched his own.

He looked up from watching Boneripper suck the marrow from a femur as his simpering, tailless servant, Issfet Loptail, pulled back the manskin door curtain and bowed in a lean skaven in the black garb and mask of a night runner. The skaven, an accomplished assassin known only as Shadowfang, who Thanquol had hired from Clan Eshin at great expense, knelt before him, head down, tail flat and meek. He only flinched a little as he heard Boneripper crack the leg bone with his teeth.

'I return, oh sage of the underdark,' whispered the assassin.

'Yes-yes,' said the seer impatiently. Wasn't it obvious he had returned? 'Speak-speak! Do you have them? Are they mine at last?'

Shadowfang hesitated. 'I… I crave your pardon, grey seer. The kidnap did not go as planned.'

Thanquol slammed his bony claw on the table, almost upsetting his inkpot. Boneripper rumbled ominously. 'You promised me success! You promised you had anticipated every contingency!'

'I thought I had, your supremacy,' said the assassin.

'You thought? You thought incorrectly then, yes? What happened? Tell me, quick-quick!' Thanquol's tail lashed with impatience.

'Yes-yes, grey seer. I begin,' said Shadowfang, touching his snout to the floor and casting a nervous glance at the rat ogre. 'The crested one blocked Mao Shing's sleep darts – he has been punished for his incompetence, I assure you – then, as I foresaw, the crested one and the yellow fur ran, fast-fast, out of the drinking place to fight. There they fell into my second trap, and success was nearly ours.'

'Nearly?' asked Thanquol, sneering.

The assassin's tail quivered at his devastating disdain. 'The fault is not mine, most benevolent of seers!' he shrilled. 'Had I been able to employ brave, proud gutter runners instead of sickly man-slaves, the targets would be even now in your noble claws. But outside in the day-sun in the over-burrow, skaven might have been discovered, so man-slaves must suffice.'

'But suffice they did not,' snarled Thanquol.

'No, grey seer,' said Shadowfang, swallowing nervously. 'They failed. The dwarf and the human kill-maimed them all, then escaped.'

'Escaped?' said Thanquol. 'Where-where?'

'I… I know not.'

'You know not?' Thanquol's voice was quickly rising to an imperious squeak. Boneripper sensed his distress and lowed unhappily. 'You know not? You, who I was told could sniff-sniff the trail of a crow through a swamp seven days after it had flown past? You know not?'

'Mercy-mercy, your eminence,' whined Shadowfang. 'I… I made a strategic withdrawal after the man-slaves died, and when I returned to the drinking place, they had vanished.'

'A strategic withdrawal,' said Thanquol dryly. 'You skitter-ran. You squirted the musk of fear.'

'No-no, your magnificence,' insisted Shadowfang. 'I merely redeployed to a rearwards position.'

Thanquol closed his eyes, so that he would not have to see the miserable excuse for an assassin that knelt before him. He was tempted to blast the worthless incompetent with a bolt of sorcerous fire, or feed him to Boneripper, but then he recalled how many long-hoarded warp tokens he had spent procuring the fool's services, and resisted the urge. He would get his money's worth out of him, and *then* he would let the rat ogre eat him.

'If I might speak, your fearsomeness,' said Shadowfang.

Thanquol sighed and opened his eyes. 'Oh yes, pray speak, enlightened one. Speak-speak. Let your wisdom shine upon us.'

Behind his mask, the assassin's red eyes blinked, confused. He was apparently a stranger to sarcasm. 'Er, had you allowed me to kill-maim the overdwellers instead of snare-catching them, even lowly man-slaves might have succeeded…'

'No-no!' shrieked Thanquol, causing Boneripper to bellow and Shadowfang and Issfet to curl their tails around them in fear. 'No! It must be I that take-takes their lives. It must be I that wreaks my vengeance upon their helpless bodies for all the pain-shame they have caused me. Only I can have that joy. Only I! You hear?'

He scrabbled among his papers until he found a stoppered bottle, then uncorked it and stuffed it up one cankered nostril. He inhaled deeply, shivering to the tip of his tail as the powdered warpstone began to spread throughout his system. Issfet and Shadowfang took a further step back as the seer's eyes glowed a malefic green.

'They will die,' Thanquol said, after he had at last controlled his trembling. 'Yes-yes, but only at my whim, and long after they have beg-cried to be free of life.' His glowing eyes snapped back to the assassin. 'Find them! Find them! And this time you must not fail to take them!'

'Yes, grey seer,' said Shadowfang, touching his snout again to the floor. 'At once, grey seer. I go, grey seer.'

'Master,' said Issfet, wobbling unsteadily on his hind paws. 'A man-spy tells me that the crested one and the yellow fur have left the drinking burrow, taking their hoardings with them. It may be that they journey again.'

'They have left?' said Thanquol, turning on him. 'Why did you not tell me this before?'

'I only just learned of it, your malfeasance,' said Issfet. 'I was coming to say when Master Shadowfang arrived.'

'But how will I find them?' whined Thanquol. 'They might vanish again for another twenty years.'

'I will send my gutter runners to every corner of the over-burrow,' said Shadowfang.

'I will question my man-spies,' said Issfet.

'No,' said Thanquol, raising a yellowed claw. 'I have it!' The powdered warpstone was once again clearing his head and allowing his genius to blossom. 'The yellow fur spoke with its brood sire today, yes-yes?'

'Yes-yes, your excellence,' said Shadowfang. 'It was from there I followed him.'

'Then to there you return,' said Thanquol, baring his teeth to admit a squeal of triumph. 'To learn what the man-sire knows of its offspring.'

MAX RAISED A glass of wine in one beringed hand. 'To fond reunions,' he said, then took a drink.

Felix raised his glass and drank in turn. 'To fond reunions.'

Gotrek just drank.

They sat in Max's handsome stateroom on board the *Jilfte Bateau*, only slightly larger, but several steps more luxurious, than Gotrek and Felix's little cabin, with mahogany panelling on the walls and coloured glass in the windows. An iron stove against one wall radiated a pleasant warmth. If it weren't for the motion of the boat upon the river, Felix would have thought himself in some tidy study.

'We all thought you dead, you know,' said Max. 'When you failed to return from that strange portal in Sylvania we lost all hope.'

Felix nodded. 'Malakai said the same thing.'

Max raised his greying eyebrows. 'You've seen him?'

'We were on the *Spirit of Grungni* when it crashed,' said Felix. 'You hadn't heard about that?'

'I heard, yes,' said Max. 'But your names weren't mentioned.'

Max had aged well, Felix thought. He was still handsome, and the grey streaks in his neatly trimmed beard added to the air of grave dignity he had always projected. His hair was mostly grey now and flowed down past his shoulders in a kingly mane.

'I have only recently returned from Middenheim,' he said. 'There was much to be done after the final battle. Much cleansing.'

Gotrek gave an angry grunt at the mention of Middenheim.

'How did the *Grungni* come to crash?' Max asked.

Felix paused. Where to begin? It was a story that could take an evening to tell. Before he could start, there was a knock on the door.

'Come,' called Max.

The door opened and in stepped the young seeress, dressed now in a much less ostentatious robe of dark blue wool with no embroidery. She inclined her head to Max. 'Good evening, magister,' she said, smiling. 'I hope I'm not intruding.'

'Not at all,' said Max as he and Felix stood.

Gotrek didn't look up.

'Let me make the introductions we were too rushed to make on deck,' said Max. 'Felix, Gotrek, may I present Fraulein Claudia Pallenberger, a journeyman of the Celestial College, and a seeress of great perception.'

Felix bowed. Gotrek grunted.

'Fraulein Pallenberger,' continued Max. 'May I introduce to you Felix Jaeger, poet, adventurer and swordsman of renown, and Gotrek Gurnisson, slayer of trolls, dragons and daemons, and the most dangerous companion with whom I have ever had the honour of travelling.'

Gotrek snorted at that.

Claudia curtseyed and smiled at Felix and Gotrek. 'I'm pleased to make your acquaintance, Herr Jaeger, and you Herr Gurnisson.'

'The pleasure is all mine,' said Felix, bowing again. 'Are you travelling to Marienburg, fraulein?'

'To Marienburg and beyond,' said Claudia as she crossed to a chair next to the stove and sat down. She raised her chin and looked mysterious. 'I've had premonitions.'

Max almost dropped the glass of wine he was pouring for her. 'This *is* a secret mission, fraulein,' he murmured.

Claudia blushed and her mysterious look collapsed. She suddenly looked closer to seventeen than twenty. 'I'm sorry, magister. I didn't think. I...'

Max smiled and handed Claudia her wine. 'Don't worry, we're among friends. But please try to be more cautious in the future.' She nodded her head, sheepish.

Max turned to Felix and Gotrek. 'You'll not speak of this.'

'Of course not,' said Felix.

Gotrek shook his head and drank again.

'Thank you,' said Max. 'Then you may tell the rest of it, seeress.'

Claudia nodded again, then looked solemnly at Felix. 'I have seen Altdorf destroyed in fire and flood. I have seen Marienburg swept from the face of the earth by a towering wave. I have seen death and ruin on an unimaginable scale, and the coming of a great dark age.'

'Ah,' said Felix. 'I see.' There didn't seem to be anything else to say.

'And I am drawn to the north by the feeling that the prevention of these events may be found there.'

'Fraulein Pallenberger's visions have been confirmed as true divinations by the magisters of her college,' said Max. 'They have also determined that she is particularly attuned to these strands of possibility, and have sent her to follow them to their source. I accompany her as mentor and, ah, protector.'

Felix frowned, confused. 'You are with the Celestial College, Max? I always thought...'

Max smiled and took another drink. 'No, I am of the Order of Light. But it was felt that, er, that a man who had seen something of the world...'

'The magisters of my college,' interrupted Claudia, her eyes flaring, 'are a lot of dusty old greybeards who never leave their rooms. Their eyes are always at their telescopes and their minds are always in the clouds. They hid behind their doors like old biddies when I asked who would accompany me.'

Max coughed to hide a laugh. 'I was chosen because, in my youthful wanderings before I found employment with the Graf of Middenheim, I had spent some time in Marienburg and came to know some of the leaders of the magical fraternity there, such as they are.'

'And because you have actually cast a spell in battle,' added Claudia hotly.

Max nodded. 'That too. Although I hope that this will be nothing more than a reconnaissance mission and that there will be no reason for violence.'

Felix frowned at Max. 'Forgive me, Max, but I'm confused now. When Makaisson said that you were at the colleges I didn't think anything of it, but weren't you...? That is, how did it come about? I seem to remember you telling me that you had, ah, broken with them. Wasn't that the cause of your "youthful wanderings"?'

Max smiled wistfully. 'There comes a time in a man's life–' He shot a sharp glance at Felix here. 'At least in some men's lives – when he puts wandering behind him, and wants some security.' He had another sip of wine. 'I was honoured by the Tsarina for my help in the defence of Praag that year. This won me the grudging acceptance of the colleges, and a few years later, after some hemming and hawing, they offered me a teaching position, and a chance to continue my studies – within reason.' He cast a look at Gotrek, who continued to stare dully into his mug. 'Adventuring wasn't the same after you two vanished anyway, so I took the job. Been there ever since.'

Claudia smiled over the rim of her glass. 'Have you all shared adventures before, then? Is that how you know each other? Were you brave friends on some noble quest?'

Felix and Max exchanged an uncomfortable glance. They had certainly shared numerous adventures, but they had not always been the best of friends.

'Herr Jaeger, Herr Gurnisson and I travelled together into the Chaos Wastes once,' said Max. 'On an airship.'

'And we fought a dragon,' said Felix.

'And the hordes of Chaos,' said Max.

'And defeated a… a vampire.' Felix stammered, wishing as soon as he said it that he hadn't spoken. He remembered the outcome of that nightmarish episode and how Max had reacted to the news of Ulrika's undeath. Should he tell Max he had seen her? Would Ulrika want him to know? What would Max do if he knew? Would he seek her out? Would she fall in love with him again? The bitter bile of jealousy suddenly welled up in Felix's heart as if the hurt had happened yesterday instead of nearly twenty years before. He fought it down, angry with himself for being ridiculous. What did he possibly have to be jealous about? Ulrika had said that love between the living and the unliving was impossible. She could no more betray him with Max than with anyone else, and yet still the wound burned. He cursed himself. Men truly were fools.

Max was looking at him curiously.

Felix flushed and turned back to Claudia, forcing a smile. 'So, yes, we have had a few adventures together, I suppose, but all many, many years ago.'

Claudia's full lips curved into a smile. 'You don't look old enough to have had adventures many, many years ago, Herr Jaeger.'

'Ah, well, I…'

'Yes,' said Max, eyeing Felix with a bemused frown. 'Herr Jaeger is remarkably well preserved.'

'Mm, yes,' said Claudia, looking at Felix from under a curtain of golden tresses. 'Remarkably.'

Felix started like he had been goosed. The girl found him attractive! That was no good at all. He shot a look at Max. The wizard was scowling. He had seen it too. Felix swallowed. This could all get very awkward. 'I think perhaps it is time for us to retire,' he said, standing quickly. 'You no doubt have many things to speak of regarding your mission. Ready, Gotrek?'

'There's no need,' said the seeress. 'Really.'

'No no,' Felix insisted, stepping to the door. 'The Slayer and I have had an exhausting day, thank you all the same.' He nodded respectfully to Max. 'Max, a pleasure to see you again.' Then he turned to Claudia. 'Fraulein Pallenberger, an honour to make your acquaintance. I bid you both a very good night.'

Gotrek stood and downed the last of his beer in one long swallow, then put the mug down and stumped out after Felix.

'Thanks for the beer,' he said.

THE JOURNEY DOWN the Reik from Altdorf to Marienburg took twelve days, according to the ship's pilot, but by the end of the second day, Felix was convinced it was more like twelve years. It seemed as if it would never be over.

Gotrek, never the most effervescent of travelling companions, had become a monosyllabic lump that sat in the dark in their cabin and stared at the wall, never leaving except to find food and beer. Without the Slayer's company, Felix had little to do but pace the decks and try to avoid the attentions of Fraulein Pallenberger, which proved no easy task.

She seemed to be everywhere: on the stairs coming down when he was coming up, stepping out of her cabin just as he was stepping out of his, walking on the foredeck just when he wanted to stretch his legs, and sipping tea in the taproom just when he was in the mood for a drink. And always, somewhere in the background, like a hovering grey owl, was Max, glaring at Felix as if it were he who was instigating things.

Felix always excused himself as quickly and politely as possible, and Claudia never made any fuss, just exchanged pleasantries and moved on, but there was something in her smile, and in the gleam of her dancing eyes, that suggested that, like a cat who waits at a mouse hole, she knew that her patience would eventually win out over his reticence.

On the third evening, when Felix had scurried to the aft deck after seeing Claudia engrossed in a book on the foredeck, Max finally sought him out, joining him as he leaned on the stern rail and looked out at the trees and fields that glided by on either side of them. The wizard filled a long clay pipe with tobacco, lit it with a flame from his finger, then exhaled a long plume of smoke.

'You would do well to keep your roving eye to yourself, Felix,' he said at last.

Felix felt his hackles raise. The accusation was unfair. And even if it weren't, who was Max to tell him what to do? 'I have no intention of allowing my eye to rove,' he said sharply. 'Nor any other part of my anatomy, for that matter.'

'I am glad to hear it,' said Max. Then he sighed. 'I'm sorry, Felix. She is a bright girl, but very sheltered. She entered the college at eleven, and has seen nothing of the world except its cloisters since. Recently, according to her masters, this has begun to chafe.'

'That's hardly surprising, is it?' said Felix. 'An energetic, inquisitive girl, coming to maturity in a monastery of – what did she call them – dusty old greybeards? You can't blame her for wanting to experience something of life while she's young.'

'No, I can't,' said Max sadly. 'I certainly wanted to see the world when I was her age. Nevertheless, I have been charged by her college to keep her safe from any entanglements or embarrassments while she undertakes this journey, and if I fail… well there will be some unpleasant political repercussions.' He looked up at Felix with a rueful smile. 'So, as a favour to your old travelling companion…?' He let the question hang.

Felix sighed and looked down the river winding away south and east behind them, as if he could see all the way back to Nuln. 'Trust me, Max. I've no interest in her, nor any woman, at the moment. My heart is locked in an iron box and I've lost the key.'

Max raised his eyebrows. 'It must be a terrible melancholy indeed to cause you to resort to metaphor.' He nodded and stood. 'Well, no matter the cause, I appreciate your understanding and restraint. I will do my best to keep her occupied, but remember what you have said here if she escapes me.'

'I will,' said Felix.

Max tapped his pipe on the rail, knocking the ash into the river, then turned to go. Felix looked after him, hesitant, then spoke.

'Max.'

The wizard looked back. 'Yes?'

'I've seen Ulrika.'

Max looked at him, his face growing still. He returned to the rail. 'She still lives?'

Felix nodded. 'If it can be called living.'

'Is she… is she well?'

'As well as can be expected, I suppose. She is still under the patronage of the Countess Gabriella. She is her bodyguard. In Nuln.'

Max twisted his pipe in his hands, his eyes far away. 'I have often thought of seeking her out, but I never had the courage.'

'I wish *I* hadn't found her,' said Felix, with unexpected bitterness.

'No?' asked Max, turning to look at him. 'Is she so changed then?'

'Not nearly enough,' said Felix. He found he had a lump in his throat. He fought to swallow it. 'Not nearly enough.'

'Ah,' said Max. 'Ah, I see.' He pressed his lips together and stared hard over the rail into the swirling waters of the river. 'Then I think that I shall not seek her out after all.' He turned away, then, after a step, turned back and looked at Felix. 'Thank you for telling me.'

Felix shrugged. 'I'm not sure it was a kindness.'

'Nor am I,' said Max. 'But I am glad to know nonetheless. Good day, Felix.' Then he turned and walked towards the main deck.

CLAUDIA CAUGHT FELIX at last on the afternoon of the fifth day.

Except for light fare in the taproom, the *Jilfte Bateau* did not serve meals. Instead, it had arrangements with inns at various towns along the Reik that would provide food and drink for its passengers. It stopped only twice a day, once in the morning and once in the afternoon, meaning that those who were inclined to be peckish at other times of day were advised to buy extra food for later. This afternoon, the riverboat had docked in the small town of Schilderheim, and the passengers had disembarked – all but Felix.

Finding himself more in need of solitude than sustenance, and seeing Max and Fraulein Pallenberger making their way down the gangplank, he had decided to remain on board, settling down in the empty taproom with a pint and the first volume of the *My Travels With Gotrek* books that his brother Otto had published during his absence. Felix had hesitated to read them these last two months, fearing that he would find that his journals had been clumsily fleshed out, or imperfectly edited, or worse, that his own youthful prose would not stand up to his scrutiny, but he could resist no longer, and at last opened the leather-bound, gilt-stamped cover and began.

He was not reassured by the title page, for there was an error even there. The publishing date was wrong – 2505. He hadn't even sent the first journal to his brother then. Someone must have used the date he had written on the inside cover of his original journal as the publishing date. But even that wasn't right, was it? It had been a few years before that. It was baffling. Out of curiosity, he pulled the other books out of his satchel and checked them. The publishing date in every one of them was the same! Whoever had typeset the books had been lazy in the extreme and left the title page untouched in each edition. Felix shook his head, then shrugged. What did he expect from a penny-pincher like Otto? He wouldn't have gone to a first-rate printer, would he?

Just as he began the first chapter, and shivered as it recalled to his mind the horrors of that long past Geheimnisnacht, a shadow fell across the page and he looked up. Fraulein Pallenberger was smiling down at him. Felix jumped in surprise.

'Herr Jaeger,' she said, curtseying and smiling at his unease.

Felix stood and bowed. 'Fraulein Pallenberger, how unexpected to find you here. I thought I saw you leave for the inn.'

'Nothing is unexpected to one of the Celestial Order, Herr Jaeger,' she said, taking the seat next to his. 'May I?'

'Certainly,' said Felix, cursing himself for not having the courage to refuse her.

He watched Claudia out of the corner of his eye as she signalled to the barman to bring her some tea. In truth, he wished he could find it within him to succumb to her charms, if only to annoy Max, but also to try to find some balm for the pain in his heart. His last view of Ulrika, running into the darkness of the skaven tunnels beneath Nuln, had been more than two months ago, and still not a day went by – not an hour! – when he did not think of her and feel the stab of regret rip through him.

Part of him wanted that never to change. The pain was all he had left of her, and that made it precious, and yet, another part of him wanted to be free of it. He longed to drown himself in the solace of loving – or at least lustful – arms. What had Ulrika said? We must find happiness among our own kind? It seemed impossible.

Claudia was beautiful, there was no denying it, and alluring as well, with her knowing glances and gleaming fall of honey-coloured hair, but though he tried his best not to, he could not stop himself from comparing her to Ulrika, and in each instance finding her wanting. Her blue eyes were bright and beautiful, but not as alive as Ulrika's – not even in her undeath. Her smile was sultry, but not as forthright as Ulrika's, her curves were lovely, even under her seeress's robes, but seemed to him girlish and unformed when compared to Ulrika's clean-limbed martial grace. Her nose... ah, but it was useless! No matter how beautiful Claudia was, and how beguiling her attraction to him, it was not *her* arms he wanted to find solace in, it was Ulrika's, and though he knew that could never be, that didn't stop him wanting it with all his heart.

'What are you reading, Herr Jaeger?' Claudia asked, leaning in to look at the cover of the book.

Felix flushed. There really was nothing more embarrassing than to be caught reading one's own memoirs. 'Ah, my brother published my journals without my knowledge. I... I'm checking to see that he didn't change them too much.'

She read the title. '*My Travels With Gotrek.*' She looked up at him. 'You and Herr Gurnisson seem an odd pairing. How did you come to travel together?'

Felix groaned inwardly. It was a long story and he didn't particularly feel like telling it just now. He held out the book. 'Would you like to read about it?'

Claudia laughed. 'I would much rather hear it from the lips of the man that lived it.'

Felix sighed. 'Well, if you insist.'

And so he told her about his student days, and the Window Tax riots, and how Gotrek had saved him from the swords of the Reiksguard – though he downplayed the slaughter somewhat – and how he and Gotrek had retired to the inn and got abysmally drunk, and how he had sworn to follow Gotrek and record his death in an epic poem.

When he finished, Claudia looked at him strangely. 'And for how many years have you followed the Slayer?' she asked.

'More than twenty,' he said.

'That seems a long time to continue honouring a vow made while in one's cups,' she said.

Felix nodded. 'Yes, it is.'

'It's a wonder you continue.'

'A vow is still a vow, no matter how long ago it was made,' said Felix.

'But what about your life!' cried Claudia, suddenly overwhelmed by emotion. 'Did you not have plans of your own? Did you not have dreams? How could you give up your life to follow another?'

Felix frowned. It was rare that he talked about these things out loud. 'I did have plans. I meant to be a poet. Possibly a playwright. I believed I would spend my life among the inns and theatres of Altdorf. But as I said, a vow is a vow.'

'But you were drunk!'

'It was still a vow.'

She shook her head, seeming truly upset. 'It must be more than that. Surely Herr Gurnisson would have forgiven you your duty if you had gone to him and asked to be released from it. I cannot believe that anyone would ask someone to hold to a promise made when they were too young or too drunk to know what it meant – when they had no idea of all the wonders that life offers for someone who is free to see them. Have you no regrets? Did you never want to leave?'

Felix wasn't sure Gotrek *would* have released him from his vow. Like all dwarfs, the Slayer was a stickler when it came to honouring pledges, but still she was right, it had been more than the vow. 'I do have regrets,' he said at last. 'And I did want to leave. Many times. I even agreed to abandon him once.' A shiver went through him as he remembered the circumstances. 'Though I didn't in the end. On the other hand, I have seen more of the world following the Slayer than I ever would have writing poems in Altdorf, and though it has often been dangerous, and I have come close to losing my life more times than I can count, I don't think I could trade it for a safer life. Not any more. I believe I have become addicted to excitement.'

'Well, I envy you that part of it, at least,' said the seeress. 'But to not be able to call your life your own. To not be able to say, "I want to go this way", or "I want to try this", or "I want to talk to this person", because you have pledged to make your life beholden to someone else for all time seems… unbearable! I don't know how you can stand it!'

Felix blinked at her. Was she talking about him any more, or herself? 'It is indeed a hard thing,' he said at last, 'to make a vow that one regrets later, but a man of honour – or a woman of honour, for that matter…'

'Fraulein Pallenberger,' said a voice.

They looked up.

Max Schreiber stood in the door, his eyes cold. 'I thought you had returned to the boat for your gloves.'

Claudia smiled brightly at him. 'And I found them, Magister Schreiber,' she said, holding up a pair of long fawn gloves. 'But then I saw Herr Jaeger here alone and thought I would take some tea with him.'

'You've missed your dinner,' said Max, sounding very much like an out-of-sorts schoolmaster.

'Sometimes a conversation can be more filling than a meal, magister,' she said, standing. She turned to Felix and held out her hand to him, smirking conspiratorially as she did so. 'Thank you for your company, Herr Jaeger,' she said. 'It is very refreshing to speak now and then to someone who still understands the yearning of youth for knowledge and experience.'

'The pleasure was all mine, fraulein.' Felix glanced at Max as he bent over her hand. The wizard was glaring daggers at him. Claudia squeezed Felix's fingers warmly before she let go.

He sighed as she rejoined Max and they turned to go. Would this journey never end? He sat down and returned to his travels with Gotrek.

FOUR

SEVEN DAYS LATER the journey did end, and not before time, as far as Felix was concerned. What with Claudia popping out at him from every corner and Max scowling at him from every doorway, he felt a haunted man by the time the riverboat reached Marienburg, and he disembarked onto the fog-shrouded docks of the Suiddock with a sigh of relief.

He and Gotrek took lodging in an inn that his father had recommended called the Three Bells, in the bustling Handelaarmarkt district – a place of shipping offices, guild halls and trade associations – and had sent word to Hans Euler that he wished to meet with him on a matter of business. While he waited for a response, he continued to read through the first volume of *My Travels With Gotrek*, which was proving better than he had feared. Every now and then he would find himself nodding at a particularly neat turn of phrase and thinking that his younger self was a better writer than he had given him credit for.

Gotrek had immediately installed himself at a table at the back of the Three Bells' long, narrow taproom and proceeded to drink himself into a stupor, just as he had at the Griffon in Altdorf. Felix sighed to see it. It was as if all the life had been sucked out of the Slayer, and all that was left was an empty husk that remembered nothing of its former life except how to drink. With Archaon's invasion repelled, was there anything now that could stir Gotrek from his melancholy? Or would he spend the rest of his days travelling from tavern to tavern, as miserable in one as he was in another?

Though he often complained when he was forced to follow the Slayer into danger, Felix didn't fancy that prospect either. It certainly wouldn't make a very exciting epic.

The next morning, when Felix came down from his room to look for breakfast, the landlord brought him a note. It was from Hans Euler. Felix opened it and read,

> *Herr Jaeger,*
> *Warmest regards, and I would be very pleased to meet*
> *you today, two hours after noon, at my house on the*
> *Kaasveltstraat in the Noordmuur district.*
> *Yours,*
> *Hans Euler*

Felix was pleased, if a little surprised, at the speed and politeness of the reply. From what his father had said of the man, he had expected to be put off or outright refused. He sent a messenger with a reply saying that he would be there at two, then went to find Gotrek.

He didn't have far to look. The Slayer was at the same table Felix had left him at the night before, staring into nothingness with a huge mug in one fist. It looked as if, once again, he had not returned to their room. Felix asked the barmaid to bring him some breakfast, then went and joined the Slayer at the table. Gotrek remained staring straight ahead.

Felix cleared his throat. 'Euler agreed to meet with me today,' he said.

'Who?' rumbled Gotrek, not turning.

'Hans Euler. The man I'm here to see.'

'Ah.' Gotrek drained the mug, then made a face. 'Grungni, that's terrible. Tastes like fish.' He signalled the barman for another.

'I was hoping you would come with me.'

'Why?'

'Well, Euler might be difficult. I might need some help convincing him to hand over the letter.'

Gotrek's single eye looked up at Felix, dim interest stirring behind it. 'A fight?'

'I hope not, but possibly. Mainly I just want him to see you, and your axe, while I talk to him.'

Gotrek pondered this, then shrugged. 'Sounds like too much bother. I'll just stay here and drink.'

Felix nearly choked. The Slayer turning away from the possibility of violence? The end times truly had come. 'But you don't like the beer. It tastes like fish.'

'It's still beer,' said Gotrek, and turned back to stare at the wall.

Felix sighed. He really wanted Gotrek along. There were few things more intimidating than a Slayer, and Gotrek was a particularly impressive example of the breed. It might mean the difference between success or failure in his negotiations. He leaned forwards. 'Listen Gotrek, I can't leave Marienburg until I resolve this matter. If you don't help me, it might take weeks – weeks of drinking fishy beer. On the other hand, if you come with me, I could have the letter today, and we could be on our way back to Altdorf, where the beer *doesn't* taste like fish. What do you think?'

As Gotrek thought this through, the barmaid brought him his next round and Felix his breakfast. Gotrek took up the fresh mug as she set it in front of him, raised it to his lips, then paused, his nose wrinkling. He grunted, drank anyway, then set the mug down again, swallowing with effort. 'All right, manling. I'll come.'

KAASVELTSTRAAT WAS A wealthy street in the middle of the quietly prosperous Noordmuur district, lined on both sides with tidy stone-and-brick three-storey townhouses, each with a white marble stoop leading up to a sturdy wooden front door, and fronted with diamond-paned windows that glittered in the chilly afternoon sun. Hans Euler's house was on the east side of the street, which butted up against a canal, and its upper storeys hung out over the water at the back. It all looked very solid and respectable, not how Felix had imagined the den of a pirate's son to look at all.

Gotrek stood behind him on the cobbled street, trying to reach an itch under his cast, as Felix stepped up to the door to knock – and hesitated. He was not looking forward to what was to follow. These sorts of situations always made him squirm. Why was he even doing this? He had never cared about his father's business. It didn't matter to him if the old man lost a portion of it to someone else. As far as Felix was concerned the whole enterprise could go up in flames. He had half a mind to go back to the Three Bells and forget the whole thing.

But he didn't. Instead, he cursed under his breath and knocked. Family was a stickier trap than any spider's web.

After a moment, a prim little butler in a high-collared black doublet opened the door. He had a spit-curl of oiled black hair plastered to his forehead, and his mouth pursed with disdain as he looked Felix up and down.

'Oui?' he said.

'Felix Jaeger to see Hans Euler,' said Felix. 'And my companion, Gotrek Gurnisson.'

The butler's eyes widened a fraction as he saw Gotrek, then he regained his composure. He made a bow that had more moves in it than a chess game. 'Please to enter, messieurs. Monsieur Euler is expecting you.'

Felix and Gotrek stepped through the door into a wood-panelled entryway with a tight spiral staircase on one side and a door that opened into a large parlour at the back. A bay window in the parlour looked out over the canal. Felix sized up the house as the butler closed the door behind them. It was small, but richly furnished with heavy tables and chairs. Dark oil paintings of men in tight ruffs crowded the walls and expensive Estalian rugs covered the polished wooden floors. It all told Felix that Herr Euler wasn't in his father's league, but he was still a wealthy man.

'Your sword, monsieur?' said the butler, clicking his heels together as he bowed.

Felix unbuckled his sword belt and handed his rune sword to him.

The butler bowed again and turned to Gotrek. 'And ze axe, monsieur dwarf?'

Gotrek just stared at him with his single, expressionless eye.

The butler held his gaze for a brief moment, and looked about to speak again, but then thought better of it. He bowed convulsively and turned away, his face pale. 'It is of no matter,' he stuttered. 'With only ze one arm, how is it possible that you might use it?'

Felix could have informed him otherwise, but let it go.

The butler put Felix's sword in a small cupboard by the door, then bowed them towards the stairs. 'If messieurs will come this way?'

They followed him up to the first floor, where he stopped at a door just at the top of the spiral stair and knocked. A muffled voice called and he opened the door.

'Felix Jaeger and companion, monsieur,' he said into the room, then bowed and edged aside, allowing Felix and Gotrek to enter.

They stepped into the middle of a long room with tall diamond-paned windows along one wall. It was in every way a much lighter room than the one below it. A fire crackled in a small fireplace opposite the door. To the left, a set of graceful Bretonnian chairs was arranged around a low table, and to the right was a grand desk with, behind it, mounted on a cherrywood sideboard, an ironbound safe of dwarf make, that seemed a bit brusque and business-like in the otherwise cultured surroundings.

Standing by the desk with an expression of welcome on his mild round face was the least piratical-looking man Felix had ever seen. He was thick and short and balding, with a shapeless lump of a nose and mild blue eyes. His conservatively tailored clothes were of the most expensive Middenland broadcloth, and he held a silver-headed cane in one pudgy hand. He looked much more merchant than pirate. Perhaps, thought Felix, in these modern times there isn't much difference.

'Messieurs, Herr Euler,' said the butler.

Herr Euler's warm smile faltered when he saw Felix in his rough travelling clothes, and fell entirely when Gotrek's half-naked, tattooed bulk sidled through the narrow door.

He turned to the butler. 'Guiot! The dwarf has his axe!' Felix decided Euler's eyes weren't quite so mild after all.

The butler turned pink and bowed vigorously. 'I apologise, monsieur, but he did not wish, and I did not think... er, that is, crippled as he is, he cannot...'

'It is you who are crippled, Guiot,' Euler snapped. 'With cowardice.' He sighed and waved a dismissive hand. 'Very well, send up Harald and Jochen with food and drink for our guests. You may go.'

'Oui, monsieur. I am sorry, monsieur.' The butler bowed again and withdrew.

Euler reassembled his smile as he turned to Felix. 'Herr Jaeger,' he said, stepping forwards and holding out a hand. 'It is good to meet you at last.'

'The pleasure is mine, Herr Euler,' said Felix, shaking his hand.

'My apologies for my outburst,' Euler continued. 'And to you, master dwarf. Your presence surprised me, that is all. Please, will you sit?'

He motioned to the fragile-looking chairs. Felix sat down with care, making sure his boots and buckles didn't scrape anything. Gotrek plopped down on another as though the exquisite thing was a tavern bench. Euler winced as it creaked in complaint, but maintained his smile.

'I must say, Herr Jaeger,' he said. 'I am surprised to see you here, and before time too. From your father's letters, I expected to be visited by solicitors or assassins, not family members.' He chuckled. 'Ah well, I suppose the old gentleman finally saw the wisdom of my offer at last.'

'Your offer?' Felix frowned. 'Your pardon, Herr Euler. What offer is this? My father said nothing of an offer.'

Herr Euler's broad brow puckered. 'Why, I offered to buy a share in Jaeger and Sons and, as he is getting on, help him with the running of the main office, as well as setting up a new office in Marienburg to facilitate his dealings with overseas merchants.'

Felix raised his eyebrows at this, then glanced over at Gotrek. If things got difficult, he was going to want his support. The Slayer was staring at the floor, paying not the least attention, his cast laying limp in his lap. Felix hoped he was paying enough attention to know when it was time to look menacing.

'My father put it slightly differently,' Felix said at last. 'He called it blackmail, rather than an offer. He said you had a letter that you meant to show the authorities in Altdorf if he failed to give you a controlling interest in Jaeger and Sons.'

There were footsteps in the hall and two men entered, one carrying a silver coffee service, and the other a tray of jam tarts. Though they were dressed in black doublets and breeches with lace at the cuffs and ribbons at the knees, Felix thought he had never seen two more unlikely footmen. They were massive men, each well over six feet tall, with bulging muscles that strained the velvet of their uniforms, hair pulled back in tarred queues, and faces that wore the scars of lifetimes of battle. The hands of the man who carried the coffee service were nearly as large as the tray he balanced it upon.

Felix looked again at Gotrek. He continued to stare at the floor, seemingly unaware as the two behemoths moved with extreme care through the room's maze of featherweight furniture and set down the refreshments on the table between Felix and Euler. Guiot the butler hovered at the door.

'It was not blackmail, Herr Jaeger,' said Euler patiently as he picked up a jam tart. 'I have no love for the dirty dealings our fathers once engaged in, and only want to make things right. What I suggested was that if your father allowed me to purchase part of Jaeger and Sons, we would, together, make amends for our mutual criminal past. But that if he refused my offer and remained in breach of imperial law, I would have no choice, as a law-abiding citizen, but to report him to the proper authorities.'

Felix pursed his lips, Euler's sanctimonious tone grating on him. It appeared his first impression of the man had been incorrect. He was a pirate after all. 'I see.'

The two giants retreated to either side of the fireplace and remained there in attendance.

'But all this is beside the point, since you are here,' said Euler, smiling. 'Have you brought the documents? Have you decided the value of the shares?'

Felix coughed, cursing his father for putting him in such a situation. He hated this sort of venal confrontation. His brother Otto would have been much better suited for the job. He would have known exactly the sort of veiled threats to use. 'Herr Euler. You misunderstand the purpose of my visit. I have not come to sell you any part of my father's company. I have come to get the letter back.'

Euler's smile disappeared as if it had never been. He shot a look at the safe on the table behind his desk, then put down his jam tart in a cold sort of way.

Felix pushed on. 'Before you say anything, I should tell you that my father has authorised me to offer you a very generous price for the letter.'

Euler barked a laugh. 'What is a one-time payment compared to the continual revenue that owning part of the company will bring me? No thank you, Herr Jaeger. There is only one way that your father may resolve this difficulty, and that is *my* way. He has seventeen days left.

Until he is prepared to sell, we have nothing further to discuss. You may go.'

Felix sighed. It was at this point in the proceedings that his father undoubtedly expected him to start smashing things up until Euler gave him the letter, but he really didn't have the heart for it. The man was vile, but no more vile than his father, and Felix had never bullied anyone for anything in his life. He wasn't a robber, and that's what he felt like here. It was embarrassing. If only he had some other kind of leverage. If only he could play the same sort of trick on Euler that Euler had played on his father.

Felix paused. Well, why couldn't he? 'I am sorry to hear you say it, Herr Euler,' he said at last. 'For I was hoping that I wouldn't have to resort to blackmail of my own.'

'What nonsense is this?' asked Euler.

Felix swallowed, and plunged in. 'Well, correspondence goes both ways. My father also has a letter from your father, in which he admits engaging in the same activities as my father did, and also, that he introduced you to the business as well.'

'What activities does he mean?' cried Euler.

Felix had no idea. 'It's best not to name them aloud, don't you think?' he said. 'Even after so many years.' He smiled at Euler with what he hoped looked like malevolent guile. 'My father wishes to assure you that, if you drag him down, you will find yourself drowning in the same sewer – and you have much more life to lose than he. But, if you are prepared to give up your letter, he is prepared to give up his. We can make an exchange, and conclude the matter peacefully.'

Euler's eyes blazed. He stroked his round chin with chubby fingers. 'The cunning old goat. I believe he would be willing to die in shame and poverty just so that he could see me ruined as well.' A sudden thought seemed to come to him. He looked at his hulking serving men, then back to Felix. 'Have you this letter here?'

Felix's eyes widened. It hadn't occurred to him that Euler would resort to violence. Despite the size of his servants, he was still a respectable man on a respectable street. He wasn't going to try anything in his own home, was he?

'Er, not on me,' said Felix. 'I left it at the inn, thinking you would be reasonable and I wouldn't need it. If it must come to this, I will go and fetch it.'

Euler smiled. 'No need to trouble yourself. I will have a servant fetch it while you wait here.'

Felix shot a look at Gotrek. He still didn't appear to be paying attention. Couldn't he feel the tension thickening the air? 'It is no trouble, Herr Euler,' he said, standing. 'We will return in an hour, shall we say?'

'I'm sorry, Herr Jaeger,' said Euler, standing as well. 'I must insist that you stay.' He gave a nod to the two massive footmen and they began to cross to the door.

Felix grunted, angry now. He was about to get into a fight over something he hadn't wanted anything to do with from the beginning. Damn Euler and damn his father both. 'You will regret holding us against our will, mein herr,' he said. 'My companion is not to be trifled with lightly.'

Euler looked at Gotrek, and Felix followed his gaze. The Slayer was a sight to instil fear and respect, his massive frame and corded muscles completely eclipsing the tiny chair he sat in, and his fearsome crest and swirling tattoos exuding exotic menace. Of course, he would have been more impressive still had he not chosen that moment to open his mouth and snore like a chain rattling through a pulley.

Euler laughed. 'Terrifying.' He turned away from him, waving a hand at the footmen. 'Take them to the cellar.'

The brutes stepped forwards. Felix nudged Gotrek with his elbow. The Slayer mumbled under his breath, but didn't wake. 'You will force me to release the letter, Herr Euler,' he said, nudging Gotrek harder.

Euler snorted. 'How can you release what you no longer have?'

The footmen loomed closer.

'Now then, sir,' said the one on the left, whose right ear was missing. 'Come quietly and we won't have to break anything.'

'Gotrek!' barked Felix, and jabbed the Slayer in the shoulder with his elbow.

The Slayer woke with a start, instinctively grabbing for his axe. The sudden motion was too much for his delicate chair. It snapped in a dozen places and Gotrek thumped to the floor in a splay of spindly kindling.

'Vandalism!' shouted Euler. 'Your father will get a bill for that!'

Gotrek was up in an instant, fists balled and turning his head from side to side like a sleepy bear. 'Who pushed me off my seat?' he growled.

'They did!' said Felix, backing up and pointing at the looming footmen.

Gotrek turned towards them, glaring and blinking.

'Come along, tipsy,' said the one on the right, who had an oft-broken nose. 'Sleep it off in the nice dark cellar, eh?' He put an enormous hand on Gotrek's shoulder.

Gotrek swung his cast and re-broke the man's nose. The footman staggered back, howling and clutching his face, and fell backwards over the low table, smashing it to flinders.

'Here, now!' said One-Ear, swinging at Gotrek.

The punch snapped Gotrek's head around, but only seemed to make him mad. He growled and doubled the footman up with a fist to the guts, then shoved him back into a side table. It exploded under his weight.

'Pillagers!' cried Euler. 'Guiot! Call Uwe and the others! Call the Black Caps! Hurry!'

The Bretonnian butler bowed and turned for the door. Felix ran for him. The last thing they needed was the watch showing up. Euler leapt in his path, twisting the head of his cane and drawing forth a slim blade.

'No, Herr Jaeger,' he said, levelling the sword-cane at Felix's chest.

Felix stepped back, then cuffed an Estalian vase off a table, right at Euler's face. When he raised his sword to block it, Felix dived forwards and tackled him to the ground, pinning his sword arm with a knee and punching him in the face. The merchant bucked and twisted under him, surprisingly strong.

'Harald! Jochen!' Euler called, struggling to get his sword free.

But the two footmen were otherwise engaged. Out of the corner of his eye, Felix could see that Broken-Nose was up again, blood streaming down his face, swinging the remains of the low table at Gotrek. Beyond him, One-Ear was holding his stomach and puking all over a set of marble chessmen.

'Gotrek,' Felix shouted, elbowing Euler in the eye. 'Forget them! Get the safe! Open it!' If Euler was going to stoop to outright villainy, Felix had no more compunctions about robbing him.

Gotrek headbutted Broken-Nose on the broken nose and pushed him aside. He turned and looked at the safe as the big man slumped peacefully to the floor behind him. 'There's no cracking that,' the Slayer said, frowning. 'It's dwarf work. You'll need a key.'

Euler wrenched his sword hand free of Felix's knee, but Felix caught it again and slammed it against the ground. Euler lost his grip and the blade bounced across the carpet. As he stretched for it, Felix saw a ring of keys on the belt at his waist. He ripped them free and tossed them to Gotrek.

'Try these!'

Gotrek caught the key ring, but as he started around the desk towards the safe, there was a thunder of boots from the passage and a flood of large bodies burst into the room.

Gotrek and Felix turned towards them. There were six of them, all dressed in the same beribboned footmen's uniforms that Harald and Jochen wore, and all apparently born of the same breed as well – huge, lumbering bashers with lantern jaws and scarred scalps, all armed with clubs and cudgels. One had a hook for a hand. Guiot peered nervously into the room behind them.

'Take yer hands off the captain,' said one with a milky left eye.

That wasn't necessary, for, distracted by their entrance, Felix had let his grip slip, and Euler crashed a fist into his jaw with a hard-knuckled hand. Felix swayed back, and Euler pushed him off, shouting at his men.

'Get them! Hold them! Keep them away from the safe!'

The six footmen waded forwards, pushing the broken furniture out of the way. Gotrek reached over his shoulder for his axe.

'Not the axe,' gasped Felix from the floor. 'No murder, Gotrek, please.'

The Slayer snarled like a thwarted badger, then lowered his hand, roared a wordless challenge at the approaching men and charged, swinging his fist and his cast with equal abandon. He disappeared in a storm of flailing, velvet-clad limbs.

Felix shook his head, trying to reseat his jaw, and pulled himself to his feet. Euler beat him to it. He scooped up his sword-cane and turned on him, raising the blade. The eye Felix had elbowed was purpling rapidly.

'I believe I've changed my mind,' he said, smiling through bloody lips. 'Perhaps the watch should find you dead when they arrive. A man must defend his home, mustn't he?'

Euler lunged, extending his arm with the grace of an Estalian diestro. Felix dived aside, alarmed. For all his padding and his bland burgher's clothes the man had been well trained in the sword. Felix rolled up and ran for the door, passing the scrum in the middle of the floor. Two of the big men were down, one with an arm bent at a sickening angle, but the rest continued to rain blows upon the squat struggling figure in their midst. Guiot, the butler, stood wide-eyed in the door, then dived sensibly out of the way.

Felix barrelled down the stairs, slipping once on the well-worn treads and nearly falling head first. He heard Euler pounding down right behind him.

At the bottom, he charged across the foyer for the cupboard next to the front door. As he threw it open, Euler careened out after him, cane sword extended in a fencer's lunge.

Felix snatched up his scabbard and leapt away as Euler's blade impaled the cupboard door. He ran for the back parlour, drawing as he went. Euler lurched after him.

The room was darker than Euler's office, and filled with sturdy, more liveable furniture. The ceiling was low and ribbed with heavy, widely spaced beams. Felix cracked his head on one as he vaulted a long red brocade couch. He turned to face Euler, his rune sword held out with one hand while he rubbed vigorously at a lump like half an onion that was forming on the crown of his skull with the other. His eyes were tearing.

Euler edged around the couch, sword high, shaking his head and unbuttoning his doublet so that he had more mobility. 'Poorly played, Herr Jaeger.' Felix could barely hear him over the thuds and bangs and crashes coming from the fight upstairs. The ceiling vibrated with them. 'Had you left the letter in Altdorf I would have been checkmated – a threat I couldn't reach. Your father would never have made such a mistake.'

'You sound like you admire him,' said Felix.

'I do,' said Euler. 'He plays the game very well.' He sneered. 'But this time he has picked a very poor pawn.'

Euler lunged, extending his sword-cane with blurring swiftness. Felix blocked it, but the lighter blade came at him again instantly. He jumped back, wishing for more space to swing his bigger sword. Euler had him at a disadvantage in the low room.

Then a horrendous thump and chorus of wild shouts from above made Felix look up. Euler's blade snaked for his throat. Felix back-pedalled furiously. Unfortunately there was a footstool behind him and he toppled backwards over it, slamming his breath out as his back hit the fine Estalian carpet.

Euler stepped over him, white flakes of plaster floating down around him from the ceiling. 'I will send your body back to your father,' said Euler, shouting to be heard over the rumpus coming from above, 'as a token of my admiration.'

Felix struggled to get his limbs to respond as Euler put his sword-cane to his throat. Then, suddenly, the shouts from above became screams, and there was a horrendous crashing from the stairs.

Euler and Felix looked towards the noise and saw a large square object bounce down out of the stairwell in a shower of wood, plaster and dust, and hit the entryway floor with an impact that shook the house. It was quickly followed by a rain of flying footmen, all spinning down and slapping loosely on the floor around it.

'My safe,' said Euler, blinking.

After the footmen tumbled Gotrek, landing shoulders first on a heaving velvet-clad stomach. He staggered up and shook his fist up the stairwell. 'Come down here, you cowards!' He was bleeding freely from the back of his skull.

Felix took advantage of Euler's distraction to roll out from under the point of his sword and stand.

Euler was beside himself. 'My floor!' he cried. 'My pan-elling! Manann's scales, the expense!' He turned on Felix, eyes blazing. 'I'll send your corpse back to your father with a bill for damages!'

He thrust at Felix with his cane-sword and Felix blocked and kicked the footstool at him.

'Gotrek!' he called. 'Here!'

The Slayer swung around and started towards him. One of the fallen men tried to rise, lifting a dagger at him. Gotrek backhanded his face with his cast and kept walking. The strike sounded like a pistol shot, and Felix thought for a moment that he had shattered the man's skull. But it was the cast that had split, a zigzag crack that ran the length of the thing. With a grunt of satisfaction Gotrek tore it off and flexed and shook out his arm.

'About time,' he growled, stepping into the back parlour and starting around the red brocade couch towards Euler. The merchant danced back, trying to keep both Felix and Gotrek in front of him. Just then, there was a rumble of boots from the spiral stair and two men ran into the room, then skidded to a stop behind the couch when they saw Gotrek.

'Sigmar's hammer, he lives!' said the one on the left, who held a blood-spattered fireplace poker.

Gotrek growled in his throat and beckoned them forwards. 'Try that again,' he rasped. 'I dare you.'

'Kill them!' screeched Euler, backing behind an elegant Tilean harpsichord.

'I'm not going near him,' said the one with the poker. 'He's mad!'

'He threw the safe at Uwe!' said the other, who was none other than One-Ear, still on his feet and now carrying a sailor's cutlass.

'Kill them or all your back pay is forfeit!' Euler shouted.

Felix stepped beside Gotrek as the two towering footmen eyed them warily.

'Can I use my axe now?' rumbled Gotrek.

'Now would be a good time, yes,' said Felix.

'Good,' said the Slayer, and drew it off his back.

One-Ear leaned towards his companion and said something out of the side of his mouth that Felix couldn't hear.

'What are you waiting for?' called Euler.

Then, before Felix could understand what they meant to do, the two giants threw aside their weapons, picked up the massive couch as if it weighed nothing, and charged Gotrek and Felix with it.

Felix stumbled back, surprised. But Gotrek roared and hacked at the brocade barrier with his axe as it raced towards them. The rune weapon bit deep, smashing through the wooden frame and the horsehair depths of the upholstery, but not deep enough.

The couch hit Felix and the Slayer amidships and drove them back towards the rear wall of the house. They tried to push back, but it was no use, the loose carpet under their boots slid across the polished floorboards and gave them no purchase. Felix's heels hit the baseboard and then, with an enormous explosion of diamond-paned glass, he and Gotrek flew backwards out of the window, trailing velvet curtains and a few red brocade couch cushions.

There was a frozen moment when Felix took in the beauty of the flying shards of glass glittering in the afternoon sun, the intricacy of the decorative brickwork on Euler's back wall, and the fluffy white clouds above it all, then the canal smacked him in the back and the water closed over his head in a freezing, silty rush.

The shock of it drove sense from his head for a moment, then he was kicking back to the surface, fighting the heavy pull of his saturated clothes. He broke the surface, gasping and kicking to stay afloat, and saw Gotrek to his left, his crest plastered down over his good eye, shaking his axe over his head.

'Craven humans!' he roared as he and Felix were drawn down the canal by the slow current. 'A couch is a coward's weapon!'

Felix looked up. From the shattered window, Euler was shouting back, his two remaining footmen at his sides, glaring murder down at them.

'This vandalism will cost you, Jaeger!' he cried. 'I will no longer settle for half of Jaeger and Sons! I will have it all!'

Gotrek returned his axe to his shoulder and struck for the side of the canal. 'Come on, manling, let's finish these furniture-throwers.'

Felix made to follow, but just then Euler and his men were joined at the window by men in the black-capped uniforms of the Marienburg city watch. Euler shouted and pointed at Felix. 'That's the man! He and the dwarf did all this!'

Felix sighed. He was almost ready to cry 'enough' and let his father take care of his own dirty business. But he *had* promised, and Euler had made him mad. The man had tried to murder him. Well, Felix wasn't going to respond in kind, but he'd find some other way to get the letter. It was a matter of pride now.

'We'll come back later,' he said. 'I need to think.'

Gotrek grunted, but then nodded. 'I could use a drink anyway.' He turned, and he and Felix swam for the far bank.

FIVE

THEY MADE THEIR way circuitously back to the Three Bells, taking alleys and lesser bridges to avoid the watch. Felix was miserable the whole way, wet and cold in the windy Marienburg sunshine, with his drenched clothes hanging off him like they were made of lead and his boots squishing with every step. Gotrek, annoyingly, didn't seem bothered in the least.

Felix slowed as they reached the last corner before the inn, worried that there would be a company of the watch waiting for them at the door. He leaned his head out to have a look, and felt a different sort of chill as he saw that there were indeed Black Caps milling outside the door of the inn. He pulled back instinctively, but then looked again, frowning. If the watch was there for them, what were they doing carrying people out of the inn on stretchers? And why were the landlord and the serving women all talking to them at once?

'Something's happened,' he said.

Gotrek had a look too, then shrugged. 'As long as they're still serving.'

He tromped forwards single-mindedly. Felix followed more cautiously, keeping his head down, but the Black Caps didn't seem interested in him or the Slayer in the slightest. They were too busy helping sickly-looking people out onto the street and interviewing the owner of the Bells. More sick people sat on the cobbles, coughing and retching. A few were weeping. People from neighbouring businesses clustered outside their doorways, talking in hushed tones.

As they neared the inn, Felix staggered, hit by a wave of horrible odour, like rotting eggs and attar of rose mixed together. He covered his nose and mouth, and continued on. Gotrek did the same. The stench was making him dizzy.

A Black Cap held up a hand at the door. 'You don't want to go in, mein herr.' His eyes were streaming and he had a kerchief over his mouth.

'What happened?' Felix asked.

'Something in the cellar,' said the watchman. 'Came up like smoke, they say, and everybody who got a good whiff fell down like they was dead.'

'They died?' Felix was shocked.

'No, sir,' said the Black Cap. 'Only fainted like, and very sick with it.'

'But what was it?'

'That's what the captain is trying to find out.'

'Sewer gas is what it was!' said a prosperous-looking merchant who appeared to have been hurried out of the inn in the middle of dressing. 'Damned city hasn't fixed those channels in decades. Manann knows what's growing down there.'

'It were cultists!' gasped a barman, looking up with bloodshot eyes from where he sat. He had flecks of bloody foam around his mouth. Felix remembered him from earlier when he had served them in the taproom. 'Cut a hole in the cask cellar floor. I saw it. Like a green fog it was. Then it got me.'

Could it have been only sewer gas? Felix looked at Gotrek. The Slayer's expression said he didn't think so.

'When did this happen?' he asked the barman.

'Just after lunch, sir,' he said. 'Right after you left in fact. I remember, because it was when I went down to bring up a new keg after you finished the old one that I saw the smoke.'

Felix exchanged another uneasy glance with Gotrek. He was willing to bet that their room had been broken into, and he wanted to see if there were any clues as to who had done it, but he didn't want to poison himself to do it.

'How long before we can go in?' asked Felix.

The Black Cap shrugged. 'Not until the captain blows the all-clear.'

IT WAS AN uneasy wait, with Felix watching the ends of the street constantly for Euler's Black Caps, and Gotrek grumbling about being thirsty, but fortunately, Felix wasn't the only one who wanted to go back in and get his things, and finally the captain gave in to the besieging guests who clamoured around him in various states of undress and distress, and said that they could all enter to retrieve their belongings, but that the inn would be closed immediately afterwards until it could be searched more thoroughly. The innkeeper looked sullen about this, but everyone else cheered and rushed in.

Gotrek and Felix followed the flow up to the second floor. The interior of the inn still smelled horrible, and the stink was worse in the confines of the narrow upper halls. Felix covered his mouth with his handkerchief, but he still felt the corridor swim around him, and had to brace himself against the wall for balance as they went along. They slowed and drew their weapons as they approached their room. Then Felix stopped altogether. The door was ajar. Had the Black Caps forced it? He certainly hadn't left it that way.

They crept to it and listened. Felix looked to Gotrek. He shook his head. The lack of noise did nothing to allay Felix's fears. It might only mean that their enemies were lying in wait. Gotrek raised his axe, then nodded.

As one, they jumped forwards and kicked the door in. It banged open and Gotrek leapt in, slashing left and right. He struck nothing. The tiny room was empty but for the expected furnishings, a bed along each wall, a wash stand and a clothes trunk. The beds had been smashed, the wash stand overturned, and the trunk had been opened and their few belongings strewn about.

Felix followed after Gotrek and closed the door behind them. Things would be awkward should the landlord come by and see the damage. He looked around. The window that was the room's only source of light was open and there were fresh splinters on the sill, as if someone had gone in or out that way. It would have had to have been a very small and agile someone, for the window was tiny, and high up on the wall. A child might have done it – or a slim woman.

He pushed that thought away and searched through his few clothes. Everything had been ripped and cut, and he feared that his armour was stolen, but then he found it thrown in a corner, still whole, but reeking like everything else from the poisonous stink. Perhaps the vandals had been unable to tear it. The Slayer's bedroll had been hacked up too, but he had no clothes to ruin. He owned no other possessions that he didn't carry on his person at all times.

'Darts, nets, poison gas,' said Gotrek. 'Only cowards use such things.'

Felix looked at him. 'You think it was the same ones who attacked us in Altdorf?'

Gotrek nodded. 'And whoever they are, they want us alive.'

Once again the image of Lady Hermione and Mistress Wither looking down at him while he was bound and helpless came unbidden to his mind, and he shivered convulsively.

ON THEIR WAY out, Felix paid the landlord double what they owed him for the room. It was his father's money, and the least he could do for the trouble they had brought upon his establishment.

As they started down the street, Felix wondered if they might not need to sleep in the open, just so they wouldn't bring a similar fate to another hostelry. He was beginning to feel like he was the carrier of some deadly plague, and that he should keep away from human society until it had run its course. They needed to face these foes and finish them, but they didn't even know who they were.

A block away from the inn, someone called their names.

'Felix! Gotrek!'

Felix and Gotrek turned, their hands drifting towards their weapons. A coach was heading towards them and Max was leaning out the window.

'I was just coming to find you,' he said, then noticed that Felix was carrying his armour. 'Have you left your inn?'

'Uh…' Felix paused, uncertain how much to tell him. 'Our room was burgled,' he said at last. 'We decided to look for other lodgings.'

Max shook his head, bemused. 'Trouble follows you two like a stray dog.'

'More like a bat,' said Felix under his breath, then spoke up. 'What did you want to see us about?'

'I have an urgent matter to discuss with you,' said Max, opening the door to his coach. 'Will you join me?'

MAX SAID NOT a word about the urgent matter in the coach as they crossed the many bridges and islands of the city to the Suiddock wharfs.

'Are we going back to the *Jilfte Bateau*?' asked Felix as the coach's wheels boomed on the wooden planks of the docks.

'No,' said Max. 'Our new companion waits for us at the Pike and Pike.'

'New companion?'

But Max would say no more.

The coach came to a stop on a busy commercial wharf, with stevedores unloading goods from merchant ships flying the colours of Bretonnia, Estalia and Tilea, as well as dozens of Imperial and Marienburg vessels. They stepped down from the coach and Max led the way to a small tavern with a river pike impaled on a spear over the door. The place smelled, unsurprisingly, of fish, but the odour lessened as they made their way through the noisy taproom to a stair that led up to a small, but neatly furnished private dining room on the first floor.

Felix nodded politely to Claudia, who sat sideways on a cushioned bench by the fire on the left wall, her feet curled underneath her, then stopped dead as he saw the other occupant of the room, sitting ram-rod straight at the head of the table that filled the centre of the room. Gotrek grunted like he'd smelled something foul. It was an elf. Felix understood suddenly why Max hadn't mentioned this earlier. He wouldn't have got Gotrek in the coach.

'Felix Jaeger,' said Max, 'Gotrek Gurnisson, may I present Aethenir Whiteleaf, student of the White Tower of Hoeth and son of the fair land of Eataine.'

The elf rose, inclining his head respectfully. He was tall, and as slender as a willow branch in his flowing white robes, but there was an air of youth and nervousness about him that made him look more awkward than graceful. He had the long, haughty features of his kind, but the nervousness showed also in his cobalt-blue eyes, which flicked about the room as he spoke. 'I am honoured, friends. Your acquaintance enriches me.'

'An elf,' Gotrek spat. He turned back to the door. 'Come on, manling.'

'Wait, Slayer,' said Max. 'If you still seek your doom, hear him out.'

'We go into the gravest danger, with you or without you,' added Claudia.

Gotrek paused at the door, his fists clenching. Felix looked from him to Max to the elf to the seeress, all waiting for the Slayer's decision.

At last the Slayer turned back around. 'Speak your piece, beard-cutter.'

'That is a myth,' snapped the elf. 'It never happened. You—'

Max held up a hand. 'Friends, please. This is perhaps not the time to bring up old arguments. We have little time.'

'You are right, magister,' said Aethenir. 'Forgive me.'

Gotrek just grunted.

Max offered Gotrek and Felix seats at the table and took one himself. Felix sat, but Gotrek remained standing, arms crossed, glaring at the elf.

'We met Scholar Aethenir last night,' said Max, 'when he came to a gathering of Marienburg magisters seeking their knowledge of the region of the Wasteland to the north and west of here.'

'The same region that my visions are leading me to,' said Claudia, leaning forwards meaningfully.

'A book was stolen from the library of the Tower of Hoeth,' said Aethenir. 'A book containing maps and descriptions of the area you call the Wasteland, and the elven cities that once graced it, as it was before the Sundering ravaged both land and sea and changed the coastline forever. I must recover this book.'

'And…?' said Gotrek when the elf didn't continue.

'And?' asked Aethenir.

'Where is my doom in this?'

'Don't you see, Slayer,' said Claudia, speaking up. 'The book details exactly the same area that my visions have told me will be the birth of the destruction of Marienburg and Altdorf. This is not coincidence. Some great evil is brewing there. We must go and prevent it.'

'It is my belief,' said Aethenir, 'that those who stole the book are agents of the Dark Powers, and seek some ancient elven artefact in one of the ruined cities. I know not what it might be, but an item of great power in the hands of the pawns of Chaos can only spell ruin and despair for the peoples of Ulthuan and the Old World.'

'I don't understand,' said Felix. 'If this is such a grave threat, why are the elves not going in force? No disrespect to you, high one, or to Herr Schreiber and Fraulein

Pallenberger, but why have you come to us? Why haven't you brought the navy of Ulthuan with you?'

Aethenir hesitated, looking down at the table, then spoke. 'As I explained to the magisters last night, the Tower of Hoeth is the centre of magical learning in Ulthuan. There, the greatest mages of the world are taught the one true art. The tomes and scrolls housed within its white walls make up the most complete, and most dangerous, library that exists in the world. The tower itself is reputed to be unreachable and unbreachable. Never has anything been stolen from it before.' Colour came into the high elf's cheeks. 'The loremasters of the tower are proud of this reputation, and do not wish it to be known that this shame has befallen them, so they have dispatched me, a mere humble initiate, to retrieve the book in secret before any know that it is missing. I have come with no escort except a few of my father's household guard, all sworn to secrecy, on the pretext of examining some pre-Sundering ruins in the pursuit of my field of study. It was felt that any larger force would call attention to the theft.'

Gotrek snorted. 'Typical elven shiftiness.'

Felix frowned. 'How soon would you be leaving on this journey?' he asked.

'Immediately,' said Max. 'Scholar Aethenir has hired a ship, and its captain is prepared to sail on the evening tide.'

Felix turned to Gotrek. 'Slayer, I still must retrieve Euler's letter.'

Gotrek nodded. 'Aye. And I've no time for elf snotling chases. I'll pass.'

He turned to the door. Felix rose to follow him, bowing to Max, Aethenir and Claudia. 'I'm sorry, but…'

'I dreamed of you, Slayer,' called Claudia, as Gotrek pushed open the door. 'I saw you in the bowels of a black

mountain, fighting foes without number. I saw blood
rise like a tide to drown you. I saw a towering abomination crushing you in its claws.'

Gotrek paused in the doorway. Felix stopped behind
him, shooting a dirty look back at Claudia. Had she
really seen these things, or was she just wooing the Slayer
with the only lure that could sway him?

Gotrek looked to Max. 'Do you vouch for this girl's seeing, wizard?'

Max nodded gravely. 'Yes, Gotrek. She has been judged
to have true powers of divination by the Lord Magisters
of her order.'

'Gotrek,' Felix said. 'I cannot go.'

Gotrek nodded, but a light had kindled in his single
eye that Felix hadn't seen since he had fought Magus
Lichtmann and his cannon daemon. 'Do what you have
to, manling,' Gotrek said. 'I won't stop you. But I must
fulfil my doom.' He turned to face Claudia, Max and
Aethenir. 'Right,' he said. 'I'll come. But keep the elf away
from me.'

FELIX FOUGHT WITH his conscience as he walked with
Gotrek, Max and the others to the wharf where their
hired ship was docked. What should he do? Did he wish
them a good voyage and have another go at Hans Euler
tomorrow, or did he go with them and forget retrieving
the incriminating letter? To whom was he more
beholden, Gotrek or his father? Which vow came first?
He had followed Gotrek for twenty years, and had never
taken another vow that contradicted the one he had
made to the Slayer. But Gotrek wasn't family. He wasn't
on his death bed. On the other hand, what if the Slayer
met his doom at last and he wasn't there to witness it?
That would invalidate their whole reason for travelling

together. It would be a terribly anti-climactic ending to such a grand adventure.

At last he sighed and dropped back to Gotrek, who had fallen a little behind.

'Slayer,' he said. 'I can't make the decision to stay or go.'

Gotrek shrugged. 'A dwarf's first loyalty is to family. I will not begrudge you this.'

Felix nodded, but continued pondering. Gotrek's permission to leave didn't actually make his decision any easier. Mad as it sounded, he would still rather go with Gotrek towards his doom. He didn't really care what happened to Euler. It was his father who had forced him into conflict with him. It would serve the old buzzard right if Felix just sat on his hands for the next seventeen days and let Euler send his letter to the authorities. And yet, he had promised. Hadn't he just told Claudia that a vow was a vow, no matter–

Seventeen days! Felix's heart lurched. That was it! That was the solution.

He turned to Gotrek. 'I've made up my mind,' he said. 'I have seventeen days to recover the letter, so I will go with you. It can't be more than a week up the coast and a week back. So we will have a day or two once we return, to take the letter back from Euler.'

'We may not return, manling,' said Gotrek.

'Then it will be fate that kept me from fulfilling my promise,' said Felix, insistent. 'Not lack of will.'

Gotrek raised an eyebrow at this but said nothing as Felix went to tell Max of his decision.

THE HOSPITALITY OF Clan Skryre Warleader Riskin Tatter-Ear, commander of the skaven burrows under the fish-stinking man-warren the humans called Marienburg, amounted to a single damp room at the far end of

an unused tunnel, barely large enough to house
Thanquol, let alone all his retinue and Boneripper, and
for which the impertinent young pup expected to be
paid a fortune in warp tokens! The gross disrespect of it
astounded Thanquol. Did he not know who he was? In
the old days a mere warleader would have bowed and
licked his hind paws in his eagerness to serve a grey seer
of his renown.

The cold welcome had done nothing to improve
Thanquol's mood, already befouled by the slow, miserable journey that had brought him here. In his day the
palanquin-bearers had been speedy and subservient.
They had known their place and how to get one to one's
destination without colliding with every skaven coming
the other way. Now it seemed more than they could do
to all move in the same direction at once. It was therefore
with little patience that he listened to his overpaid,
under-successful assassin make yet more excuses.

'My abject apologies, oh most forgiving of skaven,' said
Shadowfang from the floor where he knelt before him.
'But though our sleep-smoke missed them at the drink-
ing place, all is not lost.'

'No?' said Thanquol. 'Have you managed to poison
yourself in the process, then?'

Issfet tittered fawningly at that, and Thanquol nodded
approvingly. He liked his servants servile and obse-
quious.

'No, grey seer,' said Shadowfang. 'But we have sneak-
followed the pair to a ship, and have tortured one of the
sailors to reveal its destination.'

'And…?'

The assassin squirmed uncomfortably. 'They have no
destination, sagacious one. They hunt-seek something in
the stink-swamp, but know not where it is.'

Thanquol turned this information over in his head. It was unfortunate that Shadowfang had once again been unable to capture his two nemeses, but it would not be the most terrible of plans to follow them into the Wasteland where there would be no one to interfere or come to their rescue. Yes, perhaps it was for the best. Now he only needed some way of following them there.

He turned to Issfet. 'What manners of conveyance does this fool Riskin have at his disposal?' he asked. 'Quick-quick.'

The tailless skaven bowed and once again nearly lost his balance. 'I shall enquire, oh most effluent of masters.'

SIX

THE PRIDE OF SKINTSTAAD was a two-masted trading ship out of Marienburg that Aethenir had hired with elven gold. She was a pot-bellied little barque, slow but sea-worthy, with a grizzled, vulture-beaked captain by the name of Ulberd Breda, and a crew from every corner of the Old World.

Though happy to take Aethenir's money, Captain Breda seemed a bit uneasy about their voyage, and Felix didn't blame him. Max's instructions had been to sail north and west through the Manaanspoort Sea and on into the Sea of Chaos until Fraulein Pallenberger called a halt. They might sail all the way to the Sea of Ice if she failed to receive any vision, and a journey into those bar-barous climes was not to be made lightly by a little ship with winter coming on. Storms, Norse raiders and ice-bergs were the least they could expect if they went that far.

Felix shivered at the idea of all those days at sea, and not because of the cold or the danger. Being cooped up on the tiny ship with such a volatile mix of personalities for any length of time was sure to be a miserable experience. In fact, even before they had left the dock there had been conflict. Aethenir had come on board with seven elf warriors, taken one look at his cabin and come back out again, saying he refused to stay there until it had been thoroughly cleaned.

'It's filthy,' he said with a shudder. 'It stinks of urine and vermin. There was a rat on my bed.'

The crew snorted at that.

'Ain't a ship that sails that doesn't have rats, yer worship,' said Captain Breda.

'You've never sailed on a ship of Ulthuan, then,' said Aethenir, sniffing.

'No, yer worship, I never has. But if we was to try to chase off all the rats on *this* ship we'd never leave the dock.' He turned to one of his crewmen, an Estalian by his look. 'Doso, go and clean his worship's cabin.'

'But I swabbed this morning,' complained Doso.

'Then swab it again,' growled the captain. 'And use clean water this time.'

Doso grumbled, but did as he was told.

It was clear that, even after this extra cleaning, Aethenir was less than satisfied, but Max whispered a few words in the high elf's ear and he dropped the matter. Unfortunately, the damage was done. The high elf had earned the ill will of the crew – men that might have treated him with the awe and respect that humans generally reserved for the elder races were, in one stroke, sneering at him behind his back and spitting on his shadow.

His warriors fared better, for unlike their master, they seemed hardened veterans – cold, silent elves who wore scarred scale mail under the green and white surcoats of Aethenir's livery, and asked for no special favours. They found a place near the aft rail and talked quietly amongst themselves, and that was that.

Gotrek did what he always did on any voyage over water. He went directly to his cabin and stayed there. Felix hoped he continued this way, for that would lessen the probability that he and Aethenir would meet during the voyage, a situation to be avoided at all costs if blood was not to be spilled and the War of the Beard not to be rekindled.

Max and Claudia spoke briefly with the captain and also retired to their cabins, but Felix feared that there would be trouble from that quarter ere long, for as she started down the stairs to her quarters, the seeress cast a look back at him from under her golden fall of hair that made the hair stand up on the back of his neck.

Max's Reiksguard escort found a place for themselves along the port rail and lounged there, chatting and smoking pipes and spitting over the side, as the crew made ready to make way.

At last, with a heavy mist freshening into a light rain, they cast off the lines and were towed out of the Brynwater into the centre of the Rijksweg by boats of the Marienburg port authority. Then the sails were unfurled, and they were away, sailing past the grim fortifications of Rijker's Isle and out into the Manaanspoort Sea.

And a less breathtaking beginning to a voyage Felix could not have imagined. The sky was a dull, uninterrupted grey. The air was wet and chilly, the rain not even strong enough to be called a drizzle, and the scenery left much to be desired. The east coast of the sea, which ran almost due north towards the Sea of Chaos, was known as the Cursed Marshes, but Felix, after the fifth hour of watching them slide slowly by, was ready to rename them the Dull Marshes, because he had never seen a more uninteresting landscape in all his life – nothing but saw grass and cat-tails and stunted trees for as far as the eye could see, mile after mile after mile. Occasionally a stork would fly past, or a chevron of geese, gabbling like noisy children, or there would come the rustle and plop of some hidden swamp-dweller sliding into the still water, but that was all. It was little wonder, thought Felix, that the Empire had let Marienburg claim the marshes and the wastelands for their own. Who would want them?

THERE WAS MORE trouble with Aethenir at lunch – trouble with far-reaching repercussions for Felix's peace of mind – though at its beginning, it had only been an argument about food.

Before he had even tasted the bowl of stew that one of his warriors had brought him, Aethenir had thrown it overboard. He had come up from his cabin already agitated – presumably from the lack of cleanliness – and the smell of the food appeared to be the last straw.

'This is unacceptable!' he said in a clear high voice. 'I may be forced to sleep in filth, but I refuse to eat it.'

Felix took another sniff of his stew. It smelled fine to him, if a little strong on the garlic.

Captain Breda glared at the high elf over the lip of his bowl, his mouth full. 'You got what we all got,' he said.

'And I wonder you don't die from it!' cried Aethenir. He turned to Max. 'Is it too much to ask for fresh vegetables and fresh meat, cleanly prepared?'

Max glanced around uneasily, but before he could speak, the cook, a peg-legged Tilean with a pot belly and a black beard that would have done a dwarf proud, popped out of the galley, glaring around. 'Who say my meat is bad? I kill that pig myself, last week!'

'Last week?' Aethenir blanched. He put a hand to his forehead. 'How is it possible that humanity has risen to such heights while the noble asur have fallen? How have they even survived? Their ships are slow, their knowledge of the world contemptible, their hygiene appalling, their food poisonous...'

Max stood, trying to stem the tide. 'High one, please, calm yourself. Conditions could be better, I admit, but...'

The cook turned on Aethenir, shaking his spit-fork angrily. 'I know not what this hygiene is, but...'

'By the Everqueen, *that's* obvious,' said Aethenir as his warriors went on guard behind him. 'Look at yourself. When was the last time you washed your hands? Why did learned Teclis ever decide to grant such shaven apes the blessing of–'

'Lord Aethenir!' Max yelped, stepping between him and the begrimed cook. 'I think perhaps you would find it more congenial to dine in your cabin.' He took the elf gently by the elbow and steered him towards the door to the underdecks. 'I will have new food made for you, and I will oversee its preparation myself. It is part of the learning of my college to cleanse and purify. You need have no fears for your health.'

The high elf allowed himself to be led below with further placating murmurings. Everyone let out a held breath and returned to their meal, though there was much muttering from the crew and from Max's Reiksguard swords.

'Called our boat slow,' said a sailor.

'He throw my food off the ship,' said the cook.

'And one of my bowls,' said Captain Breda. 'That'll go on the bill.'

'Shaved apes, did he call us?' asked the captain of the Reiksguard, a knight by the name of Rudeger Oberhoff. 'Hope he doesn't think we'll be watching his back for him after that.'

His men laughed at that, but Felix didn't see anything particularly funny about the situation. If the elf got the crew too worked up, there might be mutiny or violence, and Aethenir's warriors looked like capable fellows. He was just glad that Gotrek had elected to stay below and drink instead of joining the others for lunch. Things could have gone much worse if he'd been there.

WHEN MAX RETURNED to the main deck to oversee the preparation of Aethenir's meal, Captain Breda pulled him aside and had a few words in his ear. Felix happened to be nearby, and overheard, little knowing then how those words would affect him later.

'Magister, sir,' said the captain. 'Er, it might be best, milord, if yon high one was to stay off the deck as much as possible for the remainder. Out of sight, out of mind, if you get my meaning, sir.'

'Perfectly, captain,' said Max. 'And I apologise for Scholar Aethenir's behaviour. He is young, for an elf, and has never left Ulthuan before. I'm afraid it's been a bit of a shock.'

'That's as may be,' said Captain Breda. 'But he's in for a ruder shock if he spouts off like that again, elder race or no. The men won't stand for it.'

'I understand completely, captain,' said Max. 'I will see to it personally that he stays below as much as can possibly be managed.'

'Thank you, magister,' said the captain, bowing. 'You ease my mind.'

Not exactly the most doom-laden exchange of words, but that is exactly what they were for Felix, because what keeping Aethenir below decks entailed was keeping him company. For the rest of the journey, Max spent night and day in Aethenir's cabin, discussing magic, philosophy and the nature of the world, as well as playing endless games of chess. And it was in this caretaking that the far-reaching repercussions of the 'stew incident' made themselves apparent, for with Max made nursemaid to Aethenir he was no longer able to keep an eye on Fraulein Pallenberger, and finding herself unchaperoned, she made a beeline for the target she had had her eye on since boarding the *Jilfte Bateau* – Felix.

THE BATTLE RECOMMENCED on the morning of their second day out of Marienburg. At first it seemed that it would be nothing more than a skirmish, but soon it escalated into a full-on assault, with Felix fighting a desperate rearguard action in order to get away unscathed.

The morning had begun peacefully enough, settling into what was to be the daily routine of the voyage – wake, dress, have a breakfast of oat mash, grilled flounder or pike and Tilean coffee, then watch the Wasteland go by until lunch, and then more of the same until sunset. Felix would have welcomed almost any interruption of the monotony, but not this one.

'You look sad, Herr Jaeger,' said Claudia, appearing at his side.

Felix jumped, startled. 'Sad?' he said. 'Not at all.' He had actually been in the middle of a reverie about what he might do with his father's inheritance if he did manage to get Euler's letter for him. Not that he wanted the money, of course. But if he did inherit some, what would he do with it? Visions of exquisite leather-bound volumes of his poetry dissipated into smoke as he turned to the seeress. 'Just musing.'

'Musing,' she asked, sliding closer to him along the rail. 'About what?'

'Oh, ah, nothing really. Just, well, just musing.' He looked around him for an excuse to escape, but could see none.

She touched his arm and looked at him with her deep blue eyes. 'You hide a secret grief, don't you, Herr Jaeger.'

'Eh? Oh no, not really. No more than anybody else, I should think.'

'I don't believe it,' she said.

Felix didn't have any response to that except for a keen desire to push her over the side, so he said nothing, just watched the reeds go by and hoped she would go away. Unfortunately, she did not.

'Have you ever loved, Herr Jaeger?'

Felix choked, and had to cover his mouth as he was wracked with sudden coughs. 'Once or twice, I suppose,' he said, when he had recovered.

She turned and faced him, leaning her shapely hip against the rail. 'Tell me about them.'

'You don't want to hear about that,' he said.

'Oh, but I do,' the seeress said, her eyes never leaving his. 'You fascinate me, Herr Jaeger.'

'Ah,' said Felix. And in spite of his best efforts, he found himself thinking back to the women he had shared a bed with throughout his wanderings. There had been a fair number over the years, mostly half-remembered tavern girls and harlots in lonely ports scattered from the Old World to Ind, and a few who stood out above the rest; Elissa, the barmaid at the Blind Pig, who had stolen his money, and for a time his heart, Siobhain of Albion, who had travelled with him and Gotrek in the dark lands of the east, and the Veiled One, spy and assassin for the Old Man of the Mountain, whose true name he had never learned. But there were only two he had ever truly loved: Kirsten, with whom he had thought to settle down and raise a family, murdered by the mad playwright Manfred von Diehl in a little outpost in the Border Princes, and Ulrika, with whom he had thought to travel the world, worse-than-murdered by the vampire Adolphus Krieger. The memories, one long buried and one still as raw as an open wound, brought a lump to his throat. Damn the woman. Why had she asked such a vile question? He turned away from her so she wouldn't see the pain in his eyes.

'I have only ever loved two women,' he said at last. 'And they are both dead. Is that fascinating enough?'

Perhaps he hadn't done a very good job masking his pain after all, for when he turned to look at her, she stepped back, eyes wide and face pale, and put a hand to her heart.

'I… I'm sorry, Herr Jaeger,' she said. 'I did not think… That is, I did not mean…' Her face went suddenly from white to pink, and she turned and hurried away, almost running for the door to the underdecks in her haste.

Felix turned back to the rail, cursing her for digging so thoughtlessly into his heart, but then a cheerier thought came into his mind. Perhaps this meant that she would leave him alone from now on.

Suddenly the day looked a little brighter.

ALAS, IT WAS not to be. She said nothing to him at lunch, only spooned dully at her stew and glanced at him guiltily when she thought he wasn't looking, but later in the afternoon, just when he was getting another few hours of marsh-watching in, she reappeared at his side, eyes downcast and lip out-thrust.

'I want to apologise to you, Herr Jaeger,' she said. 'I was awful to you earlier today and I feel terrible about it.'

'Forget it,' said Felix, wishing she really would. Unfortunately she persisted.

She took another step closer to him. 'Sometimes I forget that men are not books, to be opened and read like... er, books. I should not have pried and I am truly sorry for it.'

'Never mind,' said Felix, throwing a splinter from the rail into the water. 'No harm done.'

He felt a soft pressure on his arm and turned to see that she was leaning against him. The swell of her breast under her dark blue robe pressed against his elbow. 'If there is any way...' she said, looking up at him from under her long lashes, 'any way that I could make it up to you, I would be grateful for the opportunity.'

Felix stood, rolling his eyes, then turned to face her. 'I am beginning to wonder, fraulein, if you didn't use your visions to convince the Slayer to come on this journey just so that you would be able to get me alone on a ship.'

The seeress blinked at that, then drew herself up haughtily as the full meaning of what he had said sank in. 'The oath of the Celestial Order is very clear, Herr Jaeger,' she said. 'We will not use our powers for personal gain, nor will we announce false visions or predictions for any reason whatsoever!'

'Well, I won't tell if you won't,' said Felix, a little meaner than he had intended.

'Oh!' she said. Then 'Oh!' again. Then she turned and stomped away just as quickly as she had before, but with much more noise. Felix hoped this time it would stick, but he very much doubted it.

ON THE AFTERNOON of the third day, he sat down on the aft deck with his journal to fill in the so far thrilling events of their journey up the Sea of Manann. Apparently, his last insult had done the trick, for he was able to get in nearly a full hour of scribbling without any interruptions from Fraulein Pallenberger. It was very refreshing.

When he was finished he closed the journal, sighed contentedly and sat back, thinking that a little dinner would be in order shortly. But then the feeling that he was being watched crept over him and he turned, expecting to find Claudia peeking out from behind a mast. Instead, it was Max, leaning against the opposite rail and observing him with furrowed intensity as he puffed on his pipe.

Felix raised an eyebrow. What had he done this time? Hadn't he given Claudia the cold shoulder? Surely Max couldn't be unhappy about that.

He nodded politely and began to cap his ink and put away his pen. Before he finished, Max had tapped his pipe out on the rail and crossed to him, sitting down next to him on an overturned bucket. Felix hid a sigh. Was he going to get another lecture?

'Good afternoon, Max,' he said, as pleasantly as he could.

Max continued to look at him, saying nothing for long enough that Felix began to feel uncomfortable.

At last, just as Felix was about to ask what the matter was, he spoke. 'You really haven't aged a day, Felix.'

Felix sighed. 'Everyone says that. I'm getting a little tired of–'

'I do not mean it as a compliment,' said Max. 'I mean it as a fact. It is impossible that you should look this young and vigorous.' He frowned and pointed at Felix's cheek. 'You used to have a scar, just there. Do you remember?'

Felix reached up and touched his cheek – the duelling scar, taken when he had fought his schoolmate Krassner at university, and killed him.

'It's gone now,' said Max.

'Scars fade,' said Felix.

'Not a scar like that. Not completely. And yet it has.'

Felix frowned. He didn't like this scrutiny. 'But isn't that good?'

'Good?' Max shrugged. 'Yes, I suppose. But mysterious as well. Something unnatural is affecting your body – keeping it young, keeping it free from disease, allowing you to recover from wounds faster and more completely than you should. I know other hardy warriors of your age, Felix. They are strong and fit, but their knees still creak and their hands are scarred. Their faces are lined and creased. Yours is not. You no longer look a youth of twenty, it's true, but you look ten years younger than your true age and well cared for besides.'

'I think you're exaggerating, Max. But if what you say is true, what…' Felix swallowed, uncertain he wanted to know the answer. 'What do you think has caused it?'

Max leaned back, stroking his neat beard and considering. 'I don't know, but I can think of several possibilities. You will note,' he said, adopting a professorial tone, 'that Gotrek is affected in the same way. More so, in fact. There is no dwarf stronger or more massive than he. I'll wager he has the strength of ten of his kind. And he too is virtually unscarred, but for his missing eye. Perhaps something the two of you encountered during your journey to the Chaos Wastes has caused this effect. Or it might be some consequence of entering that portal through which you disappeared when I saw you last. Perhaps it is some property of Gotrek's axe. It is a weapon of great power. Perhaps it is keeping him, and you, fit for some important purpose, though what that might be, I couldn't say. Whatever it is, it is possible it could keep you alive indefinitely.'

'Indefinitely? You mean I might be...' He laughed at the ridiculousness of it. 'Immortal?'

'Or as near as makes no difference,' said Max, nodding. 'But be aware that it is not an unmixed blessing. We of the Empire are not tolerant of the unusual or the unnatural, Felix. If you continue to look as you do for another ten or twenty years, people will talk. You might be accused of being some sort of mutant, or a master of the dark arts, or even one of the undead.'

Felix blanched. He had never considered that his good health might be seen as the taint of Chaos. What was he supposed to do, get sick?

Max sighed and stood. 'I must go hold Scholar Aethenir's hand again, but think on what I have said, Felix. I believe it would be wise to face your true nature, instead of pretending you have not changed.'

'Thank you, Max,' said Felix, softly. 'I will.'

He barely noticed Max as he turned and left, so confounded was he by what the wizard had said. He didn't want to believe it. How could it be true? If something had happened to him, wouldn't he have noticed? He felt no different than he ever had. But perhaps that is what Max had meant. He should have felt different – achy, more run down, older.

What if he *was* immortal? Should he be happy about it? It was every man's dream to live forever, wasn't it? But to be made immortal without his consent by some force he didn't understand – that was more unnerving than thrilling. And did he really want to be following the Slayer into danger for ever and ever without end? Even the wildest journey must come to an end sometime, mustn't it?

A sudden thought came to him and made his heart lurch. Could he be some sort of vampire, as Max suggested? That would mean that he and Ulrika could be together after all! But no, he decided with a sigh, he doubted very much he was a vampire. He was sitting in the sun, wasn't he? And he had not, as far as he could remember, ever drunk anyone's blood. And besides, if he were a vampire, he would never have the chance to be with Ulrika, because Gotrek would kill him first.

'Sail ho!' called a voice from above. 'To the stern on our heading.'

Felix looked up. This sort of cry had been frequent on the first two days of their journey, when the *Pride of Skintstaad* had been at the narrow end of the Manaanspoort Sea and in the major shipping lane, but as they had continued to hug the east coast while most of the traders hugged the west, heading for Bretonnia, Estalia and Tilea, other ships had become fewer and fewer.

He rose and joined Captain Breda at the aft rail. Far in the distance, between the iron sea and the pewter sky, was a sharp fleck of white, like a tooth sticking up over the horizon.

'What sort of ship is it?' asked Felix.

The captain shrugged. 'Hard to tell, this far out,' he said. 'Three masts. Square rigged. Marienburg, most likely, possibly Imperial. Don't know what she's doing going north. Not much trade with the Norse this late in the year. Wouldn't be doing it myself, if it weren't for the high one's gold.'

The ship remained on the horizon for the rest of the day, not gaining and not falling back. Captain Breda left instructions for the night watch to keep an eye on its lights and wake him if it got closer, but it never did.

* * *

THE FOURTH DAY dawned grey and misty, with gusts of intermittent rain, and it was impossible to tell if the ship with the white sail was still behind them or not.

Just before noon, the *Pride of Skintstaad* sailed past the last headland of the Manaanspoort Sea and out into the great black expanse of the Sea of Chaos. The north wind, which had been softened somewhat by its passage over the Wasteland, was here a cold wet slap in the face. All the sailors donned oiled leather jerkins and shivered at their stations. Felix pulled his red cloak closer around him and looked in all directions. For all his travels, he had never sailed these waters before. Directly north was Norsca, land of longships, snow-topped mountains and fur-clad reavers. East was Erengrad and Kislev and the Sea of Claws. West was fabled Albion, the mist-shrouded isle that he and Gotrek had once visited, but never travelled to. Adventure awaited in every direction, but on the whole, it all seemed a bit chilly and unappealing.

It was a few hours later that the inevitable finally happened, and Gotrek and Aethenir crossed paths. Such a confrontation had so far been avoided because both the elf and the dwarf had spent most of their time in their cabins, and generally came up only to use the privy. Thus, it was at the privy that the meeting occurred.

The privy of the *Pride of Skintstaad* was nothing more than a round hole in a bench that hung out over the prow of the ship, directly under the bowsprit and screened off from the rest of the ship by a leather curtain. The path to it was very narrow, a little wedge of space between the looming bowsprit and the starboard rail, which had spare sails and spars and other nautical debris lashed to it.

Though Felix was not there for the beginning of the argument, it started, apparently, when Aethenir stepped out of the privy and found Gotrek waiting impatiently to go in.

The first Felix and the rest of the crew heard of it was Gotrek's rasp rising above the sounds of wind and wave.

'I'll not step aside for any honourless, tree-worshipping elf! You step aside!'

'Do you dare make demands of me, dwarf? I have paid for this ship, and you are upon it at my pleasure. Now step aside, I say.'

Felix sprang up from where he had been reading more of his travels with Gotrek, and ran for the prow. This was just what was needed. Max too was hurrying to the scene. Aethenir's household guard was not far behind. When they all reached the tiny space, they found the elf and the dwarf face to face – or face to chest, to be more accurate – and barking at each other like dogs.

'I go where I please, when I please, and no pompous, prick-eared pantywaist is going to bar my way. Now step aside before I throw you overboard!'

'Stubborn son of earth. I do not bar your way. You bar mine!'

'Gotrek,' called Felix. 'Leave off. What is the point of this?'

'Yes, Slayer,' said Max. 'Give way and have done.'

'Give way to an elf?' said Gotrek, with a dangerous edge to his voice. 'I would die first.'

'By Asuryan,' said Aethenir. 'There would be no need for this argument were you to shave that monstrous filthy beard. There would be room enough for both of us then.'

Gotrek froze, his one eye blazing. His hand slowly reached up and caught the haft of his axe. 'What did you say?'

Felix heard the scrape of steel as the high elf's warriors all drew their swords at once.

Aethenir looked up to them. 'Captain Rion! Brothers! Defend me! Save me from this mad rock hewer!'

The elves pushed forwards through the other onlookers.

'Coward,' snarled Gotrek, bringing his axe before him and ignoring the elves at his rear. 'Would you have others fight your battles for you? Draw your sword!'

'I carry no sword,' said Aethenir, backing against the privy curtain. 'I am a scholar.'

'Ha!' barked Gotrek. 'A scholar should be wise enough not to start with his mouth what he can't finish with his hands.' He took another step towards the elf.

'Turn, dwarf,' said Captain Rion, a weathered-looking elf with cold grey eyes. 'I would not slay even a tunnel-digger from behind.'

Gotrek turned and grinned at the thicket of sharp steel that faced him. 'All right,' he said. 'You first, then the "scholar".'

Felix squeezed in beside him. 'Gotrek, listen to me. You can't do this.'

'Step back, manling,' growled Gotrek. 'You're crowding my arm.'

Felix stayed where he was. 'Gotrek, please. He might deserve it, but he paid for the ship. This voyage ends if you kill him or his friends. Remember the seeress's vision? The black mountain? The tide of blood? The towering abomination? If this argument ends in slaughter we all go back to Marienburg and that doom fades away like all the others. Is that what you want?'

Gotrek stood rigid for a long moment, breathing heavily. Felix could see his jaw muscles clenching under his beard as he ground his teeth. At last he put up his axe and turned, shouldering roughly past Aethenir as the elf flattened against the rail.

Gotrek slapped aside the curtain, then looked back. 'This had better be a damned good doom!'

He turned and disappeared into the privy. There was a noise like an explosion in a brewery.

Everybody hurried quickly away.

FELIX RETIRED TO his cramped cabin that night well pleased. Though Gotrek's altercation with Aethenir had been a terrifying near-massacre that had almost ended their journey before it had really begun, afterwards, Felix had been heartened at the thought of how angry and alive the Slayer had been – trading spirited insults with the elf and challenging his whole retinue to a fight. Such a contrast to the somnambulant lump that had sat glumly in the Griffon with barely the energy to lift his tankard to his lips. The seeress's vision seemed to have worked upon him like an elixir, raising him from the living death of his depression and giving him purpose again.

As he lay down in the tiny cupboard bed and pulled the heavy quilt over him, Felix hoped that, for the Slayer's sake, the premonition wasn't a lie. After that his thoughts became scattered, and he let the swell of the waves and the creaks and groans of the ship timbers lull him into a deep, dreamless sleep.

When he woke again, it was to a soft noise. Long years of experience in dangerous awakenings had taught him not to make any sudden noises or movements. Instead he moved only his eyes, passing them slowly over the small area of dark room that he could see without turning his head. Nothing. Had he imagined it? No. The soft noise was repeated, and followed by quiet rustlings and shiftings. Someone, or some thing, was most definitely in the room with him.

He could make out the corners and edges of things now, illuminated in a dim glow of moonlight from the small, thick-glassed window. He eased his head a few inches around, as quietly as he could.

Yes, there was someone in his room, and she was stark naked, the pale light highlighting her slim, youthful curves as she dropped her robe to the deck.

'What are you doing here?' Felix asked.

'I couldn't sleep,' said Fraulein Pallenberger.

'And so you decided that I shouldn't either.'

She sighed and sat on the bed, shivering a little in the chill as she lay a hand on the covers that draped over his legs. 'You use harsh humour to hide your misery, Herr Jaeger, but I know that, beneath your cruel words, you long for solace. You drive me away so that you will not have to share your pain, but in your mind you are calling, "come back, come back".' She lay down on top of the covers and brought her face close to his. 'And so, I have.'

She closed her eyes and leaned in to kiss him. Felix turned his head so that her lips fell awkwardly on his ear.

'Fraulein,' he said, then struggled with the bedclothes and sat up. 'Fraulein, you cannot be here.'

She rolled over and looked up at him, stretching as she raised an eyebrow in what he was sure she thought was a sultry expression. He swallowed. Despite her overplaying, she did look rather fetching sprawled out like that.

'And why not?' she said. 'You long for it. I long for it. Surely you are not some prudish…'

'I do not long for it!' snapped Felix. 'And you… This has more to do with putting one over on Magister Schreiber and rebelling against your order than any attraction you have to me.'

Her languid look vanished in an angry flash of eyes and she sat up too, all semblance of desire gone. 'Why shouldn't it?' she hissed. 'Don't you see that this might be my last chance? Herr Jaeger, I am young! Young! I want to taste the world before it is taken away from me! I want to live before I die! It is my gift – my curse! – to predict the future, and I predict that the rest of my life will be a long, grey corridor, full of dust and charts and telescopes and pale, wrinkled old men!' She covered her face with one hand. 'I know I cannot leave the colleges. The Empire does not suffer a witch to live. I know I have to go back and shuffle along with the rest of them, but for now – for these few days...' She looked up at Felix with eyes that burned with a shimmering fire. 'I want to live!'

Felix sat back, torn between heartbreak and laughter. 'Fraulein Pallenberger, this is all very moving, but the Celestial Order is not a celibate order. You may marry. You may take your pleasure as you like.'

'Not until I become a magister,' said Claudia sullenly. 'And that might take until I am thirty! I will be old then. No one will want to look at me. My youth will be behind me.'

This time Felix did chuckle. 'And how old do you think I am?'

'It's different for men!' she cried, then started to weep in earnest. 'Oh, I've made a terrible mistake!' she bawled. 'I didn't want to join the order! I don't want to be a seeress!'

'Shhhh, shhhh,' said Felix, taking her hands. 'You'll wake the ship.' He groaned as he imagined Max finding them like this. 'Please, fraulein. Calm down.'

She muffled her sobs with her hands and fell heavily against his chest, nestling her head against his shoulder. He folded her in his arms and stroked her hair – not in any romantic way, he told himself – purely to comfort and quieten her. But when her hands crept around his torso and she pressed herself against him, he found desire stirring within him despite himself.

He fought it down and pried her off, but she clung again as soon as he let go.

'Do not cast me out, Herr Jaeger,' she murmured in his ear. 'Let me live. I beg you.'

'Fraulein – Claudia,' he said, trying to disentangle himself. 'You really overstate your case. Thirty, even for a woman, is not...'

Her lips found his, and then her tongue. He responded before he could remember not to.

'Claudia, please,' he said, pushing away from her at last. This wasn't right. He loved Ulrika. Her memory was still fresh in his heart. He doubted it would ever die. He didn't want anyone else but her. And since he could not have her, then he would have no one at all. It would be sacrilege to defile the memory of their love with some petty animal flailing.

Claudia's hands trailed down his torso and gripped his legs as she kissed his neck. He shivered. On the other hand, there was something to be said, in this world of trouble and pain, for taking pleasure where one could find it. Ulrika's words came back to him again. 'We must find happiness among our own kind.' He still wasn't certain that happiness was possible, but comfort might be.

With a sigh and a silent apology to Ulrika, wherever she might be, he lowered his lips to Claudia's and kissed her, long and deep. The seeress whimpered and pressed harder against him. He pulled his nightshirt off over his

head and moved his lips to her throat, kissing and nibbling tenderly. She shivered and groaned. Felix chuckled
to himself. It had been a while, but he appeared not to
have forgotten what to do. He pressed her back against
the bed and kissed her clavicle, then down between her
breasts. She moaned and clutched him, trembling as if
with fever. 'Here,' she said. 'Here!'

By Taal and Rhya, thought Felix, delving lower, no
wonder the girl regrets her apprenticeship, she's as
enflamed as a rutting cat.

'Here!' the seeress shrieked, and scrambled up out of
the bed, kneeing him in the cheek in her haste.

'Claudia, what…?' he said, then stared.

She stood in the centre of the tiny cabin, her arms
thrust wide and her eyes rolled up in their sockets, shaking like she was bracing against a high wind.

'Here!' she screamed. 'Here is the source of the visions!
I can feel it! It is from here that the ruin of Marienburg
will spring!'

Felix heard the thumps and questioning cries of his fellow passengers through the walls all around him. He
jumped out of bed and snatched her robe up off the
floor where she had dropped it. He had to get her
dressed and back to her own cabin. But it was impossible. She continued to stand with arms outstretched, as
rigid as a sword, and he could not get both of her sleeves
on her at once.

'Here!' she wailed in his ear as he tried to wrap the
robe around her nakedness. 'Here is where we will find
Altdorf's doom!'

It was in this tableau that the others found them when
they slammed open the door – Max, Aethenir, Captain
Breda, Gotrek and assorted swordsmen, sailors and elves
– all staring at Felix and Claudia struggling and naked in

the centre of the room, with the seeress's robe fluttering once again to the deck.

'Could you be quieter about it, manling?' rumbled Gotrek. 'Some of us are trying to sleep.'

SEVEN

CAPTAIN BREDA DROPPED anchor there and then, but there was little point in looking around in the dark, so they waited until first light before lowering the boats and rowing them to shore to see if they could find the source of Claudia's vision.

Gotrek and Felix set out in the boat that carried Max and Claudia and their eight Reiksguard knights, Aethenir and his elf warriors were rowed in another, and Captain Breda sent another party of sailors to look for fresh water to replenish the stores. As they all left the ship, Felix could see the sailors at the rail looking at him and elbowing each other lasciviously. His face burned crimson. They had been laughing behind his back since word had spread of how he and Claudia had been discovered. He didn't know what they had to snicker about. She had come to his cabin and not theirs after all.

The sailors' mirth was unfortunately not the only fall-out. Max had not spoken to him since. Nor had Claudia. She seemed too embarrassed to look at him. The ride to the shore was therefore silent and uncomfortable.

They pulled the boats up onto a rocky beach hemmed in on three sides by high sand dunes. A cold wind whistled through the saw grass that topped them, and clouds scudded by above them in a steely autumn sky. A few raindrops fell. Max and Aethenir turned to Claudia, expectant, while the Reiksguard and the elf warriors prepared to march and Felix shrugged into his chainmail and strapped on his sword.

'Have you further insight as to where this evil lies, seeress?' asked Max, who had grown very formal with her since the previous night. 'Or what it might be?'

Claudia shook her head, unable to meet his eyes. 'The vision has passed and I have not had another. I'm sorry, magister. It is near here, but I don't know where, or what it is, precisely.'

Max nodded. 'Very well, then we will split up and look for it. You and I will go south with Captain Oberhoff and his men along the shore. High one, will you take your kin inland and look there?'

'Of course,' said Aethenir.

Max turned to Gotrek, pointedly ignoring Felix. 'Slayer, will you and Herr Jaeger walk the coast to the north? We will search until mid-morning, then return here and compare notes. And whatever you find, let it lie until we may all examine it together.'

Gotrek nodded.

Felix stiffened at the snub, but said nothing. He had, after all, all but promised Max that he would have nothing to do with Claudia, and he had gone back on that promise – however unwillingly – so he supposed he deserved a snubbing. Still, it felt a bit petty. Maybe Max was jealous that Claudia had chased Felix instead of him. The thought sparked others. Was Max married? Did he have a mistress? Did he even care about such worldly matters any more? Felix didn't know.

As they took packs and waterskins out of the boats, Felix found himself for a moment alone next to Claudia. He leaned in and lowered his voice. 'I hope Max hasn't scolded you too much for last night's–'

'You might have covered me,' she snapped, cutting him off. 'I've never been so embarrassed.'

'I tried!' said Felix, defensive. Then he got angry. What right did she have to criticise his actions? 'And you might have stayed in your own cabin and saved us both a lot of bother!'

'Oh!' she said, and turned away without another word.

He watched her walk away and found Max giving him the evil eye again. Felix cursed silently and turned away, shouldering his pack.

Rain began to spit intermittently from the sky as Felix and Gotrek set off to the north, staying within sight of the water. This was not as easy as one might have thought. The shore was not all beaches and dunes. In fact, most of it was swampy, foul-smelling wetlands, an endless flat swamp with the occasional scrawny, leafless tree sticking up out of it like a witch's claw reaching up from a drowning pool. They slogged through brittle, knife-sharp grass – waist high for Felix, chest high for Gotrek – that grew out of rank, spongy ground, their footprints filling in with water behind them. The muck exhaled a low, foetid mist that swirled around their ankles, and clouds of midges and mosquitoes rose from it continually, getting in their eyes and noses and biting them unmercifully on every inch of exposed skin. Weird cries echoed through the humid silence, and once something big splashed heavily into a stream nearby, but they didn't see what it was.

Gotrek took the flies and the mud and the smell and the unnerving noises without apparent discomfort, but Felix was slapping and cursing and stumbling and walking into enormous spiderwebs the whole way. It seemed all of a piece with his vile mood. He couldn't get over Claudia's unfair anger at him. It wasn't his fault she had been found naked in his cabin. He had tried to get her to leave, repeatedly. It was she who had come uninvited and tried to seduce him. It was she who had decided that the best time to have a vision of the future was during love-making. Even more galling was the fact that Max seemed to think that he had lured her there, that he was some sort of low lothario that preyed upon young, inexperienced girls. It made him want to go back and shout the truth in their faces. It made him forget to look where he was going and step into a puddle that filled his boots to the top with freezing, green-scummed water.

His cursing startled a flock of ducks who flew over their heads, complaining querulously, and started a racket of strange shrieks off to the west that made his skin crawl. He cursed them too.

If only he had some idea what they were looking for, it might have made the journey more bearable. That was Claudia's fault too. Did she have to be so vague? What good was an ability that only gave half-answers? Should they be on the look-out for some ruined tower? A ring of stones? A weird tree with tentacles for branches? A fissure in the earth that radiated a ghastly glow? Without some goal in mind it all felt like some wild goose chase. Maybe Claudia had no powers of foresight at all. He had seen nothing conclusive to prove to the contrary. Maybe she made all of it up just so that she would have an excuse to leave the confines of the Celestial College. He wouldn't put it past her.

GOTREK DISCOVERED THE footprints just as they were about to turn back and report their failure. They had trudged up out of the marshland onto a hillocky plain that was covered in bramble bushes and scrub pine, and had found, carving through the brush to the sea, a narrow, clear-running stream with high, undercut banks. Below one of these banks was a line of bootprints, paralleling the stream and heading inland.

They drew their weapons and followed the prints as they weaved in and out of the water for perhaps a quarter of a mile. They stopped at last at a place where the stream widened into a pool and the banks drew back to make a muddy little beach. Here the first prints were joined by many others, and also the imprint of the keels of small boats at the waterline and the circular imprints of barrels, sunk heavily into the mud. It was clear that a landing party had been here recently and refilled their water barrels, just as Captain Breda's men were doing now further south. And the narrowness of the prints also made it clear – at least to Gotrek – who had collected the water.

'More elves,' Gotrek growled.

Felix nodded, and they turned back. It had been a discovery, but it didn't seem to be the portent of doom they had been looking for.

The rain chose that moment to begin sheeting down like a waterfall. Felix sighed. Of course it was raining. A day like today wouldn't be complete without being soaked to the skin.

* * *

As THE SKY grew darker and the downpour got heavier, they turned inland, partly to be good scouts and search new ground, but mostly to avoid the marshes during the rain. It appeared that Max and Claudia and their Reiks-guard escort had done the same, for they met them coming north about a quarter of a mile inland from the beach where they had landed. The two wizards were much the worse for wear, their cloaks and long robes muddied to the waist, their hands and faces scratched by brambles and dotted with insect bites. Felix felt a warm glow at the thought that Claudia had shared his misery. It served her right.

'Anything to report?' asked Max, raising his voice over the hiss of the rain as he mopped his face with a handkerchief. Despite the chill wind and the down-pour, he and Claudia were beetroot-red and boiling from their exertions, as were their swordsmen, who were steaming slightly, and appeared to be regretting having worn breastplates and pauldrons for the march.

'Not much,' Felix shouted in return. 'We found signs of an elf watering party at the limit of our march.'

'A watering party?' asked Captain Oberhoff. 'In this godforsaken place? Must have been desperate.'

'Or searching for something,' said Max. 'Like us.'

The clink of scale mail brought their heads up and they saw, coming over a hill to the east, Aethenir and his escort, marching in perfect double file. Felix was annoyed to see that, though wet, their surcoats were still pristine, and their boots clean. And not one of them seemed to have been bitten by mosquitoes.

'A disappointing search,' said Aethenir as the elves joined them. 'We found nothing.' He looked to Max. 'I hope you have had more success.'

Max shook his head. 'Nothing. Gotrek and Herr Jaeger have found signs of a recent elf watering party to the north, but nothing else.'

'Elves?' said Aethenir, his eyes narrowing. He turned to Captain Rion and asked him a question in the elven tongue. The captain shook his head and Aethenir looked troubled. 'I pray it was only elves,' he said to Max, then turned to look at Claudia. 'And has Fraulein Pallenberger experienced any new revelations about our goal?'

'No,' said Max. 'Not yet.'

Claudia hung her head. 'I wish I could call them forth, high one,' she said glumly. 'But they come when they come.'

The elf smiled slyly. 'So I have observed.'

Claudia turned crimson at that, and Max's eyes blazed. Even Felix felt angry. The girl might be a young fool who needed to learn restraint, but there was no need to make her feel worse about last night's embarrassment.

Aethenir turned towards the beach again, oblivious to their anger, his escort following. Max opened his mouth to speak, but Claudia grabbed his arm and shook her head, pleading silently. Felix could see her point. Protesting would only make her the centre of more excruciating attention. Max relented and they all followed the elves as they trudged up the hill into the driving rain.

Felix was slipping and stumbling down the far side and thinking that perhaps stealing his father's letter from Euler might have been the better option after all, when suddenly Claudia gasped and staggered into him.

He caught her but then lost his footing and they both went down together. It took all his will to be polite.

'Are you all right, fraulein?' he asked. 'Have you trodden on something?'

But Claudia's eyes were wide and unseeing, and she clutched her robes with spasming, white-knuckled hands. 'The flames! The sea crawls with flames!'

'Back to the boats!' snapped Max, and he motioned for two of the stronger Reiksguarders to take Claudia from Felix as he and Gotrek and the rest of the party raced towards the shore.

IT WAS DIFFICULT to see for more than ten paces in the freezing torrent and the gathering dark. Even so, all could see the flickering glow that silhouetted the last dune before the beach, and they hurried up the shifting sandy slope with anxious speed.

Felix was one of the first to the top, just behind Aethenir's elves, and he looked towards the source of the light. Out on the sea, the *Pride of Skintstaad* was a roaring pyre of sallow green flames – too far gone to even think of trying to save it.

The others joined him on the crest, Max, Claudia and the men gasping and wheezing from their run. Gotrek just stared, the green fire reflected in his single eye.

Claudia choked and wept. 'No! Why didn't I see it sooner?'

Felix was wondering the same thing.

Max pointed down to the beach. 'To our boats. We must go help the survivors.'

Felix and the others nodded and started trotting quickly down to the boats, calling for the sailors to take up their oars, but though the boats were there, the men who had rowed them ashore were nowhere to be seen.

'Where in Sigmar's name have they run off to?' growled Captain Oberhoff.

Then one of his Reiksguard pointed to the water. 'Look!' he said. 'The crew! They're swimming ashore!'

Felix looked where he pointed. It was hard to see through the rain, but he could make out the lumpy shapes of heads bobbing in the water, moving closer to the beach. Some of them were crawling through the surf.

'Praise Manann,' said one of the other Reiksguard.

But Felix frowned. Had there been so many crewmen? He only remembered a score at the most. There seemed to be twice that many heads in the water. 'Wait,' he said. 'Aren't there too many?'

The others looked again, blinking in the downpour.

Aethenir stepped back. 'Those aren't men,' he said. 'They are...'

With a feral hiss, the first wave of swimmers rose from the breaking waves and ran at the party on the beach – dark, crouching forms with water dripping from their piecemeal armour and their matted fur. Dagger teeth flashed bone-white in the gloom. Red eyes glowed. Rust-grimed spearheads glinted green in the light of the burning ship.

'Skaven!' roared Gotrek. He charged into the surf, drawing his axe from his back and sweeping it around him savagely. Skaven heads and limbs and tails spun away from skaven bodies to splash in the water.

The men and elves did not follow the Slayer's example. They fell back, shouting and drawing swords as dozens of the horrible creatures rose from the sea and scrabbled towards them, swinging wide around Gotrek and up the beach like a black tide. Felix backed off and fought alongside the others, separated from the Slayer by the seething wall of fur, filth and fangs. Spearheads flashed out of the glistening gloom, invisible until almost too late. Felix parried desperately, and slashed back, but it was like striking at shadows. A hoarse cry of pain came from his left – a curse from his right.

Felix was having a hard time getting his bearings as he fell in with the Reiksguard. Why skaven? Why now? What did they want? And where had they come from?

Then, with a shout of strange words, Max thrust up a hand and a ball of brilliant white light crackled into existence above his head. The skaven cringed back in the harsh illumination, chittering fearfully.

The Reiksguarders, hardened veterans of the recent Chaos invasion, did not flinch from this magic, nor did the elves. The Reiksguard fell in shoulder to shoulder, their swords and shields working in unison, while beside them, the elves attacked in a spinning, whirling fury, their long blades chopping through spears and furred limbs with equal ease as further spells from Max's hands shot past them and blasted the ranks of skaven with orbs of scintillating light that made them shriek and fall and writhe on the ground. But though the glowing ball made the vermin easier to see and kill, it also showed just how many there were. Felix's heart thudded as he looked out over the milling carpet of ratmen that covered the beach, while still more rose from the waves. There seemed no end to them.

The harsh light illuminated all their most hideous attributes – the patchy, scrofulous fur, the pustule-plagued snouts, the soulless black-marble eyes, the horrible, hissing mouths, the revolting trophies that dangled from their necks and belts. Nausea constricted his throat as he slashed viciously at them, all his disgust and fear of the vile creatures turning into a seething rage. His first stroke opened a ratman's stomach in a spray of blood and viscera, then he removed another's arm on the back swing. He buried the blade in the skull of a third, kicked it free and spun to face more.

On the far side of the skaven, Gotrek was doing the same, or trying to. The Slayer was as angry as Felix had ever seen him, for though he was surrounded by foes, he had no one to fight. The skaven scampered away from him like – well, like rats – and on his short legs he could not close with them. 'Stand and fight, vermin!' he raged as he ran backwards and forwards in the centre of an empty circle of sand.

Felix quickly found himself having the same problem. The skaven were staying behind their spears, prodding at him from a distance, but making no attempt to kill him. He lunged at a cluster of them, but they only parted before him, like water around a stone. He could not understand the behaviour. Skaven either fought with maddened fury or fled. There had never in his experience been anything in between.

Roaring with frustration, Gotrek gave up trying to close with passing ratmen and charged the back of the skaven line, cutting a hole through it with his axe. He only killed a few, for, as before, they jumped out of his way. The Slayer halted beside Felix, shaking his axe, his crest hanging limp from the pelting rain as he bellowed at their foes. 'Craven ratkin! Give me a proper fight!'

But they did not. The skaven continued to shy away from them. Gotrek and Felix had almost no enemies facing them at their portion of the line.

The Reiksguarders and the high elves were not so fortunate. The swordsman beside Felix crumpled, impaled by a spear, and another lay face-down on the sand. One of the high elves was stepping back behind his comrades, his left leg a bloody ruin. Though the men and the elves seemed to be killing ten skaven for every one that fell on their side, there were so many of the beasts that it didn't matter. The sheer mass of the vermin pressed the whole party back towards the dunes, step by inexorable step, and threatened to encircle it as well.

Behind the thin line of Reiksguard and elf warriors, Max wove trails of light in the air that expanded into a shimmering bubble of energy that encircled himself, Claudia and Aethenir. Within the circle, Aethenir motioned the wounded elf into the bubble and began making gestures in the air over his leg, while Claudia, looking terrified but determined, mouthed a spell and let loose a blast of lightning from her hands that caused the skaven front line to twitch and fall. So the girl had a use after all, thought Felix, uncharitably.

Just as he thought it, Claudia screamed. He looked back again. Gotrek did too. Bursting from the sawgrass at the base of the dune to their rear were black shadows, throwing metal stars and glass globes. Men and elves alike cried out as the stars bit into their limbs and torsos.

An elf warrior instinctively knocked a globe out of the air with his sword and it shattered. He and another elf went down as if shot, as green mist blossomed from the glass ball and enveloped them. The skaven hacked them savagely as they fell. Captain Rion and the other elves dodged back and covered their noses and mouths. The mist drifted into the skaven ranks and half a dozen collapsed. Two of the globes landed with a soft thud on the wet sand at Felix's feet. He picked them up in one hand and hurled them towards the sea. They left a faint familiar odour on his fingers.

Gotrek snarled and ran at the star-hurling shadows.

'Protect the wizards,' cried Felix to the swordsmen, then raced after the Slayer.

But just as they were about to close with the murky shapes, a deep bellow rose above the noise of the rain. Gotrek stopped in his tracks and looked around. A massive black-furred, rat-headed creature, nearly twice Felix's height and thick with mutated muscle, was bounding down the dune towards Max, Aethenir and Claudia. Max spun and shot a blast of light at it. The creature howled but did not slow. Claudia sent a bolt of lightning at it. It hardly seemed to notice.

The wounded high elf pushed away from Aethenir's ministrations and limped to intercept it, his teeth clenched but his sword at the ready. Captain Rion and the other elf warriors looked back, but they were engaged with the skaven front line and could not break away.

Gotrek sprinted to get between the wounded elf and the rat ogre, his one eye blazing. 'Mine, you chalk-faced thief!' he roared. 'Leave off!'

Felix ran behind the Slayer, but suddenly, with a jerk at his chest, he wasn't running any more. He was flat on his back.

He looked down at himself. There was a noose of thin grey cord wrapped around his chest. His heart thudded with sudden recognition, even as he picked himself up and turned to look where the noose led. The attack in Altdorf! It had been the skaven! And the attack in Marienburg as well! The globes smelled the same as the gas that had knocked out everyone at the Three Bells! But why did the skaven want to capture them?

'Loose me, you damned rope twirlers!' bawled Gotrek beside him.

Felix chopped through the line with his sword and turned to see that the Slayer was similarly infested with nooses. One was around his neck, another looped around his left wrist and another around his right ankle. They did not stop him by any means, but they did slow him, and the wounded elf reached the rat ogre first, his shining blade parrying the monster's massive claws with a deafening clang.

Enraged, Gotrek gathered up all the ropes that held him in one hand and pulled savagely. Black-clad skaven stumbled out of the shadows at the end of the ropes. Gotrek roared and charged them – then vanished into a pit that opened up in the sand below his feet.

Felix stared. One moment, the Slayer had been running full tilt, axe raised, the next moment he was gone, to be replaced by a dark hole in the ground with wet sand trickling down into it.

'Gotrek!' Felix ran to the edge of the hole and nearly fell in himself as the edge crumbled and fell down on the Slayer below. Gotrek clawed at the sides of the pit, half-buried in wet sand, as he tried to climb out, but the sand broke apart under his fingers and he sank back.

'Hang on, Gotrek!' cried Felix. 'I'll get you out!'

Just then a chittering from beyond the hole brought his head up. The black-clad skaven were running at him, holding what looked like a big leather bag. Felix grabbed the rope that was wrapped around Gotrek's wrist and hauled on it one-handed while lashing out at the skaven with his blade, but the Slayer was too heavy and the sand too loose. The skaven danced back out of reach, then darted in at his back and cut the cord.

He fell back as the cord snapped, then rolled to his feet, on guard, panic rising in his chest. There was no pulling Gotrek out. Not with the skaven ambushers trying to stuff him in a sack. And with the Slayer out of the fight the vermin might win, and he and Felix would be taken prisoner. He shivered at the thought. That was an unthinkable outcome. He had to get Gotrek out, but how?

Then he saw the way. Unfortunately, it meant putting himself in the path of a marauding monster. Felix hacked around at the assassins, fanning them back, then raced through the rain towards the wounded elf and the rat ogre. The skaven scampered after him. To one side, the remaining Reiksguard and elf warriors had surrounded

Max, Claudia and Aethenir, and were fighting desperately to keep the skaven horde from breaking through their circle.

Felix ran past them and hacked the massive rat beast in the side as it swung again at the elf. It roared and turned to him, and the elf staggered back in relief. He was in bad shape, barely able to move on his maimed leg, and three fingers of his left hand were missing.

'Fall back!' Felix shouted, taking a step back and slashing at the assassins behind him. 'Let me lead it away!'

The high elf nodded and stumbled aside as Felix waved his sword in the brute's face. It bellowed and lumbered forwards, swiping at him with its massive claws. Felix ducked, then turned and ran, hacking down two of the bag-wielding skaven who were creeping up behind him, and looking back to be sure the thing was following. It was – too fast! Felix sprang ahead as the monster's fists pounded the sand just inches from his heels, almost jarring him off his feet. The assassins scampered out of its path.

As he reached the hole, Felix bent down and scooped up another of Gotrek's noose ropes, then dived forwards as the rat ogre's claws whooshed over his head. He rolled to his feet and faced the towering rat ogre. It raised its arms and charged. Felix dodged aside, holding the rope and swiping at the ambushers, who were scurrying around the outskirts of the fight, still trying to put him in the bag. The beast stumbled into the rope. Felix quickly ran behind it, wrapping the cord around its legs, then got in front of it again, jerking the cord tight.

'Come on, you overgrown sewer rat!' he shouted, waving his sword. 'Come and die!'

The monster obliged, striding forwards with a savage bellow as Felix dodged back. The rope around the rat ogre's waist pulled taut behind him, and with an explosion of sand, Gotrek was dragged from the hole – by the neck!

Felix gaped, and nearly had his head taken off. He'd grabbed the wrong rope! Sigmar, had he strangled the Slayer?

Felix ducked to the side, forcing the rat ogre to stop and change direction. Its tail of rope went slack, and to Felix's great relief, he saw Gotrek stagger to his feet, cursing and clawing at the noose that had cinched his beard to his neck.

The giant beast swung its claws again. Felix dodged back, then darted in under its massive arm and stabbed it between the ribs. The point sank deep. The thing roared and twisted, wrenching the sword from Felix's hands and clubbing him to the sand with a flailing elbow.

It raised its fists over its head to deliver the death blow. Felix crabbed feebly backwards, weaponless and stunned, knowing he was dead. But suddenly the rat ogre was toppling sideways as its right leg fell away from its body in a shower of blood. It crashed down onto its back, thrashing and screaming. Gotrek stood behind it, his axe dripping gore. He raised his axe high, then chopped down through the beast's bony skull with a sickening crunch. The muscle-bloated body went slack and Felix breathed a sigh of relief.

Gotrek levered his axe out of the rat ogre's skull and ran at the skaven assassins, who were creeping in again. 'You've got a funny sense of humour, manling.'

'I grabbed the wrong rope!' said Felix, staggering up and joining. 'I didn't mean it.'

It seemed, however, that the assassins had had enough. They scattered before Gotrek and Felix like cockroaches, whistling shrilly as they ran.

The whistle appeared to be a signal, for the mob of skaven that were still pressing the Reiksguard swordsmen and Aethenir's retinue broke away from the battle and raced back towards the shore. The men and elves chased them, but the ratmen dived into the waves and swam strongly out to sea, their long snouts making streaming bow waves in the black water.

Felix stared after them as he and Gotrek strode down to the surf. 'Where are they going?' he asked. 'Do they have a ship?'

Gotrek shrugged. There was no ship to be seen except the *Pride of Skintstaad*, now burnt to the waterline and sinking fast. 'I hope they drown.'

Felix said a silent prayer for Captain Breda and his crew as he took a final look at the dying ship and turned back and surveyed the aftermath of the battle. Skaven bodies littered the beach, misshapen lumps of fur surrounded by clotted red sand. There were too many men and elves lying among the horrors, however. Two of the high elves were dead, gutted while knocked out by the skaven's sleep gas. Four of the Reikland swordsmen were dead as well, impaled by skaven spears, and a fifth was dying, a river of blood pouring from a deep gash on his inner thigh. Captain Oberhoff and two others were all that were left, and even they bled from numerous wounds. They knelt by the dying man, holding his hands and speaking comforting words to him as his face drained white and his head began to nod. Captain Rion prayed over the two elves that had fallen.

Max, Claudia and Aethenir were untouched. Their guards had done their job, and had paid for it. Aethenir cast spells of healing on the wounded elves, and Max waited for the Reiksguarders to finish saying goodbye to their companion so that he could do the same to them.

Claudia knelt on the wet sand, soaked to the bone, staring around at all the carnage, blank with shock. Felix almost asked her how she was enjoying her freedom, but decided that was too cruel and held his tongue.

Max eyed Gotrek and Felix as they neared. 'They were after you,' he said, bitterly. 'I should have remembered that you two always bring trouble with you.'

Felix shook his head. 'I don't understand it. What do they want with us? We've fought them before, but that was twenty years ago. These can't possibly be the same ones, can they?'

Max shrugged. 'Nonetheless, they want you, and they want you alive. You were the only ones they didn't try to kill. I only hope they don't come for you again until we have parted company.'

Felix nodded, fighting down a wave of guilt. Max was right. The skaven attacks had hurt everyone but their intended targets. He was about to tell Max about the attacks in Altdorf and Marienburg, when a glint of red and blue on the chest of one of the skaven assassins caught Felix's attention. It seemed out of place amidst the rest of the ratman's filthy possessions.

He stepped closer and toed aside the vermin's ragged black garment. Threaded onto a dirty string around its neck was a collection of odd trinkets – bones, coins, a human ear, bits of amber and tin, and, in the middle of this trash, a gaudy gold ring, set with sapphires surrounding the letter 'J' picked out in rubies.

Felix blinked at it for several seconds, uncomprehending. He recognised it, but it was so out of place in its current surroundings that for a moment he couldn't place it. Then he knew it, and his heart turned to a fist of ice.

It was his father's ring.

EIGHT

'WE MUST GO back to Altdorf!' Felix cried, ripping the ring from the slimy cord around the skaven's neck. 'Immediately!'

The others turned towards him, curious.

Felix held up the ring. 'This vile creature has my father's ring! It must have… It must have…' Felix found that he could not bring himself to voice what he feared the skaven must have done. 'I don't know what it has done. But I must return to Altdorf at once to find out!'

Gotrek's eyes narrowed as he looked at the ring.

Max stepped forwards, concerned. 'Felix, this is terrible. Are you certain it is your father's ring?'

'Of course I'm certain,' snapped Felix, holding it out. 'Look at it. It has the Jaeger J. The last I saw it, it was on his hand. The skaven have been in his house! I must go back as soon as possible!'

'No!' cried Claudia from behind them. 'You will not!'

They turned. She was struggling to her feet, encumbered by her wet robes.

Felix glared at her. 'Are you ordering me?' he asked, hotly.

'No,' she said again, staring sightlessly past him towards the sea, her eyes rolled up in her head. 'We will not leave.' She thrust out a trembling finger, pointing past the drifting column of black smoke that was all that was left now of the *Pride of Skintstaad*. 'We will go there! That is where the evil lies!'

Felix cursed under his breath. Damn the woman and her inconvenient visions. He was really beginning to think she did it on purpose.

The others looked out over the water in the direction she pointed. Felix reluctantly joined them, hoping against hope that there would be nothing there. Unfortunately, there was.

About a mile out, a distance they had not been able to see when the rain was at its heaviest, there was a break in the thick clouds that blanketed the sky from horizon to horizon, and the ragged edges of the hole were slowly circling like porridge being stirred by a spoon. A shaft of bleak sunshine streamed straight down through the hole. Felix shivered at the unnatural sight. It was hard to tell through all the mist and rain, but it looked like the water below the opening was swirling in exactly the same way that the clouds were.

'No, curse it! I refuse!' he said, the blood pounding strongly in his temples. 'Ancient evils from the dawn of time can wait for once! My father might be… might be *harmed*, and I intend to return to his side at once!'

'We haven't got a ship, manling,' said Gotrek.

'I don't care! I'll walk!'

'Certainly we will walk, Felix,' said Max, in the sort of patient voice one would use to speak to a pouty child.

'We have no choice now. But as we're here, we should do what we came to do. One day out of twenty won't make a difference.'

'It could make all the difference in the world!' shouted Felix, glaring around at them all. Didn't they understand? His father could be dying. The skaven might have done anything to him.

Gotrek knelt and cleaned the blood from his axe with a handful of sand. 'The rats have already done what they have done, manling,' he said without looking up. 'No matter how fast we return, we can't turn back time.'

Felix bit back an angry reply, trying to find some fault in the Slayer's cold logic, but at last, with a final kick at the dead skaven, he let out a breath. 'All right, fine. Let's go have a look at where the evil lies, but then I'm going back to Altdorf, with you or without you.'

'Thank you, Felix,' said Max.

The others turned away and began preparing to row out to the cloudbreak. Felix stepped to the dead rat ogre and began wrenching his sword out from between its ribs.

'Manling,' said Gotrek.

Felix looked around to find the Slayer fixing him with his one hard eye.

'Yes?'

'Revenge is patient,' Gotrek said, then sheathed his axe and turned away.

HALF AN HOUR later, after Max and Aethenir had seen to the survivors' wounds as well as they could, and after the bodies of the slain had been buried in the sand and the grave marked so that they could be retrieved later, the remains of the landing party set out towards the swirling clouds in a single boat. Gotrek, Felix, Captain Rion, his three unwounded elves and the two remaining

Reiksguard swordsmen manned the oars while Aethenir, Max, the wounded elf and Reiksguard Captain Oberhoff sat in the back and Claudia stood at the front, staring ahead into the wind and rain like a living figurehead. Felix once again fought the urge to push her in.

Several times during the journey he got the distinct feeling that they were being watched, but when he looked back, he could see no one on the shore, and no skaven snouts bobbing in the water, so he decided it was his imagination, though it was still a mystery where the swimming ratmen had gone.

The closer they got to the opening in the swirling clouds, the more the rain let up until, about half a mile from it, they reached the eye of the bizarre storm and all became bright and clear, with the autumn sun slanting down through the ragged aperture and shining on the dark blue water – and something else.

Standing in the prow, Claudia was the first to see it. 'There... there's a hole. In the water.'

Felix stopped rowing and turned around with the others. 'A hole?'

Max stood, shielding his eyes and looking ahead. 'A whirlpool.'

'It's... it's huge!' said Captain Oberhoff.

Gotrek grunted, as if to say that this was just the sort of thing he would expect from water.

Felix stood and looked ahead. There was indeed a whirlpool, and it was indeed huge – almost half a mile across – an exact mirror of the hole in the clouds that roiled above it. The sea around it swirled and frothed like water going down a drain, and a noise like an endlessly crashing wave reached their ears now that they were out of the rain. Felix swallowed, terrified. It was a great maw in the sea, hungry to swallow them.

'Well, there it is then,' he said nervously. 'Now we've seen it we can go back. We'll tell the Marienburg High Council a whirlpool is coming their way and they can, ah, take measures.'

'It is not the whirlpool that is the threat,' said Claudia. 'It is what's within it. I can feel it, but we must get closer.'

Felix cursed. The woman's visions kept leading them into trouble. Shouldn't prophecy warn one away from danger, not drag one towards it? 'You can't be serious! We'll be sucked in! We'll die!'

'I too can feel it,' said Aethenir. 'There is great evil here. Row on.'

Felix looked to Max for support. The wizard hesitated, but Felix could see the lust for knowledge in his eyes.

'I can't protect you from that, lord magister,' said Captain Oberhoff, piping up. 'Best to turn back.'

'Aye, lord,' said Captain Rion to Aethenir. 'Our swords are useless against such a threat.'

Finally some voices of reason, thought Felix.

'Nevertheless,' said Aethenir. 'We must get closer so that we may try to sense what is causing it. Row on.'

Max looked from Felix to Oberhoff to Aethenir. 'Perhaps a little closer,' he said at last. 'Only be careful.'

Captain Oberhoff sighed. Rion's jaw clenched. They exchanged a look of comradely suffering. Felix and the others reluctantly picked up their oars again and rowed slowly closer. There was a visible line between the choppy waves of the sea and the fast rippling current that raced around the great vortex. They edged towards the line, measuring every stroke. At last they began to feel the fatal tug of the current upon the keel of the boat.

'It's pulling now!' said Felix, louder than he meant to.

'Then retreat slightly and hold,' said Aethenir calmly, and stepped towards the front of the boat.

Felix cast a glance at his comrades as they worked together to reverse their strokes and bring the boat to a halt. The swordsmen looked nervous, Gotrek furious, and the elves as calm as milk. At last the boat came to a shaky stop, wavering restlessly in the water as the current drew it one way and their oar-work pulled it the other. It felt like they were balancing on a teetering rock. One slip and they would all go down. Felix wiped the sweat from his brow with his shoulder and kept back-stroking.

Claudia and Max joined Aethenir in the prow of the boat and closed their eyes, mumbling under their breath. A glow of light began to shimmer around Max's grey-haired head. Ripples distorted the air around Aethenir. Claudia looked up at the patch of sky that showed through the clouds, whispering fiercely.

Felix, Gotrek and the others kept pushing slowly but steadily on the oars, keeping the boat in place as the wizards' incantations grew louder and more droning. The three different spells weaved in and out of each other like some unearthly melody, and Felix felt weird pressures and unexpected emotions pushing at him from within and without. Claudia began to sway in place, and Felix feared – or perhaps hoped – she would fall out of the boat.

In the middle of it all, Captain Oberhoff raised a shout. 'A ship!'

Max broke off instantly – Claudia and Aethenir more reluctantly. Gotrek, Felix and the others turned, following the captain's finger. On the far side of the storm's eye, a dark shape was moving, just within the curtain of the rain.

'Keep pulling, human,' said Captain Rion.

Felix hastily returned to his oar, but his quick glance had shown him a black-hulled ship, small, but with a prow like a knife, with black sails and rows of long oars on both sides.

'Asuryan preserve thy noble sons,' said Aethenir, his pale skin turning even whiter. 'It is as I feared. The corsairs of Naggaroth.'

'The what?' asked Captain Oberhoff.

'The dark elves,' said Max.

'We'd better get back to shore,' said Felix.

Max nodded. 'That would be wisest, yes.'

'But the source of the prophecy!' said Claudia.

No one listened to her. Even Aethenir, staring in frozen terror at the black ship, seemed no longer interested in the whirlpool. Gotrek, Felix, and the human and elf warriors bent to their oars and began backing them again, much more quickly now. Even so, they were only barely moving away from the vortex.

'Lord Aethenir, Fraulein Pallenberger, sit down,' said Max. 'We must stay as low as possible and hope they don't see us.'

Claudia and Aethenir crouched down; she petulantly, he like a tent collapsing. He looked back at the rowers.

'Can we go no faster?' he asked.

'If you want to go faster,' said Gotrek, 'row.'

The high elf looked with horror at the last pair of oars in the bottom of the boat. 'Impossible. I have never…'

'Let me,' said Captain Oberhoff, stepping forwards and picking up one of the oars.

'And I'll take the other,' said Max as he lifted the second.

The Reiksguard captain and the magister sat on the last bench, slotted the oars into the oarlocks and began to row with the others.

Gotrek snorted at Aethenir with disgust. 'Letting an old man pull an oar. Weak-wristed little…'

His muttering drifted off as he put his back into it again. They rowed on, pulling as hard as they could while the dark elf ship continued its circular route around the eye of the storm, but even with the added help of Max and Rion they went very slowly indeed.

'What is it doing?' asked Claudia, watching the ship.

'Staying a sensible distance from that hole,' said Felix, gloomily.

'We should have tried that,' said Captain Oberhoff under his breath.

The black ship sailed closer, moving like the sweep hand of a watch around the edge of the circle. Felix found himself hunching down over his oars, trying to stay as low as possible. The druchii craft was soon near enough that, even through the curtain of rain, he could pick out the individual ropes that rose to the black sails and the elves climbing them. He saw the burnished helmet of an officer glinting on the aft deck, and the cruel emblems emblazoned on the banners that fluttered at the tops of the masts.

The ship was nearly parallel with them now. Felix held his breath. Sail on, he thought, closing his eyes. Sail on. Pass us by and continue around the circle. Another revolution and we will be gone.

Alas, it worked as well as most other childish incantations. A harsh cry echoed over the water and Felix opened his eyes again. A druchii sailor was pointing at them from the weather top and calling to the deck below.

'That's torn it,' said Captain Oberhoff with a curse.

With a swiftness that spoke of a decisive captain and a well-trained crew, the black ship arced off its course and aimed straight at them, its wet black sails gleaming like beetle shells as it broke into the sunshine of the storm's eye. It cut an oblique angle towards them across the open circle of sea, like a man laying a knife across the top of his dinner plate, and moved at an alarming speed.

'Row!' cried Aethenir. 'Row harder!'

'Why don't you use that hot air and blow?' said Gotrek, pulling powerfully at his oar.

'Don't any of you have any spells that could help?' asked Felix, before the elf could return the insult.

'All my spells are of healing and divination,' said Aethenir.

'Rowing is more helpful than anything I could muster at the moment,' said Max.

Felix turned his gaze towards the seeress. 'Claudia?'

'I... I don't know,' she said helplessly.

Felix ground his teeth as he and Gotrek and the others pulled for all they were worth. Still the little boat only crawled, while the druchii ship loomed closer with every second. It was like one of those bad dreams where one ran in place but never seemed to get anywhere.

'He means to ram us!' cried Aethenir. 'Does he not fear to go into the vortex himself?'

'He has enough speed and sailpower to pull out,' said Max. 'We do not.'

The little boat was moving faster now, as it moved further from the whirlpool's insidious grip, but still it was not fast enough. The black ship was only fifty yards away now. There was no way they could escape it.

'It's useless,' wailed Aethenir. 'We are doomed.'

'Good,' said Gotrek, throwing down his oar and drawing his axe off his back. He stepped to the prow and beckoned to the onrushing ship with one meaty hand. 'Come on, you beardless skeletons, I'll smash that floating toothpick to driftwood!'

Everyone else braced for impact. The druchii captain, however, did not attack them directly. Instead, at the last moment, he turned hard to port and shaved past them just out of reach.

But though the ship did not touch them, its bow wave did, nearly capsizing them and pushing them up and back on a mountain of white froth that threw Felix and the other rowers from their benches. Gotrek flew head over heels into the water and only prevented himself from disappearing beneath the waves by grabbing one of the oarlocks as he went over and holding on for dear life. Felix could hear haughty laughter coming from the black ship as its high hull hissed by only yards away from them.

As the others recovered themselves, Felix scrambled to his knees and grabbed the Slayer's arm, helping him pull himself back in.

'What were those villains laughing about?' said Captain Oberhoff, climbing back to his oar. 'They missed.'

'No,' said Aethenir, looking towards the whirlpool. 'They did not.'

Felix and the others turned to see what he was looking at. Felix's heart sank. The little boat was now deep within the band of rushing current that surrounded the hole. He could feel it pulling at them like an insistent lover.

'Bugger,' said Captain Oberhoff.

'Row,' cried Max. 'Quickly, friends!'

Gotrek, Felix, and the elves and men clambered back to their oars and tried to pull in unison. It was hopeless. The current dragged them sideways around the whirlpool faster than a man could run, and always a little closer to the centre. Their oars did nothing but jerk the boat this way and that. Felix's blood ran cold in his veins. There was no way out. They would die here, not beaten by some great monster or devious enemy, but by simple gravity. The vortex would pull them down into its gullet and they would drown.

The glistening slope was getting closer, so smooth and glossy that it seemed almost motionless. Felix looked around at his companions. Gotrek, Captain Oberhoff and his Reiksguarders, Rion and his warriors, all bent grimly to their oars, trying to the last. Max rowed too, but his eyes seemed far-away, as if searching for some solution. Claudia stared towards the whirlpool, eyes wide, crouching in the prow of the boat and mumbling under her breath. Aethenir seemed to be praying as well, his eyes closed and his delicate hands clamped together in supplication.

Captain Oberhoff murmured, 'Sigmar, welcome me to your hall,' over and over again, his eyes closed, and Felix found he was repeating the prayer with him.

Then they were tipping backwards down into the maw, sweeping down it at an angle like a marble spiralling down a funnel made of glittering green bottle glass. The angle of the slope steepened every second, and everyone shrank down into the boat, clinging to the sides. At last the slope became entirely vertical and they plummeted down in free fall.

Claudia screamed, and Felix was afraid he might have too. The others cursed and shouted, starting to fall faster than the boat as the drag of the hull against the watery walls slowed it. Felix clutched instinctively at one of the oar benches to hold himself in, then looked down into the green well, terrified, but determined to face his death head-on. The shock of what he saw there almost knocked the fear right out of him. Firstly, the walls of the whirlpool did not taper, as he expected, but went straight down, leaving a half-mile-wide circle of ocean floor exposed to the sky. Secondly, rising from that muddy

floor were the shattered white towers and ruined buildings of an ancient city.

'By the Everqueen!' said Aethenir.

'A city,' said Max, in awe.

A city that would be their final resting place in a matter of seconds, thought Felix.

Claudia's murmuring rose in pitch and volume. Felix
could not tell what god or goddess she was praying to,
but it seemed that whichever it was, they weren't listen-
ing.

'This is a bad doom,' said Gotrek, glaring down at the
rapidly approaching sea floor.

'I agree,' said Felix, a lump of helpless rage rising in his
throat. Now he would never find out what had happened to his father. Now he would never resolve things
with Ulrika. Now he would never finish the epic of
Gotrek's death. He put the blame squarely on Claudia. It
was her damned visions that had brought them out here
in the first place. The woman had seemed determined to
ruin his life and his peace of mind since the first moment
she laid eyes on him. This calamity was exactly what she
deserved for her foolishness. He would have laughed at
her demise if he hadn't been about to share it.

Suddenly, the seeress rose from her crouch, throwing
out her arms and diving from the boat. Felix stared. Had
she gone mad at last? Was she giving in to the inevitable?

But then she rose above them – or rather they dropped
faster than she – while at the same time she turned in the
air and swept an arm towards them. Felix felt himself
buffeted by an impossible wind – a wind that came from
below them, a wind that grabbed at his sleeves and his
cloak and tried to tear his grip from the boat.

'What is it?' cried one of the Reiksguard. 'What is the
witch doing?'

'Let go!' called Max. 'She cannot support the boat as well.'

Felix's eyes bulged, and shame flooded his heart. The girl was trying to save them, using some sort of wind spell. He fought his natural inclination to cling for safety and forced his fingers to let go of the boat.

'Push off!' Max cried.

Felix kicked away from the floor of the boat, trying to tell himself it didn't matter how he fell. It would all end the same. The others did likewise. Even Gotrek pushed off, muttering about the untrustworthiness of magic all the while.

Felix looked down as the wind blew up at him from below, and his heart dropped faster than his body. The seeress had left it too late. The ground was rushing up at them too fast. They were too close. She would never stop their descent in time.

But then the wind from below increased tenfold, blasting him like an icy furnace and beating at his face like a living thing. His clothes flapped around him deafeningly. He was slowing! They all were! She was doing it! The wind was stopping them. They were hanging in the air, almost as if they were attached to Makaisson's air catchers. Claudia floated in the midst of them, her eyes closed tight, her arms out rigidly to her sides, her lips moving furiously.

'It's a miracle,' breathed Captain Oberhoff, looking around him in terrified wonder.

It was indeed a miracle, but they were still going the wrong way. Lift us up, Felix wanted to call, but he didn't dare break Claudia's concentration. Get us out of this hole!

They continued to drift down. Was she mad? It was all very well to save them from smashing into a pulp on the ocean floor, but this unnatural whirlpool could collapse any moment.

Twenty feet above the sea floor, Gotrek dropped like a stone. He barked in surprise and fell away from the rest, landing with a wet smack in the mud.

Claudia whimpered and Felix dropped too. He yelped and flailed his arms as the wind that had been supporting him weakened to nothing, and he slammed into the mud a few feet from Gotrek. He bent his knees as he hit and found himself kneeling waist deep in blue-grey silt the consistency of wet plaster. His body rang with shock from the impact, but he didn't think anything had been broken or sprained. The others plopped down all around him, cursing and crying out, with the last being Claudia, landing ungracefully on her posterior.

Felix looked around as he tried to free himself from the sucking mud. They had landed very close to the shimmering, humming wall of water, on the very outskirts of the ruined city. The shattered remains of their boat stuck out of the muck not far away, and to their left he could see low walls, now little more than piles of seaweed-covered rubble, that might once have been a grand house. The city rose high and white and broken in the distance beyond them, like a collection of impossibly slim and delicate porcelain vases that had been smashed with a mattock. And beyond the ruined spires, lay the towering green cliff of water that was the other side of the whirlpool going up and up and up. The weight of all that water was palpable. It crushed him just looking at it. He didn't know what was keeping it up, but whatever it was, it certainly couldn't last. At some point the impossible walls would collapse and the water would come crashing back down to smash and drown them all. It made Felix want to curl up and cover his head.

Around him, the others were struggling to stand, mired to the knees or deeper in the mud, but apparently unhurt. Only Claudia remained motionless, sagging sideways, half-conscious, knee-deep in the muck. Gotrek was in the worst straits, buried up to his chest. He spat out a mouthful of mud.

'Magic,' he said, like a curse.

'Stupid woman,' snapped Aethenir as he tried to pull the hem of his robes free of the mud. 'Why did you not lift us out! We are stuck here now!'

Felix felt like punching the elf on the nose, even though he had thought the same thing just seconds before. It was different to say it out loud.

'High one, control your tongue!' said Max sharply. 'She did the best she could.'

'I'm sorry. I was too weak,' said Claudia, clutching her head as she came out of her faint. 'You were too many. I have never tried so complex an incantation before.' She turned to Gotrek, frowning. 'You were very slippery, master dwarf. Very hard to hold.'

'Dwarfs are very resistant to magic,' said Max. 'And the Slayer more so than most, I would think.'

Felix extricated himself at last and crossed to Gotrek to offer him a hand. Two of the Reiksguarders joined him.

Behind them, Aethenir inclined his head briefly towards Claudia. 'My apologies, seeress. I spoke harshly out of distress. I see you have done as much as a human can do.' He looked to Max as she glared at his back. 'But what now, magister?' he asked. 'We are still stuck here. We have only delayed our death.'

'I will try again,' said Claudia, seething. 'But I will need some time to gather my paltry human energies.'

'Let us pray then that there is time enough,' said the high elf nodding politely to her again, and apparently oblivious to her sarcasm.

'Lord magister,' called Captain Oberhoff. Max and the others turned. He was pointing to the mud a short distance away from him. 'Look, milord. Footprints.'

Max and Aethenir's eyes widened.

Max slogged forwards, the mud sucking at his feet with every step. 'Are you certain?'

'Aye, sir,' said the captain.

With Felix and the Reiksguarders' help, Gotrek pulled himself free of the muck at last, and he and Felix joined Max and Aethenir beside the captain. The holes in the mud were definitely footprints – many pairs of them – and all leading further into the city. Because the wet mud had oozed back into the holes, it was impossible to tell who or what had left them, but whatever they were, there appeared to be about twenty of them.

'Someone else has fallen down this hole,' said the captain.

'Or caused it to be created,' said Max, ominously. He turned to Aethenir. 'Do you know what place this is, high one?'

Aethenir looked around, frowning at the distant buildings. 'It is one of the elven cities that sank during the Sundering, perhaps Lothlakh, or Ildenfane. Without maps and books I cannot be sure.' He returned his gaze to the mud. 'But of one thing I can be certain. Whoever has exposed it like this, whoever has come seeking within it, can be up to no good.'

Claudia stood upright, swaying only slightly. 'Yes. This is the place. This is the heart of it. There is where the evil will be found that will destroy Marienburg and Altdorf.'

Of course it is, thought Felix, stifling a groan.

Max stroked his muddy beard and sighed. 'I suppose we better go have a look then, hadn't we?'

IT WAS HARD going, at least at first, each step a strenuous effort as the mud sucked at their feet and clung to their cloaks and robes. It got easier nearer to the city when they found the remains of a paved road. It too was covered with silt, but not nearly as deep.

It was one of the strangest environments Felix had ever travelled through – the delicate white walls of the elven buildings and the slender, jutting towers, now crumbled and covered in a wild phantasmagoria of ornament – shells, starfish and draperies of kelp, baroque filigree of dull-coloured coral, mossy algae, colonies of clinging clams, and stranger, tentacled things that looked like trees from the Chaos Wastes in miniature. Dead fish and feebly gesturing lobsters lay in the mud of ancient alleyways while water dripped from gutters that had known no rain for centuries. And above it all, the impossible green walls of seawater.

Felix couldn't help but look back at them nervously every few steps, afraid they might drop when he wasn't looking. At the gates of the city, a high white arch the wooden doors of which had long ago rotted away, he turned one last time and saw something within the water, a strange black shape bigger than a whale, gliding slowly past like a fish within a fishbowl.

'Gotrek! Max!' he cried, pointing, but by the time everyone turned around, the shape was gone, vanished back into the green murk beyond the whirlpool.

'What is it, Felix?' said Max.

'A shape,' he said. 'In the water. Like a whale.'

Max looked at the wall, waiting for something to appear, then shrugged. 'Perhaps it was a whale.' He turned and entered the gate.

The others followed. Felix scowled, feeling foolish, and took up the rear.

Within the walls, the full glory of the elven architecture became apparent. Though much of it had fallen, much more still stood, and it was glorious. The doors and windows were all tall and thin and topped with graceful arches. The columns were delicate and fluted. The streets were wide and well laid out, so that every corner was a new and breathtaking vista.

The party followed the footprints into the heart of the city, where the buildings became even taller and more ostentatious. These were obviously temples and palaces and places of public entertainment, and those that still stood were awe-inspiring in their scale and delicacy – at least to Felix.

'Flimsy elf rubbish,' grumbled Gotrek as he looked at it. 'No wonder it sank.'

Felix expected a retort of some kind from Aethenir, but he was too busy staring at the city. The elf was so fascinated by what he was seeing that he seemed to have lost all fear. 'Yes,' he said, more to himself than anyone else. 'It is just as my studies said it would be. This is definitely Lothlakh. The *Diary of Selyssin* describes the tower of the loremasters just so, but... no, if this is Lothlakh, then surely the Temple of Khaine is meant to be just to the left of the baths. Perhaps it is Ildenfane after all.'

At last the footprints led them to a sprawling, symmetrical palace with high, buttressed towers at each end and a pair of golden doors in the centre, flanked on either side by tall golden statues of regal elves holding swords and staffs. The gold of both the doors and the statues was filthy with black mud and crusted with barnacles and mussels, but they were all still whole.

Gotrek nodded approvingly. 'That's dwarf work,' he said. 'Made before the elves attacked and insulted us.'

Even that failed to raise a response from Aethenir. He was walking towards the palace like a sleepwalker, his hands waving vaguely at the various details of architecture and placement. 'It *is* Lothlakh!' he said. 'It must be. This is the palace of Lord Galdenaer, ruler of Lothlakh, described exactly in Oraine's *Book of the East*. To think that I have lived to see this.'

'It is indeed beautiful,' said Max. 'But we should perhaps approach it with more caution. It appears that those we seek may be within.'

Aethenir looked down at the footsteps leading to the golden doors, and a nervous look appeared in his eyes as he awoke from his scholar's dream. 'Yes,' he said. 'Yes of course.' He turned to the captain of his house guard. 'Rion, take the lead.'

The elf captain bowed and his elves moved towards the broad, muck-covered marble steps to the golden doors. The others followed. Gotrek and Felix and the Reiksguard took up the rear, watching all around.

The doors had been pulled open – by what means Felix couldn't guess – just enough to allow them passage one at a time. The first of the elves slipped through the opening while the others waited. After a moment he reappeared and beckoned the others through. The party followed him into an enormous entry hall. Felix and the rest looked with wonder upon the gold-chased columns, the crumbling obsidian statues, and the high arched ceiling. Windows that had once been filled with coloured glass were now gaping holes, through which watery green sunshine streamed in, giving the impression that the palace was still under the sea.

The mysterious footprints led across the silt-covered marble floor to a wide stairway that descended into darkness. Max created a small light – less bright than a candle – that he sent ahead of the elf warriors so they could follow the footprints. The silt was heavier here, making the stairs treacherous. Felix gripped the marble banister to steady himself. One flight down, Captain Rion held up his hand and everyone stopped. From below came the faint sounds of movement and conversation, and a bright noise of metal rubbing on metal, like someone endlessly scraping a dagger around the inside of a bell. Felix strained his ears, but could not make out the words or the language that was being spoken. The high elves looked at each other, but said nothing. They continued down the stairs, as silent as cats. Felix and the others tried to do the same.

At the base of the stairway there was an archway that glowed with a strange purple light. The high elves crept to one side of the archway, keeping out of sight, then leaned their heads out cautiously. Felix, Max and Gotrek followed their example.

Through the arch was a moderately large chamber with decorative pillars running down both sides and, at the far end, at the top of three wide marble stairs, a pair of enormous steel, granite and brass doors. Standing on the broad dais before the doors were a number of tall, thin figures, silhouetted in the glow of a purple light that hovered over the head of the one nearest the door – an elven woman in long black robes with black hair to her waist. Her hands were raised towards the door, and weird words poured from her lips in a sinuous melody. Five other robed women surrounded her, while surrounding them were twelve warriors in black enamelled scale mail and helms that were faced with silver skull masks. The tallest of the women wore an elaborate headdress and held a metal wand aloft, spinning a silver hoop on it. It was from this that the metallic ringing sound came.

Aethenir shrunk back behind the arch. 'Druchii!' he hissed.

'Sorceresses of Morathi's cult,' said Rion, his hand tightening convulsively on the hilt of his sword. 'And Endless, the Witch King's personal guard.'

'At last,' rumbled Gotrek. 'Elves I can kill.'

Rion turned to Aethenir. 'Lord, we humble house guards are no match for such as these. Even swordmasters of Hoeth would find themselves in difficulty here.'

Aethenir returned his attention to the room, biting his noble lip. 'We may have no choice,' he said, his voice quavering.

At the vault, the sorceress with the waist-length hair finished her incantation on a high, sustained note and then stepped back. With a rumble of hidden counterweights and a grinding of stone on stone, the massive doors began to swing out. She turned and smiled at her black-clad companions, motioning them to enter.

When he saw her face, Aethenir gasped and staggered back. 'Belryeth!' he whispered. 'It can't be!'

NINE

MAX TURNED AND looked at the high elf, raising a questioning eyebrow. 'You know this dark elf?'

Captain Rion was looking at Aethenir with a much colder look on his face.

Aethenir looked from one to the other, stepping back. 'I didn't know she was druchii.'

Captain Rion's eye got colder yet. 'I believe that requires explanation, Lord Aethenir.' He motioned the elf back up the stairs, out of sight of the door.

'Yes,' said Max, following. 'I believe it does.'

The others crept back up to the first landing with them, then everybody turned to face the high elf.

'Now, my lord,' said Rion. 'Pray continue. How do you know this druchii?'

Aethenir swallowed. 'Ah, yes, well, you see, when last she came to me, she claimed to be a maiden in distress. Belryeth Eldendawn she called herself, and she told me–'

'You mistook one of the fallen ones for a true elf?' asked Rion, his voice like ice.

'She didn't look like she does now!' squealed Aethenir. 'Her hair was blonde and she had a beautiful, noble face, and a voice like the sweetest, saddest song ever sung by...'

The high elf caught Captain Rion's eye and faltered. Felix had never seen an elf blush before. From down the stairs came crashings and smashings and the tinkling of broken crystal. It sounded like the druchii were tearing the contents of the vault apart.

'Go on, my lord,' said the elf captain.

Aethenir nodded. 'She came to me,' he said, 'begging for help. She said that her family was in disgrace and could not approach the tower directly, but she must learn something hidden in one of the volumes in the library. Her grandfather, it seemed, had lost a precious family heirloom during the Sundering when he was stationed in one of the cities of the Old World. Recovering it was the only way she could fend off an odious marriage, now that her father had lost the family's fortune and all honour in a disastrous trading scandal. Her misfortunes moved me to tears.'

Felix rolled his eyes. The poor sheltered elf had obviously never seen a Detlef Sierck melodrama.

'She swore that all she wanted was the information contained in one book,' Aethenir continued. 'A book that told of that time and of those cities.'

'Do you mean the book that was stolen from the tower?' asked Max. 'Did she learn its location from you? Is she the thief?'

Aethenir hung his head. 'It was not stolen from the tower. As I said before, none may find the tower if the loremasters do not wish them to.' He hesitated, then went on. 'I borrowed it from the tower, and she stole it from me.'

Rion went rigid, his eyes blazing. 'What?'

Aethenir shrunk before that terrible gaze. 'I swear I didn't know until now! She promised me that we would always look at the book together and it would never leave my sight, but the night I brought the book to her we were assaulted by masked assassins. I saw her killed! Then they leapt at me, knocking me out. When I awoke from my swoon, her body was gone, and so was the book.' He looked down the stairs towards the vault. 'All this time I thought her dead.'

Max coughed. 'I had always read that no books were allowed to be borrowed from the Tower of Hoeth. That they were never to leave the premises.'

Neither Rion or Aethenir acknowledged that he had spoken. They seemed to have forgotten that anyone else was there.

'My lord,' said Rion, with a dangerous softness. 'You told me that you had discovered that the book was missing, and that the loremasters had sent you to find it as a test of your worthiness to be taught the arts of Saphery. You told your *father* this.'

Aethenir covered his face with a shaking hand. 'I lied,' he whispered, so low Felix almost couldn't hear him.

'So the loremasters of Hoeth know nothing of the truth?' Rion asked.

Aethenir shook his head. 'I ran away from the tower. It has been my hope that I might, with your help, find the book and return it to the library before they know it is missing.'

Captain Rion's head sank and his fists clenched. 'My lord,' he said, 'were it not my sworn duty to protect your life, I would kill you here and now.'

Aethenir paled and stepped back at that, but Rion made no move against him.

'You have not only compromised your own honour,' the elf captain continued, 'but by asking your father for money and assistance in this misbegotten quest, you have compromised his honour, and the honour of all House Whiteleaf. Not to mention jeopardising the safety of our beloved homeland.'

Aethenir hung his head. It looked like he was sobbing.

Rion carried on mercilessly. 'Recovering the book will not win back House Whiteleaf's honour, my lord. The crime is too great. But it must be recovered even so, for to leave it in enemy hands would be an even greater crime.'

'Yes,' said Aethenir, still looking at the ground. 'It must be done. It is the least that I can do.'

'I am pleased that you think so, my lord,' said Rion, stepping closer to him. 'Because if you swerve from the path of honour – if you fail in the duty to your father and your house,' he curled the front of Aethenir's robe in his fist and jerked it up so that the young elf's jaw came up and he was forced to look the captain in the eye, 'I *will* kill you.'

'I won't fail, Rion,' said Aethenir, trembling. 'I promise you.'

Rion stepped back and bowed, very formal. 'Thank you, lord. That is all I ask.'

'Just a moment,' said Max. 'I wish to be clear. Ulthuan has no knowledge of this quest? You are not here by the authority of the Tower of Hoeth, as you previously implied? You are not an initiate?'

'No, magister. I am the merest novice.'

'And you are entirely on your own in this?'

'Yes, magister.'

Max sighed. 'Had I known this, I would not have so blithely...' He paused, then shook his head. 'Never mind. What's done is done. The danger is still the same and we must still face it.'

Gotrek grunted. 'Are you through? Can we kill some elves?'

Captain Rion turned and glared at him, seemingly displeased with his turn of phrase, but then nodded. 'Aye,' he said. 'Whatever these fiends mean to do, it can only mean dark days for Ulthuan if they succeed.'

'Good,' said Gotrek. He turned on his heel and started down the stairs again.

'Slayer,' whispered Max after him. 'We must be cautious! It is the sorceresses who maintain the whirlpool. If they die...'

But Gotrek was already striding through the arch into the antechamber. Felix and the others trailed in his wake, whispering after him urgently, as the sounds of smashing and shifting continued from the vault.

'Wait, Gotrek,' said Felix.

'Stop, dwarf,' hissed Captain Rion. 'We need a strategy.'

'Bring him back,' cried Aethenir.

'Here's your strategy,' rumbled Gotrek. 'We kill everyone except the one with the stick and the hoop, then force her to take us out the way she got in.'

'Very good,' said Max, trotting along beside him. 'But how?'

'Like this,' said Gotrek and strode up the low stairs to the half-open vault doors. 'Come on, you corpse-faced scarecrows!' he roared. 'Show me you've got more courage than your white-livered cousins!' Then he charged into the vault.

Aethenir gasped. Max groaned. The Reiksguard and Rion's elves exchanged grim glances and prepared to follow him in.

'Wait!' hissed Felix. For once he had an idea of how to take advantage of the Slayer's bullheadedness. 'Hide. Let them think he's alone. Max, Claudia, Lord Aethenir, prepare your most deadly spells. Captain Rion, be ready to attack. Captain Oberhoff, protect the magisters.'

Oberhoff and his men obeyed, as did Max and Aethenir. Rion looked at Felix like he was a dog who had suddenly begun to sing opera, but then motioned his elves to the left of the vault door as Felix peered into the vault.

'Firandaen,' Rion said to the elf whose leg had been maimed by the skaven. 'You will stay with the magisters.'

The skull-masked Endless were charging Gotrek from all sides, swerving around overturned treasure chests and mounds of dumped treasure. Beyond them, the sorceresses stared at the Slayer, shocked. The only person who seemed entirely undisturbed was the sorceress who spun the silver hoop on the metal wand, a tall, ageless, hard-faced beauty who watched coolly as Gotrek and the Endless met in the centre of the room with a deafening crash and a flurry of flashing steel.

The Slayer disappeared as his taller foes swarmed around him, hacking and stabbing with their long slim swords. One of them fell back, a scarlet trench dug through the armour and flesh of his chest, spraying blood everywhere.

'Magisters! Captain Rion! Now!' cried Felix.

Max and Claudia stepped to the gap between the doors, thrusting their hands through and propelling streams of light and crackling lightning into the room. Felix, Rion and his three unwounded warriors ran in right behind the blasts. The masked druchii screamed and fell back as the blue fire and blinding light attacked their bodies, then Felix and the high elves slammed into them and five more went down, Gotrek killing two, Rion and the elves killing two more between them, and one dying fried to a crisp by Claudia's lightning. Half of them dead already! Felix rejoiced. This might be easier than he had expected.

Felix lunged at his bedazzled opponent, but the dark elf recovered with alarming speed and Felix's sword only scraped his armour as he blocked and whipped his blade into a blurring riposte. Felix barely brought his sword up in time. The next attack came almost before the first had finished, aiming straight for his eyes. Felix back-pedalled desperately, panic sweat prickling his skin. In two seconds Felix knew the dark elf was the best swordsman he had ever faced. There was no question of going on the offensive. Felix couldn't keep up with his attacks. He counted himself a better than average swordsman, but he was only human. He had only been fighting with a sword for twenty-five years or so. The dark elf, on the other hand, had probably been studying the blade for two hundred years, and was of a race naturally more agile than mankind to begin with.

Felix blocked again, but the druchii slipped under his guard and stabbed him at the crux of his right shoulder and chest. Felix's chainmail stopped most of it, but still the point sank an inch into meat before striking bone, driving links of mail with it. Felix fell back, barking with pain, and landed gasping on his back. The world dimmed and throbbed before his eyes. He waved his sword weakly above him with his off hand, but the druchii had turned away from him and was attacking Rion's warriors.

The arrogance of it cut through Felix's pain. Was he really so negligible a threat that the dark elf would turn away without finishing him off? He had never felt more dismissed. Felix struggled to get up and go on guard, then understood the druchii's confidence. The attack had been a carefully calculated crippling blow, goring the muscle that allowed him to lift his sword. He couldn't use it.

Beyond the melee, the woman with the wand and the silver hoop called out an order in a slithery voice, and two of her five sorceresses began scribing spells in the air. The others, Aethenir's Belryeth included, returned to searching through the stacks of treasure chests, as they had been doing before Gotrek's interruption – casually dumping them and kicking through their contents.

Determined to stay in the fight, if only to prove to the dark elf that he was still a threat, Felix switched his sword to his barely competent left hand, and charged him again. The Endless didn't even look back, just threw his leg out behind him in the middle of a lunge and kicked Felix precisely on the wound.

Felix smashed to the ground, hissing and curling up in a ball. By the gods, I'm useless, he thought as he fought to remain conscious through the pain.

His eye was caught by a cloud of boiling blackness that roiled towards the combat from the two druchii sorceresses. The pain of the wound was instantly eclipsed by a greater one as the black cloud enveloped him, and a burning like red-hot brands seared through him, seeming to cook him from the inside. He screamed and beat at himself like he was on fire, though there were no flames. The high elves were affected in the same way. They fell back, cursing and wailing and blocking desperately as the Endless lunged in to take advantage. Only Gotrek fought on unaffected.

But almost as quickly as the black cloud was upon them, a bubble of light pushed it back, dissolving it in its radiance. The pain receded from Felix's limbs as the bubble expanded beyond him. He looked to the door and saw Max and Aethenir standing within it and working in tandem, sending pulses of white and golden energy into the room as Claudia shot more lightning at the sorceresses.

The bubble of light expanded to surround the high elves, allowing them to recover, but for one it was too late. He was crumbling, blood pouring down his white and green surcoat as Captain Rion and the other two elves fought on at Gotrek's side, surrounded by five skull-masked Endless.

Felix rolled out of the way of the combatants and staggered to his feet, while all around him invisible forces flexed and strained as the sorceresses and the magisters cast and countered each other's spells. With one arm useless, he couldn't hope to fight the dark elves directly, but he could at least take up his old position and guard Gotrek's sides. He limped behind the Slayer and immediately put his sword in the way of a slashing druchii sword. It was amazing to see how much trouble the Slayer was having. He who had fought armies of orcs and hordes of skaven single-handed, and who had faced down daemons and vampires, wasn't able to get a single strike in on the three druchii he held at bay. Though his axe was everywhere and his face was red with effort, he could not touch them, and shallow gashes covered his chest and arms.

The three druchii that fought him looked the same, blooded and winded. Their eyes, barely seen through the eye holes of their skull masks, were wide with offended surprise that any foe could last so long before them.

Rion and his remaining elves were drenched in sweat and blood, and fought their opponents with doomed desperation, for though, being elves, they might best any man alive at the sword, compared to the Endless, they were fumbling beginners. There was no question what the outcome of their fights would be, and Felix shuddered at what would happen when they had died and all the Endless were able to turn their attention on Gotrek. Against five such enemies, even the Slayer could not hope to prevail.

Suddenly, from atop a stack of treasure chests to the right of the door, Belryeth cried out in triumph and raised a sinuously curved black object over her head. The other sorceresses cheered. She turned towards the door of the chamber and smiled at Aethenir. 'Look, beloved, the Harp of Ruin, which you have helped us find!'

Aethenir shouted something back at her in the elvish tongue, but she laughed at him.

'No,' she said. 'I will speak so these fools can understand and know your humiliation. Bewitched and beglamoured, you have given into the hands of your enemies the greatest weapon of a lost age. One pluck of these strings can cause earthquakes that raise mountains from valleys or sink highlands lower than the sea bed. With this will the druchii create a wave that will sweep all the asur from Ulthuan. With this will we raise lost Nagarythe and rule the world again from our true homeland! You have doomed your people, and all for a love that never was!'

She reached into her robe and drew out something thick and square, then threw it so that it skidded across the floor to stop at Aethenir's feet. It was a book. Aethenir stared at it, then stooped and picked it up.

'Please thank your masters for the loan,' called Belryeth, laughing. 'It was everything I'd hoped it would be.'

The sorceress who spun the silver ring on the wand barked something that sounded to Felix suspiciously like 'enough gloating', and Belryeth and the other druchii women began making their way towards the door of the vault as they began new incantations.

With five of the sorceresses turning their attentions on them now, Max, Aethenir and Claudia were overwhelmed. Beams of darkness, like shafts from a black sun, smashed through their protective bubble. Felix saw Max stagger and Aethenir fall back, clutching his throat. Claudia wailed and tore at her face as if she were staring into the abyss. The Reiksguarders fell to the floor, screaming. Firandaen, the wounded elf who had stayed back to guard the spellcasters, pulled Aethenir and the magisters behind the vault door as blood poured from his nose, mouth, ears and eyes.

Gotrek and the elf warriors glanced towards the women, but could not disengage from the Endless, who would have cut them down the instant they lowered their guard to run. Only Felix was free. Though he knew it was death, he sprinted towards the women, his shoulder screaming with every jarring step. Belryeth turned casually and waved her free hand at him. A ripple of air rushed from her fingers and blew over him. It was as cold as death. He dropped, frozen to the bone, his teeth chattering. He couldn't move. His very blood seemed to have turned to ice. Frost rimmed his eyelashes.

Belryeth paused, smiling, as her sisters filed out the vault door. 'You are fools helping a fool on a fool's errand, and you will die a fool's death as a result.' And with a merry laugh, she turned and followed the others out.

Though the cold would not let him turn his head, Felix could hear screams and raving from the antechamber and he knew that the Reiksguard were trying, and failing, to prevent the sorceresses from leaving. He willed his limbs to move, wanting to go to their aid, but they would not. They were frozen stiff.

After a moment the cries fell silent and all that he could hear was the clashing of sword on sword and axe, and the heavy breathing and stamping of the fight behind him. And that will end soon enough, he thought, miserably.

But then, to Felix's surprise, Max appeared in the gap between the doors of the vault, clutching them for support and looking near death. He raised a feeble shout over the clamour of the battle. 'Your mistresses have left you to die, warriors. Will you still fight for them?'

A cold voice came from the depths of the skull helmet of one of the Endless. 'For the ruin of Ulthuan and the rebirth of Nagarythe, we are proud to die.'

'Then die you shall,' said Max. He forced himself upright and summoned his sorcerous energies, though it seemed to age him to do so. With a grunt of pain and effort, he unleashed a stream of swirling lights at the druchii. It was weak compared to his earlier attacks, but it was enough. With the sorceresses gone, the Endless could not defend themselves from it. The lights danced in front of their eyes, blinding and confusing them.

It was their end. Gotrek and Rion and his warriors beat down their swords and chopped through their armour with brutal ease. Gotrek dismembered the three who had defied him, as the others fell to the elves.

'Damned dancers wouldn't stay still,' growled the Slayer as he and the three elves stood over the pile of limbs and heads, breathing heavily.

Felix uncurled slowly as the effects of the unnatural cold faded and the stab wound in his shoulder throbbed to prominence again. He bit his cheeks against the pain.

Max sagged against the vault doors. 'No time to rest,' he said. 'We must go after the sorceresses.'

Aethenir appeared behind him, swaying like an aspen. 'Yes, hurry. They carry the doom of the asur in their hands.'

'Then let them go,' said Gotrek, shrugging.

'Vile dwarf,' said Aethenir. 'Would you doom the rest of the world to satisfy your grudge against the elves?'

'Why not?' said Gotrek. 'You doomed it for a druchii kiss.'

'I told you,' cried Aethenir. 'I did not know that she–'

'Their leader holds the key to escaping this trap alive,' said Max, interrupting their sniping angrily.

Suddenly not even Gotrek had any objections to going after the sorceresses.

Felix, Gotrek, Rion, and his elves followed Max and Aethenir out of the vault and found a bloodless massacre. Firandaen was dead, a look of wide-eyed horror on his noble face. Captain Oberhoff and the last of the Reiksguard were dead too, icicles like daggers growing out of their mouths and eyes, and stabbing through their breastplates from within.

Felix for a moment thought Claudia was dead too, her little body huddled in a ball at the base of the low stairs, but then he saw her twitch. He and one of Rion's remaining warriors helped her up and supported her between them as the party moved towards the stairs. She whimpered and flinched at their touch, and her face was shredded where she had clawed at herself after the sorceress's attack.

As they hurried across the antechamber, Aethenir turned to Rion, holding up the stolen book. 'I know this is not enough,' he said. 'Not any more. I vow that I will not rest until I recover the harp and prevent the sorceresses' plan.'

Rion nodded, but did not look around. 'That is the path of honour, my lord,' he said coldly.

Aethenir's eyes were downcast as they entered the stairwell.

The two flights to the entry hall was one of the most terrifying distances Felix had ever travelled, for he expected at every moment for a roaring torrent of water to pour down them and bury them beneath the sea. It was also one of the most painful, for with every step the wound in his shoulder staggered him afresh. The blood from it was soaking his shirt and padded jerkin and turning the rings of his mail red. He nearly lost his grip on Claudia several times as the pain made him faint.

The others were in equally bad shape. Max's face was pale and drawn, as if he had aged twenty years since the beginning of the battle. Aethenir was shaking as if with fever, sweat standing out on his pale skin. Rion and his last two elves moved with grim precision, staring fixedly ahead of them as their wounds bled into their surcoats. Only Gotrek seemed fit and ready for another battle. Though he bled from a score of wounds, his step was firm and his eye was clear and angry.

They reached the silt-filled entry hall and ran to the golden doors, then slipped through them onto the wide porch at the top of the marble steps, looking around anxiously for the sorceresses. Felix didn't see them, and it looked as if it would be impossible to follow them, for the streets of the city were flooded with water, and it was rising swiftly, already halfway up the palace's grand marble steps.

'The water!' wailed Aethenir. 'She has loosed the walls!'

'If she had loosed the walls, scholar,' said Max, with barely concealed impatience, 'we would be dead by now. They are whole, you see? She is losing concentration, that is all.'

'And that is better?' asked Aethenir.

Over their voices Felix thought he still heard the now familiar chime of the sorceress's silver hoop, faint, but still audible. 'Shhh!' he said. 'The ringing. Listen!'

Everyone listened, but it was hard to pinpoint where the sound was coming from, and it was getting fainter, lost in the deep distant roar of the whirlpool's spinning sides.

'Where is it?' said Aethenir.

'There,' said Claudia, looking straight up at the sky with dull eyes.

Everyone followed her gaze. At first Felix could see nothing – only the glare of the sky shining down into the gloomy green well of the whirlpool. But then, as his eyes accustomed themselves to the light, he saw them – six black dots, levitating up towards the top of the well like they were being drawn up on ropes – the sorceresses. They rose in a circle, with one of their number in the centre.

'Bring them down!' cried Aethenir. 'Stop them!'

'But we'll die,' said Felix.

'Still I think I must,' said Max. 'For the safety of the world.' He took a deep breath and began an incantation, pulling power from the air around him with his hands.

He was too late.

Before he was halfway through his droning, the shrill ringing stopped, like a chiming glass pinched silent.

There was a short pause in which Felix could hear half a dozen frightened gasps – one of them his – then, with a sound like the world ending, the whirlpool collapsed, the green walls caving in and an avalanche of water thundering towards the centre to fill the unnatural hole in the sea.

TEN

AETHENIR SCREAMED.

Gotrek cursed.

Claudia stared.

Felix turned to her, shouting though she was right next to him. 'Seeress! Lift us up! Levitate us!'

Claudia didn't appear to hear.

The titanic waves were already crashing into the city, smashing buildings and toppling towers in their wake, and the shallow water in the street began rising much more rapidly.

'Back to the vault,' rasped Gotrek.

'Back to the vault?' cried Felix. 'But that's suicide!' The Slayer was insane! They would be trapped underground, under water. They would die!

Gotrek was already pushing through the narrow gap between the doors. 'It's the only thing that isn't,' he shouted.

'Follow him!' said Max, and hurried in with Aethenir and his escort.

Felix and the elf who was helping him support Claudia hustled her through the door as quick as they could, but she was still too slow. The water from the street was already spilling into the palace. She would never make it to the vault, and neither would they. With a curse, Felix scooped Claudia up, slung her over his unwounded shoulder and raced across the entry hall after the others. The pain was still almost more than he could bear.

'Thank you, Felix,' said Max, then turned back and held out his hands towards the palace doors.

Felix heard them grind shut as he plunged into the stairway. A useless gesture, he thought. Even if they held, the palace was full of broken windows. As Max caught up with him, the roar of the approaching water drowned out every other noise. The party splashed breakneck down the last flight, slipping and clutching at the walls as water pushed at the back of their legs and rained down from above.

Then, just as they reached the bottom, with a noise like the world ending, a cataclysmic impact shook the palace, knocking them all off their feet and sending huge blocks of masonry crashing down from the ceiling all around them. Felix landed on top of Claudia, his shoulder screaming and his ears nearly bursting as a horrible pressure slammed them.

The whirlpool had closed.

Gotrek picked himself up from the knee-high water as rocks and dust continued to splash down. 'Run!' he roared.

Felix found his feet and pulled Claudia up after him, slinging her over his shoulder again and slogging across the antechamber after the Slayer, dizzy from the pain and weaving drunkenly. A deafening thunder roared behind them. The palace doors? Felix didn't dare look back.

After several endless seconds Felix trudged up the three steps to the vault with Claudia and stumbled through the half-open doors. Water was lapping over the raised threshold and spreading out in a puddle towards the treasures.

'To the side!' called Gotrek.

The elves and humans splashed to the right. Felix started to follow but tripped over the body of a dead elf and dropped Claudia again. The pain as he crashed down almost made him black out. He tried to rise, but his head was swimming too much. Then Gotrek's powerful fingers grabbed his collar and pulled him across the floor. Rion was doing the same to Claudia. The whole room was shaking.

Felix looked back towards the vault doors as the Slayer dragged him aside. A frothing wall of water was blasting out of the stairwell towards the vault faster than stampeding horses. It's over, he thought, cringing away from the sight. This is the end.

But then, just as he expected the full weight of the sea to burst in and batter them all to death against the walls of the vault, the doors slammed shut with a deafening boom, closed by the force of the water, and there was silence.

The elves and humans all looked at the doors in shock. They had held. Gotrek looked smug.

'We... we're alive,' said Aethenir, as if he didn't quite believe it.

'Good thinking, Slayer,' said Max.

'Dwarf work,' Gotrek grunted with a nod towards the doors. 'The only doors I could trust not to break in this elf hovel.'

Aethenir sniffed. 'That's all very well, dwarf, but now you've trapped us under the sea. How am I to honour my pledge to Rion and make recompense for my crimes if we all die of asphyxiation down here?'

'Not asphyxiation, my lord,' said Rion, looking towards the doors. 'Drowning.'

Everyone turned. The doors had held perfectly, but there was a knife-thin arc of water spraying through the narrow gap between them. The puddle on the floor continued to spread.

'Shallya's mercy,' moaned Claudia, staring with dull eyes. 'You've made it worse. We might have been dead already. Now we must wait for it.'

Gotrek snorted. 'You can all die down here if you like, but this will not be my doom. I'm getting out.'

'How?' asked Aethenir, in a voice tinged with hysteria.

'I'm still working that out,' said the Slayer, sitting down on a treasure chest and looking thoughtfully around the room.

Felix looked around with him. He had been too busy fighting or running until now to take in its details. Though the druchii had made a mess of it during their search for the harp, it was still a place filled with beauty. Below the witchlight chandeliers hanging above were neatly stacked treasure chests, ranks of statues carved from marble, alabaster and obsidian, jewelled suits of armour, beautiful swords, spears and axes, so delicate and exquisite that it seemed impossible that they could be used in battle, paintings, rugs, a throne of gold, complete with a deep blue canopy, and in one corner, a gilded war chariot – and all of it as bright and clean and unweathered as if the doors of the vault had closed yesterday and it had not spent the last four thousand years under the sea. Some elven magic, no doubt.

Aethenir threw up his hands. 'He's still working it out? You ordered us down here and you didn't have a plan?'

'Would you have rather stayed above?' snarled Gotrek.

'I would rather you had waited for us to form some strategy before charging impetuously into battle with the druchii, dwarf,' snapped Aethenir.

'High one, please,' said Felix, trying to be a voice of reason so that he wouldn't succumb to panic too. 'We cannot change the past. Do you have any spells that might help us? Can you make us able to breathe water? Can you create a bubble of air?'

Aethenir blinked. 'I... I can do none of those things. My few skills, as I said before, are in healing and divination.'

Felix turned to Max. 'Max?'

The wizard shook his head. 'Such spells exist, but they are not the purview of my college.'

Felix looked to Claudia. 'Fraulein Pallenberger? You can make the wind blow. Can you not make air?'

She shook her head dully. 'I require air to make a breeze. I cannot make it out of nothing.'

Felix sagged. No air. They were doomed. Even if they could get out of the sealed vault, their lungs would burst long before they reached the surface. Damn magic and damn all magicians too! All they seemed to be able to do was kill people and predict disaster. Never anything useful.

'Ha!' said Gotrek, standing.

Everyone, even the stoic Rion, turned to him with the eager light of hope in their eyes.

Gotrek strode past them towards the vault's treasures. 'Collect nine of the largest wooden treasure chests, the biggest rug, as much rope as you can find and the chains from those chandeliers.'

The others stared after him, dumbfounded.

'But, Slayer,' said Max, struggling for calm. 'What do you intend to do? How will this get us to the surface?'

'Just do it!' snapped Gotrek, upending a treasure chest the size of a courtesan's bathtub and spilling golden treasure in every direction. 'We don't have much time.'

BY THE TIME Felix, Rion and his elves had assembled the nine largest wooden treasure chests they could find, the water in the vault was up to their ankles. Gotrek collected the chandelier chains by the simple expedient of chopping through the winches mounted on the walls by which the chandeliers could be raised and lowered. They crashed to the ground in an explosion of delicate silver and crystal as the witchlights shattered. Aethenir wailed at this and the hundreds of priceless lost treasures uncaringly dumped on the floor, but the vandalism continued.

While Felix and Gotrek and the elves worked, Aethenir and Max called them over one at a time and used their healing arts on them. Felix bit a piece of leather against the pain while Max used a pair of tweezers to tug bits of cloth and broken links of chainmail from the wound Felix had received from the druchii swordsman, all the while murmuring spells of cleansing. Then Aethenir attended to him, and though by this time Felix was of the general opinion that the elf needed his neck wrung at the earliest opportunity, in this at least he was a useful addition to the party. Felix watched amazed as his long, slim fingers weaved over the wound and seemed to sew it up without touching it. The skin around the puncture glowed from within and the wound began to knit together at the ends, and then gradually close towards the centre, until finally there was nothing left but a pink scar and a deep ache.

'It is still weak,' said the high elf when he had finished. 'You must rest it for a few days.'

Felix looked around at where they were. 'I don't know if I'll have the opportunity, high one.'

Nonetheless he did his best not to tire it – leaving most of the heavy lifting to Gotrek and the elves, and instead pulling the gold tasselled ropes from the canopy of the throne and coiling them. The elves stripped the ropes and leather straps from the gilded war chariot. Claudia, recovering slowly from the druchii sorceresses' mind blasts, sat cross-legged on a chest and untied the cords that held ancient war banners to their poles. Max searched the vault and determined that the largest rug was rolled up in the back right corner, but by the time they found it, it was half-soaked in the rising water and it took Gotrek, Felix and Rion's elves to carry it out to the corner into the open. Felix's head spun with every step, his shoulder aching like a hammer blow.

When everything was brought together, Gotrek laid three of the gold tasselled ropes parallel on the ground near the door, each about a long pace apart – actually they floated in the water, but there was no dry space left to lay them now, so it had to do. Then he hacked the lids of the chests off with his axe and set the chests upside down on top of the ropes in three rows of three, wedged as close to each other and the door as possible. They bobbled and bumped a bit in the water, floating. Gotrek nailed the ends of the ropes to the sides of the chests with gold-headed nails pried from the golden throne.

'Now unroll the rug over the chests,' said Gotrek.

Felix, Rion and the elf warriors did as he asked, pushing and lifting the heavy rug until it covered the nine chests completely. Felix was still unsure what Gotrek was up to, but at least staying busy kept his mind off their impending drowning.

'Now the chains.' Gotrek picked up the end of one of the chains and started pulling it around the covered chests. Felix grabbed the other end and pulled the other way. They met on the far side of the chests with several feet of chain to spare. The elves did the same with the second chain.

'Tuck the carpet as close to the chests as you can while I pull,' said Gotrek, taking the two ends of one of the chains.

The rest of the party stepped to the chests, folding and pushing down on the carpet all around the edges of the chests as if trying to tuck in the sheets of a bed. All the while, Gotrek hauled on the ends of the chains, taking in the slack.

'I think I begin to see what you intend, Slayer,' said Max as they were at it. 'The wooden chests will float, and also hold air, and binding them together keeps *us* together, and makes it harder for any of the chests to flip over and spill its air.'

'Aye,' grunted Gotrek, heaving again. 'And the ropes underneath are to hold on to.'

'But I don't understand,' said Aethenir. 'Even if this bizarre contraption works, we will never get out of the vault. There are hundreds of thousands of pounds of water holding the doors shut!'

Gotrek snorted. 'And you call yourself a scholar. When the vault fills with water it will equalise the pressure.'

'When the vault fills with water we will drown!' cried Aethenir.

Gotrek didn't dignify this with a reply, though Felix wished he had, because he wanted to know the answer too.

When the carpet and the first chain were as tight to the sides of the chests as they could make them, Gotrek attached a jewelled, dwarf-made crossbow to one end of the chain and hooked the cleat into the other end, then used the ratchet to winch the chain even tighter. When it was so tight Felix feared that a link would break, Gotrek lashed the crossbow in place with a length of the leather chariot reins and did the whole thing again with the second chain and another crossbow. By the time he was finished, he was cranking the crossbow's handle under a foot of water, and the nine chests were floating like a raft.

Max looked at the raft uneasily. 'Slayer, I foresee a problem. When the water rises so will this. And the roof is far above the top of the vault doors. It will press against the ceiling. How will we get it out?'

Gotrek didn't answer, only stepped to the nearest full treasure chest, picked it up as if it weighed nothing, then carried it to a corner of the raft and set it down. The raft dipped down into the water at that end.

'Ah!' said Max. 'Excellent.'

'Space them evenly,' said Gotrek. 'The raft must be just heavier than the air and wood.'

'How do you think of these things, dwarf?' asked Aethenir, shaking his head as Rion and his elves lifted a single chest between them and staggered with it to the raft.

'Dwarfs are practical,' said Gotrek. 'They look at the ground. Not the sky.'

'Which is why they so rarely soar,' sneered the high elf.

'They don't drown much either,' said Gotrek dryly.

Felix scratched his head, still not quite understanding. 'I assume we'll float up on other chests as the water rises in here, but then how will we swim down to the raft? I'm not sure I can dive so deep, and I doubt Fraulein Pallenberger can.'

'I have never swum at all,' she said in a small voice.

Gotrek grinned and nodded towards the ranks of beautiful ceremonial armour along the left wall. 'We will carry armour for weight,' he said. 'Though you should put your own armour on top of the raft, or you won't be light enough to float when we rise.'

As Felix struggled out of his armour and threw it onto the raft with the treasure, he marvelled once again at the change that had come over the Slayer. Only two weeks ago he had been slumped in the Three Bells, unable to string more than three words together, and now he was solving problems of engineering and survival of which Felix would never have been able to conceive. It was an amazing transformation.

THE WAITING WAS the hardest part. With all the work done, there was nothing to do but watch the water rise. They sat inside empty treasure chests, rising slowly with the water, hour after hour, inch by incremental inch, with the elven armour that Gotrek had insisted they use for weight belted around themselves so that they could swiftly drop it when they needed to later.

'What do you know of this Harp of Ruin, Lord Aethenir?' asked Max as they rose. His voice echoed strangely in the enclosed space.

Aethenir looked guilty at the mention of the thing. 'Nothing more than Belryeth said,' he replied. 'I believe I might have read the name in some old texts, but I remember nothing else. There were many weapons created out of desperation during the first rise of Chaos that were later deemed too dangerous to use safely, and also too dangerous to destroy.' He looked around the flooded room. 'Thus they were locked away and often forgotten.' He sighed. 'One would have thought that this harp was doubly safe, hidden in this vault and buried as it was beneath the sea.'

'Yes,' said Rion bitterly. 'One would have thought.'

Aethenir hung his head in shame.

After that, conversation faltered and they all just stared at the walls, glum and silent. With the water of the deep sea all around them, the vault, which had been chilly to begin with, now grew painfully cold, and they all shivered and hugged their knees. Only Gotrek, shirtless though he was, bore it without any sign of discomfort.

When it got too much to bear, Max cast a further spell of light which gave off a mild pleasant warmth as well. It wasn't nearly enough.

Eventually the water rose above the doors, and its climb slowed even further. Still Gotrek told them they must wait, saying that the pressure must be completely equal or the doors wouldn't budge. Now that the air wasn't escaping through the crack that the water was coming in through, the air started to become compressed, and Felix could feel it pushing on his eardrums and his chest. A while later it seemed to be pressing against his eyes. His head ached terribly, and the others were similarly affected. Aethenir got a spontaneous nosebleed that he had difficulty stopping.

Finally, after an hour where Felix's pulse pounded in his temples like an orc war drum and they had to hunch down in their floating chests to avoid knocking their heads against the carved and gilded beams of the vault's ceiling, Gotrek nodded.

'Right,' he said. 'Into the water. When you're on the floor, lift the raft over your heads and set it down over your shoulders. Walk forwards and push the chests against the door. When we're free of the palace, drop the armour. I'll shift some of the treasure off the top too so we'll rise.' He looked around at them all. 'Ready?'

Everyone nodded, though they didn't look particularly ready.

'Go,' said Gotrek, and, taking a deep breath, he leaned to the side, tipped out of his chest and sank like a stone.

Rion and his warriors followed his example instantly, but Felix, Claudia, Max and Aethenir all hesitated a moment, looking around at each other with unhappy eyes, then they too took deep breaths, capsized their chests and plunged into the icy water.

The cold shock of it was like a blow to the head, and Felix fought a desperate urge to flail back to the surface. He opened his eyes. Max's magical ball of light shone just as well under the water as above it, and suffused the sunken vault with an eerie greenish light, suspended silt sparkling like diamond dust in the murky water. Gotrek was already on the floor, the elves landing with dreamlike slowness all around him. Felix saw Max, Claudia and Aethenir sinking as well, their robes billowing around them like living flowers, then they too were on the floor and stepping with strange, bouncing strides to the treasure-laden raft, which hovered at about knee height.

Felix touched down a second later, his slow impact raising a puff of silt. His lungs were now crying for air, and the pressure on his chest was like a crushing fist. He bounced to the front of the raft and grabbed for an edge. Gotrek's hand stopped him and he looked up.

The Slayer held up a hand and looked around at everyone, then, when he had their attention, motioned for them to lift all at once. The raft, which not even Gotrek would have been able to lift by himself on dry land, came up with ease and they raised it above their heads, then shuffled around until they were all under one of the upside-down chests – Felix, Gotrek and Rion in the first rank, Aethenir and the two remaining elf warriors in the middle rank, and Max and Claudia in the corner chests of the last rank.

Felix's blood was beating in his throat now, and black spots danced in front of his eyes, so it was a great relief when they pulled on the underslung ropes and lowered the strange contraption down over themselves. Felix gasped in great gulps of air as his head broke the surface, then he tried to slow his breathing as he realised how little air was within the inverted chest. Though it might save his life, the little cubicle was terrifyingly small, and he felt more closed in here than he had pressing against the roof of the vault. He hoped that none of the others suffered from a fear of small spaces.

There was a loud rap from Gotrek's side of the chest and Felix started walking forwards. He looked down through the water and saw that Rion was doing the same, but Gotrek's short legs were pedalling uselessly above the floor. He heard a muffled dwarf curse through the wood.

Another step and the raft boomed hollowly against the vault's left-hand door. Felix placed his hands on the front wall of his chest and pushed with all his might. His feet scraped and slipped, struggling to gain purchase against the slick marble floor. Through the water he could see Rion doing the same, and the chests creaked as the others behind him applied pressure too.

The doors didn't move. Felix strained harder. Still nothing. Panic began to rise in his chest. He heard another curse from his right, then a small splash. He looked down into the water again and saw Gotrek, out of his chest, pushing at the door with both hands. Still nothing happened, and Felix's panic grew worse. Had the doors locked when they closed? Was the pressure still too unequal? Were the doors just too heavy to move without magic?

Then, with agonising slowness, Felix saw the bottom edge of the door inch forwards. He let out a breath he hadn't known he had been holding, loud in the confines of the chest, and pressed all the harder. Slowly, but then more swiftly, the door began to swing open. Gotrek gave a final push, then leapt back up to his chest, and Felix heard hoarse breathing coming through the wood.

The door opened all the way with a shuddering thud that reverberated through the water and they were free. The raft shot ahead, the momentum almost dragging them across the antechamber towards the archway. They slowed by the time they reached the stairs, and began to ascend. After the first few steps, Felix noticed that the front of the raft started to angle up – only natural as they were on stairs – but alarming, as he heard the heaps of treasure above him shift, and a stream of bubbles escaped under the leading edge of his chest.

He heard another curse from Gotrek's chest, then an angry slap.

'Crouch down, manling!' came Gotrek's blunted voice. 'Crawl! Tell the elf!'

Felix rapped at the left side of the chest. 'Crouch down!' he shouted. 'Crawl!' Then he started pulling down on the rope that underslung the chest. To his relief, the elf did the same, and the raft's angle slowly evened out again. Felix, Gotrek and the elf began crawling up the stairs like turtles sharing the same shell.

At the first landing, Felix cautiously rose again. Fortunately, both the stairs and the landings were built on a grand scale, and they had no trouble manoeuvring around to start crawling up the next flight.

By the time they reached the entry chamber, the air inside the chest was rank and humid and thin. Felix tried to stop his heart from pumping in panic. It would be the cruellest of jokes if, after all of Gotrek's genius invention, they died of asphyxiation just short of the surface.

They pushed quickly across the entry hall. Felix had a momentary flash of panic as he remembered that Max had closed the palace doors, and he ducked down into the water to look ahead. He needn't have worried. The doors lay, splintered and bent on the marble floor, ripped off their hinges by the wall of water that had rocked the palace. Felix and the others walked over their twisted remains, then out onto the wide front steps, where Gotrek banged on the chests for them to stop.

'Drop the armour!' he called. 'Pass it on!'

Felix rapped on the high elf's side of his chest. 'Drop the armour! Pass it on!' He reached down into the water and undid the belt that held the elaborate elven ceremonial armour around his waist. It dropped away and he felt his toes rise off the steps.

Beside him, the Slayer's thick legs disappeared again and he heard heavy thuds and clunks above him. He looked up, then down as something bumped his boot. One of the treasure chests was settling down sideways on the steps, spilling bubbles and golden treasures.

A thud to the rear of the raft told him that Gotrek was being careful to dump their ballast in a way that wouldn't raise one side of the raft before the others.

And the raft was indeed rising. Felix was busy thinking how much treasure was being lost forever, and didn't notice at first, but then he was up to his chin in the water instead of his chest. He caught at the underslung rope and pulled himself up into the chest again as his feet floated off the steps. After another second he heard a splash and a gasp and a smug chuckle from Gotrek's chest. The Slayer had reason to be proud. Everything he had planned seemed to be working.

Felix tried to look down at the city as they rose, but couldn't see any distance through the ripples on the surface of the water in the chest, so he took a breath and ducked his head under again.

The sight below him was an eerie wonderland. What had looked like a sad, crumbling relic of lost glory when exposed to the air and the harsh light of day was, by the light of Max's glowing globe, a beautiful blue dream of ruined towers and swaying seaweed taller than cedars. The coral and the strange undersea plants which had looked so dull and dry out of the water were now bright and lurid. Things like jewels glowed in the shadows with their own luminescence. It was a city where mermaids should live.

He pulled himself back into the air of the chest, gasping as his lungs burned, and found that the air within was hardly enough to give him relief. The spots in front of his eyes remained, and the blood pounded against the roof of his mouth, demanding to be fed.

He clung to the rope, trying to breathe as shallowly as possible and praying for the raft to rise faster. How deep was the city below the waves? A hundred feet? A hundred yards? A hundred fathoms? He had no idea. Deep enough that no sailor had ever seen or suspected the elven towers below.

The black spots began to crowd his eyes. His fingers tingled with pins and needles. He couldn't feel the rope and had to look to be sure he was holding it. Then his heart leapt with hope. The sea around them was becoming brighter and Max's light paler. They must be nearing the surface. He could hold on a little longer knowing that.

Then something heavy pushed past his legs. At first he thought it was Gotrek, heading for the back of the raft for some reason, but when he looked down he saw a thick grey trunk and a sharp tail. His air-starved mind took a second to put those things together, and then he gasped.

A shark!

Just as the realisation came to him, he heard a muffled scream from behind. He dropped his head down into the water and looked back. Beyond the kicking, dangling limbs of his companions, a shark the size of the *Pride of Skintstaad's* long boat had an elf warrior in its jaws and was shaking him back and forth violently. The elf's limbs flopped like a doll's as plumes of red billowed from his body.

Felix fumbled for his sword, holding on to the rope with one hand. He looked towards Gotrek. The Slayer was in the water too, readying his axe and kicking towards the shark as Rion and the other warrior drew their swords and guarded Aethenir. Max and Claudia looked like they were trying to crawl up into their chests. Then Felix saw something beyond and below them that stopped his heart. Rising up from the murky, tower-pierced depths were more moving shadows – a whole school of sharks. Manann preserve us, he thought, we're all dead.

Gotrek caught the shark by the tail and swung his axe, burying it in the creature's slate-coloured side. Blood blossomed into the water and the shark flinched and spun, dropping its mangled prey to face this new threat. It lunged at Gotrek with a mouth the size of a rain barrel. Gotrek kicked up, trying to get out of the way, and the thing butted him in the stomach with its snout, smashing him back twenty feet. Felix slashed at it uselessly as it rushed past, and saw, to his horror, that a smaller snout was growing from the side of the shark's head, complete with eyes and mouth, and its needle teeth were clamped down on the golden bracelets on the Slayer's left wrist. Was not even the sea free from the taint of Chaos?

Through a storm of black spots, Felix watched as the Slayer rained blow after blow on the head of the massive grey monster. The other sharks were close enough now that Felix could see their beady eyes gleaming through the murk. Rion and his last elf stayed close to Aethenir and turned towards the monsters as their dead comrade spun lazily down and away, red blood and white and green surcoat trailing gracefully behind him. Some of the sharks turned towards him, but most came on.

Suddenly Felix felt the rope go slack in his hand. He looked up, frightened. The raft had stopped rising. Had they hit some obstruction? Was something holding it down? Then he saw the dapple and shine of sunlight on water. They were at the surface!

Every fibre of his body screamed for him to climb to the air, but he couldn't leave the others to the mercy of the sharks. He looked back and saw Rion and his last elf pushing Aethenir to the edge of the raft. Max was doing the same for Claudia. Felix clambered hand under hand to them and caught the seeress's other arm. He and Max reached the side and lifted her up so that her head broke the surface. Felix's face hit the air a second later. He took one gasping, glorious breath, saw that Claudia was doing the same, then ducked back down and grabbed her left leg as Max grabbed her right. Together they raised her up until her torso flopped on top of the raft.

Felix looked back towards Gotrek. The Slayer had hit some vital spot on the shark and it was flipping and flailing down through the water, a curling column of blood erupting from its side, while Gotrek frog-kicked back towards the surface, his left arm also spewing blood.

Half the oncoming sharks turned towards their wounded cousin but the rest still came on. Felix looked around. All he could see were the flailing legs of the others clambering onto the raft. He joined them, kicking up out of the water and gripping the soggy carpet with desperate fingers. He could feel the wound Aethenir had just healed ripping internally as he humped himself up. Max was crawling out beside him, hampered by his water-logged robes. Rion and the other elf were rolling Aethenir up onto the chests by brute force. Felix flopped himself out at last and immediately turned back to the water. Gotrek's head broke the surface and he sucked air as he kicked forwards, chopping his axe into top of the raft to try to pull himself up. Felix saw deep gashes in the Slayer's left wrist as he rushed to help. Half the gold bracelets upon it had been crushed so badly by the shark's bite that they pressed deep into his flesh. Felix grabbed Gotrek by the shoulder, and hauled at him. The Slayer surged up and crashed to the carpet, breathing deeply.

'Friends, help me!' called Aethenir.

Felix and Max crawled to where the high elf and the last elf warrior were trying to pull Rion out of the water. Felix caught him under the left arm, while Max grabbed his right.

But suddenly the elf captain jerked down in the water, nearly torn from their hands. He gasped, his eyes bulging.

'Rion!' cried Aethenir.

Gotrek joined them and all pulled desperately at Rion as something below tried to drag him down in the water. Then, with a horrible scream, the elf captain came up all at once and they fell back in a heap.

'Rion!' cried Aethenir again, scrambling up. 'Are you…?' His words ended in a cry of horror and he collapsed again.

Felix sat up to see what had happened. Rion's right leg was covered in blood. His left leg was… gone. The ragged stump pumped gore all over the wet carpet in thick gouts. Max and Gotrek cursed. Claudia looked away.

Aethenir crawled to Rion and cradled his head. 'Rion, I… I am sorry. I never…'

The dying captain reached up and clutched at Aethenir's sleeve. He looked hard into his eyes. 'Follow… the path of honour.'

'I will,' wept Aethenir. 'I promise you. By Asuryan and Aenarion, I promise.'

Rion nodded, apparently satisfied, then closed his eyes and sank back, dead. Aethenir sobbed. His last elf hung his head. Felix found a lump blocking his throat, and fought down the unworthy thought that he would rather that it had been Aethenir who had died and Rion who had lived, for the captain had been the epitome of elven virtue that Aethenir should have been.

The last elf warrior began to pull Rion's body to the centre of the carpet, but before he could take a step, a huge grey snout full of picket-fence teeth surged up out of the water and smashed the little raft, raising it out of the water and sending everyone flying. Felix crashed down on his wounded shoulder and nearly rolled off. Only Max's sprawled body stopped him. The wizard tottered at the edge. Felix grabbed him and pulled him back. Nearby, Gotrek and the elf warrior were doing the same for Claudia and Aethenir.

'Thank you, Felix,' Max gasped.

The survivors crawled to the centre of the pitifully small raft, while all around cruel triangular fins circled them and hidden predators bumped them from beneath.

Gotrek surged up, shaking his axe and beckoning towards the water. 'Come on, you skulking cowards!' he roared. 'I'll kill the lot of you!'

But then Claudia saw something that the others had been too preoccupied to notice.

'A… a ship,' she breathed.

Everyone looked up. Felix's heart pounded with fear that it was the dark elves' black galley swooping in to ram them again, but it was a different ship altogether – a fat merchant ship flying the flag of Marienburg, not half a mile away from them, its white sails a reddish gold in the late afternoon sun.

Felix jumped up, waving his arms. 'Ahoy!' he cried. 'Ahoy! Save us!'

Another bump from the sharks knocked him flat again, but the ship was turning their way.

'Praise be to Manann and Shallya,' whispered Claudia with tears in her eyes.

But suddenly Felix wasn't so sure the ship was salvation. The covers were being raised from the forward gun ports and the black muzzles of cannons were pushing into the sun.

'Oh come,' wailed Aethenir. 'This beggars belief! Does everyone in the world seek to kill us?'

'Bring 'em on,' said Gotrek.

Twin puffs of smoke obscured the prow of the ship. Everyone but Gotrek ducked. A second later, the boom of the guns reached them and two huge plumes of water shot up about a dozen yards away.

Felix let out a sigh of relief. 'They missed.'

'No,' said Max, looking around. 'I believe they hit what they intended.'

Felix followed the wizard's gaze. The shark fins were gone from the water, vanished as if they had never been.

'You think they mean to save us?' asked Aethenir.

'I hope so,' said Max.

And so it seemed, for no more shots came from the approaching ship, and it banked its sails and eased in gently to their side. Ropes dropped down to them. Felix and Gotrek and the elves grabbed them and pulled themselves tight to the ship's towering hull.

Felix called up to the deck above. 'Have you a ladder? We have women and wounded.'

A short round man leaned on the rail and smiled down at them as several dozen large and unsmiling men appeared at either side of him and aimed a profusion of pistols and long guns in their direction.

'Good evening, Herr Jaeger,' said Hans Euler. 'What a pleasure to once again make your acquaintance.'

ELEVEN

'So it's guns now, is it?' Gotrek growled at Euler. 'Couches weren't cowardly enough?'

Felix stepped quickly in front of the Slayer. 'Herr Euler. How unexpected.' He recognised some of the gun-wielding crewmen as Euler's massive footmen, who had since traded their black velvet doublets for leather jerkins and red bandanas.

'Yes, I suppose you would think so,' said Euler, pleasantly. 'But some friends of mine in the Suiddock overheard the sailors of your hired ship say you were going north seeking treasure, and I decided to come along and learn if this was true.'

'It isn't treasure we seek,' said Aethenir. 'It is–'

Max trod heavily on his foot.

'It had better be treasure, high one,' said Euler. 'Herr Jaeger owes me considerable recompense for the damage he and his uncouth friend did to my house. I intend to collect from him one way or the other.'

'Come down here,' said Gotrek, 'and you'll get more of the same.'

'Is it wise to threaten me, dwarf?' said Euler, raising an eyebrow. 'I can easily leave you here. There is blood in the water now. The sharks will soon return.'

'Herr Euler,' said Felix. 'There is indeed treasure. Look.' Felix turned and searched the rug they stood on. As he had hoped, a few spilled treasures remained. He picked up a gold and silver ewer of elven design that lay next to Rion's corpse, then turned and tossed it up to Hans. The merchant caught it and examined it with the practiced eye of the connoisseur. 'We had a holdful of it, but it was stolen from us.'

'Stolen by whom?' asked Euler. 'Where have they taken it?'

Aethenir opened his mouth to speak, but Max once again crushed his foot. The high elf glared at him.

'That,' said Felix carefully, 'I will not tell you until you allow us to come aboard. But they are not far away.'

Euler paused, greed warring with caution behind his eyes. He ran his hands over the fine filigree of the elven ewer and sighed. 'Very well, Herr Jaeger, but I must first receive vows from every member of your party that you will not harm me, my property or my crew, if you come aboard – particularly the dwarf,' he added, glaring at Gotrek.

Max, Claudia and the elves swore quickly enough, but Gotrek growled under his breath. Felix knew it was no small thing for a dwarf to make an oath.

'Make oath with a liar and a blackmailer?' he said. 'I won't.'

'Gotrek,' said Felix. 'We can't stay on this raft. We must follow your prophesied doom, remember?'

Gotrek grunted, annoyed. 'Very well, manling.' He turned and looked up at Euler. 'I will swear to do no harm to you, your property and your crew, unless harm is done to us first.'

'I swear to that as well,' said Felix.

Euler glared down at them, but finally sighed and waved a hand. 'Fine. I agree to those terms.' He motioned to his men. 'Throw down a ladder.'

A few minutes later they were all aboard, standing on the deck and shivering in the cold breeze. Claudia leaned against Max, her lips blue and her limbs shaking, but Euler had yet to offer them any food or shelter or dry clothes.

He stood in front of them with his arms crossed above his round belly. 'Now then,' he said. 'Who stole this treasure and where did they go?'

Felix looked at Max and Aethenir. They nodded.

'It was dark elves. They sank our ship and headed...' Actually he couldn't be sure where they had headed, but Euler had come from the south and would have seen them if they had gone that way, so north was a safe bet. 'They headed north. Our seeress can divine their location if,' he said pointedly, 'she doesn't die from exposure first.'

'Dark elves?' said Hans, hesitant.

His men looked uneasily at each other.

'Not a war ship,' said Felix hastily. 'A scout, smaller than your own ship.' He coughed, then lied through his teeth. 'They carry enough elven gold to repay you for your house and buy another just like it, as well as provide handsome shares for us and your men.'

Euler fingered his chin, thinking. 'One ship?' he asked.

'One ship,' agreed Felix.

'Any wizards?'

'Not a one,' said Felix. It wasn't technically a lie. Sorceresses were different than wizards, weren't they?

After another second, Euler nodded. 'Very well, Herr Jaeger, but if you have deceived me in this, I will find some other way to make you pay.' He turned to his men. 'Find quarters and food for them.' He turned away, then glared back at Felix. 'Bring me the word of the seeress as soon as she learns their location.'

Felix bowed. 'Of course, Herr Euler.'

WHEN EVENING MESS was served, Gotrek, Felix and Claudia brought their plates to Max and Aethenir's lantern-lit cabin to discuss their plans. Only the elves and the wizards had been given private quarters, probably more out of fear than hospitality. Gotrek and Felix had had to find places on deck to sleep, for none of Euler's surly crew would give up an inch of hammock space below.

Now they were all wedged into a cramped little cabin with two narrow cots along the side walls. Felix sat on an overturned bucket by the bulkhead. Gotrek stood near the door, legs braced wide.

'I don't believe,' said Max, between mouthfuls of beef stew and peas, 'that Herr Euler will be very pleased when he learns we have deceived him.'

Felix ate greedily as well. Whatever his shortcomings as a human being, Euler did not skimp when feeding his crew. The food was easily among the best Felix had ever had on board a ship.

'Who cares?' grunted Gotrek.

'*I* do, dwarf,' said Aethenir with a sniff. 'If this man is our only way home once we have wrested the harp from the druchii, then we cannot afford to anger him.'

Gotrek sneered as he shovelled a hunk of beef into his mouth. 'After what you did, you should be ashamed to go home. A dwarf would have shaved his head and sworn to die.'

'I am prepared to die,' replied Aethenir, raising his head and trying his best to look noble. 'But I am also prepared to live, and continue to make recompense for my crime.'

'Such a shame demands death,' said Gotrek.

Aethenir shook his head pityingly. 'That is why the dwarfs have fallen. Their greatest warriors are always shaving their heads and killing themselves.'

Gotrek lowered his wooden spoon, glaring dangerously at the high elf.

Max coughed. 'Friends, please, if we could return to the matter of Captain Euler. Some of us have no great shame to be expunged and would like to return from this journey alive. Have you any suggestions?'

For a moment there was nothing but the sound of chewing.

'We can't fight his crew without casualties,' said Max at last. 'And we can afford no more casualties.'

'Could we take the druchii ship?' asked Felix.

Max shook his head. 'There are too few of us to crew it.'

Claudia looked up from the bowl of stew that she cupped in both hands. Her eyes were still dull, but the colour had returned to her cheeks. 'Could… could we make sure the druchii ship sank?' she asked. 'So that Captain Euler would think the treasure sank with the ship, and would not know we lied?'

Felix nodded, approving. The girl was quick – mad, of course – but quick. 'It would be surer than facing them hand to hand.'

Aethenir, however, was frowning. 'Sink the ship? And lose the harp?'

'Isn't that the general idea?' growled Gotrek.

'Are you mad, dwarf?' cried Aethenir. 'A treasure like that cannot be lost again. There would be much we could learn from it.'

'Being a student of history, scholar,' said Max to the high elf, 'you must certainly know that treasures like that have a way of being used for terrible things, no matter the intentions of those who preserve them. Perhaps it would be best to let it sink.'

'But what guarantee is that?' the high elf asked. 'The druchii raised it from the sea once. What is to stop them from doing it again?'

'You won't tell them where it is next time,' said Gotrek dryly.

'Will you leave off, dwarf!' snapped Aethenir. 'I am doing what I can to amend the fault.'

'How would we do it, though?' asked Max, forestalling Gotrek's reply. 'Euler would be suspicious if he saw any of us deliberately trying to sink it.'

'Some spell, perhaps?' asked Felix.

Max's brow wrinkled as he thought. Claudia pursed her lips, but in the end they shook their heads and the others returned to thinking.

'Well,' said Max when no one came forwards with a suggestion. 'We will think more upon it. Go and sleep. Perhaps the answer will come to us in the morning.'

As HE WAS following Gotrek up the stairs to the deck, Felix felt a hand on his arm and turned. It was Claudia. She looked up at him, biting her lip.

'I seem always to be apologising to you, Herr Jaeger,' she said finally.

'Er, there's no need,' said Felix, edging back.

'But there is,' she insisted. 'I was vile to you this morning, and I feel terrible about it. I snapped at you when you were only asking about my welfare.'

'Oh, it was nothing,' said Felix, taking another backwards step up the stairs.

'But it was. I could see how I had hurt you. And yet…' Her voice caught in her throat. 'And yet, when the waters came crashing in, you picked me up and carried me to safety, though you were grievously wounded. Such selflessness, such charity in the face of my rude behaviour…'

'Well, I couldn't let you drown, could I…?' Felix tripped as the next step caught his heel. He stopped himself as Claudia reached to catch him. They ended up very close.

She looked up at him with her wide blue eyes, smiling shyly. 'I have caused you considerable anger, pain and embarrassment, Herr Jaeger, but I believe you were beginning to warm to me before all this. Captain Euler has given me a private cabin. If you would like a more comfortable berth than the deck…'

'Ah, I wouldn't actually,' said Felix, sweat breaking out on his brow as he backed up onto the first step. 'Thank you all the same. As delightful as I find your company, I don't think that either of our reputations would survive a repeat of last night's events. Now, if you will excuse me…'

'It doesn't happen every night,' said Claudia, pouting.

'Yes, but if it did,' said Felix, still backing up. 'All in all, I think the risk is too great.'

Claudia's eyes began to burn into him with an unsettling keenness.

'Not that I don't appreciate the honour,' he continued. 'But, er, it's for the best, I think, don't you? Good night.'

And with that he fled to the main deck, feeling her angry gaze upon his back all the way.

* * *

GOTREK AND FELIX bedded down on the foredeck, laying out their bedrolls on either side of the cages that held the ship's goat and chickens. The barnyard stench was enough to make Felix's eyes water, but they were out of the way of the crew and, more importantly, for Felix anyway, out of Claudia's reach.

Felix stretched his cloak across the rail and the cages to make a little tent over his bedroll before he lay down, for the night was cloudy and cold and there was a chilling drizzle wetting the deck. The goat stared reproachfully out of its cage at Felix for a while, but then lost interest and curled up in its nest of hay.

Felix found it difficult to sleep. The day had been so full of terror and danger that he hadn't had a moment to think, but as he lay there, all the thoughts that fighting for his life had pushed from his mind now flooded back and preyed upon him. Was his father unharmed? Did he still live? What had the skaven done to him? He wanted desperately to get back and learn the answers to these questions, and yet, in the heat of the moment, he had convinced Euler to go the other way, chasing after the dark elf ship. Knowing the scope of what the sorceresses intended to do, he knew it was the right thing to do. The needs of the many outweighed his need to discover his father's fate, but it was still agony to be sailing in the opposite direction from Altdorf.

Part of his concern for his father was undoubtedly guilt. He had wished the old man dead on many occasions, and now that it was possible that he actually might be, Felix felt responsible, as if one of his petty wishes had come true. But it wasn't just that. He truly *was* responsible, for the skaven had undoubtedly visited his father while hunting for him and Gotrek. Gustav Jaeger – if he was indeed dead or hurt – was just another victim of the plague of vermin that had been trailing Felix since Alt-dorf – which was only a lesser strain of the epidemic of mayhem and bloodshed which followed Gotrek and Felix wherever they went. Truly, he thought, it was prob-ably best for the Empire that we stayed away for twenty years. The land would likely have half its current popu-lation had we remained.

At last exhaustion won out over worry and guilt, and dragged him down into a dark and anxiety-haunted sleep.

HE WOKE AGAIN, as he had the morning before, to nearby rustling in the dark, and at first his foggy mind thought that it must be Claudia again.

'Really, Fraulein Pallenberger,' he mumbled. 'Your tenacity is alarming.'

The rustling stopped and he heard a grunt that sounded very little like Claudia. He froze and opened his eyes. It was still night, and very dark, but a faint yellow flicker reached him from the lanterns hung on the main deck, giving him just enough light to see by.

The first thing that he saw was the goat, almost eye to eye with him, and staring at him again. Felix let out a relieved breath. It had only been the goat. Then he paused. The goat had not blinked. And it was lying on its side. And it had a rusted metal star sticking out of its throat. And blood was soaking the straw beneath it. From somewhere nearby came another muffled grunt and then thrashing and thumping sounds.

'Gotrek?'

Through the goat cage he could see flashes of violent movement on the far side. He heard hoarse cries of sur-prise from the main deck and looked that way. A crewman was slumped across the taffrail, three metal stars sticking from his back.

'Gotrek!'

Then he heard the rustling again, directly behind him. He twisted around. A black shape with glittering black eyes crouched by the rail, clutching something in its bony little hands. The hands darted forwards and the something was jerked down over Felix's head.

Felix gasped and inhaled a horrible smell – the smell from the glass globes the skaven had used. Immediately his head started to swim and his limbs began going numb. A horrible seasick nausea made his stomach roil. He cried out and swung his scabbarded sword. There was an impact and he heard a squeak and a thud. He snatched the bag off his head and staggered up, falling against the goat cage. His hands and face were sticky with the foul, narcotic paste.

The skaven assassin was up as well, and reaching towards him with hooked metal claws curling out over its true claws.

Felix threw an unsteady foot out and booted the creature in its narrow chest. It squealed and toppled backwards over the side of the ship. But three more skaven took its place, carrying ropes with what looked like fish hooks on the ends. The vermin seemed to distort and stretch as they approached. In fact, the whole ship was twisting and melting around him like it was made of hot wax.

Felix stumbled back, his gorge rising, as the world swam around him. On the far side of the goat cage, Gotrek was on his feet, legs braced wide, slashing around with his gore-smeared axe and struggling to pull a bag from his head while scrawny black shadows capered around him, swinging the barbed ropes at him. Unfortunately for the Slayer, one of the ropes was wound around his neck, pulling the bag tight. Incoherent roaring came from within. Three black forms lay dead at his feet, their guts spilling across the deck.

Sharp pains stabbed Felix's arms and legs, bringing him back to his own predicament. Fish hooks pierced his clothes. Another bit into his bare wrist as he tried to lift his sword to cut them away. The dancing black shapes wobbled and oozed like they were behind warped glass as they wrapped him up in a cocoon of ropes.

Felix surged towards them with the slowness of a dream, the acrid smell of the drug paste filling his nose. Pain erupted all over his body as the hooks dug deep into his flesh, but it felt like it was happening to someone else. The shadows squirmed out of the way, wrapping him tighter and dragging him towards the rail. He struggled feebly, fading in and out of conciousness, and seeing the chaos around him in a series of long blinks, surrounded by moments of blackness.

In one blink, he saw Euler's crew running in panic from skittering black shapes as big as dogs. In another blink, he saw spindly shadows carrying something wrapped in a bed sheet as the last elf warrior fought towards them through a crowd of spear-wielding ratkin. In a third blink he saw Gotrek drop to one knee, using his axe to hold himself up, the leather bag still tight around his head. In a fourth blink, he saw Claudia running out onto the decks in a nightdress, anguish in her eyes as Max tried to hold her back.

'I saw it!' she wailed, fighting to get free of him. 'I saw it! Oh, gods, forgive me!'

In the next blink the night clouds were above Felix, and he felt his feet go out from under him. The disorientation made him vomit all down the front of his chest. Hard little hands were lifting him over the rail, and he saw more rising to take him as he was lowered, upside down, towards the waves.

The last thing he saw before unconsciousness swallowed him was a glinting green shape humping up out of the water like the back of a verdigrised brass whale. The beast had a huge black blowhole in the centre of its back, and skaven were crawling in and out of it like ants.

FELIX PUKED HIMSELF awake, the rising of his gorge so painful in his raw throat that it tore him from the leaden grip of unnatural sleep. It was the worst waking of his life.

The first thing he was aware of, beyond the dripping of sputum down his chin, was the throbbing in his head. It felt like someone was slowly and methodically cutting into the back of his skull with a carpenter's saw. His vision pulsed in time with the throbbing, going from dim to painfully bright with each thud of his heart. His mouth tasted like an orc's armpit, and his body ached from head to foot – most particularly his arms, which seemed to be drawn back so far behind his back that he could barely breathe. His ankles throbbed too, and he couldn't feel his feet at all. The pain of it all made him wish he had stayed unconscious.

When his vision cleared somewhat, he saw a puddle of filthy water below him, floating with what looked like a film of fur. The view did not improve when he raised his head. He was in some sort of low-roofed metal room, the walls and ceiling crawling with grimy pipes and strange brass reservoirs that sprouted taps and spigots from every surface. Every bit of it looked like it had been salvaged from a dwarf engineer's rubbish tip. Rats fought over something in one corner.

The room was nearly as hot as the pouring room at the Imperial Gunnery School at Nuln, but as humid as a jungle of the Southlands. Water sweated from the pipes and dripped from the ceiling, and from all around came a howling, booming roar that made the room – and Felix's head – vibrate horribly.

Then Felix heard a familiar grunt to his left. He turned his head and nearly vomited again, for the movement had triggered what felt like an avalanche of boulders inside his skull. When he could breathe and think again, he blinked away the tears and looked left.

Gotrek was beside him, his huge arms bound tightly behind him around a heavy, corroded brass pipe. His ankles had been bound as well, in such a way that his feet did not touch the ground. There were deep cuts and gouges all over the Slayer's body, and his beard was clotted with blood and filth. His head hung low, but Felix could see that he was conscious, and looking around the room with his single eye.

A third figure hung limply from another pipe beyond Gotrek – Aethenir. He was less battered and bloody than Gotrek, but just as covered in filth, and with a purple bruise on his left cheek that bled at its centre.

None of them had their weapons.

'So, you live, manling?' said Gotrek.

'Aye,' said Felix.

Gotrek looked up at him. Trails of bright green mucus ran from his nose and the corners of his mouth. 'I'm sorry to hear it.'

Flashes of the fight on Euler's ship returned to Felix's mind as he tried to work out why Gotrek would say such a thing – rat faces and ropes, Max and Claudia shouting, the elf warrior fighting shadows, claws pulling Felix over the side.

'The others,' he said. 'What happened to them? Do they live?'

Gotrek shrugged. 'Alive or dead, they're better off than we are.'

'Eh? Why?'

'Because this will be worse than death.'

Aethenir jerked awake with a cry of fear, then lifted his head and blinked around. 'Mercy of Isha,' he moaned as he took in their surroundings. 'What hell is this?'

'It's a skaven submersible,' said Gotrek.

'A... a what?' asked Aethenir.

'A ship that travels underwater.' Gotrek snorted contemptuously. 'Damned vermin stole the idea from the dwarfs, and got it wrong, naturally – powered by warpstone instead of black water. I'm surprised it hasn't exploded.'

'Skaven again?' said Aethenir. 'But what do they want?'

Before Gotrek or Felix could answer, splashing footsteps made them all look up. Through a circular opening on the far side of the metal chamber came a figure out of a nightmare. It was a skaven – the oldest Felix had ever seen – and decrepit beyond imagining. Felix had seen undead who looked healthier. It was skeletally gaunt, with gnarled hands and matchstick arms sticking from the sleeves of its dirty grey robes. Its paper-thin flesh was stretched skeletally across its angular, spade-shaped skull, and its snout seemed to have rotted away, the area around its nostrils nothing more than a gaping hole of black, corrupted meat. Horrible cysts and warts grew from shrivelled, scabrous skin gone mostly bald with mange. Only a few clumps of wispy white fur clung to its head and arms.

It limped towards them with the aid of a tall metal staff topped with a glittering green stone. A retinue of other skaven followed it. Four big black brutes in polished brass armour, a crouching, scurrying ratman clad head to toe in black, a round, pop-eyed skaven that tottered unsteadily after the rest and seemed to have no tail, and behind them all, ducking to pass through the room's low round opening, a huge albino monster of the kind that Felix and Gotrek had fought when the skaven had attacked them on the beach. It went and sat in a corner, scratching itself. Aethenir moaned when he saw the thing.

The ancient skaven glanced at the high elf and paused. It muttered a question to the skaven in black. The assassin bowed obsequiously and replied in kind, motioning from Felix and Aethenir and back with nervous paws and pointing to their hair.

The old skaven raised its head and hissed a laugh, then snapped its gaze back to Gotrek and Felix. Its laughter ceased as if it had never been. It limped forwards and looked them up and down with glittering black eyes that contained all the life the rest of its body seemed to have been drained of.

'So long,' it crooned in a voice like a broken flute, as it smiled at them both with cracked yellow fangs turned brown with decay. 'So long I have waited for this day.'

TWELVE

GOTREK LUNGED FORWARDS, snarling savagely, the violence of his motion making the pipe creak at its joins.

Felix strained forwards too, shouting as fury boiled within him. 'What have you done to my father, you filth?'

The ancient skaven leapt back from them, squeaking with alarm, and the rat ogre stood, rumbling dangerously and looking around. The seer turned to its minions and screeched in its own language, pointing a trembling claw at Gotrek.

'Answer me!' shouted Felix. 'What did you do to my father?'

One of the armoured guards backhanded Felix across the cheek with a mailed gauntlet as the black-clad assassin hurried towards Gotrek, taking a coil of thin, grey rope from its belt. The blow snapped Felix's head around and made his head ring with agony. He could feel blood trickling down past his ear. He decided he would wait to ask any more questions about his father until he had the ancient skaven at sword's point.

'Loose me, you skull-faced bag of sticks!' Gotrek grated.

He snapped at the assassin with his teeth as it wound the rope tightly around his chest and shoulders and the pipe, and the old skaven squealed orders from a safe distance. Aethenir stared around at all this as if it might be some strange nightmare.

The assassin hauled at Gotrek's ropes until Felix saw the thin strands bite deep into the Slayer's flesh, drawing blood in places, then it tied them off and backed away. Gotrek struggled but couldn't move an inch. With a grunt he seemed to resign himself to his situation, conserving his strength.

The old skaven breathed a phlegmy sigh of relief, and stepped forwards again, gazing at them triumphantly.

'My nemeses,' it whispered. 'At last I have you in my claws. At last you will pay for all the indignities you have heaped upon me.' It hissed, like steam from a kettle. 'Horribly, you will die, yes-yes, but slowly, slowly. First, you will pay for all the long years I have suffered by your cruel schemes.' The mad ratman's eyes shone with wild glee. 'For every defeat, a snip-cut. For every setback, a blood-bruise. For every misery, a bone break.' It stepped closer, its tail and its frail limbs twitching with fevered excitement, until Felix could smell its acrid breath with each whispered word. 'You will beg-beg for mercy, my nemeses – but to no avail.'

'But…' said Felix, completely at a loss. 'But, who are you?'

The ancient skaven stopped. It blinked and stepped back. 'You… you know me not?'

Felix looked to Gotrek questioningly.

The Slayer shrugged. 'They all look alike to me.'

Felix turned back to the skaven and shook his head.

The ratman staggered back, eyes rolling, and collided with its tailless servant. The servant squeaked and the ancient whirled on it, swiping at it with its staff and spitting shrill abuse. The servant cringed back, then scurried unsteadily out of the chamber, leaving the old skaven screeching after it. The rat ogre lowed anxiously and thumped the deck with its huge paws.

The skaven spun back towards its captives again, shaking with rage and tearing at the few tufts of fur on its skeletal head. 'Madness! Madness! Can it be possible that you do not remember me? Can it be possible that you have masterminded my failure-fall by accident? Did you not destroy my works in the Nuln warren, oh those many years gone by? Kill-killing my plague priests, burnsmashing my gutter runners and my engineers, killing even my first gift of Moulder?' It clenched its paws in rage. 'Close-close I came to killing you then, in the brood queen's burrow. But for that cursed man-mage, my torment would have ended before it had begun!'

Felix gaped, wide-eyed, remembering. This was that skaven? The ratkin sorcerer who had attacked them during Countess Emmanuelle's costume ball twenty years ago? The one Doctor Drexler had saved them from? It was impossible! Surely skaven didn't live that long. It had been ancient then. How old must it be now? And what sustained it?

Felix glanced at Gotrek. The Slayer was glaring at the skaven with new loathing, and straining harder against the cruel ropes.

The skaven paid neither of them any attention. It continued gibbering away, pacing back and forth before them, its limbs and tail atremble, lost in its memories. 'Did you not then follow me north, foiling my every attempt to capture the earth diggers' flying machine? Did you not twist-taint my servant-slave and turn him against me when you flew to the Wastes? Did you not rip-take the machine from me when my magic had it in its grip?' The creature clutched its forehead. 'Impossible! Impossible that you do not know me! Impossible that all is by chance! My whole life! My whole *life*!'

With a whimpering wail, the old skaven began to scrabble furiously at its robes, checking pockets and sleeves, and finally raised a small stone bottle in its shaking paws. It pried out the stopper, tapped a mound of glittering powder in the hollow between its thumb and foreclaw, then inhaled it through the ragged wet hole that served it as a nose.

For a moment after it had ingested the stuff, the skaven shook even worse than it had before, and its escort of armoured troopers took a nervous step back, but then, with a final seismic shake, the tremors stopped and it stood straight, taking a deep, if thready, breath.

It turned back to them, calm and composed, a stream of blood and mucus trickling unnoticed from its nosehole as it glared at them with eyes that blazed with green fire. 'If that is the case, then my shame-rage is even greater, and therefore so will be your suffering. You will know agony-fear that no overdweller has ever endured, and yet by my magic you will heal to be tortured again-again, until you share all of my torture despair–'

'Ah, your pardon, ratkin,' said Aethenir, his voice quavering. 'But, does this mean that you have captured me by acci–'

'You dare to interrupt?' squealed the skaven, snapping around. 'I am speak-speaking, miserable prick-ear!'

'Indeed,' said Aethenir. 'But, er, as your feud appears to be with my companions and not myself, perhaps you could be so gracious as to let me return to the ship upon which–'

'What do I care for your wishes?' screamed the seer. 'You are mine-mine to do with as I please!' It limped to the elf, looking him up and down and stroking its cankered chin. 'It was an accident that you were taken, yes-yes. Your misfortune to have yellow fur like the tall one. But never-never have I experimented on a prick-ear. Never have I put one through my mazes, or fed one with poisons. Never have I cut-snipped its flesh and examined its organs.' It leaned in, its ruined nose almost touching the elf's high-bridged one. 'You will be the first.'

Aethenir flinched away, gagging, as the skaven turned from him and chittered furiously at its escort.

'Just like an elf,' snarled Gotrek out of the side of his mouth. 'Only thinking of himself.'

'I do not think of myself,' said Aethenir, as one of the armoured guards scampered out of the room on the old skaven's orders. 'But of my duty. Did I not promise Rion that I would let nothing stop me from righting the wrong I have caused?' He ground his teeth. 'I must recover that terrible weapon or the destruction of Ulthuan will be upon my head. Surely a dwarf will not begrudge me doing all that I can to restore my honour?'

'Elves have no honour to restore,' snarled Gotrek.

Just then the old skaven turned back to Aethenir, its eyes gleaming. 'What-what? Terrible weapon? What is this?'

The elf's eyes went wide as the ratman advanced on him. 'I… I know not what you mean. I said nothing of any weapon. You misheard me.'

'I did not mishear,' said the skaven. 'No-no. I heard perfectly.'

Just then the tailless skaven returned, a box under one arm which appeared to be made entirely of bone, etched all over with crude-looking glyphs. The little creature hurried to the ancient, making trembling obeisances, and held out the bone box with quivering paws.

The old skaven turned the clasp of the box, which looked to have been fashioned from a human finger bone, and opened the lid. Inside it, Felix could see a ter-rifying collection of steel and brass tools, none of them very clean. The ancient ran a claw over them, then selected one and held it up. It looked like a scalpel, but with a serrated edge, and it was orange with rust. The skaven turned towards the high elf, showing its teeth in a travesty of a smile.

'Now, prick-ear,' it hissed. 'Now you will tell-tell what I misheard.'

FELIX HAD TO admit that Aethenir held out much longer than he expected, but in the end he cracked, just as Felix had feared he would. He remained strong through the knives and the saws and flames and the collar that fit over a finger and increased pressure on it with a screw until it snapped. He had even kept silent when they had fixed a cage around his head and filled it with diseased rats, murmuring only some endlessly repeated elven cantrip that allowed him to remove himself into some interior chamber of the mind so that the excruciations of his flesh did not reach him.

Felix looked away when torture began, though hearing the sounds was nearly as bad as watching. The clever skaven was serving a dual purpose with its treatment of the elf, extracting information while at the same time attempting to build terror in the hearts of those who would next face its ministrations. Felix couldn't speak for Gotrek, but the ploy was working on him. With every moan and scream that came from the elf, cold dread dripped into Felix's heart. He could feel every cut, anticipate every twist of the screw. He wanted to scream, 'Tell him! Tell him!' to make it stop.

Of course, it would be worse when the skaven started on him and Gotrek, for the seer wanted no information from them. There would be nothing they could tell it to make it stop. Their torture itself was the creature's goal, and Felix could think of no way to escape it.

It was when the wizened ratkin attacked Aethenir's mind directly, dabbing a glowing paste of warpstone in his held-open eyes and then blasting him with spells that brought the poor elf screaming out of his mental stronghold, that he finally broke, whispering and weeping words in the elven tongue that Felix was glad he couldn't understand.

'Make them stop,' he whimpered finally to the skaven sorcerer. 'Make them go away. They are eating my knowledge… eating it.'

'I will banish them if you speak-speak,' said the skaven.

And at last Aethenir spoke, weeping as he did. 'It is called the Harp of Ruin,' he moaned, as Gotrek snarled curses at him. 'A weapon that can cause earthquakes… tidal waves… raise valleys and lower mountains. The druchii mean to use it on fair Ulthuan.'

The old skaven stared past the elf as it digested this information, scratching distractedly at a patch of scaly skin on its withered neck as it mused. 'A great weapon indeed,' it said at last. 'What the skaven might do with such a weapon. What *I* might do with such a weapon!

The warrens of the overdwellers I would crash low, and raise-lift skaven cities in their place! I would show the council the greatness of my power! They would bow-scrape before me! At last I would rise-return to my true stature!'

Its eye refocused on Aethenir. 'Where is this harp?' it snapped. 'Quick-quick! I must have it!'

The high elf looked like he was going to resist again, but the ancient had only to raise a hand that glowed with green fire and he spoke again, babbling in his fear. 'A druchii ship takes it north. Six powerful sorceresses guard it. Their destination may be Naggaroth, or Ulthuan itself.'

The skaven nodded and began to pace. 'The ship I spied. Small-small – easily taken. But six sorceresses.' It looked hesitant. 'The prick-ears are great in the ways of magic. Equals nearly of the skaven. The whirlpool. Could even I have created such a…?' It shook its head, as if banishing the thought. 'How to accomplish this without risk-pain to myself. There must some trick weapon I could deploy that…' its eye fell suddenly on Gotrek and Felix. It paused, looking at them appraisingly, then turned away again, angry.

'No,' it said. 'Never-never! Not when I have them at last. I have waited for this too long. They are mine, mine, to do with as I wish.' It looked at Aethenir. 'And yet… and yet will vengeance win me power? Is it better to use them as tools to reclaim my former position? Better, isn't it, to set them against my enemies as my enemies once turned them against me? Yes-yes! That is the skaven way! They will smash-kill the tainted prick-ears, and I will pluck pick the harp from the wreckage.' It looked at its captives and a hissing giggle escaped it. 'You will be the cheese in a trap for rats!'

It turned to its guards and chittered something to them in its own tongue. They bowed and went to a metal locker in one corner of the room.

When they turned back to the prisoners they held leather sacks, crusted on the edges with green muck.

FELIX OPENED HIS eyes, then blinked with shock. There were white clouds above him, drifting across a blue sky. He felt a cool breeze on his cheek, and a gentle rocking as if he were in a hammock. This was a decided improvement on the humid skaven torture chamber he had woken in last. Were they free? Had some incredible miracle happened? Had it all been a dream?

All at once the pain returned, worse than ever, blinding him with its savagery, and he nearly blacked out again. When he had mastered it, he raised his head like a man might raise a brimming mug, afraid the slightest motion would cause some of the contents to slop out. Again his vision was distorted, as if he was seeing the world through an imperfect mirror, and nausea and vertigo threatened to overwhelm him with each turn of his head.

He tried to sit up and realised that his hands and feet were still bound. With a lot of grunting and cursing he finally managed to get up on one elbow and look around. His heart sank.

They were indeed free. The gentle rocking he felt was waves, lapping at the sides of a small wooden rowboat. There were no skaven in sight. In fact there was nothing in sight. All he could see, in every direction, was endless cold grey ocean. Aethenir lay in the bottom of the boat, his head down, trussed as Felix was, but with Gotrek the skaven had taken no chances. He was still cocooned to the pipe that he had awoken on. It had been freed from its moorings and now lay across the rowing bench. The

Slayer hung from it like a meaty, but particularly ugly, chicken on a spit.

'The knife,' the Slayer rasped.

'Eh?' said Felix, looking around. 'What knife?'

A curved dagger, rusted and filthy, had been stabbed, point first, into the edge of the boat. It pinned a piece of vellum to the wood.

Felix flopped over painfully and began wiggling it from the wood.

'Don't drop it,' said Gotrek.

'I won't' said Felix, then dropped it. Fortunately it clattered into the boat instead of out. The folded vellum fluttered down next to it. Felix picked up the vellum and unfolded it. He frowned.

'What is it?' asked Gotrek.

'A note.' Felix struggled to read the jagged script. 'Druchii... coming. Fight... well.'

Felix groaned, then scooped the dagger up and started towards Gotrek. Humping across a wobbling boat with one's wrists and ankles tied and a knife in one's hands was no easy task, and more than once he fell forwards and nearly impaled himself before he reached Gotrek and began sawing.

'Cowards,' he said as the strands of rope began to part. 'Wouldn't free us even though we were unconscious.'

'Aye,' said Gotrek. 'They lead from the back.'

'This time they lead from under the water.'

After another minute of sawing, the heavy ropes came free, and Felix moved to the thin grey cord. This parted more quickly and soon Gotrek thudded heavily to the bottom of the boat. He grunted, then closed his eye and lay where he had fallen, massaging his cruelly abraded arms and flexing his fingers to get the blood back into them.

Felix turned to Aethenir and began sawing at the ropes that encircled his wrists. He winced when he looked at the elf's injuries. Aethenir looked as if he should be dead. The old skaven had robbed him of his beauty and done terrible things to him. His face was a mass of cuts, his nose was broken and both eyes blackened, the skin of his right forearm was black and blistered from fire, the pinkies and middle fingers of both hands bent at unnatural angles, and Felix knew that more atrocities were hidden beneath the elf's blood-smeared robes.

Aethenir twitched and whimpered as his last rope fell away, then opened his eyes. 'The fiend has killed me,' he moaned.

'He would have if you had any honour,' said Gotrek from where he lay. 'Instead, you talked.'

Felix scowled at that. Gotrek's words seemed a bit unfair. The elf had held out a long time – longer than he would have. He wasn't sure he could have stood half what the elf had endured, but he hesitated to say anything. Gotrek would just think him weak.

Though he was free, Aethenir continued to lay in a stupor, so Felix put the knife between his knees and tried to saw through his own wrist cords.

'I'll do that, manling,' said Gotrek.

Felix looked around. The Slayer was sitting up and rolling his shoulders. The marks the ropes had left on his arms, chest and wrists looked like deep scars, but there was colour in his hands again.

He crawled to Felix and took the knife, then cut swiftly through his bonds. Felix hissed in agony as the blood rushed back into his fingers. The pins and needles were more like daggers and spikes. He couldn't imagine how much pain Gotrek must have been in when all his ropes had come off, and yet the Slayer had shown no emotion or discomfort at all.

'Where are we?' murmured Aethenir, blinking up at the sky.

'You got your wish, high one,' said Felix. 'We are free.'

Aethenir raised his head and looked around. He moaned and lay back. 'But, where are the druchii? Where are the skaven?'

Felix reached a tingling hand to the vellum note and handed it to the elf. Aethenir took it with his three unbroken fingers and read it. He sighed, disgusted.

'And do they think we will win their battle for them like this?' he asked. 'Have they even given us weapons?'

'You're lying on them,' said Gotrek.

Aethenir and Felix looked down. There was a lumpy canvas sack under the elf, also tied up securely.

'Not taking any chances, were they?' said Felix.

He took the knife from Gotrek and cut open the sack. Inside it were Karaghul, Felix's chainmail and Gotrek's rune axe, as well as all their belts, clothes and packs. There was also a slim elven dagger that Felix had never seen Aethenir draw.

After that there was little to do but prepare themselves for the arrival of the druchii. Aethenir summoned his magic and did his best to cleanse and heal his and Felix's wounds. When he took off his robe and shirt to attend to the wounds the skaven seer had given him during its interrogation, Felix had to look away, and found he had to reappraise once again his estimate of the elf's fortitude.

Aethenir's spells of healing were not as powerful as before, but they closed up most of the open wounds and burns on his face and torso, and eased Felix's aches considerably. The elf's four mangled fingers however were too badly broken for him to fix with spells, so Felix helped him set and bind them with canvas from the sack that had held their weapons. The elf took the manipulation of his bones with closed eyes and gritted teeth, but neither cursed nor wept. Gotrek refused to be magicked and just washed his cuts and bruises in the ocean.

Felix mopped his face clean the same way, hissing as the salt water attacked his wounds. He rinsed out his doublet and cloak too, as they were filthy with muck from the skaven ship, then put them on and pulled his chainmail over them, so that he would be ready when the druchii came.

Then they settled in to wait.

And wait.

After an hour of nothing, they discovered that the skaven had not provided them with water or food, nor oars. Felix had a little water in the skin he'd had when the vermin had captured him, but that was all.

'So,' said Aethenir, sighing. 'We will go into battle hungry and athirst, and if the druchii fail to see us and sail by, there will be no battle at all, and we will float here until we die of starvation.'

'I'll kill you long before that,' muttered Gotrek, then turned away and stared out to sea as the high elf glared at his back.

Felix had nothing to add, so he looked off in the other direction and tried to pretend he wasn't thirsty.

IT HAD BEEN mid-afternoon when they had regained consciousness on the boat, and still no ship had appeared from any direction as they watched the sun set in the west and a thick fog roll in from the north on the back of a cold breeze. An hour later, with the light fading to purple, the fog wrapped its cold, clammy arms around them and they could see no more than twenty feet from the boat. Then darkness fell completely and they couldn't see at all. The druchii ship could have passed within spitting distance of them and they would never have known it.

Gotrek took first watch, and Felix and Aethenir curled up to sleep as best they could in the bottom of the boat.

AFTER A SURPRISINGLY deep sleep, Felix woke to Gotrek tapping his shoulder. 'Your watch, manling,' he said.

Felix grunted and pushed himself up, hissing at the stiffness in his limbs. He felt miserable. Every part of his body ached. His muscles were sore from the fighting and the swimming and from being tied up for so long, his head still hurt from the skaven's horrible sleep drug, his lips were cracked and bleeding, his tongue thick from lack of water, and he was starving.

He pulled the cork from his waterskin and took a sip, but only a small one. There was less than two cupfuls left, and it might have to last, well, forever.

He looked around him as Gotrek lay down in the back of the boat. The fog had thinned somewhat, becoming a fine mist that he could see into for nearly forty feet, with thicker drifts roiling slowly by in patches that glowed a sickly green in the dim light of Morrslieb, shining almost full above them. The sea was dead calm, as if the fog had pressed it flat, and the silence was eerie, just the soft slap of wavelets on the hull of the boat and, after a few moments, Gotrek's snores.

Felix sat on the oar bench and put his sword on his knees, ready, and tried not to think about how hungry he was. It was impossible. His mind drifted back to grilled chops in taverns, to pheasant in noble houses, to rabbit stew and wild vegetables on the march, to grilled sea bass in Barak Varr, to strange spiced dishes in the lands to the east. He cursed as his stomach growled.

It had only been a day since he'd eaten last. He had gone longer than that. Much longer. And longer without water too. Now his mind flashed back to a less savoury time – the brutal brazen sun, the sea of sand, hiding in the shade of the ancient statues and waiting for the cool of night.

He cursed again. Now he wanted a drink! His hand reached for his water skin. Just one more sip, just to rinse the taste of hot sand from his mouth. But no, he mustn't. He must save it for morning when the sun would rise again.

He leaned forwards on his knees and stared out into the misty nothingness. The curls of fog suggested menacing shapes in the darkness, but then dissolved into nothing again. He sighed. It was going to be a long night.

FELIX JERKED HIS head up and blinked around, instantly angry with himself as he realised that he'd fallen asleep. It couldn't have been for long. The sea hadn't changed, the mist hadn't changed, and Morrslieb was still in the sky. But something had woken him up. What had it been?

He turned on the bench, checking behind him. Gotrek and Aethenir were both asleep, and there was no black ship prow looming behind the little boat.

Then he heard it again – a quiet splash somewhere far off in the fog. He looked in the direction he thought the sound had come from, but he could see nothing, just the drifts of mist billowing silently by. What was it? It could have been anything – a wave, a fish breaking the surface. A…

'Hoog!'

Felix froze. That had not been a fish. A seal perhaps, but not a fish. Once again he tried to pinpoint the far-off sound, but he could not. It had seemed to echo from every direction at once. He stood, drawing his sword. At least it had been far away. Perhaps whatever it was would miss them in the fog and pass on.

The hooting came again, closer now! Much closer! He stepped over the oar bench to Gotrek and Aethenir and shook them, whispering in their ears.

'Gotrek, high one, wake up. Something said "hoog".'

Gotrek grimaced and yawned. 'What's that, manling?' He scratched his chin through his beard.

Aethenir rubbed his eyes with his splinted fingers and groaned. 'Something said what?' he murmured.

'Hoog!'

Gotrek and Aethenir leapt up at the sound, almost capsizing the boat. Gotrek had his axe in his hands. Aethenir clutched his delicate dagger. Felix gripped his sword. They stared out at the fog.

The high elf swallowed, his eyes wide. 'I know that sound,' he hissed. 'I have read a description of it in the diaries of Captain Riabbrin, hero of the Lothern Sea Guard. It is the hunting cry of the menlui-sarath, used as scout beasts by the druchii corsairs.'

'The what?' asked Felix. Was that something moving in the fog? He couldn't be sure. He strove to listen, but the pounding of his heart was too loud.

'The menlui-sarath,' repeated Aethenir. 'The hunter of the deep. A sea dragon. If such a thing is abroad, then the black ships cannot be far behind.'

'HOOG!'

They spun around. Out of the fog loomed a towering silhouette, a supple swaying trunk like a swan's neck, but as thick around as a tree and rising higher than a house.

'By Sigmar, it's enormous,' said Felix.

'And still only a juvenile,' breathed Aethenir. 'The adults are large enough to pull ships.'

Perched on top of the supple trunk was an angular, asymmetrical mass that Felix at first mistook for some gigantic misshapen head. Then it drifted closer and he could see that the silhouette was not just a beast, but a beast and rider.

The beast was a sleek silver-green serpent with a blunt reptilian head the size of a cask of ale, and a chin full of dangling, tentacle-like feelers. Its glistening hide was made of thick overlapping plates, and rippling ribbons of fin ran down its flanks. Felix hated it on sight. The rider was a dark elf in black plate armour, sitting on an elaborate saddle strapped just behind the monster's head. She carried a long curved sword in one hand, and a strange conical shield in the other, like the pointed roof of a castle tower, made of polished steel.

The rider saw them at the same moment as they saw her, and her reaction was instantaneous. She shouted a harsh cry and jabbed her spurred boots into the sea dragon's neck.

With another deafening hoot, the beast's head shot down like a fist, straight at the boat. Felix and Aethenir leapt aside, yelping. Gotrek swung as he dived the other way. Felix couldn't tell if he connected, because the dragon smashed its huge skull into the boat and sent them all flying in an explosion of water and spinning timbers.

Felix came down on something hard, then bounced off it into the water. His armour and heavy clothes dragged him down and he grabbed desperately at what he had hit. He caught it and held on. It was the boat – half the boat, rather – the prow end, upside down in the water.

He sucked in a gulp of air as he tried to pull himself on top of it. Aethenir thrashed and coughed in the water beside him. Felix caught him by the collar and pulled him to the broken boat. The elf clung desperately, panting and wheezing. A few yards away, Gotrek clawed up onto the stern half of the boat.

Of the sea dragon and its rider, there was no sign except the ever-widening ripple where it had plunged beneath the sea.

'Where is it?' snarled Felix. 'I must kill it!' He found himself boiling with rage and righteous fury. 'On land or sea, dragons are the bane of mankind!'

'Herr Jaeger,' said Aethenir, still breathing hard. 'The runes of your sword are glowing.'

Felix looked down. Aethenir was right. The dwarf runes engraved along Karaghul's length, which Felix hardly noticed most of the time, were glowing with an inner light. He cursed. This was the source of his sudden hatred of the sea dragon. Once again, the sword was trying to take over his will, trying to force its purpose upon him. It hadn't happened often, but when it did, it infuriated him. His mind and his will were his own, and any attempt to wrest control from him was an intimate violation of his self.

On the other hand, he never fought better than when the sword awakened and he surrendered his will to it. He had killed the Chaos-twisted dragon Skjalandir with it, had he not? Of course, he had nearly died in the doing of that mighty deed, something that he didn't think the sword cared about in the least.

The sea dragon had still not reappeared. Felix, Gotrek and Aethenir looked around warily, dripping with freezing water. Had the dragon rider left them to drown? Had it decided they were too insignificant to fight?

'Gotrek,' called Felix. 'Are you all–'

With no warning, the end of the boat Felix and Aethenir clung to exploded upwards as the dragon's head smashed up through it from below. Felix and Aethenir pinwheeled through the air as the long neck shot up like a geyser. Felix came down hard, still clutching a splintered plank, and bobbed to the surface, gasping for breath, in time to see the massive beast looping back on itself to plunge at Gotrek, who balanced, legs bent, on the capsized stern of the boat, roaring a dwarfish challenge.

'Over here, damn you!' Felix cried, filled with the sword's purpose, but to no avail.

The rider tucked herself behind her conical shield, and dug her spurs into the dragon's flanks. The beast's battering-ram head rocketed down towards the Slayer. At the last second, he dived to the side, swinging his axe behind him.

Dragon and rider smashed down through the stern and disappeared into the water. Now Felix understood what the conical shield was for. It pushed the water aside so that the rider wasn't punched off the back of its mount every time it dived beneath the waves.

Then he noticed that the dragon seemed to have taken Gotrek with it. The Slayer had vanished.

'Gotrek?'

The serpent and rider shot up again. Gotrek came with them, his axe hooked behind the rider's leg. The rider slashed down at him with her curved sword and the Slayer blocked with his armful of gold bracelets, then grabbed the rider's leg and freed his axe.

The rider hacked down at him again, but Gotrek's weight on his leg ruined her balance and she missed. Gotrek swung the axe over his head and buried it in the rider's gut, punching through her armour with a bright clang.

The rider screamed and tumbled from the saddle. She and Gotrek splashed down in a spinning tangle and disappeared under the waves. The sea dragon plunged after them, roaring its anger.

Felix waved his sword at it. 'Face me, dragon!' he shouted.

The serpent ignored him, intent on killing he who had killed its master. It dived down into the water, then came up again, looking around. Gotrek bobbed up behind him, one arm over the remains of the rowing bench.

'Down here, sea wyrm!' he roared. 'My axe thirsts!'

The sea dragon howled and lunged down at him, jaws agape. Gotrek kicked aside, letting go of the bench and swinging his axe two-handed. There was a crack of impact and then both dragon and Slayer vanished beneath the water in a violent splash.

'Damn you, Slayer!' called Felix. 'The dragon was mine.'

Only echoes returned to him. The sea was quiet. The ripples were spreading and fading.

'Perhaps they have slain each other,' said Aethenir, looking around with worried eyes.

But then Felix noticed that the runes on his sword were glowing brighter. 'It's coming back!'

The sea dragon surged out of the sea right beside them, its scales flashing by so fast that they blurred. It thrashed its head back and forth like a terrier trying to kill a rat, and Felix feared the worst, but when he got a good look, he saw that Gotrek was not in its mouth, but hanging from the beast's back, one leg caught in a loop of its bridle, and flopping about like a banner in a high wind. The Slayer's axe was buried in the side of the sea dragon's snout, and it was this that was causing it to writhe so wildly.

It weaved towards Felix and Aethenir, and Felix kicked towards it, clinging to his plank.

'Yes! To me!' he cried, then slashed at it as it collided with him. Karaghul bit deep, cutting through the dragon's protective scales as if they were made of cheese, and opening it to the bone. Blood and black bile spilled from the gaping wound and the serpent howled in pain, turning to face its new attacker.

Felix roared up at it as it rose above him, its eyes meeting his for the first time. 'Come, drake! Your death awaits!'

Beside him Aethenir screamed. 'No, you lunatic! You'll be killed!'

Felix didn't care, as long as his blade got another chance to strike. The serpent reared back. Felix saw Gotrek catch its reins and begin to pull himself upright.

'HOOG!'

The head shot down at Felix like a ball from a cannon. He raised his sword, howling in anticipation. A hand grabbed his collar and jerked him back. The head smashed down into the water an inch from his chest. Even so, the momentum of the beast pulled him under and he spun in a jumble of water, bubbles and whirling timber.

The hand still had a hold of him when he came back, sputtering, to the surface. He turned to find Aethenir gripping him and a section of the broken rowboat.

'Interfering elf!' he spat, water shooting painfully from his nose. 'I nearly had it!'

'I saved your life,' said Aethenir.

'Did I ask for it?'

The elf shook his head, wonderingly. 'You're both mad.'

Just then, with an enraged 'HOOG!' the sea dragon exploded from the waves again, twisting and snapping at something on its back. Felix and Aethenir could see that it was Gotrek, his short, powerful legs clamped around the serpent's neck just behind its head, his axe raised high, roaring a wordless battle cry as water flew from his crest and beard.

Just as the sea dragon rose to its highest height, the Slayer slashed down and buried the axe's blade deep into its brain-pan, spraying blood in all directions.

With a last soft 'hoog' the fires died in the sea dragon's eyes. For a brief moment, as Gotrek struggled to wrench his axe free, it hung motionless in the air, then toppled, Gotrek still clinging to it, as slow and inevitable as a tree falling in a forest, right for Felix and Aethenir.

'Flee! Swim!' cried the elf, and kicked wildly while clinging to the timber.

Felix kicked with him. The serpent slapped down beside them with a smack that hurt the ears and pushed them forwards on a surging swell. Its huge body slipped swiftly beneath the waves, leaving little eddies and whirlpools in its passing. It also seemed to have taken Gotrek with it, for he was nowhere to be seen.

Felix turned in a circle as the seconds ticked past. Had the Slayer not managed to free his axe? Was he still caught in the beast's bridle straps? Had he found his doom at last?

But then, after it seemed that there could no longer be any hope, a familiar head broke the waves, gasping and choking and flipping its crest out of its eye.

'Gotrek! You live!' said Felix as he reached a hand out.

'Aye,' said Gotrek catching his hand. 'Worse luck.'

Felix pulled him to the floating plank and the three of them clung to it and just breathed for a while. With the death of the sea dragon, Karaghul's runes faded out, and so too did Felix's all-consuming hatred for dragonkind, to be replaced by sick fear at all the suicidal risks he had just taken. Had he really shouted in the dragon's face and waited for its attack?

He turned to Aethenir. 'Thank you, high one, for pulling me aside. And I apologise for insulting you.'

Aethenir waved a dismissive hand. 'You were ridden by the sword. I took no offence.'

Around them, the grey light of pre-dawn was beginning to push back the darkness. The mist continued to lift and the sea remained calm. The miserable night was over. Not that it mattered. Though they had survived the fight with the sea dragon, they were as dead as if it had eaten them, for without a boat, the cold of the sea would kill them long before their thirst or hunger ever did.

'Perhaps the skaven will save us,' said Aethenir. 'Perhaps they've been watching all along.'

Gotrek spat into the water. 'Saved by skaven. I'd die first.'

Then little more than a mile away, silhouetted against the pearl-grey horizon, Felix saw jutting black crags rising from the sea. 'An island!' he cried, pointing. 'Look! We're saved!'

The others followed his gaze and peered into the half-light.

Beside him Aethenir moaned. 'No, Herr Jaeger, that is no island, and we are not saved.' He shivered and lowered his forehead to the shattered plank. 'We are doomed.'

THIRTEEN

FELIX TURNED TO Aethenir, confused. 'What do you mean? Certainly it's an island. Look at it.'

The high elf shook his head. 'It is a black ark, a floating city, a piece of sunken Nagarythe held above the water by the profane magics of the druchii. It is a moving fortress from which the black ships of the corsairs spill to pillage and enslave. And it is coming our way.'

Felix blinked at Aethenir, aghast, then turned back to the island. Fear gripped his heart. It was closer now, much closer, and he had a sudden understanding of its scale. It rose hundreds of yards out of the sea, and must have been nearly a mile across. Towers and thick-walled fortifications jutted up all along the tall crags, and palaces and temples and citadels climbed steeply towards the centre, where a massive black keep glowered down on the rest of the island like a black dragon surveying its chosen domain.

Felix turned in the water, looking around for some escape. There was none. 'This is madness,' he said. 'We were after one tiny ship! The cursed skaven put us in the way of the wrong druchii!' He lowered himself again so that only his head showed above the water. 'Perhaps they won't see us. Perhaps they will think we are dead and pass us by.'

'No, manling,' said Gotrek. 'They will not.'

Felix looked at him. The Slayer's single eye blazed.

'This is what I have been waiting for,' Gotrek said, never looking away from the ark. 'This is the black mountain the seeress promised. This is my doom.'

And mine too, thought Felix. For if Gotrek met his death on that floating rock there was no way Felix would ever make it off alive.

As they watched, a piece of darkness broke off from the craggy island and became a black ship with a lateen sail.

'Are they looking for us?' asked Felix, swallowing.

'They are looking for the rider,' said Aethenir. 'They will have heard the beast's battle cries, and are coming to investigate.'

And so it seemed, for the sleek ship rowed straight for them while Gotrek chuckled under his breath.

'Once we kill these,' he said, 'we sail it back to the island. Then the real slaying begins.'

Felix looked at Gotrek agog. The Slayer was serious. 'Putting aside that it may be difficult to kill a whole ship full of druchii, not to mention an island,' he said. 'Three men aren't enough to sail us there.'

'The galley slaves will row us back,' said Gotrek.

'And why would they do that?' asked Aethenir.

'To see their masters die.'

The ship was getting close now, slowing and arcing towards the wreckage. Gotrek watched it like a wolf

eyeing an approaching sheep, seemingly unaware that he
was the prey and the ship was the predator.

'Closer,' he murmured. 'Closer.'

Aethenir, on the other hand, seemed to be praying.
Felix joined him.

The ship heaved to a considerable distance from them
and sat in the water, drifting slowly. It was a low, evil-
looking craft, with a blood-red sail, rows of sweeps and
giant, bow-like bolt-throwers lining both rails. Felix saw
a flash of reflection from the deck. Someone was observing them with a spyglass.

A muffled command echoed across the water and one
of the bolt-throwers turned their way.

'They're going to fire!' cried Aethenir.

'Dive!' said Gotrek, and disappeared below the water.

Aethenir dived, but before Felix could follow there was
a sharp clack, and something shot from the weapon. It
wasn't a bolt. Halfway through ducking down, he paused
to watch the strange, amorphous shape come towards
them, twisting and blossoming as it came. A net!

Panicked, he let go of the floating timber and dropped
under the water, then panicked again as he remembered
he was wearing chainmail, and was starting to sink. He
kicked and flailed desperately with his arms, clawing his
way back to the surface, and finally caught a hold of
something, but it wasn't the wreck. It was the net. He
grabbed it gratefully anyway and pulled his face up to the
air, sticking his head up through the weave of ropes.

Gotrek and Aethenir had risen too, and were also
clinging to the net.

'To the edge,' said Gotrek. 'Before they draw it in.'

But as they tried to pull themselves along the underside of the net, they realised that their hands were stuck
fast to the ropes they had first touched. They pulled and

yanked, but it was no good. It was worse than tar, and it wasn't just their hands that were trapped. The strands that lay upon Felix's shoulders were stuck to his chainmail. A strand that had fallen across Gotrek's head was stuck to his scalp and his crest. Aethenir's long blond hair was caught in it, as were the sleeves of his robes.

Gotrek growled a curse as he tried to pull his hand away from the stickum. He could not. He brought a foot up and hooked it in the rope for leverage, then heaved mightily. After much straining and grunting, his hand tore free, leaving a patch of skin, but then his boot was stuck.

'Grimnir take all tricksy elves!' he cursed as he tried to free his foot. Without thinking, he grabbed the net for leverage and was back where he started. He roared with frustration.

The black hull of the corsair ship suddenly loomed up beside them, and ropes and grapnels snaked out from the deck and splashed in the water. The grapnels hooked the net and winches lifted it slowly clear of the water.

Felix, Gotrek and Aethenir came up with it, hanging at awkward angles and getting more entangled as more of the net touched their bodies and their clothes. Gotrek was the most tightly held, for he had struggled the most, and by the time the net had been swung over the deck, he was covered from head to toe in the sticky ropes.

As the winches lowered them to the deck, figures in ragged clothes spread out a canvas tarpaulin that shone greasily, and it was onto this that they were dropped – none too gently – on their faces.

A chorus of laughter rang out as they crashed down, and Felix turned his head to see that they were surrounded by tall dark elves in close-fitting grey surcoats, over which they wore heavy cloaks that looked as if they had been made from the hide of the sea dragon Felix and

Gotrek had just fought. The corsairs looking down at them with sneering smiles on their long, gaunt faces.

'You'll be laughing with your necks when I get free,' snarled Gotrek from where he lay.

A pair of red-heeled boots strode through the crowd of legs and stood before them. Felix looked up. A tall druchii with an amused smirk on his lips looked down at him. He wore a red sash belted around his surcoat and his long, braided hair was pulled back into a queue with silver wire.

'What strange fish my net has caught,' he said in heavily accented Reikspiel. 'An Old World flounder, a cave-dwelling rock fish and an Ulthuan minnow – and none of them market fresh by the smell of them.'

'Free me and face me, you corpse-faced coward,' said Gotrek.

The dark elf's eyes widened in mock amazement. 'By the Dark Mother, a talking fish! And with such an ill-favoured tongue.' He stepped forwards delicately to the edge of the oiled tarpaulin and kicked Gotrek savagely in the cheek with his high heel.

Gotrek snarled and lunged, blood welling from a deep gouge, but trussed as he was, he could do nothing.

The druchii stepped back. 'I am almost curious enough to ask how three such strange companions came to be floating out in the middle of the sea alone, but not quite. No matter where you come from, you all go to the same place.' He turned away and said something to his lieutenants, waving a dismissive hand.

One of the lieutenants bowed and, in turn, gave orders to the ragged human slaves who spread the tarp, but then another corsair pointed at Gotrek and said something that caused the druchii captain to turn back and look at him again.

The crouching humans were padding towards the captives, holding strange objects that looked something like oil lamps, but the captain waved them back again. They shrank away as he began to circle the net, staring at Gotrek intently. Felix couldn't figure out what had caught his attention, but Aethenir understood the murmured exchanges between the druchii.

'He is interested in your axe, dwarf,' whispered the high elf. 'And your sword, Herr Jaeger. He recognises them as powerful weapons and knows collectors who will pay well to own them.'

Gotrek snarled at that. 'No one touches my axe. No one.'

But there didn't seem to be much he could do about it at the moment. The axe was on his back, and his arms were so entangled in the sticky ropes that he couldn't reach it.

After circling the net twice, the dark elf stepped back and waved the slaves forwards again. Felix thought he had never seen sadder-looking men in all his life – emaciated, dead-eyed creatures with patchy, close-cropped heads and permanently stooped shoulders. They came and crouched next to Felix, Gotrek and Aethenir, deftly avoiding the sticky ropes while they held up the strange lamps and began smearing black paste into a little metal reservoir above the flames.

'Brothers,' whispered Felix. 'Help us. Free us and we will free you. We will slaughter these slavers and return you to the Old World.'

The men didn't even turn their heads, just kept at their task as if he hadn't spoken. Wisps of smoke began to rise from the black paste as the little pan that held it heated up.

Felix tried again in the few words of Tilean he knew, and then in halting Bretonnian. The men made no response.

'Damn you, are you deaf?' snapped Felix. 'Do you not want to be free?'

'Leave them be, Herr Jaeger,' said Aethenir. 'They have been so long under the druchii lash that they have forgotten what freedom is.'

The smoke was rising thickly now from the black paste, and a sweet, cloying scent reached Felix's nose. His eyes watered. The slaves quickly covered the lamps with ceramic caps that looked like tobacco pipes with two stems. Felix had no idea what the strange devices were for until the slave who knelt next to him put one of the stems to his lips and pointed the other at Felix's face.

A stream of sweet smoke shot from the stem, right at Felix's nose. He pulled back and tried to turn his head, but the ropes held him too tightly. He couldn't get away from it.

'The black lotus,' said Aethenir, choking. 'They seek to drug us!'

Felix held his breath, but a second slave, a little boy of no more than nine or ten, reached forwards and pinched Felix's nostrils shut while the first punched him in the stomach. Felix gasped and sucked in an involuntary gulp of smoke. He choked and sputtered as the resinous poison filled his lungs, but then had to inhale again just to breathe, and took in more smoke. He could hear Aethenir and Gotrek coughing and cursing as well.

The third lungful was easier, and the fourth was actually pleasant, the smoke slipping silkily down his throat and spreading sweet languor through his veins. The cold and the discomfort of the ropes felt far away, cushioned by a delicious warmth that felt like the heat of a summer sun radiating from his lungs. By the fifth lungful he was straining forwards to catch as much of the smoke as he could.

Aethenir's choking protests quietened as well. Only Gotrek continued coughing and cursing. Felix wished he would stop. The Slayer's struggles were disturbing his lovely lethargy.

A moment later, Felix's pipe slave got up and went to blow smoke in Gotrek's face instead, as did Aethenir's. Felix was sad that the smoke was gone, and he was angry with Gotrek for being so greedy, but sadness and anger took too much energy to maintain, and he quickly let go of them, content to relax into the sluggish current of contentment that flowed through his veins.

After a while even Gotrek's struggles subsided, and then more slaves came, this time with buckets of some foul-smelling grease that they rubbed into the ropes to loosen their hold. Felix watched with idle interest as his sword was carried away, followed by Gotrek's axe. There was some sort of seismic convulsion behind him at this, and another when further slaves carried away the Slayer's golden bracelets, but both times the eruptions subsided again in a rumble of slurring curses.

Then the grease was rubbed on the rest of the ropes and Felix, Gotrek and Aethenir were pulled from the net. More slaves helped Felix to his feet and took off his armour, jerkin and shirt, then put shackles on his wrists and his ankles that were connected by a chain so short he couldn't stand upright. He thought the shackles were silly. He didn't want to go anywhere. He just wanted to lie down again. Unfortunately, they wouldn't let him. They locked his chains to a ring on the central mast and left him there with Gotrek and Aethenir. It wasn't comfortable, but he was too happy to care. He just stared ahead as the high crags of the black island loomed closer. It quickly filled his vision from edge to edge. It must be the size of Nuln, he thought dreamily. He wondered if they had a college of engineering too. That would be nice.

After a time he could differentiate between the island's jagged grey granite cliffs and the towering black basalt walls that topped them. Tall, crenellated watchtowers rose up at every turn of the wall, each crowned with a halo of wind-whipped fire. For a moment Felix thought that they were going to crash right into the granite cliffs, and he giggled at the druchii's foolishness. They would smash their pretty boat. But then he saw that what he had taken for a dark shadow next to a craggy outcropping was actually the mouth of a black cave. Felix's head tipped back and back as the roof of the cave came closer and closer, then swallowed them entirely. For a while all was dark, and he found that restful, but then an orange glow appeared in the darkness before the ship, a flickering light that reflected on rough stone walls and a baroque filigree of stalactites that thrust down from the ceiling high above them.

Then the dark channel opened out into a vast underground bay, at the far end of which great fires blazed in giant braziers mounted on towers that rose above a long line of docks and wharfs. It reminded Felix of Barak Varr – not nearly as big, or as brightly lit, but just as full of ships. There must have been more than thirty low-slung galleys docked in the harbour, as well as many smaller ships and boats, including some that looked like Old World merchantmen. Felix thought the light of the flames dancing on the black water as their ship rowed towards the braziers was the most fascinating thing he had ever seen.

THE CLAN SKRYRE skaven at the periscope turned and bowed to Thanquol, who stood in the centre of the bridge of the mighty skaven submersible, trembling with excitement.

'They have been taken into the ark, grey seer,' said the sailor.

Issfet smiled up at Thanquol fawningly. 'It has happened just as you hoped, oh most geriatric of masters,' he shrilled.

'Yes-yes,' said Thanquol, rubbing his paws together. 'Now we must only be patient, for surely, where my nemeses go, ruin and confusion must follow.'

It had better, he thought darkly. For he had paid dearly for the use of the submersible, in oaths of alliance, promises of warp tokens and pledges of future services rendered, none of which he was in any position to deliver. If he failed to recover the Harp of Ruin, he was ruined.

By THE TIME the dark elf ship docked, and Felix, Gotrek and Aethenir were prodded down the gangplank to the busy stone dock by spear-wielding druchii, the lotus smoke's sweet euphoria had soured and gone flat. The warmth that had filled Felix's veins had turned to a dull numbness, and his fascinated gaze had become a blank stare. It was hard to think, hard to remember to move until the butt of a spear thudded into his back. His feet, as he shuffled through the crowded streets of the cave-roofed port with the others, felt encased in mud, and he tripped often on the too-short chains that rattled between them. When his captors stopped to talk to guards who stood at either side of a great arch set in a rock wall, he stopped and stared straight ahead until they pushed him forwards again, too torpid to care about his surroundings.

He passed unseeing through wide, crowded corridors, looking neither right nor left. Only once did he look up, when he heard a garbled mumble from Aethenir and saw the elf staring dully ahead of them. Felix swung his head around heavily and saw, coming up the wide passage that they were shuffling down, a tall, scarred druchii noble in beautiful black and silver armour, accompanying a proud, cold-eyed druchii woman in flowing black robes and an elaborate headdress. They were escorted by a double file of silver-masked warriors who shoved aside anyone who didn't get out of their way.

Felix blinked at the woman. He knew her. His lotus-smothered brain churned as he wondered how. Then he remembered. It was the sorceress who had spun the silver ring on the metal wand. The one who had let the ocean close on top of them. Fear tried to fight through his lethargy, tried to tell him to look away so that she would not see him and recognise him, but the warning reached him much too late, and he didn't look down until the sorceress and her noble companion had already passed him. It hadn't mattered. They had spared not a glance for chained slaves. They hadn't even noticed their existence.

Their guards led them down a long zigzag stairway into the depths of the floating island, which got colder and damper the deeper they descended, until they passed through a gate into a chamber lit with thickly smoking torches, then through another gate, and finally into a low square chamber with iron doors in its walls. A number of wooden railings sectioned the floor of the room off into paths that led to the doors. Felix couldn't think what they reminded him of until a dim memory of his father taking him to a stockyard in Averheim formed in his head. The cows had been forced into runs just like this as they were divided into lots.

Druchii guards in leather armour came out of a room to one side, followed by another in robes who prodded forwards a bent-over slave with what looked like an enormous book strapped to his back. The robed druchii talked with their captors briefly, examined Felix, Gotrek and Aethenir from all sides, then stepped to the slave and opened the book on his back. He made some notations in it, then gave their captors some sort of receipt. The slavers left the way they had come as the guards led Felix, Gotrek and Aethenir to one of the iron doors, unlocked it, and prodded them into a pitch-dark cell, then slammed and locked the door behind them.

Felix could see nothing at first, and could hear nothing but rustling and a constant low buzzing. His nose wasn't so lucky. The reek of human waste hit him like a solid wall, forcing its way through his smoke-deadened senses and making him gag. Then his eyes became accustomed to the dim reflected light of the torches outside, and he saw the source of the smell.

The room was like a tunnel – long, low and dark – with what appeared to be a raised bench running down the centre at knee height, and it was packed with more people than Felix had ever seen in so small a place. Emaciated men, women and children covered the filth-smeared floor like a carpet, sitting, squatting or lying as best they could – the short chains between their wrists and ankles making it impossible to stretch out. Hundreds of dull eyes turned to look at him and Gotrek and Aethenir, blinking at them with empty misery.

Felix, Gotrek and Aethenir stared back at them. They were horrible-looking wretches, dressed in rags, covered in filth and gaunt with starvation. Many of them showed open, untreated wounds and trembled with fever, and Felix realised that the buzzing he had heard was the sound of the thousand, thousand flies that crawled all over them, feasting.

A man halfway down the left wall stood and glared at them. 'Stolen treasure, you said!' he rasped, shaking his chains. 'A tiny druchii scout ship, you said!'

It took a moment for Felix to realise that the haggard wreck who was spitting so venomously at him was Hans Euler.

FOURTEEN

Surprise fought through Felix's drug-induced dullness. 'Herr Euler?'

'Aye, you lying little trickster!' said Euler, as the remnants of his crew began to stand all around him. 'First the damned rats come for you, then an entire fleet of dark elves. By Manann's deeps, I curse the day you walked into my house, you wrecker!'

His men glared at Felix menacingly. Felix saw Broken-Nose and One-Ear among them. He didn't know how much damage they could do with their wrists and ankles shackled, but he didn't want to find out. He shot a glance at Gotrek. The Slayer was still staring straight ahead, apparently oblivious to everything around him.

Felix put his hands as high as the chains would let him. 'Herr Euler, please. I didn't lie. I just didn't know all the facts. I thought the scout ship was alone.'

'A likely story,' sneered Euler.

'But what happened?' asked Felix. 'Are Magister Schreiber and Fraulein Pallenberger with you? Did they survive?'

'Does my guard, Celorael, live? Asked Aethenir.

Euler shrugged. 'The elf died fighting the rats. The magisters were alive when we were brought here, but they were taken away.'

Felix's heart sank at that. Where had they been taken? What had been done to them? Did they still live?

'*They* did well by us at least,' said Euler. 'Didn't sneak off like some I could mention when the going got rough. Although the little seeress is a regular little nutcase, I have to say.'

'How do you mean?' asked Felix.

'Jumped in the sea when she'd found you'd disappeared during the fight with the rats. Thought they had taken you.'

Felix blinked. 'She jumped in the water?'

'Aye,' said Euler. 'We'd chased the rat-things away and found you were missing. Magister Schreiber insisted that we come about and look for you, thinking you had fallen overboard, but the seeress said the rats had you and that we had to swim down to their ship and save you.' He shook his head. 'There was no ship to be seen, but she said it was under the water and that it was all her fault. She dived in with all her clothes on, and we had to get a hook out before she drowned.'

Felix blinked again. 'That... *does* sound peculiar.' What could Claudia have meant, saying it was her fault? Surely she hadn't summoned the skaven. They had been after him and Gotrek all along.

'But she did well when we found the dark elves. She and the magister blasted them with light and lightning like they were sun and storm, but it wasn't enough.' He shook his head. 'We'd nearly chased down your little scout ship when out of the fog came five black galleys. We turned and ran, but we were no match for their sweeps. The magister and the girl loosed their spells over the aft rail as we peppered them with the nine-pounders. Her lightning set one of the galleys alight and it crashed into another, but then the scout ship came to the fore and six elf women stepped into her prow.' He spat. 'That was the end of your friends, and then the end of us. Weird black clouds balled them up and dropped them to the deck, choking and puking – and with them gone, we didn't stand a chance.'

Aethenir muttered something at this, but Felix didn't hear what it was.

'I'm sorry, Herr Euler,' said Felix. 'I had no idea it would end like this.' Much as he disliked the man, he wouldn't wish this fate on anyone. Of course, if the fool hadn't come chasing after them looking for treasure, he would be at home nibbling on jam tarts in his cosy little office.

'Never mind your damned "sorry",' said Euler. 'We'll settle what's between us if we somehow manage to escape this pit.' He sat back down against the wall. 'Until then, just stay away from me and mine. You're bad luck.'

Felix nodded, then picked his way awkwardly through the close-packed bodies of his fellow prisoners towards the opposite wall to find a space to sit. Gotrek and Aethenir clanked dully after him.

FELIX WOKE SOME unknowable time later, his mouth dry and foul, his head aching, but at last clear of the black smoke's lulling lethargy. He looked around blearily. The torch-tinged darkness of the cell was unchanged, so it was impossible to tell how long he had been asleep. The filthy bodies of other prisoners pressed against him from all sides. Most lay curled up in sleep, though others moaned with pain, or sat and stared straight ahead, or shivered and twitched in the throes of sickness as the flies rose and fell in clouds all around them and the dark shapes of bold rats squirmed through the crowd. Aethenir had his head on his knees next to him, his splinted, fettered hands curled in his lap. Gotrek lay on his side. No one spoke. No one raged. No one tried to free themselves from their fetters.

And why should they? The reality of their situation hadn't truly sunk in for Felix before. The lassitude of the drug, the surprise of seeing Euler there, the story he had told – all had momentarily pushed it aside. But now, waking among the lost and the damned in a slave pen in the depths of a floating dark elf island, no doubt sailing at this moment towards the far shores of Naggaroth, with their weapons taken from them and numberless dark elf warriors and sorceresses between them and the dubious escape of the sea, he could understand their despair. There was no hope. None at all. They would die here, or as slaves in some dark elf city. He wished he had more of the black smoke. Everything would be better with a few whiffs of blissful oblivion.

To his right, Aethenir shifted, then raised his head and opened his eyes.

He closed them again with a groan. 'So it wasn't a dream.'

'You aren't pleased?' asked Felix sourly. 'Didn't you want to find the dark elves so we could recover the harp?'

'Do not make jokes, Herr Jaeger,' said the high elf. 'There is no hope for us now. It would have been better for us to have died by the teeth of the sea dragon, for the death the druchii give their slaves is cruel by comparison.' He shivered.

Strangely, though he had been thinking much the same thing only seconds before, hearing Aethenir say it out loud stirred Felix's contrary nature.

'While we have life there is hope,' he said, trying to sound like he meant it.

'We have no life,' said Aethenir. 'We were dead the moment the druchii net settled over our heads. Our corpses still twitch, that is all.'

Gotrek woke with a snort to Felix's left. He blinked his eye and looked around, then instinctively tried to reach over his shoulder for his axe. His chains stopped him. He tugged harder.

'It's gone, Gotrek,' said Felix.

'Where is it?'

'The dark elves took it.'

Gotrek struggled to sit up, fighting the shackles. He stopped as he looked down at his blood-caked bare arms. 'Where is my gold?'

'They took that too.'

Gotrek went still, his hands clenching so tight that the bulging of his thick wrists made his manacles creak. 'I will kill every elf in this place.'

He stood, growling, and gripped the chain that connected his wrist manacles to his ankle fetters, preparing to wrench it.

'Wait, Gotrek,' said Felix. If he was going to pretend to be hopeful, he had to pretend to do his best to turn that hope into a reality. 'We need a plan.'

'Damn all plans,' said Gotrek, wrapping the chain around his bound wrists. 'I will not be chained.'

The other prisoners were looking around sleepily at the Slayer.

'Shut up, can't you?' said a tired voice.

'Gotrek,' Felix whispered quickly. 'If you reveal your strength now, the druchii will kill you before you get a chance to use it. Hide it until we can do something useful with it.'

'What's more useful than killing druchii?'

'How many will you kill unarmed?' Felix asked. 'A few jailors? Is that enough? Wouldn't you like to die with your axe in your hands?'

Gotrek paused and turned to Felix, his eye blazing. 'Aye. I would.'

'Then wait. We may find a way to escape this cell and find it.'

'And if not?' asked Gotrek.

'Then you're more than welcome to break free and kill as many as you can.'

Gotrek grunted and let go of the chains. 'And do you have a plan, manling?'

Felix shrugged. 'Not at the moment. No.'

Aethenir raised his head. 'I know where your weapons are,' he said. 'And your gold.'

They both turned on him. 'Where?' they said, in unison.

The high elf drew back at their attention. 'Ah, that is to say, I know who has them. The corsair captain who took them. His name is Landryol Swiftwing. I overheard him say that he plans to sell your things to a collector in Karond Kar.'

'What good does that do us?' growled Gotrek.

Aethenir shrugged. 'Knowing his name, we might learn where his quarters are, and then...' He paused, then looked around the dank, crowded cell again, and the stout iron door. 'And then...' He sighed and lowered his forehead back to his knees. 'Never mind.'

'Landryol,' rumbled Gotrek, sitting down again. 'He will be the first to die when I take back my axe.'

Suddenly Aethenir's head jerked up again. 'Asuryan! I forgot!'

'What is it, high one?' asked Felix, hoping against hope that the elf had just remembered some magic spell that would miraculously get them out of this situation.

'The high sorceress,' he said, turning to them. 'She is here. I saw her as we were brought to this place!'

'I saw her too,' said Felix, remembering.

'If she is here, the harp is here!' said Aethenir. He turned to Felix. 'Perhaps we *could* recover it.'

'We'd be dead long before we reached her,' said Gotrek. 'There are foes without number between us,' he murmured, his single eye far away.

'Then we must avoid them!' cried Aethenir. 'All that matters is the harp. If we don't take it back, Ulthuan is doomed!'

Gotrek grimaced at the high elf's shrill tone. 'Good riddance,' he rasped.

Aethenir stood, angry, then staggered when his chains caught him as he tried to draw himself up to his full height. 'Dwarf! Your stupidity amazes me. If the druchii destroy us, they will come for you next and, armed with the harp, they will crush your holds one by one until there is nothing left of your race but rotting corpses in buried ruins. You must promise me–'

Gotrek swung his chained hands and knocked Aethenir's legs out from under him, then clamped his fingers around the high elf's throat. 'A dwarf makes no promise he can't keep, elf. I will seek the harp, but I will make no vow. My doom awaits me somewhere on this ark. If it finds me first, then the defenders of Ulthuan will have to fight their own battles for once.'

He shoved the high elf away with an angry grunt. The prisoners around him were looking towards him, frightened by the violent outburst.

'What of Max and Claudia?' Felix asked, trying to calm things down again. 'Do we try to save them? Or do we try only for the harp?'

Aethenir coughed and sat up, massaging his throat and glaring at Gotrek. 'We have no hope of reaching the harp without them. Their magic will help us immeasurably.'

Felix shook his head. It all sounded convoluted and impossible. 'So, let me see if I have it. If we escape the cell, we look for our weapons, then for Max and Claudia, then seek the harp and fight until we reach it or die trying. Yes?'

Aethenir nodded.

Gotrek shrugged. 'If we escape the cell.'

Felix nodded. Nice to have a plan.

They all settled back to wait for an opportunity to escape to present itself.

No such opportunity arose in the next few hours, and Felix drifted between consciousness and sleep, finding it almost impossible to distinguish between the two. The monotony of sitting there with nothing to do but breathe the foul wet air and wave away the flies was the same in either state. After a while Felix had to relieve himself and discovered that there was a narrow gutter that ran along the base of the wall. A thin stream of water trickled through it.

He paused when he saw it, all the thirst that had tormented him in the boat coming back to him now more strongly than ever. He wanted a drink more than anything he had ever wanted in the world, and yet, it was water at the bottom of a piss gutter. It turned his stomach to think of drinking it. Still, if they were going to be ready to fight when the time came – if it ever did – he would need all his strength. Perhaps it wouldn't be so bad.

He finished his business and let the water run on for a moment, then squatted down and reached a tentative hand towards the stream.

'Don't,' murmured a voice beside him.

Felix looked over. A middle-aged woman, horribly gaunt, lay on her side, looking up at him.

'It's salt,' she said. 'All the new ones make that mistake.'

Felix withdrew his hand from the gutter and nodded to her gratefully. 'Thank you.' He sighed. Salt water. The druchii truly were as cruel as they were depicted.

The woman closed her eyes and curled up again. 'They'll come with our food and water soon enough.'

Felix nodded and sat back to wait.

Another unguessable while later, there came voices and a rumble of heavy wheels from outside the door. Everyone looked up or woke up at this and crowded towards the raised bench that ran down the centre of the room, pushing and shoving to be close to it. Those too weak or too injured to move lay behind them, raising quivering hands and moaning to be brought forwards. Some didn't move at all. Felix didn't understand what it was all about, and stayed with Gotrek and Aethenir along the wall.

A key turned in the lock and the door swung open. Four druchii guards, armed with drawn swords, filed in and stood to either side. After them came a whip-wielding overseer leading six strong-looking slaves. Two of them were dwarfs, one gnarled and greying, the other very young, who carried a huge metal cauldron between them, hung from chains hooked to a long metal pole that they bore on their broad shoulders. The other four slaves were human, and they split into pairs and walked down the length of the cell carrying torches and prodding any of the prisoners that didn't move.

Gotrek growled, deep in his throat. Felix looked around to see what the matter was and found the Slayer staring at the dwarfs.

'What's the matter?' whispered Felix.

'Dwarf slaves,' rumbled Gotrek. 'The most despicable creatures in the world. They are without honour.'

Aethenir looked up at that. 'Surely even a dwarf can't blame someone for being captured by slavers.' He smiled sadly. 'We ourselves are guilty of that.'

'A dwarf should die before capture,' Gotrek snarled. 'And no true dwarf should live as a slave. He should kill himself first.'

He spat, then sat with his knees up, glaring at the dwarfs, his single eye glittering balefully. Felix decided it was wisest to keep silent on the subject, and watched them too.

The dwarfs carried the cauldron to the raised bench and then tipped it so that the contents spilled into it. Felix recoiled as he realised what was happening. The bench was in reality a food trough. They were being slopped, like pigs.

A thin grey gruel flowed down the channel and the prisoners scooped at it with their hands as it passed, daubing it into their mouths and gulping it down. Even proud Euler and his crewmen mucked in with the rest, elbowing weaker men and women out of the way. It didn't seem enough to feed them all, and it wasn't. When the dwarfs had emptied the first pot, they went out and carried in a second pot and spilled that down the trough as well.

Felix knew that there would come a time when he would be fighting for a mouthful of the muck just like all the others, but just now it turned his stomach and he stayed where he was. Gotrek and Aethenir seemed similarly disinclined to try it.

As the dwarf slaves finished pouring the slop into the trough, the human slaves continued their examination of the prisoners. If a prisoner didn't respond to their prodding, they kicked him. If there was still no response, they grabbed him by the wrists and dragged him to the door.

Felix's heart leapt when he saw this. Here was the way to escape! All they had to do was play dead and they would be taken out of the cell! His heart sank again when he saw the overseer take out a curved dagger and cut the throat of every prisoner the slaves brought to him, before allowing them to take the body out the door. So, they had thought of that one. He sighed.

The dwarf slaves went out again and returned with a third cauldron on their shoulders, but this one they did not immediately pour. Instead they waited at the end of the trough, and Felix took the time to study them. Both were strong, and both had their hair cropped to patchy stubble. They had beards too, but only just. These had also been trimmed to little more than an inch all over. Not since poor Leatherbeard had Felix seen more naked-looking dwarfs. They wore breeches and filthy aprons, but no shirts or shoes, and their eyes were as dead and emotionless as those of zombies.

After a moment, the overseer cracked the whip over his head. 'Hurry up, you filthy cattle!' he cried in Reikspiel. 'I've twelve more cells to feed!' The prisoners at the trough flinched and scooped faster.

Half a minute later, the overseer decided he had waited long enough and snapped his fingers. The two dwarf slaves lifted the last cauldron and tipped it into the trough. This time it was water that rushed down the trough, and the prisoners stuck their faces down into it and guzzled greedily.

Felix's thirst got the better of him and he shoved forwards. He couldn't yet imagine eating the food, but he needed water desperately. Gotrek and Aethenir joined him, and they squeezed to the trough. Other prisoners whined and complained when he shouldered past them, but he was too thirsty to care. He stuck his head down in the trough and sucked at the thin current of water that ran down the channel. He had never tasted anything so good in his life. Gotrek and Aethenir slurped on either side of him. They sounded like pigs. It didn't matter. Water was all that mattered.

With the last cauldron empty and the last corpse dragged from the cell, the slaves and the overseer went back out through the door, followed by the guards with drawn swords. Then the door swung shut with a clang, and Felix heard the key turn in the lock.

Gotrek raised his head from the trough and glared at the door, and Felix wondered if he was thinking about how difficult it might be to break through, or how many of the guards he could kill before they raised the alarm.

'Filth!' barked Gotrek. 'Kissers of pale arses. Your ancestors disown you.'

AFTER THE PRISONERS had drunk and licked the trough clean and settled back to their places, Felix asked the woman who had told him about the salt water how often they were fed.

'Twice a day,' she mumbled. 'Leastways, it might be. No telling the days now.'

Felix thanked her and turned to his companions. 'We have to talk to the slaves,' he said.

'The dwarfs? Never,' growled Gotrek.

'The dwarfs or the humans,' Felix insisted. 'They're our only way of finding out what's going on beyond the door. They might be able to tell us where the corsair captain lives. Where Max and Fraulein Pallenberger are.'

'And where the Harp of Ruin is,' said Aethenir.

'I'd sooner kiss a troll,' sneered Gotrek.

Felix sighed. 'Well, I'll talk to them.'

A FEW HOURS later, Felix began to regret not eating. It wasn't that the cell did anything to arouse the appetite. The reek of unwashed bodies and human waste was nauseating, the cold wet air made him shiver and sweat at the same time, and the constant pestering of the flies was enough to drive him mad. He felt fevered and close to vomiting, yet his stomach wouldn't be denied. He tried to remember the last time he had eaten. It had been before the skaven had captured them. Had that been two days ago? Three days ago? His limbs trembled with weakness just sitting there. He snapped awake several times, never realising that he had fallen asleep.

At last, several hours after Felix had given up hope of the overseer ever coming again, the sound of rumbling wheels woke the prisoners and they rushed to the trough. This time Felix, Gotrek and Aethenir joined them. Felix fought forwards to be the closest to the food slaves. It wasn't easy. Weak as he was, he was stronger than the other prisoners, whose confinement and poor diet had wasted them away, but there were more of them and they were just as desperate as he – a scrabbling mass of frenzied skeletons. Felix was elbowed in the face and kneed in the ribs as he shoved closer. They squirmed around him and under him like sickly wolves.

Then suddenly, his path was cleared. A woman with mottled bruises all over her naked arms and legs was plucked out of his way. A man in the uniform of the Marienburg coastal patrol was dragged back. Felix looked around. Gotrek had entered the fray, picking prisoners up and putting them firmly behind him. The Slayer didn't look at Felix, but he seemed to be making sure that Felix would get an opportunity to talk to the slaves. Felix said nothing. Speaking of it might anger Gotrek and make him change his mind.

With the Slayer's help he bellied up to the trough right at the end, closest to the door, harvesting a crop of dirty looks for his pains. Gotrek and Aethenir were right next to him. Euler and his crewmen, the strongest men on the left side of the pen, were directly across from him.

Euler smiled wickedly at him over the trough. 'Decided to join us for dinner this time, have you?'

Felix opened his mouth to speak, but just then the key turned in the lock and the guard and the overseer filed in, followed by the human and dwarf slaves.

He waited anxiously as the slaves carried the first cauldron to the trough, its chains creaking as it swung from the pole they shouldered. To his relief, the slaves were the same dwarfs as last time. They stepped forwards and tipped the contents of the cauldron into the trough. Felix paused as he reached down to scoop up his first mouthful. Hungry as he was, he almost backed away.

It was thin oat gruel, more water than meal, but had that been its only sin, Felix would have dug in with a will. Unfortunately, it was rotten as well, made with mouldy grain, and a sweet reek of mildew rose from it. In addition, Felix could see fat weevils and rat droppings floating in the gruel.

Felix heard Aethenir retch, but Gotrek began shovelling the stuff into his mouth with both hands. Felix did his best to follow his example, though it was an act of will to put it in his mouth and he wished he could have kept it from touching his tongue. More than once he had to fight down the urge to vomit.

He did not attempt to communicate until the dwarfs had poured the second cauldron and returned to wait by the trough with the cauldron of water. Felix shot a quick look at the overseer, who prowled impatiently near the door as he had before, then, as he bent down and pretended to scrape at the last smears of the porridge in the bottom of the trough, he spoke in low tones.

'My friends, we need your help. The fate of your homelands and holds hangs in the balance. We seek the location of the quarters of Corsair Captain Landryol Swiftwing.' Felix risked a glance up at the slaves. They were staring ahead as if they hadn't heard. He looked down again and continued. 'And also where two recently captured human wizards are being held – a man and a girl. If you have any fondness for your old lands, I beg you, bring us this information and–'

A pain like liquid fire exploded across Felix's back and he reared up, crying out.

The overseer was drawing back his whip for another strike. 'No talking, vermin! I'll have your tongue!'

The prisoners scattered away from Felix like terrified rats. Euler and his men stared at him and backed away.

The overseer lashed out again. Felix put up a hand, but the tip of the whip licked past it and striped his shoulder and neck. The pain made his eyes water, and he instinctively reached out to grab the leather strand and yank it from its wielder's hand.

Gotrek shouldered him hard and he missed.

The druchii laughed. 'That's it, human dog. Take a lesson from the rock-eater. Fight the lash and die. Obey and live.' He cracked the whip over their heads. 'Now back!

You've had your fill. For today and tomorrow. Neither of you will eat for the next two feedings.'

Felix clenched his fists with pain and rage, but forced himself to lower his head and turn away from the trough. Gotrek and Aethenir followed him. As they sat, Felix cast another glance at the cauldron slaves. Neither of them had shown any reaction when Felix had been whipped, and they remained stone-faced now, staring straight ahead as they tipped the cauldron full of water into the trough. Had they heard? Had they understood? Did they care? Would they do anything? Or were they too scared or too dulled by their years of captivity to try?

The two dwarfs emptied the cauldron, then turned to the door without a backwards glance. Felix waited until the overseer and guards had followed them out and locked the doors behind them, then let out a long-held breath.

From across the room came a cackling laugh. 'Serves you right, Jaeger! What were you playing at, you fool?'

Felix looked over and saw Euler and his men grinning savagely at them. He grunted and turned away, probing gently at the whip cut on his neck. 'I hope that was worth it.'

Aethenir shook his head. 'The slaves will do nothing. They are too cowed. They have lived too long under the lash.'

'And we will have to wait two feedings to learn one way or the other,' said Felix bitterly. He looked at the high elf. 'At least you will get to eat tomorrow.'

Aethenir made a face. 'A debatable pleasure,' he said.

The Slayer shrugged and motioned for them to return to the trough. 'Water is more important than food. Drink.'

* * *

FELIX WONDERED HOW he was going to survive without eating again for a full day. He had managed to choke down only a few handfuls of the miserable porridge, and he was hungry again almost immediately after he had finished it. The thirst was excruciating as well. His head throbbed with it, the pain a dull counterpoint to the singing agony of his whip cuts, which prevented him from leaning against the wall or lying on his back.

When he heard the rumble of wheels again he almost couldn't bear it. He fought the urge to charge the trough and get as much gruel down his throat as he could before they pulled him away. But he couldn't do that. If they wanted to have any hope of getting information from the slaves, he had to make the overseer forget he existed.

He wondered if that would be possible. The druchii looked his way as soon as he came in the door, then laughed when he saw that Felix and Gotrek were staying away from the trough.

'Good dogs,' he said. 'A slave who is quick to learn can rise high with us. Just ask these fellows.' He turned and slapped the shoulder of the younger dwarf slave as he was pouring the gruel into the trough, causing him to slop some on the ground in surprise.

The druchii hissed and clubbed the dwarf on the back of the head with the brass-pommelled handle of his whip. 'Clumsy cur! Dare you waste food?'

The dwarf lowered his head and said nothing, merely continuing to hold the cauldron steady as he poured, though blood ran down the back of his head to his neck. Felix heard Gotrek growl at this, and his fists clenched, but he remained where he was.

After that, the overseer's anger seemed sated, and he returned to pacing impatiently as the slaves went back for the second cauldron and the prisoners gobbled and slurped noisily at their meal. Felix was disgusted with himself when he realised he was envious of them.

As the dwarf slaves waited with the cauldron of water and the human slaves dragged the morning's bodies away, Gotrek did a strange thing. He hadn't moved or said a word since the overseer had struck the young dwarf, but now he leaned forwards and, without looking up, slapped the filthy floor three times, then twice more.

The noise was hardly loud enough to be heard over the noise of the prisoners feeding, and no one seemed to notice. Felix was about to ask him what he was doing, but the Slayer shook his head. After a few seconds, he slapped the floor again, no louder than before, and in the same pattern. And then once more a few seconds later.

The third time, for the briefest of seconds, the dwarf slaves' eyes flicked up, wide, then dropped again instantly. The older dwarf frowned and stared fixedly at the trough, but the younger dwarf's eyes suddenly looked alive. Felix looked from the two dwarfs to Gotrek, unsure what had just happened. Then he saw the younger dwarf's finger silently tapping on the rim of the cauldron. Was it the same rhythm, or was it just idle motion? Felix glanced nervously at the overseer. The druchii didn't seem to have noticed the exchange.

'Don't look, manling,' Gotrek muttered under his breath.

Felix looked away, though his curiosity was killing him. Gotrek patted the floor again, much softer than before, and in new and different patterns. It reminded Felix of something, but he couldn't quite place it.

A moment later, the overseer snapped his fingers, and the slaves poured the water into the trough and left, followed quickly by the overseer and the guards. Felix waited impatiently until he heard the lock turn and the rumble of wheels fade away, then turned to Gotrek.

'What was that?' he asked. 'What passed between you?'

Gotrek stood and started pushing to the trough. 'Water first,' he said.

Felix grunted with annoyance, but followed Gotrek. Aethenir came too, and they all drank as much as they could, as well as scraping up the few meagre grains of gruel the others had left.

When they had finished, Gotrek sat back down near the wall. 'The mine code,' he said. 'For talking through walls with picks and hammers.'

Felix slapped his forehead. 'Yes! I remember now. Hamnir used it to communicate with the dwarfs inside the lost... hold...' He trailed off as Gotrek turned a cold, angry eye on him, and Felix realised that it was the first time he had mentioned Gotrek's former friend in his presence since they had left Karak Hirn. Apparently the wound was still fresh. Fear and embarrassment made him flush. 'I'm sorry,' he said quickly. 'I didn't mean to interrupt. What did you tell them?'

Gotrek gave an angry snort. 'I told them that they were cowardly oathbreakers who should have taken their own lives rather than become slaves to elves. Then I told them to tell me where our weapons are, and where Max and the girl and the harp are, the next time they come, or I'd return to their holds and let their clans know what had become of them.'

Aethenir sniffed derisively. 'That's sure to get results.'

'You told them all that in a few slaps?' asked Felix, incredulous.

Gotrek shrugged. 'More or less.' He lay down on his side and closed his eye. 'Now we wait and see.'

* * *

FELIX FOUND IT hard to be so calm about it. He was restless and jumpy, hunger gnawing at his belly while impatience gnawed at his mind. He started wondering what they would do with the information if they got it. Could they even break out of the cell? With Gotrek's strength and fighting prowess, he didn't doubt it, but how far would they get after that? He could not remember the way from the harbour to the slave pens or how many guards were beyond the cell door. His brain had been too fogged with the smoke of the black lotus at the time, and none of it linked together.

His restlessness and the pain from his whip cuts wouldn't let him sleep, so he got up and shuffled as quietly as he could to the door. There was a viewing port in it about the size of a playing card. The chain between his wrists and his ankles was so short he could barely lift his head high enough, and he had to twist it at an uncomfortable angle to see out into the area outside the cell.

It was a square room lined with cell doors. At the far end, a narrow area was separated off from the rest by a cage of iron bars that protected the door to the hallway and two smaller doors. The main area was further divided by low wooden walls that were meant to channel prisoners from the cage door to the doors of the various cells. The hallway door was a lattice of bars through which he could see a short hall that led to a larger torchlit area in the distance. That was as far as he could see, but he vaguely remembered that they had come into the torchlit area by coming down some stairs.

He sighed. That stairway might as well have been on Morrslieb. There were at least three locked doors between him and it – the cell door, the cage door and the hallway door – and there were guards to deal with as well. In the left-hand room beyond the cage he could see the office where the robed clerk worked, while in the right-hand room he could see half a dozen guards lounging. The gods only knew how many more might guard the stairway.

He almost gave up and went back to the wall to sit with Gotrek and Aethenir, but if they were going to try something, it would be imperative to know everything they could about the world beyond the cell. He watched a little longer, though it was putting a terrible crick in his neck. Nothing happened. The guards laughed and occasionally walked through the caged area to speak to the clerk in the other room, but that was all.

Felix lowered his head and crouched beside the door. This wasn't telling him enough. He needed to see what happened when the food came, which guards had keys, what doors were opened and when. He sighed and sat down to wait.

He found that the other prisoners were all looking at him, wondering what he was doing. Euler's gang were glaring at him and whispering amongst themselves. But after a while, when he did nothing but sit, they lost interest and returned to sleeping or staring at nothing.

Felix did his fair share of sleeping and staring as well, but finally, after what seemed to his tortured mind to have been several weeks, he heard the rumble of distant wheels and commotion among the guards. He pushed himself back to his feet, groaning at the stiffness in his shackled arms and legs, and raised his eye cautiously to the little port again.

The hallway door was swinging out, and one of the druchii guards was opening the cage door with a key. Eight other guards stepped into the main area of the room, then turned and watched as the overseer and a procession of carts rolled in from the hall. There were three carts, and the first two were enormous – taller than a dark elf and consisting of sturdy wooden frames from which hung the heavy iron cauldrons that held the gruel and the water. Dwarf slaves pushed these, straining mightily. The third cart was an empty box on wheels, pushed by humans, and Felix couldn't think what it was for until he remembered that the human slaves took dead bodies out of the cells.

Once the eight guards and the overseer and the carts were all inside the main area of the room, a guard at the cage door locked it behind them. Four of the guards remained near the door, watching, while the other four travelled with the overseer and the carts as they began to move from cell to cell. Felix watched the whole process unhappily. The druchii weren't taking any chances. The hallway door and the cage door had been locked before any of the cell doors were opened, and the guard with the key to the cage door remained outside it, and Felix wasn't sure who had the key to the exit door or how it was opened.

He sighed and went back to Gotrek and Aethenir. It wouldn't do for the overseer to find him crouching by the door.

'What did you see, manling?' asked Gotrek.

As briefly as he could, Felix sketched out the layout of the central chamber and the guards who stood between them and the exit.

'It's impossible,' moaned Aethenir.

Gotrek stroked his beard thoughtfully.

Then the cart wheels rumbled close and the prisoners rushed to the trough. Aethenir looked as if he meant to stay with Gotrek and Felix, who were still on starvation punishment, but Gotrek pushed him forwards.

'Go,' he said. 'Can't have you weaker than you already are.'

Aethenir made a face, but he went.

Felix waited in anxious anticipation as the key turned in the lock. If Gotrek had got through to the dwarf slaves, they might have brought them information. But when he looked at them, Felix moaned with disappointment. Neither of them looked their way, nor did they betray any signs of nervousness. They weren't tapping their fingers or feet. They weren't doing anything except their job, emptying the cauldron of watery meal into the trough and going back for the second.

'Eyes down, manling,' murmured Gotrek.

Felix forced himself to look at the floor, though it killed him to do it. He wanted to know.

Beside him, Gotrek patted the floor as he had done before, then waited. Felix's ears strained. Had he heard a faint tap-tap in response? With the sounds of shuffling and slobbering that filled the room it was hard to tell. Several times he caught himself in the act of looking up and jerked his head back down.

Finally it was over and the slaves and the guards filed out. Gotrek gave a grunt of satisfaction as the door slammed shut once again and Felix looked up at him.

'Well?' he asked.

Gotrek nodded. 'I know the way to our weapons and to Max and the girl.'

'You know the way?' asked Aethenir. 'You mean you can lead us there?'

'Aye,' said Gotrek.

The high elf looked amazed. 'How is that possible?'

'That is the purpose of the code,' said Gotrek. 'Guiding dwarfs through mines at a distance.'

'But what about the Harp of Ruin?' Aethenir asked. 'Do you know where it lies?'

Gotrek shook his head. 'They didn't know. They hadn't heard of it.'

Aethenir hung his head. 'Of course they wouldn't. They are only slaves after all.' He sighed. 'Well, it is a beginning. Perhaps we can question some druchii along the way.'

Gotrek chuckled evilly. 'Aye. Good idea.'

They all looked up as they heard the rattling of chains coming their way. Euler was shuffling towards them with One-Ear and Broken-Nose at his back. He stopped in front of them and looked down, a suspicious look on his jowly, unshaven face.

'What are you up to, Jaeger?' he asked.

Felix did his best to look uncomprehending. 'What do you mean?'

'Don't think we haven't noticed,' Euler sneered. 'Trying to talk to the slaves. Looking out the window. Whispering to each other. You're thinking about making a break.'

'Doesn't every prisoner?' said Felix.

'It's impossible,' Euler snorted. 'We had a look too, the first day. You'll never get past the cage. Even if you do, the second door will stop you cold. Do you know how it opens?'

'I haven't a clue,' said Felix, trying to sound uninterested, though it would indeed be nice to know.

'There's no key – just a lever inside the clerk's office,' said Euler. 'We saw it when they brought us in. He looks through a little window into the hall and only pulls it if all's well. You haven't a chance.'

'If you didn't think we had a chance,' rumbled Gotrek, 'you wouldn't be pestering us.'

Euler smiled slyly. 'Ah, so you *are* thinking about it.'

Gotrek looked up at him, his face expressionless. 'And if we were?'

Euler exchanged a look with his men, then turned back to him and leaned in. 'If you can get us to the harbour, we can get you away.'

Felix's heart leapt. He had been prepared to die when there didn't seem to be any option, but if Euler could get them off the ark...

'How?' he said, perhaps too eagerly.

Euler glanced at his men again, then shrugged. 'I suppose there's no harm, seeing as you couldn't manage it without us.' He squatted down and began drawing with his fingernail in the filth of the floor. 'That tunnel that leads to the underground harbour,' he said. 'Very clever. Hard to find if you don't know it's there. Keeps the weather out too. But...' He tapped his sketch. 'It's very narrow. If one were to sink a ship in it, all the rest would be bottled up tight.' He smiled up at Felix. 'You help us get to a ship, we'll get you home, Herr Jaeger.'

It could work, thought Felix. We might be able to leave after all! Then he paused. 'Didn't you say you would settle what was between us if we escaped?'

Euler looked embarrassed at that, then shrugged. 'I'm prepared to put that aside if you are, Herr Jaeger. What are petty grievances in a situation like this? We need each other.'

'Well, then I...' Felix paused again and looked over at Gotrek. What would the Slayer think of him leaving? Would he count it as a betrayal? As cowardice?

The Slayer didn't seem to notice his hesitation. He turned to Euler. 'Are you prepared to fight when the time comes?'

'Oh aye,' Euler said. 'If you can get us through the doors we'll fight every long-ear between here and freedom.'

Gotrek nodded. 'Then we have a deal.'

Euler smiled. 'Excellent. Just give us the nod when you're ready.' He inclined his head to Gotrek and Felix, then turned and shuffled away, his men flanking him.

'WE CAN'T TRUST him,' said Felix, when Euler had returned to his own side of the cell. 'He still wants his vengeance, despite all his smiles.'

'We can trust him as far as the harbour,' said Gotrek. 'And we need him no further, unless you mean to go with him.'

Felix paused, his face flushing. 'I... I haven't decided.'

'You swore to record my death, manling,' Gotrek said. 'Not to die with me. I won't stop you.'

Felix bit his lip, still conflicted. Every sensible part of his brain was saying that he should go with Euler, but his loyalty to Gotrek and his desire to see the story to the end were once again making him think twice.

Just then, the key turned in the lock. Everyone looked up, because it had been much too short a time for another feeding and they hadn't heard the rumble of the cauldron carts. The door opened and a double file of uniformed druchii marched in, longswords drawn. There were eight of them, each with an elven rune stitched into the breast of his dark purple surcoat. They moved with grace and precision, holding themselves erect and alert. Felix marked them as several cuts above the guards who usually visited the cell.

They were followed by two richly dressed druchii who held scented pomanders to their noses. A handful of slaves accompanied them, some carrying witchlight torches and others brooms. The male druchii was shorter than most elves Felix had so far seen, and with a weaker chin. He wore a heavily brocaded black coat over a dark red velvet jerkin and had so many rings on his fingers that Felix was surprised he could lift his hands to his face. The rune the guards wore was stitched into his jerkin as well. The female was beautiful in a heavy-lidded, sleepy sort of way, and wore a massive sable fur coat over a sea-green silk slip that hugged her voluptuous body and seemed more suited for the boudoir than the slave pen. Her hair was piled on top of her head and held in place by what looked like half a dozen miniature stilettos.

The man bowed the woman into the cell and then snapped his fingers. Two of the slaves hurried forwards and swept and scraped the stone floor in front of them clear of filth and then sprinkled what smelled like rose-water on the bare flags. The couple stepped fastidiously into the cleared area, then the man snapped his fingers again, and two larger slaves pushed into the huddled mass of prisoners, shoving a witchlight torch into the dark corners of the cell.

While they waited, the two druchii chatted to each other in their own tongue, occasionally laughing or shaking their heads at something the other had said. Felix looked to Aethenir and saw that the high elf was concentrating very hard on what they were saying.

After a moment, the two big slaves dragged a handful of young girls and boys out of the crowd, shoving back their wailing mothers and fathers, and brought them before the druchii. The man gestured to the children like a horse trader trying to sell a horse, seemingly pointing out height and build and other qualities. The woman ignored the man's words and gave each of the children a thorough going over, pulling back their lips to see their teeth, snapping her fingers in front of their eyes and watching them blink. Then she gestured to the slaves and they tore the children's clothes off one by one and turned them roughly around in front of her. An angry murmur rippled through the cell.

Felix's hands clenched, and his heart thudded in his chest. He heard Gotrek rumbling beside him like an angry bear.

Felix leaned in to Aethenir. 'Is she buying them?' he asked.

Aethenir nodded. 'She is from a brothel. The other druchii owns us.'

'A brothel!' Felix wanted to leap across the cell and strangle both of them, and he must have given in to the urge, because suddenly Gotrek was holding him back.

'Easy, manling,' he murmured. 'Now is not the time.'

'But they're taking children,' whispered Felix.

'And they'll take them just the same after they've killed you,' said Gotrek. 'Save your strength until it can do some good, you said.'

Felix sat back again reluctantly. How was it possible to sit by when he knew what would be done to those children? And yet Gotrek was right, attacking now was futile. He would be cut down and the children still taken. He watched in sullen silence as the druchii woman examined each of them from top to bottom, rejecting more than half of them for various flaws – scars, sickness, deformity or insufficient beauty – the lucky ones.

When she was done with the first batch, another few were brought up, and another, until the slaves had worked their way through the whole room, and the woman had seventeen boys and girls lined up behind her.

Men and women screamed and rushed forwards as the slaver's slaves began leading the children out.

'You won't take my daughter!' roared one man.

'Animals!' cried a woman. 'Beasts! What are you going to do to them?'

The prisoners were kicked back and bludgeoned down by the slaver's guards, who did not bother to use their swords on such weak foes. The parents fell back weeping and cursing as the children were prodded out and the druchii and their guards followed.

Felix shuddered with horror and loathing as the door clanged shut again. He ought to have done something, but he couldn't think what.

Aethenir sighed and ran his broken fingers through his filthy hair. 'Most disturbing.'

Felix nearly hit him. 'Children are sold into prostitution and all you can say is "most disturbing"?'

The high elf shook his head. 'I wasn't speaking of that. I was speaking of what the druchii said.'

Felix snarled. 'What could they have said that would be more disturbing than that?'

Aethenir raised his head and looked at him. 'They are angry with Lord Tarlkhir, the commander of this ark, because he has acquiesced to the wishes of High Sorceress Heshor – the leader of the sorceresses we met in the sunken city – and is sailing the ark to the Sea of Manann, instead of home to Naggaroth. They fear the delay will cause them to be frozen out of the Sea of Chill and unable to return until spring, something that will lose them both much business.'

Felix raised an eyebrow. 'We are sailing back to the Sea of Manann? Why?'

Aethenir shrugged. 'The slaver didn't know, but the whore had heard a rumour from one of her customers that High Sorceress Heshor intended to somehow close off the sea. She didn't know how this would be done, but I believe I can guess. It appears the sorceress wants to test her new toy.'

Felix's eyes widened with horror. 'She's going to use the harp to raise the land at the mouth of the sea! By Sigmar, it's…' His mind boggled at the consequences of such an act. Blocking the Sea of Manann would cut off Marienburg from all trade, which would in turn cut off the Empire from all trade. The country would be landlocked. 'She will have destroyed the economy of the Empire in one blow,' he said when he could speak again. 'She will do more damage than even Archaon did!'

'And it won't be just trade she destroys,' said Aethenir. 'The tidal waves and earthquakes created when so much land suddenly thrusts up out of the sea will undoubtedly swamp and shatter Marienburg, and the storm surge could travel up the Reik all the way to Altdorf and beyond, flooding as it goes.'

Felix stared at him. 'Fraulein Pallenberger's prophecy.'

'Indeed,' said the elf.

FIFTEEN

'WE HAVE TO destroy the harp,' said Felix, his heart racing. 'It is no longer a matter of fighting our way out and hoping. We *must* reach it.'

'Aye,' said Gotrek.

'How quickly one's attitude changes when one's own lands are in danger,' said Aethenir dryly.

'Never mind that,' said Felix impatiently. 'How do we do it?' He looked up at the roof of the cell. 'This high sorceress must surely keep it with her, somewhere above us, but where?'

'She will live among the highest of the high, for in the hierarchy of druchii society, her rank is even above that of the commander of this ark.'

'So how do we reach her?' asked Felix.

'We do not,' said Aethenir. 'It is impossible.'

'Nothing is impossible,' growled Gotrek.

'Certainly it could be accomplished by an army,' said Aethenir. 'But not by us. The druchii are often as much at war with each other as they are with the world, and so their houses and palaces are guarded against invasions and assassinations of all kinds. There will be a hundred guarded gates between here and her, and thousands of druchii going about their business on the streets – every one of which will know us for intruders. We will never make it.'

Felix shot him a look. 'I thought you were the one who was urging us to go?'

Aethenir nodded his head. 'It must be tried, if I am to remain on the path of honour, but we have no chance of success.'

'No wonder you're a dying race,' muttered Gotrek.

Felix had to agree. 'Perhaps we'd have a better chance if you put your great scholar's mind to work on a solution instead of bemoaning our fate.'

The elf sniffed. 'I shall think on it.'

'Well, don't take too long,' said Felix. 'Who knows how close we are to the Manaanspoort Sea.'

They fell silent as each began mulling the problem over in their heads. Mad ideas came to Felix – schemes out of the worst sort of melodrama.

They would wait until the slaver came back, then kill all his guards, dress Aethenir up in one of their uniforms, then deliver themselves to the high sorceress. No. Could even Gotrek kill eight armed guards barehanded? And even if he could, what were the odds the slaver would come back before the ark reached the Manaanspoort Sea?

They would fake their deaths so well that the overseer wouldn't bother cutting their throats, and escape after they had been wheeled out with the other bodies. No. The overseer cut every corpse's throat, regardless.

They would tell the overseer that Aethenir was a lore-master of Hoeth, who could tell the high sorceress secrets of Ulthuan's magical defences if they brought him before her. No. Even if they were believed, the overseer would take Aethenir away and leave Gotrek and Felix behind.

Felix hung his head in despair. He could think of nothing. Aethenir was right. It was impossible. They had too little knowledge of what was outside their cell. There was no way to make realistic plans. They didn't even know if they could get past the first three gates.

He looked up at Aethenir and Gotrek. They didn't seem to be having any better luck. Aethenir just sat there, running his fingers through his filthy hair and murmuring over and over again. 'I must stay on the path. I must stay on the path.'

Gotrek just stared ahead, his single eye blank and distant, cracking his knuckles absent-mindedly.

Felix sighed and sat back, closing his eyes, determined to go through it again. There had to be some way. There had to be.

FELIX WOKE TO Gotrek grunting and sitting up. He opened his eyes and looked around. Nothing appeared to have changed. The prisoners lay coughing and moaning and snoring on the ground as usual. There were no strange sounds from outside the cell. The key was not turning in the lock, and yet Gotrek was looking around, alert and awake.

'What's happened?' Felix mumbled sleepily.

'The ark has stopped,' said Gotrek.

'Stopped?' said Felix. 'How do you know?'

'Trust me, manling,' said Gotrek. 'A dwarf's stomach knows when a ship sails – and when it doesn't.'

Felix's heart dropped. 'Then we've reached the Sea of Manann,' he whispered. 'We're out of time!'

On the other side of Felix, Aethenir raised his head. 'What do you say? The ark has stopped?'

Gotrek nodded as he stood. 'We must act now.'

Felix groaned but nodded, resigned. They had no choice.

Aethenir sat up and pushed the hair out of his eyes. 'You assume much, dwarf. Can we be certain this is why we have stopped? It might be for another reason.'

'It might be,' said Felix, getting to his feet beside Gotrek. 'But can we risk it if it isn't? The sorceress might play the harp at any moment. We may already be too late.'

'But we still have no plan,' said the high elf, querulous. 'It won't work.'

'Then we will die gloriously,' said Gotrek, gathering his chains in his hands. 'There are two hours to the evening feeding. We will go then, and fight until they kill us.'

Felix looked at him. 'You'll wait two hours?'

Gotrek looked towards the cell door. 'It would take me more than two hours to get through that door with no tools, and they would stop me in two minutes. We have to wait.' He stood up sharply and the chain that connected his wrists to his ankles snapped like it was made of dry biscuit.

Aethenir sighed. 'I had hoped for a chance to rectify my sin. This will only be pointless death.'

Gotrek glared at him as he strained to snap the chains between his wrists. 'Better a pointless death than a life of shame.' The chains parted with a bright ping. He turned to Felix and broke his chains for him in a matter of seconds. 'Tell Euler to bring his men and I'll do the same for them.'

Felix nodded, but first he stood tall and stretched, raising his arms over his head. It felt glorious! Then he walked through the crowd and around the trough to the other side of the room. Taking long strides was another joy. He felt like he had been living like an old man for the last few days, hunched over and eating gruel. He felt more optimistic already.

Euler and some of his men were playing a game with pebbles and a circle scratched in the floor. The others slept or stared at the walls.

The balding pirate looked up at him as he approached, noting his dangling chains. 'So it's time then, Jaeger?'

'Yes,' said Felix. 'We go when the cart comes again. Go to Gotrek and he'll break your chains.'

Euler's men cheered at this and started to stand. Felix was about to turn and go back to Gotrek when he paused and faced Euler again.

'Uh, Euler.'

'Aye?' said the merchant, struggling to his feet.

'Listen to me a moment,' said Felix. 'The druchii sorceresses you fought. They have a weapon – the Harp of Ruin – a magical instrument that can raise and lower mountains. They mean to use it to close off the Manaanspoort Sea.'

'Eh?' said Euler. 'What's this?'

Some of his men were turning to listen.

'They're going to raise the sea floor and block the mouth of the sea,' said Felix. 'It will cause a tidal wave that will destroy Marienburg and possibly Altdorf, not to mention stop all ship trade.'

'Is this a joke, Jaeger?' said Euler. 'Because I don't find it amusing.'

Felix shook his head. 'It's no joke. It is the reason we tricked you into going after the sorceresses in the first place – to try to wrest it from them before they could use it.' He looked Euler in the eye. 'They are going to use it now, unless we stop them. Will you help us? Will you fight with us to the top of the ark and find the sorceress and the harp?'

'What?' Euler snorted. 'That's suicide.'

'Yes,' said Felix.

Euler held up a hand and turned away. 'Sorry, Herr Jaeger. No heroes here. We part at the harbour as planned.'

'Can you really stand by and watch Marienburg destroyed?' asked Felix angrily. 'That is what will happen if the sorceress unleashes the power of the harp. Your city will be swept away. Your precious trading empire will be no more.'

Euler shrugged. 'What will I care if I die helping you?'

'Have you no family there? Will you allow them to die by your cowardice?'

The pirate looked up, glaring, his chains rattling as he balled his fists. 'You fooled me once with your lies, you wrecker, but I won't be fooled again. If you want to go above decks looking for treasure, or whatever it is you're after, that's your business, but you won't drag me into it again. I'm not going to sacrifice my life and my men for the sake of your greed.' He laughed, sharp and angry. 'A harp that raises mountains. You couldn't think of a better lie than that?'

He shouldered past Felix and started around the trough towards Gotrek, his men following, though some of them looked back, frowning thoughtfully.

Felix sighed, wondering if he should try one more time to convince Euler. There didn't seem to be any point. The man's heart was so larcenous that he could not believe that everyone else wasn't larcenous at heart as well.

He shuffled back towards Gotrek behind the pirates. The Slayer had snapped Aethenir's chains and was now surrounded by a crowd of prisoners, amazed by this feat of strength. They pushed in on all sides, men and women holding out their wrists towards him. Gotrek snapped them as they came, untiring – three sharp pulls freeing each one.

Then Euler's men pushed through the weaker prisoners and stepped up to Gotrek, grinning. Gotrek snapped their chains too, not even looking up to see who he was freeing.

Felix looked around at the throng of prisoners pushing forwards. Most of them were so malnourished and weak that they could barely stand. Only a few were better than animated corpses. They would be worth hardly anything in a fight. Still, without Euler and his men, Felix, Aethenir and Gotrek were only three, and three wouldn't get far alone.

Felix pushed through the crowd and stood beside Gotrek to address them. 'The dark elves mean to destroy Marienburg and the Empire,' he said. 'If you can swing a sword, we need volunteers to help stop them. It will be death, but you will be saving your families back home.'

Only a very few came forwards. Most seemed too numbed to understand what he was saying, and only wanted to be able to move their arms and legs.

Felix sighed and let it go. He had tried.

THE KEY TURNED in the lock and the four guards filed in, swords drawn as usual. Felix looked nervously at his fellow prisoners, hoping they wouldn't jump too soon. If anything, they hesitated too long, watching nervously as human slaves started through the room, looking for bodies, and the dwarf slaves trudged in, the heavy cauldron hanging by its chains from the iron pole between them. Gotrek, Felix and Aethenir started for the trough, shuffling and holding their wrists together to hide that their chains were broken as, on the other side of the trough, Euler and his biggest men did the same, taking the positions closest to the cauldron. The rest of the prisoners surged in behind them. Most of them remembered to keep their wrists and ankles together.

Felix exchanged nervous nods with Euler and Aethenir as the dwarf slaves stepped up to the trough and started to tip the cauldron. This was it. Much as he would have liked to, they could not wait to eat. Their deception would be discovered as soon as they tried to dip their hands in the gruel.

With an animal roar, Gotrek leapt up and shoved the young dwarf back. The slave staggered back, the iron pole slipping off his shoulders and the cauldron slamming to the floor, splashing gruel. Before the overseer or the guards understood what was happening, Gotrek grabbed the big pot by its chains and swung it around him as the dwarfs dived away, alarmed. The overseer shouted, running in, only to be smashed to the floor by the thing, his knees a shattered ruin.

The guards cried out, raising their swords, but Felix, Euler and the others were moving and mobbed two of them, dragging them to the floor and smashing their heads on the flagstones. The other two foolishly stepped into the arc of Gotrek's spinning cauldron and were knocked flat, arms and ribs broken. Gruel slopped everywhere. The corpse collectors also turned, calling out in surprise, but the prisoners jumped them and dragged them down.

Aethenir wisely stayed out of the way.

Felix rose again and saw that the overseer was trying to push himself off the floor, scrabbling for his sword. Felix leapt on him and slammed him back down with all his weight, then snatched the druchii's dagger from his belt and stabbed it into his stomach, jerking it up under his ribs.

'That's for the whip cut,' he hissed in his ear as he died.

He took the overseer's sword and tore the key ring from his belt. He tossed it to one of the other prisoners. 'Open the other pens when we go.'

He looked around. Euler and the others were finishing off the two guards they had dragged down, and Gotrek was raising the cauldron and dropping it on the head of the second guard he had flattened. The druchii's skull cracked with a sickening pop. The other one's brains were already oozing across the flagstones. The prisoners had killed the corpse collectors.

Felix shook his head, amazed. They had done it! No more than thirty seconds had passed and the guards and the overseer were dead. But now there were shouted questions from the room outside – the four backup guards. Felix turned to the door as Euler, One-Ear, Broken-Nose and one of the other crewmen armed themselves with the dead guards' swords. Gotrek took up the iron pole that the slaves had used to carry the cauldron. Felix swallowed, afraid of what came next. This fight had only been the beginning, and already his limbs were trembling from exhaustion and hunger. He felt too weak to lift the sword.

'Slayer,' said the young dwarf slave, standing and bowing before Gotrek. 'Let me come with you. I can help you find your way.'

'Farnir, you fool!' said the older dwarf. 'The masters will kill you!'

Gotrek pushed the young dwarf aside. 'You already told me the way, oathbreaker,' he said, then gathered up the chains of the cauldron in his left hand and started for the door, holding the iron pole in his right hand and dragging the heavy pot behind him with his left like it was the head of some giant's flail.

Felix and Euler pushed out into the big room after him, the pirate crew hard behind and Aethenir timidly bringing up the rear. The four backup guards were advancing warily towards the open cell, swords out, while three more guards and the clerk watched and cried questions from behind the cage. The two huge carts sat near the cell doors, each loaded with giant cauldrons. Two well-muscled dwarf slaves stood by one, staring in amazement.

The four guards shouted and charged forwards, raising their swords. Gotrek roared in response and again swung the mighty cauldron around himself, then let go of the chains. It flew towards the guards, bowling one over and sending the others leaping over the low wooden rails that divided up the room. Felix, Euler and the others rushed forwards to attack them before they recovered.

Felix hacked one of them in the neck as he tried to rise, then parried a wild slash from another. His arm was so weak the second druchii's blow almost drove his sword back into his face. He fell back, blocking another stronger attack by a hair's breadth. Felix cursed. It seemed even lowly druchii prison guards were better, faster swords than he. He made a desperate chop at the guard's flickering blade and knew it wouldn't be enough, but then an iron pole slashed down and crushed the druchii's head like an egg.

Felix looked around. Gotrek was roaring past him to where Euler and three of his men were trying to bring down the last guard, who fought them furiously.

One of the pirates stumbled back, screaming, his guts spilling from a tear in his belly. Gotrek shoved him aside and slammed the yoke down on the druchii's arm, snapping it and knocking his sword to the ground. The pirates ran the druchii through, then hacked him to pieces in a release of pent-up fury.

Behind the melee, the prisoners were stumbling out of the cell and blinking around in somnambulant wonder. The prisoner Felix had given the ring of keys to opened another cell door and waved his arms at those within.

'Free! You're free!' he cried.

Felix wondered for a brief second if he was doing the poor, half-starved wretches any favours freeing them. They would probably be killed by the guards for escaping. There was no time to think about it.

The pirates took the swords and daggers from the dead guards and advanced on the cage. Gotrek and Felix joined them, pushing to the fore, just in time to see the three guards spill from the guard room holding odd-looking crossbows. The clerk had vanished into the other room, and Felix heard the brazen clangour of an alarm bell.

Gotrek, Felix and the others slammed into the cage bars, stabbing through them at the guards, who jumped back out of reach and fired their crossbows. One missed Felix by a hair's breadth, and one of the pirates fell back, screaming and clutching his face. Felix's stomach dropped when he saw new bolts appear in the slots of the bows and the bowstrings draw back by themselves. They would be slaughtered!

Felix and the pirates swiped at the guards with their swords, but only Gotrek, with the length of the iron pole, could touch them. He knocked the crossbow out of one guard's hands and struck another on the shoulder, ruining his aim.

The guard with the keys on his belt fired at the Slayer, but Gotrek ducked and the bolt struck a prisoner. The Slayer stabbed at the key guard again, but missed. He dodged back, turning for the guard room door with his companions, who were realising too late that they should have stayed back. Gotrek flailed after him with the pole, but hit another instead, knocking him to the floor.

Cursing, Felix shoved up to the bars, reversed the overseer's dagger in his hand and flung it end over end. The knife struck the key guard pommel-first on the back of the head and he careened off the wall to fall to the floor next to the other fallen guard.

'Good work, manling,' said Gotrek.

Unfortunately, the blows hadn't been enough to knock either guard out. They started picking themselves up again instantly, but they had fallen too close to the bars of the cage and the pirates ran them through as they stood. The key guard collapsed to the floor again, his left foot tantalisingly within reach.

Felix shot an arm through the bars, reaching for the druchii's ankle as the last guard grabbed him under the arms and tried to pull him back into the guard room. Felix pulled the other way, grunting with effort, the guard's ankle slipping from his grip. Then Gotrek's yoke shot forwards and poked the last guard in the chest. He fell back, sucking wind.

Felix pulled for all he was worth – which wasn't much just then – and dragged the dead guard an arm's length closer to the bars. He let go and reached for the keys. They were just an inch from his fingertips.

The last guard sat up, gasping, and crawled forwards to grab his dead comrade's arms again, but with a thwack that made Felix's ears ring, Gotrek's yoke came down across the druchii's shoulders and dropped him to the floor.

Felix pulled again on the dead guard's ankle and brought him another foot closer. He thrust out his hand and this time closed his fingers around the key ring. It had two keys. He ripped it off the guard's belt and pulled it through the bars, then tossed it to Aethenir, who hovered anxiously behind the pirates.

The high elf stepped to the cage door as Felix, Gotrek and the pirates kept their eyes on the doors. He tried one key. It didn't work. Euler cursed.

He tried the other and there was a satisfying click. Euler and Felix shoved past him, slamming the door open and stabbing all the fallen guards again just to be sure.

As the pirates stripped the dead guards of their swords and crossbows and pushed past to loot the guard room, Gotrek stumped to the exit door, a lattice of heavy iron slats, and shook it. It barely rattled. Through it Felix could see worrying movement at the end of a short corridor.

'Come on, dwarf,' snapped Euler uneasily. 'Don't tell me we're finished before we've begun. I thought you had a plan.'

Gotrek examined the edges of the door with care, ignoring him. Both the lock and the hinges were hidden behind the fitted stone of the door frame.

'Damned dwarf slaves built too well for their masters,' the Slayer growled. 'Might be tougher than I thought.'

A black-shafted arrow glanced off a slat and rattled into the room. A few more clattered off the lattice, but did not come in. Felix jerked back and looked through the door again. Half a dozen guards were lined up at the end of the short corridor, aiming repeating crossbows at them.

'Manann's depths,' groaned Euler. 'We're done for.'

'Not yet. Come on.' Gotrek turned away from the door and jogged back into the larger portion of the room, pushing through the milling crowd of freed prisoners and striding for the massive cauldron carts. 'And clear the door!' he called.

Felix, Euler and his pirates trotted after the Slayer, curious. Gotrek checked both carts. Each was taller than a man, and each carried twelve of the cauldrons – six below and six above – all hanging by their chains from stout wooden racks built into a heavy frame. On the first cart – the one that had fed their cell – all but two of the cauldrons were empty, but on the second cart, all were full.

'This one,' said the Slayer, slapping it. 'Turn it round.'

Felix and a few of the pirates inched the heavily laden cart until it faced the door as Gotrek stepped to the other cart and lifted one of the empty cauldrons off its rack. He carried it to the full cart and used the chains to hook it to the front, like the nose of a battering ram, then came around the back and joined the rest at the push bar.

Farnir, the young dwarf slave, and the two dwarfs who had pushed the cart approached them.

'Let us help,' said Farnir. 'Please.'

Gotrek turned his back on them without a word.

From the cell door, the old dwarf slave cried to the others. 'Don't! Stay here! Wait for the masters!'

'Clear the way!' called Felix, waving at the aimlessly wandering prisoners.

'Now!' said Gotrek, and shoved at the bar. Felix and the pirates joined him. The cart started rolling, swiftly picking up speed as it rumbled across the flagstones. They ran faster. The hanging cauldrons swung back a little, creaking and sloshing.

If the door doesn't open, thought Felix, this is going to hurt.

The cart hurtled through the open cage door with inches to spare on either side, and slammed into the outer door with a sound like dwarf ironclads colliding. The twelve full cauldrons swung forwards, adding a second impact and sending gruel and water splashing everywhere. The racks cracked and splintered, and some of the cauldrons jumped their hooks and crashed to the floor.

The lattice door, unfortunately, didn't open. Felix and the others crashed into the back of the cart. Felix's cheek smashed against the wooden frame, loosening teeth, and his ribs were crushed against the push bar as the pirate behind him slammed into him. He had been right. It hurt.

Groaning and cursing, Gotrek, Felix and the pirates stepped out from behind the cart to survey the damage to the door. The lattice of slats bulged out in the centre where the nose-cauldron had smashed into them, and the door's iron frame was bowed in, but the hinges still held, and the bolt of the lock had not quite slipped its collar.

'Again!' called Gotrek, and began pulling back on the push bar.

It was clear, as they hauled it back into the big room, that the cart had lost much of its structural integrity. The wheels wobbled and some of the cauldrons hung off it at odd angles, nevertheless it still rolled. When they had it in position, Gotrek fitted it with another nose-cauldron – the first one had cracked and was squashed nearly flat – and they pushed at it again.

This time it rattled and shuddered as it bounced across the floor, and they had to fight to keep it going straight.

One of the cauldrons banged off the edge of the cage door as they charged through, but they made it, and slammed into the outer door again. The noise was even worse this time, and cauldrons and timbers flew everywhere, but with a deafening clang, the outer door flew open and they were through and staggering into the wide corridor after the rapidly disintegrating cart.

'Keep on!' shouted Gotrek.

Felix and the others obeyed the order and sprinted down the corridor towards the thin line of archers as arrows ricocheted off the swinging cauldrons and stuck in the shattered spars. The rest of the pirates followed in their wake, crouching in ragged double file behind the cart's bulk, some of them holding more cauldrons in front of them like shields, others firing back with crossbows purloined from the guards and the guard room.

Felix heard a shouted order and the archers fell back before them, disappearing to the left. Then, about ten strides from the end of the hallway, the front right wheel of the cart fell off and wobbled away as the cart slammed down on its axle end, scraping a groove in the flagstones. Gotrek and Felix and the other pushers unfortunately didn't stop pushing in time, and the cart swerved wildly, pivoting on the dragging axle, then toppled slowly forwards to crash on its side. It skidded noisily to a stop as cauldrons and bits of wood bounced away ahead of it, and a tide of water and mouldy gruel spread out before it.

The escapees halted just before the end of the hallway, not wanting to run into a hail of arrows, and edged forwards. Felix peeked left and right, trying to see the lay of the land.

The room was large and octagonal – the junction of four corridors – all identical to the one they were in. The archers had retreated to the mouth of the corridor to their left. In the angled wall to their right was another iron gate – this one guarding a broad stairway that led up into darkness. Six guards stood at the ready behind it, armed with swords and crossbows.

'A crossfire,' said Felix, his heart sinking.

'And another gate for which we have no key,' said Aethenir.

'Don't think the cart is going to be much use this time,' said Euler.

Gotrek was glaring at the gate with his single eye, edging out further than Felix thought safe to have a good look. It was not a lattice this time, but a line of close-set iron bars that stretched from floor to ceiling, with a wide, vertically barred door in the centre. Much easier to shoot through, thought Felix, swallowing nervously.

But Gotrek didn't seem daunted. 'Easy,' he said at last, then turned to Euler. 'Cauldrons for shields around me and crossbows in the middle.'

Euler nodded and whistled up four of his pirates. They took up four of the cauldrons, wrapping the chains around their arms so they could hold them like shields, then clutched crossbows in their opposite hands. Felix grabbed a fifth cauldron, groaning with the weight. Even when empty the things were staggeringly heavy, and yet Gotrek had swung a full one around like it was a mace. Then Felix and the four pirates formed up in a tight circle around Gotrek, as the rest of the pirates and prisoners made ready to run for it the instant the door was opened. Felix noticed that the three young dwarf slaves had joined with the rest.

'Now,' said Gotrek.

Felix and the others ran out and right, aiming for the gate. Crossbow bolts immediately began spanging off the cauldrons and skittering past their feet and Felix was hard pressed to slow his pace to Gotrek's. The temptation to run from the shooting was almost overwhelming.

As they reached the gate, the pirates fired their crossbows through the bars at the guards behind it, forcing them back towards the stairs. Gotrek stabbed forwards with the iron pole. The frame of the door was nothing but four long iron bars, forged into a rectangle, and the space between it and the door was about two fingers wide. Plenty of room for Gotrek to wedge the end of the iron pole and pull, which is what he did. He jammed the end into the gap just above the square plate that hid the deadbolt, and began to pry sideways, trying to bend the door frame out far enough that the deadbolt would pop out of its socket and the door would spring open.

Gotrek crouched down and heaved mightily. The frame shrieked. Felix and the other shield carriers crouched with the Slayer, trying to hide as much of their bodies behind the cauldrons as they could as they fired over them at the druchii archers behind the gate. The archers backed up the stairs and fired back. More bolts clanged off Felix's cauldron. The tip of one punched through. One of the pirates howled as an arrow pierced his naked foot and he almost fell.

Gotrek kept pulling. The door frame was bending out, but not enough. The pole was bending more than the frame. Felix was afraid it was going to snap.

'I thought you said this one would be easier,' said Felix.

'Shut up, manling,' Gotrek rasped.

A guard tumbled to the ground, a bolt through his chest. Another turned and fled up the stairs, out of bolts, but the other four kept firing. A hot stripe of pain burned across Felix's shin as a bolt tore a trench in it. Another skipped off the stone floor and buried itself in Gotrek's calf. He grunted, but kept pulling.

'Hurry, dwarf,' gritted one of the pirates.

Felix heard the slap of bare feet rushing towards them, but before he could turn to look, someone shoved through two of the cauldrons. Felix almost struck out with his sword, but checked when he saw that it was the young dwarf Farnir. A bolt stuck from his back.

Without a word, the slave grasped the pole about midway along its length and added his strength to Gotrek's. The door frame groaned. Felix readied his sword in anticipation. The pirates fired the last of their bolts at the guards.

'One, two, THREE!' rasped Gotrek, and he and Farnir heaved together. The metal screamed and suddenly Gotrek and Farnir were staggering sideways as the door sprang open.

The guards on the stairs dropped their crossbows and rushed down to hold it shut, but they were too late. Felix and a pirate slammed through behind their cauldron shields, knocking them back and slashing at them before they could draw their swords. Gotrek and the others charged in behind. The Slayer swept the legs out from under two of the guards with the pole, and Felix bowled another down with his cauldron. He stabbed the dark elf in the throat as he stepped over him, then turned to face another. There were none left to face. The pirates had finished them all off.

Felix threw aside the cauldron with a relieved sigh. His shoulder felt broken from carrying it. There was a thunder of running feet. Felix turned to see Aethenir, Euler and the rest of the pirates, as well as a mob of prisoners, breaking cover and running towards them. A handful fell to the arrows of the druchii in the far corridor, but the rest kept coming.

Gotrek pulled out the bolt that had pierced his calf as the first pirates pushed through the door and armed themselves with the weapons of the dead guards. Aethenir selected a crossbow.

'Well done, dwarf,' called Euler.

The Slayer shrugged and turned to the stairs. 'This is only the beginning.'

Felix and Aethenir joined him and they started up the stairs into darkness with Euler and his pirates and the rest following behind.

FELIX FEARED THAT they would find the ark's entire garrison waiting for them at the top of the stairs, but though they heard alarm drums booming in every direction, the reinforcements were apparently still on their way. He was glad of it. It had been six flights. His legs were like jelly from the climb and he was soaked with sweat.

Aethenir leaned against the wall, his eyes half-closed. Beside him, Euler was gasping for breath, hands on his knees, as his pirates recovered around them, looking anxiously up and down the wide, high-ceilinged corridor.

After a moment Euler collected himself and stood. 'Right,' he said. 'Which way is the harbour?'

'You certain you won't change your mind, Euler?' asked Felix.

Euler laughed. 'Very.'

Gotrek pointed left down the hall.

Euler bowed to him. 'Thank you, herr dwarf. You've done us a great service.' He turned to Felix, smiling. 'Well, Herr Jaeger. It seems this is goodbye.'

Felix nodded, not about to join the pirate in his false bonhomie. 'Goodbye, Euler. Good luck, I suppose.'

Euler's smile broadened. 'You don't understand, Herr Jaeger. This is *goodbye*!'

And with that, Euler and his pirates attacked.

SIXTEEN

FELIX FELL BACK, throwing up his sword in a desperate parry, and barely turned aside Euler's blade. Beside him, Gotrek roared as a sword striped him across his back, then spun in a circle, swinging his iron pole and fanning the pirates back. To one side Aethenir cowered against the wall.

'Euler!' cried Felix, turning another attack. 'What is this?'

'After all you've done to me,' snarled Euler, 'do you think I would let the long-ears have the satisfaction of killing you?' He laughed, harsh and breathless. 'I meant to wait until I had you on my ship, but since you've chosen suicide, it was now or never.'

He pressed in, attacking feverishly, his breathing ragged, his eyes wild. As Felix blocked the crazed stabs, he saw one of Euler's men fall back from Gotrek, screaming, his arm bent at an unnatural angle. Two others were on the floor, clutching their shins.

'This is madness, Euler,' said Felix, as the alarm drums continued to boom. 'You're ruining your chance to escape. The druchii are coming. Leave off and go!'

'Not until I've finished you!' Euler beat Felix's sword aside and did a running lunge, straight at his naked chest, but the pirate was winded and weak from captivity, and the attack was slow. Felix knocked it away and shoved him past.

Euler turned, roaring and weaving, and slashed down wildly. Felix thrust over his arm and ran him through the heart. Euler gasped, his eyes going wide.

His sword dropped to his side and he looked Felix in the eye. 'You really are a curse, Jaeger.'

He sank to his knees, then fell back and collapsed, sliding off Felix's blade. Felix looked pityingly at him for a brief moment. Haggard and scruffily bearded, his corpse looked nothing like the plump, proud man Felix had met in the study of his prosperous Marienburg townhouse.

Felix turned to help Gotrek, but found that the pirates were stepping back from him and holding up their hands. Five lay on the ground around the Slayer, legs and arms broken.

Gotrek snarled at the rest, beckoning them forwards. 'Come on, you cowards. Finish what you started.'

One-Ear backed up, shaking his head. 'It was the captain that wanted this. Now he's dead, we only want to leave.'

'Then go,' growled Gotrek. 'And good riddance.'

The pirates let out relieved breaths and turned and ran towards the harbour – at least most of them did. About a dozen of them hesitated, looking uncertainly from their departing comrades to Gotrek, Felix and Aethenir. Broken-Nose was among them.

One of the other pirates nudged him forwards. 'Ask him, Jochen.'

Broken-Nose turned to Felix. 'It is true what you said about Marienburg?'

'It's true,' said Felix, who then suddenly looked up, his blood freezing. In the distance he heard the steady tramp of marching feet. The druchii were answering the alarm at last. The others heard it too. Aethenir whimpered. Gotrek growled.

'I have a wife and two boys there,' Jochen said. 'They will die?'

Felix nodded, anxious to be away. The marching was getting closer every second. It was just around the next corner. 'They will if we don't stop the sorceress.'

Jochen looked at the other pirates who had hesitated. They nodded. He turned back to Felix. 'We are pirates, but we are Marienburg pirates. We will come with you.'

'Then hurry,' said Gotrek. 'This way.' He turned to the right.

'Master Slayer, don't,' said the young dwarf slave. 'You won't make it that way now.' He stepped to a small door in the wall where the two other dwarfs waited. 'The slave corridors. No druchii goes here.'

Gotrek hesitated, his brow lowering, then turned and followed the slaves through the door. Felix, Aethenir and the pirates followed.

THE SLAVE CORRIDORS were quite a contrast to all else that Felix had seen of the black ark. Even in the slave pen area, filthy as it was, the stone had been cleanly cut and finished, and the corridors broad. Not so here. These passages were little more than clawed out tunnels, narrow, low and choking with smoke from the torches that were used to light them. No witchlights for the slaves.

The floors were uneven and damp, and littered with trash and the stubs of old torches. They branched and weaved this way and that in a bewildering maze, with steps and ramps in unexpected places and doors everywhere from which one could hear kitchen or laundry noises or smell sawdust or horse manure or food or perfume.

Felix, Gotrek, Aethenir and the dozen pirates who Jochen had brought with him followed the dwarf slaves through the tunnels uneasily. Felix couldn't stop looking over his shoulder, expecting to hear shouts and the rumble of running boots behind them at any moment, but they never came. Whatever consternation the escape of the prisoners was generating in the main corridors had not penetrated here. The only sign that anything unusual was happening was the faint pounding of the alarm drums, pulsing though the rock walls, but the passing slaves – almost all human – paid it no mind. They hurried past on various errands – carrying baskets of food or clothing, trundling barrows full of trash, loaded down with heavy tomes or chests, or shuffling along in work details, armed with mops or brooms or shovels, eyes down and arms close to their sides.

As they hurried on, young Farnir fell back and bowed respectfully to Gotrek. 'Can you tell me, master Slayer, what is this threat to the holds? Is it the same thing that you say will destroy the city of Marienburg?'

'I will not speak to you, coward,' said Gotrek, staring straight ahead. 'You are a disgrace. You should have died before allowing yourself to be captured.'

The young dwarf flushed. 'Forgive me, Slayer,' he said, 'but I was captured when I was an infant. I was raised here.'

Felix had never seen Gotrek brought up so short in all the time he had travelled with him. The Slayer turned on the slave, his eye bulging. 'What?'

Farnir cringed before his gaze. 'But my father has taught me much about the old ways and our noble ancestors. The mine code, the book of–'

Gotrek cut him off with a curse. 'Your *father*? Your father is a–' He bit off what he had begun to say and returned his gaze to the way ahead, his fists clenching and a thick vein pulsing in his temple as they continued on.

Without exception, the slaves they passed were pale, miserable things, with close-cropped heads and down-cast eyes, gaunt from undernourishment and hunched as if they expected to be whipped at any moment. It made Felix's heart sick just to see them. Many times in his life he had seen men and women in much more miserable straits – chained, starved, diseased, wounded, mad or suffering from horrific mutations, but the look of hope-lessness in the eyes of the slaves, the dull acceptance that their life would never change, that salvation would never come, was almost more than he could bear. These peo-ple had sunk below despair to an empty blankness that made them more like the undead than any living, breathing thing. Here they were, in a part of the ark that the druchii never visited, and still the slaves did not talk to each other or allow themselves to relax. They just hur-ried on, eyes fixed on the path ahead and glancing neither left or right. They hardly gave Gotrek and Felix a second look.

At the intersection with a slightly larger corridor, Farnir paused and turned to his dwarf companions. He whis-pered in their ears and sent them off in different directions, then turned and beckoned the escapees on.

After another few minutes, they came to a straight corridor that had evenly spaced doors all along its left side.

Farnir stopped at the third one and turned to them. 'Captain Landryol's house.' He said. 'This is the kitchen.'

Gotrek strode forwards, raising the iron pole.

'Wait, master Slayer,' said the slave. 'No need.' He motioned them out of sight.

'Betraying us will be the last thing you do,' said Gotrek.

Farnir nodded, cowed, then stepped to the door and knocked as Felix, Gotrek and the pirates stood against the wall.

After a moment a slot opened in the door.

The dwarf slave bowed. 'A delivery for Master Landryol. Wine from Bretonnia. Three casks.'

'One minute,' said a flat voice.

The slot closed, and then a latch clacked and the door swung out.

'Who sent it?' said a human cook in an apron, stepping out. 'I don't remember–'

The dwarf slave wrenched the door out of the cook's hands and slammed it open. Gotrek, Felix, Aethenir and the pirates shoved quickly past them and into a dark, low-roofed kitchen.

'Hoy! What are you–' said the cook, but the young dwarf clamped a big hand over his mouth and shoved him inside. Felix closed it behind them.

The kitchen was lit by torches and the fires that burned in ovens and hearths. Gape-mouthed kitchen slaves stared at them from long work tables, where they were preparing trays of food and drink. A serving man almost dropped a tray of silverware. But all these details were overwhelmed and obliterated by the delicious, overpowering smell of cooked food. Felix's stomach rumbled and growled like a caged lion at the scent of it.

'Who are you?' asked the cook, looking wide-eyed at them and their weapons. 'What do you want?'

'Nothing of you,' said Felix, fighting down his hunger and returning to the business at hand. 'We only want a word with your master.'

The serving man yelped at that and ran for a set of stairs, but Jochen leapt after him and shoved him down, then stood in front of the stairs with his sword drawn.

'We'd rather we were unannounced,' said Felix. He turned to the cook. 'Is the captain in?'

The cook said nothing, only stared at him, trembling, until Gotrek grabbed him by the shirt front and pulled him down so he could speak in his ear. 'Answer him,' he said softly.

'Y-yes,' said the cook. 'He's in.'

'Does he live alone?' asked Felix.

'Yes. Alone.'

'Any guards?'

'Two men from his crew. They live above stairs.'

Gotrek shook him again. 'Where?'

'At the back. Left at the top of the stairs.'

'Any other slaves?' continued Felix.

'The master's body slaves. Four girls.'

'Where are they?' demanded Gotrek.

'Usually in his room.'

'Right,' said Gotrek. He turned to Jochen. 'You'll stay here and keep these quiet.' He looked at Aethenir. 'You too, elf. The manling and I will deal with this corsair.'

The pirates nodded.

'But first,' said Gotrek, turning to the tables where the food was being prepared, 'we eat.'

Felix's heart leapt at the prospect. The pirates laughed. They advanced like wolves towards a downed deer.

'You mustn't!' said the cook. 'That is Master Landryol's food. We'll be whipped.'

'He won't be wanting it,' said Gotrek, and tore the leg off a roasted chicken. 'And bring more.'

Felix and the others attacked the platters ravenously as the servants backed away to obey Gotrek's demand. Even Aethenir ate like an animal, shoving food into his mouth with both hands and guzzling down wine and ale like all the rest.

'You're going to kill him!' said the serving man. 'We must raise the alarm! They kill slaves who fail to protect their masters!'

'And we kill slaves that warn their masters,' said Jochen.

After that, the servants watched in silence as the intruders ravaged their master's meal, and then his larder.

Felix moaned with pleasure as he choked down bread and meat and fruit and washed it down with something that he suspected was Averland wine. Never in his life had food tasted so good. After the days of rotten gruel and filthy water it was like ambrosia. He practically wept as the smell and the taste filled his mouth, and he had to force himself to remember to chew and not just gulp it down like a snake.

Then, only a minute after they had begun, Gotrek stepped back and wiped his mouth with the back of his hand.

'That's enough,' he said. 'We can't waste time.'

Felix groaned. He was only getting started. He never wanted to stop. His stomach was still howling for more. With aching reluctance, he stuffed one last piece of ham into his mouth and turned away, wiping his hands on his filthy breeches and taking up his curved sword as Aethenir and the pirates continued to feast.

'Coming,' he said with a sigh.

Gotrek grabbed the serving man by the front of his jerkin and shoved him towards the stairs. 'You lead us,' he said. 'And no tricks.'

The slave whimpered and started up the stairs. Gotrek and Felix followed, their weapons at the ready. They came up into a dark hallway between, on one side, a dark-panelled dining area filled with small round tables and low chaises, and on the other, what appeared to be some sort of study. Maps covered its stone walls, and a large desk with scrolls, books and more maps sat in its centre. On this floor, they could better hear the alarm drums, still sounding faintly in the distance.

The slave led them to the far end of the hallway, where it opened out into a high-ceilinged entry chamber, an ironbound oak door at its front, and a straight, iron-railinged stairway rising up to the second floor.

They went up the stairs to a second floor, passing closed doors, and then up another stair to a third, but before they had reached the top, they heard a terrific explosion, far off, but still very loud.

Felix exchanged a glance with Gotrek.

'Euler's men are putting up a fight,' he said.

'Aye.'

The third floor was a single corridor, very dark, with doors on either side.

The slave stepped to a door on the left, then hesitated, shaking. He looked back at Gotrek and Felix, eyes wide with fear. 'Have mercy, sirs,' he murmured. 'If you kill him, we will die. They will kill us.'

'Step aside, craven,' sneered Gotrek.

He pushed past the quivering slave to the door and turned the handle. It was unlocked. He readied his weapon and looked over his shoulder. Felix gripped his stolen sword and nodded. They pushed in.

'Is that you, Mechlin?' came a voice speaking sibilant Reikspiel from within the dark chamber. 'Where in the name of the Dark Mother is our dinner? And what was that damned noise?' Felix recognised the voice as if from a dream.

The entrance was curtained off from the rest of the room by heavy brocade drapes, but Felix could see through a gap hints of panelled walls and dark wood furniture glinting red in the light of a banked fire.

Gotrek drew the drapery aside a few inches to get the lay of the land, and they saw their quarry sprawled naked on a fur-covered sleeping platform with his head propped up on a tasselled bolster and his arms draped around the sleeping forms of four beautiful young human girls, completely bald, and clad only in delicate silver fetters at throat, wrists and ankles. They curled like cats around him. The scent of black lotus smoke hung heavy in the air, and Felix could see enamelled pipes and braziers glinting by the bed.

'Stop cowering and come in, Mechlin,' drawled Landryol. 'I won't bite.' He chuckled and looked at his bedmates. 'Not you, anyway.'

'They seek to kill you, master!' shrieked the slave from the corridor. 'Protect yourself!'

Gotrek cursed and ripped aside the curtain, then charged across the dark room with Felix beside him as Landryol struggled to sit up and the four beauties raised sleepy heads.

Gotrek leapt up onto the sleeping platform and caught the druchii captain around the neck with one massive hand. Felix stood beside him and put his sword to Landryol's chest. The pleasure slaves shrieked and spilled off the bed in all directions.

Gotrek raised the iron pole over his head. 'Where is my axe?'

'And my sword,' said Felix.

'How do you come here?' asked Landryol, blinking drug-fogged eyes and looking back and forth between them. 'No one escapes the pens.'

Gotrek shook him like a doll. 'My axe!'

The druchii raised a trembling hand and pointed to a curtained alcove on the far side of the room. 'Under the floor.'

Gotrek shoved Landryol back down and sprang from the bed, looking back at Felix. 'Watch him.'

Felix nodded and moved the tip of his sword to the druchii's throat as the Slayer disappeared behind the curtain.

Footsteps thudded somewhere below them. Felix glanced to the door.

'Guards coming!' Felix called.

'Good,' said Gotrek from behind the curtain.

'You will never leave here alive,' said Landryol.

'We know that already,' said Felix, looking towards the door again. The footsteps were thundering up the stairs now.

There was a sound of splitting wood from the alcove and then a grunt of satisfaction. The curtain jerked aside and Gotrek strode out brandishing his axe in one hand and carrying Felix's scabbarded sword in the other.

'My arm is complete,' the Slayer said.

With a clatter of boots, two druchii corsairs ran in, swords drawn, and skidded to a stop at the scene that met their eyes.

'Kill them!' said Landryol.

The corsairs needed no encouragement. One charged Gotrek while the other leapt onto the bed and lunged at Felix. Felix whipped his stolen sword around and parried a blade aimed straight at his face, but Landryol kicked him behind the knee and he crashed down on the bed. The corsair slashed down at him. Felix rolled off onto the floor, sending one of the bed slaves scurrying for a corner. He scrambled up as the corsair came after him.

'Manling,' called Gotrek.

Felix looked up just in time to see his sword arcing towards him, thrown by the Slayer as he blocked the other druchii's attacks.

Felix's opponent knocked Karaghul out of the air and stabbed at him again. Felix cursed and hopped back, then kicked the table with the pipe and brazier at him. The corsair stumbled back, trying to avoid the hot coals, and Felix flung his stolen sword after him then dived for Karaghul, drawing as he rolled to his feet. The corsair charged and they clashed again.

On the other side of the bed, Gotrek blocked another blow by the second druchii, then kicked him in the stomach. The druchii curled up, retching and exposing his neck, but Gotrek only cracked him in the face with the heel of the axe and stepped back as he fell. 'You will not die yet,' he said.

He turned to Landryol, who had caught up a jewelled sword, and stood at the foot of the bed, entirely naked.

'I vowed that you would be the first to die when I recovered my axe,' said the Slayer, striding towards him.

Landryol's lip curled in derision as he dropped into guard and extended his blade. 'You may try, dwarf. But I am reckoned quite a formidable–'

Gotrek's axe hacked the slender sword in two and buried itself in the dark elf's breastbone, and the rest of the boast went unsaid.

The corsair facing Felix gaped at his master's sudden death. Felix ran him through before he recovered.

Gotrek wrenched his axe from Landryol's chest, then turned on the corsair he had cracked over the head. The druchii was still struggling to stand.

'*Now* you die,' said Gotrek, and beheaded him with a casual backhand.

The room was suddenly silent, the only noise Felix and Gotrek's breathing, and the soft weeping of the bed slaves. Felix wiped his sword clean on the bed furs and returned it to its scabbard. It felt good to have it again, but this was only the first part of what they must do.

He turned to Gotrek. 'Are you ready?'

'One moment, manling.'

The Slayer crossed back to the alcove and disappeared, then came back with an open wooden chest. The contents glinted in the dim firelight. He lifted out a heavy shirt of chainmail and handed it to Felix. It was his!

Under it was a profusion of golden bracelets, armbands and chains.

'Your gold,' said Felix.

'Aye,' said Gotrek, obviously pleased. 'Besmirched by elven hands, but all here, Grungni be praised.'

Gotrek slipped it all back on his meaty wrists while Felix pulled his mail on over his head, then they strode back out into the hall. The slave who had brought them there still cowered by the door. Gotrek glared at him for a second, as if contemplating killing him for his betrayal, but then snorted and continued to the stairs.

'The druchii will do worse to him,' he said.

THE KITCHEN SLAVES, all pushed into one corner by the pirates, stared in horror as Gotrek and Felix came back down the stairs to the kitchen holding their weapons.

'You killed him,' said the cook.

Felix nodded.

The slaves moaned in misery. A scullery girl burst into tears. 'We'll be sold off now! To who knows who! How could you be so cruel?'

Another patted her on the shoulder, comforting her. Felix glared, angry, though he knew not at whom. Shouldn't slaves be happy that their master was killed?

Jochen stepped up to them, looking grim. 'We were right to come with you, it seems. The others didn't make it out of the harbour. Blown up with their own powder.'

'Where did you hear this?' asked Gotrek.

Jochen nodded towards the dark end of the room, where the slaves' meal table was. Farnir sat with the two dwarfs he had sent off earlier there, as well as two other dwarfs, a grizzled elder with a stiff brush of short grey hair, and a youngster with downcast eyes and a balding horseshoe of ginger hair. The newcomers' beards were little more than grown out stubble. They rose in silent awe as the Slayer turned to face them.

'What is this?' asked Gotrek.

Farnir opened his mouth to speak, but the grey-haired dwarf spoke first, stepping forwards. 'Farnir sent word to us that you'd broken the pens, and we came to see it for ourselves.'

'Never would have believed it,' said the balding dwarf, shaking his head.

'Never would have tried it,' grunted Gotrek.

The older dwarf bowed his head respectfully to Gotrek. 'I am Birgi, father of Farnir. And this is Skalf. It is an honour to meet a true follower of Grimnir.'

Gotrek glared at him with cold contempt. 'Your shame is twice that of the others. You live as a slave, and you raised a son into slavery. You are lower than grobi.'

Birgi hung his head, 'Aye, Slayer. We know what you think of us, but you'd be crest-deep in druchii at the moment if it weren't for Farnir bringing you through the slave corridors, and it was us who told him the way to this house and to where the wizards are held, when you asked, so you might be polite.'

Gotrek snorted, and looked about to retort, but then Jochen stepped forwards.

'The dwarfs say the magister and the seeress are locked up downstairs in the druchii barracks,' he said. 'Is that true?'

Gotrek nodded. Felix sighed at this news.

'I want to save Marienburg,' Jochen continued, 'but is it necessary to walk into the middle of the whole damned dark elf army? Can't we leave them?'

'We won't stand a chance against the sorceresses without them,' Aethenir said, looking up from where he was cleaning himself fastidiously at the kitchen's pump.

'We can lead you there,' said Birgi. 'There are service tunnels down to the barracks level, but you can't enter the barracks themselves without passing through a guarded gate.'

'We don't need a guide,' snapped Gotrek.

Everyone looked to him.

'I will not be in the debt of honourless dwarfs,' he growled.

'Slayer, they want to help,' said Felix. 'And we need help.'

Birgi nodded. 'We'll do anything we can,' he said.

'Except put your lives at risk,' growled Gotrek.

The balding dwarf raised his head at that, angry, but Birgi put a hand on his arm.

'Easy, Skalf,' he said, then turned to Gotrek. 'If our deaths would make a difference, Slayer, we would die. But if we rose up, if all the slaves on this ark rose up, the druchii would only kill us and replace us with new slaves. They are too strong.'

Gotrek snorted at that. 'The death of one elf is difference enough.'

The old slave continued, undaunted. 'We will gladly help you stop this threat to our old holds – for it is there that our hearts lie – but even if you succeed, this ark will go on, the few druchii you kill forgotten when the next fleet of hakseer corsairs comes to reinforce it. Nothing will change. Nothing has ever changed, for four thousand years.'

'Where are the wizards inside the barracks area?' Felix asked before Gotrek could respond. There was no time for argument.

Birgi coughed and turned to him. 'Er, well, they're being held by the Endless, the cold bastards that High Sorceress Heshor brought with her. We had to fix up a pair of old barracks for them. Refitted one for new officers' quarters, new rooms carved, fine furniture – only the best for our guests from the mainland.'

'Why have they held them? Why weren't they locked up with the rest of us?' asked Felix.

Birgi shrugged. 'I don't know about that, only the Temple of Khaine don't allow wizards as slaves. Kill 'em as soon as they're taken. So I'd guess the Endless are hiding them from the witches. No guess as to why.'

Felix couldn't quite understand all that. Weren't the sorceresses witches? What was the difference? It didn't matter now. What mattered was how they were going to get past the barracks guards.

'Does this Heshor have a lot of power here?' he asked.

Birgi and the other dwarfs laughed.

'She's turned the ark upside down since she's come,' said Skalf, the balding dwarf. 'Making us sail this way and that like she owned the place. Twisted old Tarlkhir around her finger like a ribbon.'

'Orders from Naggarond,' said Birgi. 'Whatever she's here for, she's doing it on the authority of the Witch King himself.'

'So things done in her name would carry weight?' Felix asked.

The old dwarf nodded. 'Aye, but...'

Felix turned to Aethenir and Gotrek. 'If we dress the high one as a druchii and pretend to be his prisoners, and if he says that he is bringing slaves captured during the pirates' attack on the harbour to the Endless by Heshor's orders...'

'It won't work,' interrupted Aethenir. 'I look nothing like a druchii!'

The others gave him a look.

He groaned. 'Well, I *sound* nothing like a druchii. My accent...'

'Then you better start practising,' said Gotrek. 'And go find some clothes.'

Aethenir sighed, but reluctantly went up the stairs to look through the dead druchii's closets as Gotrek and Felix fell on the remains of the food.

NOT LONG AFTER, they wound through the tunnels again, following Aethenir, who wore Landryol's armour, helm and sea dragon cloak, as Birgi trotted at his side, telling him the name of the captain of the Endless and other important names a corsair would know. Felix wondered if it was all for naught. The ark had stopped hours ago – at least two hours before they had made their break – and it seemed hours more since they had fought Euler's pirates, though in fact it was probably no more than half an hour. Could it be possible that Heshor hadn't plucked the harp yet? Did harnessing its terrible power require more than just playing it? Was there some ceremony involved? He expected at every step to feel the ark shake or sway and hear the far-off rumble of land being born from the waves. But perhaps he wouldn't have felt a thing. Perhaps Heshor had already done it!

He sighed to himself. If it had already happened, then they would take what revenge they could, though it could never be enough.

At last they neared the door that Birgi said opened near the front gates of the druchii barracks. They stopped some distance from it and made their final preparations, putting all their weapons and mail in a sack Felix and Gotrek would carry between them, and manacling themselves to a long slave chain that they had found among Landryol's belongings. Felix and the pirates didn't like this measure, and Gotrek hated it, for it meant that he would not be able to get to his axe quickly if anything went wrong, and also that he was putting all his trust in Aethenir, who, as their 'captor', held the only key to unlock them. But it was a necessary measure, for no captured prisoners would be allowed to keep their weapons, and if they were to get through the gate, they must be able to pass an inspection by the guards. Simply looping the chains around their wrists and pretending to be locked up wouldn't do.

As Aethenir struggled to get a pair of manacles around Gotrek's massive wrists, Birgi gave them detailed instructions for finding their way through the barracks area to the lodgings of the Endless, then he and the other dwarfs gave them a dwarfen salute.

'Good luck, Slayer,' said the old dwarf. 'Good luck to you all.'

Gotrek sneered and said nothing.

Suddenly Farnir stepped to Birgi. 'Father, I'm going with them.' He turned and offered his wrists to Aethenir.

Birgi blinked, stunned. 'Farnir, you have already risked much. Don't be…'

'Did the stories you told me about brave dwarf heroes of old mean nothing?' asked Farnir insistently.

'Of course they did,' said Birgi. 'But…'

'This is for the holds of our homeland,' said the young dwarf, backing away. 'This is for the honour you told me we once had.'

'But… but it will fail, Farnir,' called Birgi, his face sagging with despair. 'It won't make any difference.'

'I'm sorry, Father. I must.' Farnir turned away, stone-faced, and allowed Aethenir to add him to the line of 'prisoners'.

Gotrek laughed over his shoulder, scornful. 'Ha! A beardling shames them. They should all shave their heads, the lot of them.' He turned away as Aethenir stepped to the head of the coffle. 'Lead us out, elf. It stinks in here.'

Aethenir took a deep breath then stepped to the door and opened it. As Felix shuffled out after him with the others he cast a last look back at the four dwarfs who had stayed behind. They stood with their heads hung low, unable to look towards Gotrek or each other. He felt for them. Offered the choice of death and torture or serving as a slave, he wasn't sure what he would have done, either.

Aethenir looked back at Felix and his other 'prisoners' as they approached the gate. 'Put your heads down, curse you,' he hissed. 'Look defeated.'

Felix did as he was told, although the temptation to look forwards and see what was transpiring was hard to fight. He could tell by the tremor in the high elf's voice that he was terrified – which made Felix terrified, for if

Aethenir betrayed his fear to the guards they would be exposed, and that would be the end. They would be killed here, unable to defend themselves, and never find Max and Claudia or stop the sorceresses.

They were crossing a broad, cave-roofed plaza in front of the barracks area. Druchii spear and sword companies hurried past towards the gate, some bearing the wounded behind them on stretchers – casualties from fighting the pirates, Felix thought. Other companies marched out in quickstep behind their captains – looking for them, perhaps?

The barracks gate was a wide portcullised doorway with defensive towers on either side. It looked like the front of a castle built into the end of a cave. A double rank of well-armoured guards stood outside it, their captain passing companies in and out, and a dozen archers walked an artillery platform above. As Aethenir and his line of slaves approached, the captain held up a hand and asked a question in the druchii tongue.

Aethenir answered, keeping his voice clipped and hard and, thankfully, remarkably steady. Felix couldn't understand a word of the exchange, but he heard the high elf mention the names the old dwarf had give him – High Sorceress Heshor and Istultair, the captain of the Endless – and seem to make demands in their names. Felix had hoped that the magic of their exalted influence would usher them smoothly through the gate, but this did not happen. The guard captain seemed unimpressed, and walked down their line with his hands folded behind his back, examining them one at a time. He paid particular attention to Gotrek, and stopped at him again when he came back up the line. Gotrek's fists clenched at the attention and Felix held his breath.

The guard captain turned away and said something to Aethenir in a sly tone. Aethenir answered haughtily, but Felix could hear a tremor at the edges of his voice. It's all going wrong, Felix thought, and sweat began to pour down his sides. The guard captain came back with a jovial yet menacing reply. Aethenir repeated his refusal, and the guard just shrugged and waved him away.

Aethenir paused, in what appeared to be angry indecision, then finally stepped to Gotrek. 'Do not kill me, dwarf,' he murmured. 'He requires a bribe.'

He reached out and began to tug on two of Gotrek's smaller golden bracelets. Gotrek growled and jerked away. Aethenir cursed in the druchii tongue and slapped the Slayer hard on the ear. 'Insolent cur,' he shouted in Reikspiel. 'Dare you resist? You have no possessions! All that you are and own belongs to High Sorceress Heshor now!'

Felix nearly fainted. The Slayer was going to kill the high elf, and then they would be chopped to pieces by the guards. But amazingly, Gotrek held his temper, doing nothing more than grinding his teeth and balling his fists as the high elf pried the two bracelets from his wrists. Felix could see that the self-restraint required to keep still was nearly killing Gotrek. A vein pulsed dangerously in his forehead and his face was blood-red.

Aethenir tossed the bracelets to the guard captain as if they meant nothing to him, and the druchii bowed them through the gate.

'I will take the price of that gold out of your hide, elf,' growled Gotrek when they had passed out of earshot.

'I had no choice,' whimpered the high elf. 'Surely you can see that.'

'You could have bargained better,' said Gotrek.

Inside the gate, they came into a large open parade square with a high roof and rows of doors and windows cut into the stone walls on either side – the barracks themselves – and passages leading off in every direction. The place was a swirl of activity – companies forming up in the square under the barked orders of baton-wielding captains, and other companies falling out and laying their wounded in neat ranks along one side as surgeons and healers and slaves moved among them. It reminded Felix of what one saw when one stirred up an ant hill, only much more orderly.

Birgi had told them that the barracks he and his crew had refitted for the use of the Endless was in a left-hand passage that opened off the far end of the parade ground. Felix swallowed nervously at the idea of walking shackled and unarmed through so many of the enemy, but thankfully, the druchii paid them no mind, except to shove them aside if they got in their way. Felix held his breath again, afraid that Gotrek would explode into violence at such treatment, but he kept his head down, muttering Khazalid curses all the while.

At the end of the square, Aethenir found the left-hand passage and they entered it. There was no one in it, and the noise of the parade ground fell away behind them as they turned a second corner into another row of barracks. Aethenir paused in the shadow of the passage and they looked out, examining the long corridor. Most of the barracks appeared to be unoccupied – the windows boarded up and the steps that led up to the doors dusty. The first two on the right, however, were freshly scrubbed, with new doors and open windows but, unsettlingly, no sign of activity.

'Strange,' said Aethenir. 'I expected to see guards, or at least slaves.'

'Maybe they're all inside,' said Jochen.

'Let's have a look,' said Felix.

Aethenir got to work with his key and they all shucked their manacles. Gotrek opened the sack full of weapons and drew his axe from it while Felix pulled on his mail and buckled Karaghul around his waist. The pirates followed suit and they all crept forwards, only this time with Aethenir taking up the rear.

Felix and Jochen raised their heads and looked through the first window they came to. Inside was a barracks room like any other – except that the walls were carved from solid rock. Cots ran down each wall, each with a small iron-bound chest at its foot. There was one door at the back of the room and another in the side wall. A few slaves were cleaning the floor, and a few young druchii were sitting on the cots and polishing armour, boots and belts. The Endless were not there.

'Yer wizards might be behind one of them doors,' said Jochen when they had crouched down again.

'Let's check the other barracks first,' said Felix.

They crossed to the second barracks and looked through those windows. These were clearly the officers' quarters. There was a well-appointed entry way, the stone walls covered with ebony panelling and mounted with witchlights, and a central corridor leading away into darkness. No one was in sight.

'This one first,' said Felix.

Gotrek stepped to the door. It was unlocked. He pushed it open and stepped through. Felix, Aethenir, Farnir and Jochen's pirates followed him in. They padded silently down the corridor. It had two lavishly carved doors on each side and a plain one at the far end. Felix and Aethenir listened at each of the carved doors in turn, but heard nothing. They continued on.

Gotrek listened at the door at the end of the hall, then tried it. It too was unlocked. A feeling of unease crept over Felix. They should have been challenged by now. They should have met some resistance.

On the other side of the door was a narrow set of stairs going down into darkness. Aethenir made a tiny ball of light with a snap of his fingers and Gotrek started down. Felix and the others followed.

They came down into a supply room, bedding and candles and sundries stacked in crates along the walls. At the far end of the room was a heavy door. There was a chair and a table outside it, and the remains of a meal drawing flies.

'That's it,' said Gotrek, and started forwards.

Felix and the others crept along behind him, weapons at the ready. Felix held his breath, expecting hidden druchii to leap out of the shadows at every step. No attack came.

Gotrek put his hand on the latch and turned it. It opened easily. He threw the door wide, revealing blackness beyond.

Aethenir sent his light in before them. The room was small and bare but for two piles of filthy straw. Gotrek and Felix stepped cautiously inside. It smelled of urine and sweat and rotting food. There were grimy, blood-spattered rags on the floor. Some of them might have once been deep blue, others might have once been gold and white, but of Max and Claudia there was no sign.

SEVENTEEN

A DRUCHII VOICE called a question behind them and they turned. A young dark elf stood upon the stairs, a witch-light torch in one hand.

Aethenir called to him, beckoning him forwards, but the youth, seeing them all with their weapons, sensed something wrong and ran back up the stairs, shouting warnings.

Felix cursed and sprinted after him, pounding up the stairs and into the hall. A door opened halfway down, and the youth, looking back towards Felix, ran smack into it and fell reeling to the ground. A slave looked out from the open door, then shrieked and darted back, slamming it behind him.

Felix pounced on the young druchii before he could recover himself and pinned him to the floor, putting his sword across his throat.

'The mages!' he hissed. 'Where are they? Where have you taken them?'

The youth babbled in the druchii tongue. Felix shook him. 'Reikspiel, damn you!'

There were footsteps behind him and Gotrek and Aethenir joined him, followed closely by the pirates.

Aethenir asked something in the elf tongue and the youth stared at him, then spat on his boots. Aethenir kicked him in the ribs. Felix pressed his sword harder against the druchii's neck. Gotrek stepped forwards and raised his axe over him, his single eye cold and dead.

The youth blanched at the sight of Gotrek and blurted out something. Aethenir asked a few more questions and got short replies.

He sighed and turned to Felix and Gotrek. 'The sorceresses came and took them away several hours ago. The Endless went with them.'

'Where?' asked Felix. 'Where have they gone?'

'He doesn't know,' said the high elf. 'Only that they took the stairs at the end of this avenue, which go only down.'

'Further down?' said Jochen, looking uneasy. 'Let's give up on these magisters.'

'What is below us?' asked Gotrek, ignoring him.

'The menagerie of the beastmasters,' said Farnir. 'And those flesh houses reserved for officers and the nobility.'

Felix blinked. 'Are they going to feed them to wild beasts? Are they going to…?' he couldn't complete the thought.

The dwarf slave suddenly paled. His eyes widened. 'It is rumoured among the slaves that there is a secret temple in the depths of the ark, with its entrance somewhere inside one of the flesh houses. They say many are taken there, never to return.'

'What sort of temple?' growled Gotrek.

'None dare say,' said the dwarf.

'A temple with an entrance in such a house can only serve one god,' whispered Aethenir, looking sick with fear.

'What house is it in?' Felix asked Farnir.

He shook his head. 'I know not.'

'Then we'll have to check every one,' said Gotrek.

'There are more guards before the stairs,' said Farnir. 'You will need your disguises again.'

'We'll need a new disguise,' said Gotrek, thinking. He turned to Aethenir. 'Trade that armour for Endless kit, elf. And hurry.'

'What do we do with this fool?' asked Jochen, pointing to the young druchii still cowering under Felix's sword.

Gotrek dropped his axe and buried it in the young dark elf's face, shattering his head and splashing blood everywhere.

'That,' he said, and turned away.

A FEW MINUTES later, once more locked to their chain, and with their weapons once more bundled in the sack, they shuffled down the long corridor between the unused barracks towards the menagerie stair gate, trailing behind the trembling figure of Aethenir, dressed as an officer of the Endless and wearing a silver skull mask.

This time there was no bribery required. The guards at the gate seemed awed by the uniform of the Endless, and bowed Aethenir through without question. The high elf led them to a narrow stairwell that zigzagged down into the rock for twelve flights before ending in a broad, low-roofed corridor that reeked of animal dung and rotting meat.

The roars of fierce beasts and the crack of whips echoed all around them as they started down it. The sounds and the smells came from a wide archway on the left-hand wall, sealed by elaborate wrought iron gates, and guarded by druchii in uniforms adorned with leopardskin capes and carrying long, wickedly barbed spears.

Aethenir ignored them and continued on, as he had been instructed to by Farnir, and soon they came to a much smaller archway with no gate and no guard. The sounds and smells that wafted from this arch were of an entirely different sort of wildlife. Felix smelled wine and perfume, incense and the smoke of the black lotus, as well as sweat and sex and death. Raucous laughter and strange discordant singing reached his ears, mixed with far-off shrieks of pain.

They filed through the arch and stopped dead at the scene that opened before them. The street, or tunnel – it was hard to make the distinction – was narrow and tall, with houses carved from the solid rock rising three storeys on either side. The high arched roof of the tunnel was cut back deeply, so that the houses had roofs and rooftop gardens and verandas. Witchlights blazed purple and red in iron lanterns hung from baroque facades, and the sights illuminated by this blood-coloured light were enough to turn Felix's stomach. He had been in the red light districts of cities from Kislev to Araby, but never had he seen a place so dedicated to pleasure, pain and perversion. Usually, even in the loosest of cities, the joy houses kept a somewhat respectable front. Such a pretence was apparently unnecessary here.

Friezes and statues depicting the most lewd and vile acts decorated the fronts of every establishment. Some places had iron cages hung above their doors, within which dull-eyed human slaves flagellated one another or performed listless acts of coitus. In front of every house stood armed guards dressed in fanciful armour that seemed to have more to do with titillation than protection.

Strolling from house to house were the flower of druchii society – tall, cruelly handsome lords, sultry, sway-hipped ladies, swaggering officers, naked, silver-masked courtesans, exquisite persons whose gender it was impossible to tell, and pushing through the crush to the sound of cracking whips, covered palanquins carried by stooped, scarred human slaves, transporting those who wished to keep their identities secret.

'Asuryan protect me,' murmured Aethenir. 'This place is an abomination.'

'For once we agree,' said Gotrek. 'Even for elves this is disgusting.'

Felix concurred, but the thing that concerned him more than the vileness of the place was its vastness. The street curved away into the smoke-shrouded distance before them and more streets branched from it on either side, and every house that they could see was a house of pleasure. They might search for the next three days and not find the house that hid the entrance to the secret temple.

His fear was unfounded, however, for as he and the others stood staring around slack-jawed, Farnir called to a female slave who was displaying herself lewdly in a window cage.

'Sister,' he said. 'Did a troop of Endless and a party of sorceresses pass this way?'

'Aye,' said the woman, not ceasing her gyrations.

'What house did they enter?'

The woman didn't know, but she told them that the procession had turned the corner to the left, a few hours ago.

It was in this way that they proceeded – Aethenir marching along as if he knew where he was going, while Farnir whispered questions to the slaves they passed – and they were legion – to learn where they should go. At last, after several more lefts and rights, they were directed to a house known as the Crucible of Joy.

Just before they reached it, Aethenir marched them into a dark alley between two houses and began unlocking their shackles. 'What am I to say?' he whimpered. 'What if we are turned away?'

'Then we fight at last,' said Gotrek.

'What if it isn't the right place after all?'

'We still fight,' said Gotrek.

'Tell them…' said Felix, trying to think. 'Tell them, "She awaits". If it is the right place, they will lead us to the sorceress. If it isn't, we haven't compromised ourselves.'

They left the unlocked shackles loose around their wrists and followed Aethenir out of the alley and up to the guards that stood before the door of the Crucible of Joy. From the outside at least, it looked little different than any of the other flesh houses. Its sign, if one could call it that, was a bubbling crucible hung over a fire in an alcove cut in the front wall, out of which spilled something that looked – and smelled – very much like blood. The guards were towering druchii women, dressed only in stained leather blacksmiths' aprons, golden greaves and gauntlets, and helmets crested with pink and purple feathers that looked like flames. They came to attention as Aethenir stopped in front of them.

Again, Felix could not understand what passed between them, but the guards seemed to treat him with the utmost deference. They bowed to him, and then one went to the door and spoke to someone within. After a moment, a human slave clad only in a purple loincloth came out, bowed almost to the floor, then motioned for them to follow.

The interior was everything that Felix had feared, and worse. The fire motif continued through a hexagonal entry chamber where braziers blazed with purple flames. A druchii woman, topless, but wearing a black veil, bowed to Aethenir as the slave led them into a corridor painted with black and purple flames. From above and below and all around Felix could hear sounds of ecstasy and excruciation – moans and screams and whimpers of fear. A girl pleaded heartbreakingly for mercy in Bretonnian. A male voice laughed or screamed, Felix couldn't decide which.

Through open archways only partially curtained, Felix saw glimpses of fire and flesh and murder being done. He flinched from brandings and scarrings and knives that glowed a cherry-red. Memories of fighting in the cellars of the Cleansing Flame, and the fires that Lichtmann had attacked them with, came unbidden to his mind and made him shiver. In one room he saw a ring of druchii men and women passing around an enamelled pipe as they watched molten gold being dripped from a crucible onto the face of a bound woman, one drop at a time. They laughed dreamily at each scream and convulsion.

Felix heard Gotrek growling beside him, and realised that he was echoing him with growls of his own.

The house slave led them down a winding iron staircase that was hot to the touch. Three flights later he bowed them into a square black marble chamber with doors on each wall and a chandelier of purple-flamed torches hanging above. Veins in the marble glinted pink in the flickering light. The door directly opposite the stair was grander than the others, framed by fluted columns and topped by a decorative arch, into which was set a white stone face of cold, immaculate beauty. Three Endless stood before the door, rigidly at attention.

Aethenir slowed when he saw them.

'Go on, elf,' muttered Gotrek.

'But surely they will know that I am not one of their fellows,' said the high elf.

'They will if you cower back here,' said Felix. 'Be bold.'

The elf snorted angrily at this, but it seemed to have some effect. He straightened his shoulders and strode towards the guards. Felix held his breath and loosened the mouth of the sack that carried their weapons. The guards eyed Aethenir as he approached, motionless and impassive behind their silver masks. Then the centre one spoke.

Aethenir replied, but apparently the answer was not to the Endless's liking. He asked a second question. This time Aethenir faltered in his response.

The hands of the guards dropped to the hilts of their swords and the centre one motioned for Aethenir to remove his mask.

'Right,' said Gotrek, throwing off his chains and dropping the sack with a clang. 'That's it.'

The Endless turned, drawing their swords as Gotrek and Felix pulled their weapons from the sack. Gotrek roared and charged them, shoving the paralysed Aethenir behind him. Felix followed the Slayer in, though he knew from past experience that it was hopeless. The slave in the loincloth ran shrieking back up the stairs as Farnir, Jochen and the pirates snatched up their weapons and joined the fray.

The Endless in the centre died on the first pass, parrying perfectly, but totally unprepared for the Slayer's strength. The flashing axe drove his blade back into his helm, staggering him, and Gotrek hacked him in the side, cutting through both armour and ribs like they were brittle shale.

Felix's first exchange with the druchii he faced was almost exactly opposite. He slashed with his sword, only to find that the druchii had moved and was stabbing at his chest with an overhand thrust. Felix twisted, and the sword grazed his ribs. He fell back, slashing desperate figure-eights in the air. The druchii followed and he thought he was dead, but then Farnir, Jochen and the pirates came to his rescue, hacking and stabbing and howling.

The druchii didn't bat an eye. He blocked every wild attack and returned with a riposte that skewered a pirate's neck. Felix lunged at him again, but his sword was turned neatly aside in passing as the druchii gashed another pirate's wrist and turned to face Felix again.

Felix fell back, then felt himself shoved aside, as Gotrek stepped in, swinging his axe up from the floor. The druchii saw him and spun to counter, but Gotrek was faster. The axe split the dark elf from crotch to chest and his guts slapped wetly on the polished floor. He crumpled on top of them.

Felix and the pirates stepped back, looking for the last druchii. He was already dead – his head missing. Another pirate had fallen as well, pierced through the heart.

'Well done, friends,' said Aethenir, stepping forwards.

'You might have helped,' said Jochen, looking around at his dead and wounded comrades.

'Better he didn't,' said Gotrek with a sneer.

The pirate searched the dead dark elves for the key to the door as Felix pulled his mail from the sack and put it on. There was no key. Whoever had entered had locked it behind them.

Gotrek shrugged and stepped to the door. 'Get ready,' he said.

Felix, Aethenir and the remaining pirates lined up behind him. Farnir armed himself with one of the druchii blades and joined them. Felix took a deep breath and got a firmer grip on Karaghul.

The door was of heavy, intricately carved wood. The lock was protected by a sturdy, black iron plate. Gotrek was through it in three swings of his axe, then kicked open the splintered panel and strode in, on his guard.

Inside was a large and entirely empty bedchamber.

Felix stared around him, confused. This was not the secret temple to some foul god that he had been expecting. This was – by druchii flesh house standards at any rate – a perfectly ordinary boudoir. A nightmarish mural of carnal atrocities was painted on the four walls above intricately worked ebony panelling. Fetters, whips and instruments of torture were displayed on racks to the right and left. Against the wall in front of them rose a massive sleeping platform, piled with furs and pillows, all in disarray, and so high that it was reached by a set of shallow black marble steps. At its four corners were hung columns of red velvet drapery, and torches were set into the wall on either side of it. All very grand and nasty, but a dead end.

'This can't be right,' said Jochen.

'We have been led astray somehow,' said Aethenir.

'Is it a trap?' asked Felix, looking back at the door.

Gotrek snorted. 'Men and elves are blind.'

He stumped across the room to the torch on the left-hand side of the sleeping platform and pressed the wood panelling below it. There was a click, and everyone stepped back, wary.

Felix watched the wall beside the torch, expecting to see a secret door open in it, but then movement caught his eye and he turned. The entire sleeping platform was slowly rising like the lid of a treasure chest, and folding back against the wall. The underside of the bed was revealed to be a large marble panel, carved into a bas-relief of a graceful figure that appeared to be both masculine and feminine, and who danced upon a mound of naked copulating bodies, all of them maimed in the most horrible ways. In the flickering torchlight of the room it almost seemed as if the figure and the bodies that it trod on writhed and squirmed lasciviously.

There was a hole in the raised platform where the bed had rested, with marble stairs that led down into darkness.

'Sigmar and Manann preserve us,' said Jochen.

Felix had the sinking suspicion that they would shortly need the help of every god they could call upon.

THE STAIRS WENT straight down for so long that Felix was afraid they would come out at the bottom of the floating island and be dumped in the sea again. There were no torches mounted on the walls. They felt their way down in utter darkness but for a reddish glow far below them that bobbed and weaved with each step. The further down they went, the thicker the air became – a cloying soup of incense, lotus smoke, and something sharp and bitter.

Then another, closer glow began to light their steps. Felix looked around and saw that the runes on Gotrek's axe were pulsing as if fire was coursing through them.

'Gotrek…' he said.

'Aye, manling.'

As they descended further, the red glow resolved itself into the reflection of crimson light shining upon a black marble floor at the base of the stairs. Gotrek and Felix stepped cautiously down to it and looked along a short corridor that ended at a pair of half-open, unguarded doors, through which came the red light, accompanied by the sound of voices raised in a high, wailing chant that set Felix's teeth on edge.

With the others edging forwards behind them, Gotrek and Felix crept to the doors, a pair of heavy gold panels crusted with rubies, amethysts and lapis lazuli in patterns that depicted thousands of naked bodies entwined in impossible, painful ways. Felix looked through the gap between them, then jerked his head back, startled, for a face was staring directly at them.

'It's only a statue, manling,' said Gotrek.

Felix looked again. The air inside was so hazed with violet smoke that it was hard to make out details, but directly ahead of them, in the middle of a circular, brazier-lit chamber, was a statue of a six-headed snake that reared up twice as high as a man. Each of the snake heads was fronted with a beautiful white marble druchii face of indeterminate gender, one of them looking directly at the door with eyes that glittered like living onyx. Half-hidden behind the statue, on the far side of the room, was a pillared archway that opened into a further chamber, within which Felix could see shadows of sinuous movement that seemed to follow the rhythms of the chanting.

Gotrek pushed through the obscene doors and entered. Felix tried to follow, but as he put his hand on the door, his mind whirled with unbidden emotions. All in an instant he wanted to weep and rage, laugh and kill, love and torture. A vision of writing the Slayer's story in the Slayer's blood on vellum made from the Slayer's flesh crawled up into his brain, and he found he could not push it away.

'This is an evil place,' said Aethenir, behind him.

The words brought Felix back to himself. He forced the horrid visions back down into his subconscious and followed the Slayer into the chamber. Aethenir, Farnir, Jochen and the pirates edged in even more reluctantly. The pirates huddled together like frightened cattle, and Farnir clutched a stolen sword like it was a lifeline. Under his druchii helm, Aethenir's eyes showed white all around, and he murmured a constant stream of elven prayers.

The chamber was perfectly circular. Walls of pink stone glittered like mica, and it throbbed with low moans of pain and ecstasy, counterpoint to the wailing chant that continued to grate on Felix's ears. Purple flames leapt in golden braziers set at regular intervals around the walls, and the floor was a mosaic of golden tiles with a large offset ring of purple tiles within them, surrounded by strange runes. The six-headed snake sat at the centre of the room, with its pedestal touching the arc of the offset ring.

As they crept across the golden floor towards the far archway, they passed close to the statue, and Felix saw around its base offerings of wine, blood, ink and other intimate liquids shimmered in little golden dishes amidst pink, red and purple candles. The pirates skirted warily around the thing, spitting and making warding signs.

Beyond the archway was the second chamber. Thick purple smoke made it hard to tell just how large it was, but if there was a back wall Felix couldn't see it. It appeared though to be another circle, with pillars ringing a sunken central area in which there was a broad circular platform. Braziers as big as shields were set between the pillars, within which smouldering mounds of incense raised columns of curling smoke that seemed to form into semi-human shapes if Felix looked at them too long.

Behind drifting veils of smoke, High Sorceress Heshor stood facing away from them in the centre of a circle drawn on the marble surface of the raised platform, her arms raised in supplication. The Harp of Ruin sat upon a tall black iron table before her. A much larger circle bordered – but did not intersect – hers. There was a crude stone table within the larger circle, and something – or some things – lay upon it, obscured by the haze.

Strange, many-limbed shapes writhed to either side of Heshor, and it took Felix a moment to see that the shapes were Heshor's five sorceresses, lying along the edge of the platform and coupling wildly with five of the Endless, naked but for their skull masks, and drenched with sweat. The lovers tore at each other constantly with sharpened fingernails, and all bled from long weals that criss-crossed their bodies, yet they moaned in a chorus of rising ecstasy. They looked as if they had been at it for hours. Felix shivered in disgust at the sight, and yet it was impossible to deny a horrible arousal as well.

The participants in the strange ceremony were guarded by seven armoured Endless, standing on the steps that descended to the centre, and watching the proceedings while at attention, their swords drawn and point-down on the floor before them.

'Magister Schreiber,' breathed Aethenir. 'And Fraulein Pallenberger.'

Felix frowned, for he had no idea what the high elf meant, then he followed his gaze and saw that the lumps that lay upon the stone table within the larger circle were indeed Max and Claudia, cruelly strapped down with leather ropes and with their mouths bound and gagged.

He choked when he saw them. They were almost unrecognisable. They were naked and emaciated, and both had been shaved entirely bald, even unto the eyebrows. Paint had been applied to their faces and their bodies in purple and red swirls, and runes had been carved into their skin with knives. Max looked a hundred years old, Claudia's ribs stood out through her lacerated skin, and their eyes were shut tight as if in pain.

Gotrek spat, disgusted at the sight.

'Sigmar,' murmured Felix. 'Are they are alive?'

'They are alive,' said Aethenir dully. 'They are sacrifices to the Great Defiler.'

'Sacrifices!' said Felix, horrified.

Aethenir shuddered. 'It appears she intends to raise a daemon, though what purpose that would serve in using the harp I know not.'

Gotrek's eye lit up. 'A daemon!'

'Control your lust for glory, dwarf,' said Aethenir. 'If Heshor succeeds in calling something out of the void, your friends will be killed.' He trembled. 'Though it must surely mean our death, we must strike before the ceremony is finished.'

The moans of pleasure coming from the archway were growing higher and more urgent, as was Heshor's chanting. 'That might be very soon,' Felix said, swallowing.

'Leave the skull-faces to me,' said Gotrek. He turned to Felix and the others. 'Kill the hags and save Max and the girl.'

Jochen and his men looked at him like he had suggested they run into a burning building, but they nodded. Felix nodded too, though he wondered if it would go quite as neatly as that.

Felix, Farnir and the pirates lined up on either side of the archway, weapons at the ready. Aethenir stood further back, readying spells of healing and protection. Felix was finding it difficult to concentrate. The cries of ecstasy were getting louder and wilder, and try as he might, they were stirring dark thoughts and desires in his depths. He could see that the pirates were affected as well, twitching and grunting and shaking their heads like bulls beset by flies.

Gotrek stepped to the centre of the archway, running his thumb along the blade of his axe until it drew blood. The axe's runes blazed like the glow of a furnace. Gotrek raised it over his head and opened his mouth to roar a challenge, but before he could speak, with simultaneous shrieks, the coupling druchii all climaxed together, while in the same instant, Heshor shrieked the final words of her summoning.

There was a crack like thunder and the room shook, nearly knocking them off their feet. Suddenly the air was filled with the cloying scents of roses and ambergris and sweet milk, and Felix felt the presence of a terrifying intelligence looming within his brain. His vague stirrings of desire were suddenly an all-encompassing lust. He wanted to race into the summoning room, not to kill, but to tear off his clothes and join the druchii in their orgy. Only past experience with alien thoughts invading his mind allowed him to resist the urges and understand that they were not his own. He shook like an aspen as he concentrated on hating the intruding emotions and casting them out.

The pirates, unfortunately, had not encountered such violent attacks on their consciousness before, and knew not how to resist. They shrieked and tore at themselves and their clothes. Some of them pawed at each other like lovers, while others stumbled through the arch towards the chamber, their breeches around their ankles.

'Come back!' called Jochen, though it was clear he was only inches from following them.

Felix reached after one to drag him back, and looked into the chamber. He regretted it instantly.

Standing in the large circle before Heshor and wreathed in rose-coloured fog was the most beautiful being Felix had ever seen. She – he? – it? – towered more than twice the height of a man and appeared to be neither male nor female but, unsettlingly, both – a voluptuous icon of lust that looked directly at him and beckoned him hither with violet eyes and luscious lips.

'What do you desire of me?' it asked in a voice like honeyed thunder.

High Sorceress Heshor replied in the druchii tongue, her arms spread wide. Felix cursed her. It was speaking to him, not her! Felix stepped forwards, trying to see the beauty more clearly. He caught glimpses of writhing tentacles, or perhaps swaying snakes, graceful limbs and clawed hands, that seemed to flicker in and out of existence. He couldn't decide if the beauty had two arms or four, if it had breasts or a powerful chest, if its legs were those of a shapely woman or those of a goat.

'Back, manling,' said Gotrek.

Felix was jerked roughly back. He turned, snarling at this intrusion into his luscious dream, then blinked. Gotrek had pulled him behind him. He had been halfway into the summoning chamber though he had no memory of moving forwards. A dozen Endless were streaming up the curved steps towards them, half still naked, swords high, cutting down the enraptured pirates as they passed them.

Gotrek bellowed a challenge and slashed with his axe as three armoured Endless reached him. The first blocked the blow, but the force of it pushed him into another, staggering both of them. Felix ran one through before he recovered, but that was the last blood he drew. The rest of the Endless swarmed around him and Gotrek, Farnir, Jochen and the pirates, swords flickering faster than the eye could follow.

Aethenir huddled in the shadow of the arch, waving his hands, though whether he was casting spells or only flailing in fear Felix couldn't tell.

'Out of my way!' Gotrek roared at the Endless. 'I've a daemon to kill!'

The Slayer lashed about him in a blur of steel, his axe's rune-glow trailing behind it like a comet tail, but he was the only one fast enough to return the dark elves' attacks. Half the pirates were dead in seconds, and Jochen had a gash on his forehead that showed bone. Even firm of mind and in the best of health they would have been no match for the Endless. Starved on gruel and distracted by unnatural lusts, they fell like wheat before the scythe.

Another Endless went down before Gotrek, but the end was inevitable. There were too many of them. It was just Felix, Farnir, Jochen and the Slayer now. Then Jochen died with a foot of steel sticking from his back. Felix took a savage cut on his left forearm and suddenly his sword felt like lead. Two Endless were stabbing at him at the same time. He couldn't block both. He fought to raise his sword, knowing that he was going to die.

The two druchii suddenly stumbled aside, their swords missing him. In fact, all around him the druchii were turning and falling and shouting in confusion. Felix blinked, surprised, but didn't fail to take advantage. He ran one through the neck, then turned to see what had staggered them. He gaped. The chamber was suddenly chest deep in dwarfs, all attacking the Endless.

Gotrek turned as he cut down another masked druchii. 'You,' he said.

'Da!' cried Farnir.

Birgi saluted them with a bloody shovel. Skalf raised a framing maul. Their heads were bald and bleeding from dozens of little cuts. It looked like they had shaved them with butchers' cleavers. Felix looked around. All the dwarfs in the room had shaved their heads and had armed themselves with what makeshift weapons they could find – picks, hammers, fireplace pokers, frying pans, pitchforks and roasting spits, and they battered the Endless with them with terrifying fury. Felix was amazed and relieved.

'We've heeded your words, Slayer,' Birgi said. 'Go take your doom. This is ours.'

EIGHTEEN

'ABOUT TIME,' SAID Gotrek, but his voice was gruff. 'Come on, manling!'

He turned from the newly made Slayers and started towards the summoning chamber. As Felix followed, he saw that the sorceresses had risen and were joining Heshor in a new chant, all calling out an endlessly repeated phrase while extending their arms towards the harp and sending energy pulsing towards it. The daemon too thrust its hands forwards, feeding the harp with its power, and the instrument glowed within a pink and purple aura. Two of the abomination's other appendages were held out towards Max and Claudia, and curls of white and blue vapour rose from their bodies and trailed towards the daemon.

'It's killing them,' said Felix.

'Worse,' said Aethenir, stepping up behind them. 'Much worse.' He trembled as he fell in with them, but he did not falter. He held a druchii sword in his hand.

The sorceresses – still naked – were all facing away from them as Gotrek, Felix and Aethenir strode into the chamber, concentrating their attention and their energies on the harp. The daemon too was fixed on the harp, but Felix could feel its attention everywhere at once, a beacon that charred what it illuminated.

'Your warriors have failed you, daughters,' it said as Felix, Aethenir and the Slayer ran down the stairs into the circle. 'Your enemies draw near.'

Heshor did not turn or slacken the flow of energy she was pouring into the harp, but by some silent command, two of her sorceresses did. One was Belryeth, Aethenir's nemesis, and she laughed when she saw him.

'Dearest, you return to me!' she said as she wove her incantations. 'Love, it seems, conquers all.'

'Honour conquers all,' hissed the high elf, and leapt up onto the platform straight at her, sword high.

She and her sister shot streamers of black mist at him and Gotrek and Felix. Aethenir screamed and dropped his sword as it enveloped him, but pitched himself headlong into Belryeth and they went down together on the platform. The Slayer shrugged off the mist and bulled on, but Felix staggered as it blew over him, every inch of his skin screaming as if he was being both frozen and cooked at the same time. His muscles tensed to the point of snapping and he crashed to the floor before the platform.

Gotrek leapt onto the platform and slashed his axe at the second sorceress in passing, his eye never leaving the daemon. She shrieked and fell as it bit into her side.

With her death, the black cloud dissipated, but the effects of the spell lingered, needles of fire and ice stabbing into Felix, and he could only watch as Gotrek plunged across the platform straight for the daemon.

Heshor and the other sorceresses broke off their chanting and shrieked at this interruption, but the daemon smiled down at Gotrek as he leapt across the warding line that bound it within its circle.

'Ah, little one,' it purred. 'You save me from boredom. Excellent.'

It slashed down at Gotrek with a crab-clawed arm it had not possessed a second before. Gotrek blocked the blow with the flat of his axe and was bowled back like a hedgehog hit with a spade. He bounced twice before he spun off the platform and slammed to the floor of the chamber.

'Come, try again,' laughed the daemon. 'I haven't experienced a wound in millennia.'

Felix fought to his feet. On the platform, Aethenir and Belryeth were rolling back and forth in a parody of ecstasy as they fought for control of her dagger, while Heshor and her coven blasted the Slayer as he pushed himself up to his knees, shaking his head. The spells seemed only to anger Gotrek, and he roared as he rose to his feet.

Felix saw his chance. Though every sane portion of his brain told him to turn and run the other way, he jumped up onto the platform, weaved through the angry sorceresses and ran into the daemon's circle – being careful, even in his mad rush, not to disturb the warding line, which appeared to have been drawn with some kind of purple powder – and aimed for the table upon which Max and Claudia were bound.

He didn't make it. The daemon turned its full attention upon him as he crossed the purple line and he stopped as if he had run into the wall, held by the power of its regard.

'Have you come to steal my sacrifices, beloved?' it murmured, reaching hooked claws out towards him. 'Or to join them?'

Felix's mouth went slack, overwhelmed by the daemon's majesty. He stumbled towards it, spreading his arms to receive its cruel embrace. He had never longed for anything more than he longed to be rent apart by those beautiful glistening claws.

Suddenly the daemon shrieked, and Felix collapsed as its pain broadcast through the chamber, sending waves of searing agony through his mind. He hit the ground screaming and writhing and saw that Aethenir and the sorceresses were too. Even Max and Claudia struggled and spasmed in their bonds. Only Heshor remained upright, shaking and tearing at her hair and gouging her face with her nails.

The daemon was falling back before the Slayer, who had somehow climbed back onto the platform. Purple blood spewed from a deep wound in the daemon's leg, and the edges of it boiled and sizzled as if they had been splashed with acid.

'Exquisite,' rumbled the apparition's beautiful voice, as it slashed at Gotrek with an enormous black sword that it plucked from thin air. The Slayer ducked the blow and chopped at its other leg. A new claw parried the blow, and a suddenly appearing mace smashed down at him from above.

Felix's waves of pain subsided as the daemon's attention was narrowed to fighting Gotrek, and he found he could move again. He crawled to the stone table and pulled himself up on it. Close to, Max and Claudia looked even worse than they had at a distance. Their cheeks were hollow and their skin slack and filthy. Scrapes and bruises and ritual cuts covered them from head to toe, and their fingernails were cracked and bloody, as if they had tried to dig their way through stone. Max had a black eye and Claudia a split lip. The seeress was unconscious, and Max only a little better. His eyes rolled madly when he saw Felix and he mumbled something behind his gag.

Felix reached trembling hands forwards and sawed through the silk cords that held the gag in place, then pulled it from his lips.

'My hands,' mouthed the wizard, his voice rattling like paper. 'Then I can defend you.'

Felix almost laughed at this. Max didn't look like he could defend himself against a strong wind, let alone daemons and sorceresses. Nonetheless, he went to work on the braided leather that held Max's wrists. He didn't get far, for the daemon wailed again and its pain drove all thought and ability out of Felix's head. The screams of the sorceresses told him that they too were affected.

One of the daemon's arms was effervescing away and it staggered back to the limits of its circle as it defended itself against the Slayer with three other limbs.

'That axe,' it moaned. 'I know it now.' It shifted the weight of its attention to Heshor. 'Release me back to the void, mortal. I crave sensation, not destruction.'

'No!' shrieked the high sorceress, some resonance with the daemon's all-encompassing consciousness allowing Felix to understand her though she spoke in the druchii tongue. 'You must fulfil your bargain! Finish the dwarf and resume!'

'You will hold me to your regret, hag,' it rumbled, as Gotrek attacked it again.

Felix recovered himself and finished cutting through Max's wrist bonds and started on Claudia's. He looked back. The sorceresses were standing again.

'Kill the human!' cried Heshor, pointing a black-nailed finger at him. 'He must not disturb the sacrifices!'

She and the three still-standing sorceresses turned towards him, spouting vile incantations as Max mumbled a protection, moving his hands weakly through the ritual motions.

But then, before either spells or counter-spells could be completed, the daemon smashed Gotrek in the chest with an armoured fist the size of a boulder and sent him flying back again. This time the Slayer hit the platform shoulder-first and skidded backwards towards the edge – straight through the purple powder boundary of the binding circle, wiping it away. Blood welled from the Slayer's nose and mouth as he came to a stop. He didn't move.

Heshor and her sorceresses gasped and faltered in their incantations at this momentous accident. The daemon laughed.

'Did I not say?' it chuckled, then strode out of the circle, straight towards Heshor. 'Come, daughter, I will make you a guest of my realm, as you have welcomed me to yours.'

The sorceress screamed and backed away, snatching up the harp as her remaining sisters stepped before her to guard her retreat, blasting the daemon with their black sorcery.

The daemon appeared to relish the attack, moaning with pleasure but slowing not one whit. It caressed the three sorceresses with probing tentacles and they collapsed in paroxysms of ecstasy so intense that they snapped their own spines.

Heshor turned and ran with the harp, but then a bloody figure rose up and tackled her, stabbing at her with a dagger. Felix was shocked to see that it was Aethenir.

'For Ulthuan and the asur!' he cried as they slammed to the ground, the harp between them. 'For Rion and the path of honour!'

'No, scholar,' shrilled Belryeth as she stood and leapt to defend her mistress. 'You will win no redemption.' She dragged Aethenir off Heshor as the daemon stepped closer.

The high sorceress scrambled to her feet as the high elf and the young sorceress fought once again, and fled for the door.

The daemon came after her, laughing melodiously. 'Do you abandon me now, dear heart? Have you not pledged your undying love to me?'

It trod on Aethenir and Belryeth as it followed her, and they screamed, though whether in pain or delight, it was hard to tell. They continued flailing and fighting as the daemon slashed down at Heshor with an arm like a bone scythe.

Heshor leapt away, but the tip of the appendage gashed her trailing leg and she fell on the steps that led to the outer chamber. The daemon loomed over her, raising new arms, but then, just as her fate seemed sealed, a red-crested figure staggered out of the shadows, then leapt up and buried its axe in the base of the daemon's spine.

'Die, spawn of the abyss!' roared the Slayer, blood bubbling from his mouth with every word.

The daemon shrieked with a thousand tortured voices, and its agony once again crushed Felix to the ground with its vastness. It turned and staggered back from the Slayer, bits of it fading in and out as it bled pink mist. The wound in its lower back grew larger as Felix watched, sharing its agony, the edges eating away like parchment attacked by fire.

The daemon glared down at Gotrek as the Slayer stumped doggedly after it. 'No, little one. I will not fight you. This is not my fate. One greater than I is to die killing you. In the meanwhile, I will relish your disappointment.'

And then, between blinks, it was gone, and the chamber was silent, the sudden vacuum of its absence almost as painful as its presence had been. It felt for a moment as if all the joy and colour and excitement had been bled from the world – as if life wasn't worth living. Felix almost wept.

Gotrek, on the other hand, roared with rage, slamming his axe down and shattering the marble floor. 'Craven hellspawn!' he bellowed. 'Leavings of the void! Will you rob me of my death? Will you rob me of glory? Come back and face me!'

Felix looked up, terrified, but the daemon failed to reappear. Gotrek bent over and coughed blood all over the floor, the glow fading from the runes on his axe.

Recovering, Felix looked around for High Sorceress Heshor. She was gone – and so was the Harp of Ruin.

'The harp,' he said, struggling to stand. 'We…'

'Felix,' came Max's feeble whisper. 'Claudia's bonds.'

Felix returned to the stone table and finished cutting Claudia free. She did not move or open her eyes.

Felix checked her pulse. 'We had hoped to save you before this,' he said. There was a faint flutter beneath his fingers. 'But they moved you.'

Max sat up as if he was made of dry twigs. 'I am frankly surprised to see you at all. The last we saw of you…'

'Friends,' came a weak voice from behind them. 'Help me. Something has happened.'

Max and Felix turned. Aethenir lay where the daemon had stepped upon him and Belryeth. He was under the sorceress and pushing at her.

'Release me, cursed asur,' whined the sorceress, flailing in his grasp.

Max and Felix limped wearily to the two elves, but as they came closer, Felix staggered and nearly vomited. Max choked.

Something had indeed happened. It had appeared from a distance that Belryeth lay on top of Aethenir. This was not the case. In truth, they had become one. The touch of the daemon had fused them in a permanent lovers' embrace. Their bodies were melted together at the torso, Belryeth's head looking forever over Aethenir's shoulder, and their arms and legs intertwined.

'By the gods,' said Felix, gagging.

'Horrible,' agreed Max.

'Please, friends,' said Aethenir, looking up at them with frightened eyes. 'Do something.'

'Take him away,' whimpered Belryeth.

Gotrek stepped up and looked down at them. He snorted. 'A fit punishment for causing all this,' he said.

Felix glared at him.

'Don't be cruel, Slayer,' said Max.

'Taking your example, Slayer,' said Aethenir, 'I had hoped to die to atone for my sin, But this… this is not to be borne.'

Felix looked at Max. 'Is there nothing to be done?'

Max shook his head. 'The unmaking of this would be beyond the greatest of magisters.'

'Do you still wish for death, elf?' asked Gotrek.

Aethenir swallowed, then nodded. 'Aye, dwarf.'

'Then pray and die well.'

Aethenir looked around at them all and spoke. 'Let it be said that, though I strayed from it, I died upon the path of honour.' Then he closed his eyes and murmured a prayer as Gotrek raised his axe.

When the scholar's prayer was finished, the Slayer let the axe fall and beheaded him. Aethenir's face was peaceful when his head rolled to a stop.

Felix silently bade the high elf farewell. He might have been a fool, and perhaps not the bravest of his race, but, as he had said, in the end he had not flinched from doing what he could to rectify his foolishness.

'Come on,' said Gotrek, striding towards the outer chamber. 'There's still the sorceress.'

'Wait!' cried Belryeth. 'You can't leave me like this! Kill me like you killed him.'

They all looked down at her, then at each other.

'It would be much more fitting to spare your life,' said Max.

'Barbarians!' she cried. 'You will pay for this indignity!'

They ignored her. Felix draped one of the naked seeress's discarded black robes around Claudia, picked her up and put her over his shoulder, then hurried after the Slayer. Max donned the surcoat of one of the Endless and joined them.

In the outer chamber the Endless were dead, but so were the dwarf slaves, their bodies strewn about the room with great wounds hacked through them by the Endless's longswords. By contrast, the druchii had been dragged down and bludgeoned to death. Not one of them still had a face. The mosaic floor was a lake of blood.

Kneeling in the middle of the lake was Farnir, cradling the head of his father in his lap. The young dwarf was near death. There was a wound in his chest that made red bubbles when he breathed. Birgi was dead, a wound in his side opening him up to his spine.

Farnir looked up. There were tears in his eyes. 'Have we saved the Old World?' he asked.

Gotrek looked at him, then towards the door that led to the stairs. 'We will, beardling. Rest easy.'

'Aye,' said the slave. 'Aye, good.' He closed his eyes and slumped over the body of his father and died.

Gotrek bowed his head. 'May Grungni welcome you in his halls.'

They hurried on, splashing through the blood to the stairs. Felix found it impossible to dismiss Farnir's face from his mind as they started up the endless flight of stairs. The young dwarf had lived almost his entire life as a slave of the druchii. He had seen nothing of the world except the inside of the black ark, and yet he had died gladly for a homeland and an idea of honour he knew only from a few old stories told to him by his father. He had died to preserve a whole race's freedom, a thing he had never known himself.

BY THE TIME they had followed Heshor's trail of blood spatters to the top of the stairs, Max was crawling on his hands and knees, Felix's legs were like jelly, and even Gotrek, suffering from the daemon's last hammer-blow punch to the chest, was wheezing, wiping blood from his mouth with the back of his hand.

A few steps from the top the Slayer paused. Twittering voices and the sound of hurried movement came from the room above.

'Put down the girl and ready your sword, manling.'

Felix did as he was ordered, giving Claudia over to the care of Max, and sucking in deep breaths to strengthen himself. Then, at a nod from Gotrek, they ran up the stairs and into the druchii boudoir.

A crowd of slaves and harlots and pleasure house guards swarmed around what looked like a litter in the centre of the room. Several of them turned as Gotrek and Felix burst in, and Felix saw that the litter was in fact a low divan, and that Heshor lay on it, clutching the Harp of Ruin as a slave tried to bind the wound in her leg.

The guards shouted and charged Gotrek and Felix, while a majordomo cried orders and four burly human slaves picked the divan up at its four corners and ran towards the door as the whores and slaves shrieked after them.

Gotrek hewed through the guards like they were tall grass. Even Felix cut one down – they were hardly the elite fighters the Endless had been. The fight slowed them down nonetheless, and by the time the last guard fell to Gotrek's axe, his head dangling from a string of neck flesh, Heshor's makeshift stretcher was out the door.

Gotrek tramped towards it resolutely. Felix looked behind him. Max was just rising from the opening in the bed platform. Claudia's arm was draped over his shoulder, but she was moving under her own power.

'Go,' said Max. 'We'll catch up.'

Felix nodded and hurried after Gotrek. They ran out into the hallway just in time to see the slaves and the divan disappearing up the iron stairs opposite.

They charged after them, though Gotrek was wheezing and Felix felt like an anvil sat on his chest. At the top of the stairs they saw Heshor's bearers running down the long purple hall to the foyer and started after them, but it was clear that the sorceress would escape the pleasure house before they caught up with her.

Gotrek skidded to a stop, cocked back his arm, and threw his axe. It spun end over end down the hall and bit into the back of the slave holding the back left corner of the divan with a sickening chunk. The slave screamed and fell. The divan dropped at his corner and Heshor squawked and let go of the harp to steady herself. It bounced across the marble floor.

The other slaves screamed in fear and ran on, steadying the divan. Heshor screamed orders and pointed back at the harp, but they didn't heed her and ran out through the open door.

Gotrek and Felix thundered into the hexagonal foyer seconds layer. Gotrek wrenched his axe from the dead slave's back and raced with Felix to the door, but as they burst out onto the shallow front porch they drew up sharply. The street was filled in every direction with what appeared to be the black ark's entire complement of spear companies, lined up in orderly ranks and all facing the front door of the pleasure house. In their centre, next to an imperious druchii in elaborate armour who Felix deduced must be Lord Tarlkhir, commander of the ark, Heshor sat up on her divan and pointed a trembling finger at Gotrek.

Gotrek chuckled deep in his throat and readied his dripping axe. 'Foes without number,' he said, grinning savagely.

At an order from Tarlkhir, the druchii lowered their spears and started to advance.

Felix looked back through the door to the harp, which still rang on the marble floor near the middle of the foyer and seemed, strangely, to be getting louder rather than diminishing.

'Gotrek,' he said. 'Wait. Perhaps we should destroy the harp first, just in case they get through us.'

Gotrek grunted, but he could see the logic in this, because he jumped back through the door, then turned and strode for the harp.

'Lock it, manling,' he said.

Felix slammed and locked the door just as the first druchii mounted the house's steps, then crossed to the Slayer, who was looking down at the harp, which was ringing even louder now, dancing on the tiles of the floor. Felix could feel the vibrations through his feet. The foyer moaned with sympathetic overtones that made Felix want to pop his ears.

'Foul thing,' said Gotrek, as the sound of spear butts thudded on the door behind them.

Felix had to agree. Its growing note was a discordant howl that hurt the ears, and its twisted, black, U-shaped body was vibrating so much now that its edges were blurred. Its translucent strings quivered like strands of saliva.

Felix stepped back as Gotrek lifted his axe over his head for a mighty stroke.

A weak voice came from the purple corridor. 'Slayer, no!'

Gotrek and Felix looked around. Max was limping up the corridor towards them with Claudia stumbling along beside him. 'Break it, and the energies released could kill us all!' said Max.

Gotrek raised an eyebrow. 'Truly?' An evil smile spread across his ugly face. 'Good.'

He reached down and grabbed for the harp, but he had trouble reaching it. His thick fingers stopped inches from it, as if blocked by an invisible wall, and his hand and arm shook. He cursed. Dust began sifting down from the roof of the chamber, shaken loose by the harp's vibrations, and the braziers that ringed the room rattled in their alcoves, spitting sparks.

'Filthy magic.'

Max looked at the harp with fear. 'Its strings have been struck. It is releasing its power.'

With bared teeth Gotrek forced his arm forwards, his muscles bulging and the veins popping out on his forearms and neck, then closed his hand around the harp's vibrating frame. It continued to ring, making his fingers blur as he turned to the door, which was shuddering from the blows of the druchii spears.

'Open it, manling,' he said through clenched teeth.

Felix stared at the harp. Pebbles and mortar were now pitter-pattering down along with the dust, and he could feel the vibrations in his chest and heart as if he were standing beside a company of kettle drummers. His knees shook with it. He couldn't imagine how it must feel to hold it.

'Manling!'

Felix snapped out of it and ran to the door. He drew the bolt, then pulled it open and jumped to the side. A wave of druchii spearmen stumbled in, caught off balance, and Gotrek slammed into them, chopping one-handed with his axe as he held the roaring harp in the other.

The druchii soldiers fell back before the savagery of Gotrek's bloodthirsty attack and the instrument's horrible noise, retreating to the bottom of the steps and holding their ears, ten of their fellows dead in as many seconds. Gotrek strode out and looked across to Heshor, who was staring at him from her divan next to Commander Tarlkhir on the far side of the street.

'Here's your harp, witch!' he bellowed, holding it up. It looked like the thing was shaking the meat from his arm. 'Come get it.'

He threw it down on the porch in front of him.

It was possibly not one of the Slayer's better ideas.

The harp clanged off the flagstones, and a shockwave like a mortar impact rocked the building and knocked them all to the ground. The witchlight globes in the foyer's chandelier exploded and rained crystal shards down upon them. Cracks ran up the plastered walls, and the steaming crucible that was the symbol of the house jumped its hooks and clattered to the ground, spilling boiling blood across the cobbles. The street was pelted with falling masonry and black slate roof tiles. Spearmen were clubbed to the ground by stones. The floor Felix lay on split and buckled. The harp rang in his ears like a hundred temple bells. His sword sang as if it was being struck with a mallet, and shook so hard he could barely hold it. His guts churned. His heart hammered in his chest.

'Fool of a dwarf!' shouted Heshor in Reikspiel. 'Surrender it before it buries you in rubble. Only I can stop it. Only I can save you.'

Gotrek picked himself up, laughing as more masonry smashed down all around him. 'Save a Slayer? I'm taking you all with me!' He picked up his axe and started to raise it. Heshor shrieked. The druchii soldiers scrambled back, trying to get away. A block the size of a cow slammed down from above, crushing three of them.

Gotrek cackled maniacally and raised his axe high above his head, but just as he started to slash down, something bright shot down past him from above and jerked the harp aside. Gotrek's axe missed it, and shattered the black marble of the porch instead.

Gotrek ripped his axe from the stone, cursing, and swung again at the harp, but it hopped into the air like a puppet and his axe swished under it. Felix gaped as it rose higher. It was hooked to a crossbow bolt with flanges like a grapnel, swinging at the end of a grey silk cord.

Felix and Gotrek stared after the harp as it shot up towards the rooftops. Heshor and Commander Tarlkhir shouted and pointed. Halfway up, it clanged against the wall of a house, and this time the impact rocked the whole ark, making it boom like a giant drum. The street lurched and dropped, knocking everyone to the cobbles, and the roaring throb that filled the air drowned out even the sounds of half-ton stones tearing from the ceiling and smashing druchii to a pulp in the street. From the depths of the ark came a sound like muffled thunder and a deep tectonic rumbling.

Felix looked up through the rain of debris that was falling from the cave ceiling, searching for the harp. Then he saw it – a glittering, bouncing spark, hanging from the barbed bolt that had whisked it away, dragged, banging and clanging across the shaking, shattering rooftops of the pleasure houses behind a pack of scrawny scampering black shadows.

NINETEEN

'SKAVEN!' SHOUTED FELIX, pointing.

'After them,' roared Gotrek.

Heshor and Commander Tarlkhir were shouting the same thing to their troops, and the druchii spear companies hared off down the street, following the leaping shadows.

Gotrek and Felix ran after them, but it quickly became clear that it was impossible. The skaven were already out of sight, and there were thousands of druchii spears in the way, all trying to do the same thing.

Gotrek stopped when they reached the first intersection, watching Heshor and Tarlkhir's forces hurry away ahead of them. 'This won't work,' he shouted.

'No,' Felix shouted back.

Though they no longer stood beside the harp, the walls and streets around them still throbbed with deafening sympathetic vibrations, and they were getting worse. It

was like being inside a snoring giant's nose. Blocks of
stone and spear-tip stalactites dropped all around them.
Felix had a vision of the harp getting louder and louder
and its resonances and reverberations stronger and
stronger until at last it shook the whole world apart. The
ark would only be the beginning. When it shattered, the
harp would fall to the ocean floor and continue vibrating, causing earthquakes and tidal waves that would
drown the Old World, the northlands and Ulthuan
beneath the waves. The high elves had been right to lock
the vile instrument in a vault. Perhaps they had even
sunk the city on purpose to hide the horrible thing away
for all time.

'They're going out. So we go out,' called the Slayer. 'This
way.'

The Slayer turned around and stomped back towards
the flesh house, pushing through the crowds of druchii
gallants and whores and half-dressed officers who were
spilling out of the houses and screaming orders at each
other and the jostling throngs of slaves – all so frightened that they ignored Gotrek and Felix entirely.

Max and Claudia stood in the door of the crumbling
pleasure house when they returned to it, looking fearfully out at the rain of debris. Gotrek beckoned to them
and continued on down the street, back the way they had
originally come. The magister and the seeress ducked
their heads and limped out after them.

'The skaven have stolen the harp,' said Felix as they fell
in beside him. 'We went after them but it was impossible.
We're getting out.'

'An admirable idea,' said Max.

Felix took Claudia's arm, hurrying her along and keeping her steady as the ground continued to vibrate
beneath their feet.

'Are you well, Fraulein Pallenberger?' he shouted over the din of destruction.

'I… I no longer know,' she said dully. 'But I am glad you live.'

Felix looked at her with concern. Her voice was utterly devoid of life or spark. Had her experiences shattered her mind? Imprisoned and abused by the druchii, attacked by the blackest of magics and exposed to the reality-altering presence of a daemon, it would be little wonder if they had.

Gotrek led them back towards the stair to the barracks, but before they had gone two blocks, another titanic crack rocked the ark, sending everyone lurching sideways as the street tilted violently to the left. Felix caught Claudia before she fell, then almost fell himself. Ahead of them the facade of a building toppled forwards and sloughed to the ground like a spill of gravel, crushing dozens of druchii and their slaves.

Max looked pale. 'The harp's vibrations have disrupted the magics that hold the ark level. I don't think it will survive.'

'Good,' said Gotrek.

Water started to stream down from the ceiling.

They all looked up, as did the druchii and the slaves all around them.

'What's happened?' asked Felix.

'We're under the harbour,' said Gotrek. 'It's sprung a leak. Keep moving.'

'Not again,' murmured Claudia, but when Felix asked her to repeat herself, she had sunk back into dull silence.

Too soon the water was ankle deep and rising steadily. Great columns of it poured down from the cracks in the roof, and carriage-sized stones were breaking away around the rifts and thundering down to smash houses to bits.

They reached the narrow door to the corridor that passed the beastmaster's menagerie and found scores of druchii and slaves running out of it, shouting and waving others back. Gotrek and Felix pushed through against the tide and pulled Max and Claudia in after them.

The crowded corridor echoed with frightened animal roaring and the screams of terrified humans and druchii. In the shadowed distance near the menagerie gates, fur-cloaked druchii were struggling with some mammoth beast that Felix couldn't quite make out. He got the impression of mass and violent movement, and a dark elf flew through the air and smashed against the wall, but it was too dark and congested in the corridor to see what had thrown him.

Felix paused. 'Do we find another way?'

'Any other way will be under water by the time we reach it, manling,' said Gotrek, and pressed on.

Felix looked down. The water was knee deep now. He followed with the others.

As they got closer the shapes became clearer. Druchii with whips were trying to lead a pair of massive reptilian beasts out of the gate towards the stair. Felix quailed at the sight of the monsters. He had never seen the like – lizards that walked on their hind legs, taller at the shoulder than a man. Their sinewy forelegs ended in cruelly hooked claws, and their heads were enormous bony things with spear-tip teeth gnashing in roaring, slavering mouths.

Gotrek chuckled dangerously when he saw them, and stomped forwards eagerly.

'Slayer,' said Felix, following unhappily. 'Now is perhaps not the time.'

'Don't fret, manling,' said Gotrek. 'Get along the wall, and be ready to run.'

Felix led Claudia and Max to the right wall, edging towards the confusion as Gotrek splashed openly down the centre of the corridor, shoving frightened druchii and slaves out of the way. The beastmasters didn't look around. They were too busy trying to control their charges, who seemed to have been driven to a frenzy by the noise, the rising water and the ground shaking and tilting beneath their feet. Already two of the trainers were down, one lying in a broken lump at the foot of the left wall, half-underwater, the other kneeling and holding a crushed arm close to his chest.

The others were hauling on long leads attached to the beasts' saddles and bridles while a few brave souls whipped them and shouted commands at them, trying to make them turn towards the stairwell. The beasts were having none of it, bellowing and whipping their heads around and snapping at anyone who came close.

Ten paces behind them, Gotrek crouched down, axe ready, then looked to Felix, Max and Claudia, continuing to inch along the wall in the shadows of the milling beastmasters. Felix nodded. He still didn't know what the Slayer intended, but they were ready to run from it, whatever it was.

Gotrek grinned in a worrying way, then turned back and charged, silent. The two closest druchii turned at his splashing steps, and died before they could open their mouths to scream. They went down in a spray of blood, the leads slipping from their hands.

By Sigmar, thought Felix. The lunatic is freeing the beasts!

Gotrek swung into two more beastmasters, chopping through their padded leather armour like it wasn't there. They collapsed into the water, screaming.

The giant lizards roared and turned towards the scent of blood, dragging their handlers with them. The beast-masters screamed and shouted. A druchii with a whip lashed at a monster's face. It lunged and snapped him in half.

Gotrek ran between the beasts, ducking under a massive tail, and pounded for the end of the tunnel. 'Now, manling! Now!'

Felix took Claudia's arm and propelled her forwards. Max ran with them, skirting the edge of the chaos as the beastmasters fled and fell before the rampaging monsters. One beast brought down two of them in a terrifying hop, then nosed in the water for their corpses. It came up with a head.

Felix didn't look back to see more, just splashed with Max and Claudia into the shadows again, the roars of the monsters and the shrieks of the eaten echoing in their ears.

'Well... well done, Slayer,' said Max, as they hurried on.

Gotrek snorted. 'I could wish the same for the entire race.'

By the time they reached the stairwell the water was hip deep – rib deep on Gotrek – and rising faster than before.

'The water appears to be sinking the ark,' said Max. 'The druchii's magic cannot support the added weight.'

'Then hurry,' growled Gotrek. 'There are twelve flights to this stair.'

They started up as quickly as they could, Felix half-carrying Claudia along with her arm over his shoulder while Gotrek did the same for Max. Even so it was slow going. The stairwell shook and twisted like a tent in a high wind, the walls and ceiling groaning and cracking and falling apart, making every step a challenge. At the fourth landing they had to climb over a portion of wall that had buckled and filled the landing almost to the roof, on the next flight there was a cavernous booming from above and they flattened themselves to the walls just in time to avoid being crushed by a massive boulder that bounced away down the stairs. Ominously, they heard it splash only a few flights below them.

A little further on, Felix felt Claudia staring at him and turned his head to her as they walked. 'Yes, fraulein?'

She looked away, flushing, but then, after a few more steps, she spoke up.

'Herr Jaeger,' she said. 'I have a confession to make.'

'Oh yes?' he said, as he helped her over a spill of rock.

'It is my fault that you were taken by the ratmen,' she said, and her lower lip trembled.

Felix frowned. 'I think you might be mistaken, fraulein. They had been following us from Altdorf. In fact, you might say they have been following us for twenty years.'

'You don't understand,' she said, hanging her head. 'I... I saw it. I saw the attack, before it happened. I saw you fighting shadows on the deck of a ship. I might have warned you, but...' She sobbed suddenly. 'But because you had... had spurned me, I... I was angry with you, and I decided I wouldn't speak!'

Felix stopped climbing the stairs and stared at her. 'You... you saw that I was to fall into the clutches of the skaven and said nothing?' His heart was pounding in his chest.

Above them Max and Gotrek paused and looked back.

'I didn't see that!' she wailed. 'I didn't see so much! Only that you would be fighting! I thought... I thought you might be hurt a little, or...' She faltered and sobbed again. 'I didn't think you would be taken away! I only wanted you to have a fright, a petty vengeance for your coldness. Oh what a fool I am! I thought I had killed you.'

Felix clenched his fists and started up the stairs again, pulling her more forcefully than necessary. 'You nearly did kill Aethenir,' he snarled. 'In fact he would most likely have preferred it. Those fiends tortured him, broke his fingers, cut into the muscles of his chest and–'

'Felix!' snapped Max, as Claudia went white. 'Enough!'

Felix turned to him. 'Enough? After what she's done? She should be charged with aiding the enemies of mankind! You didn't see what those vermin did–'

'She made a terrible mistake, Felix,' said Max, stepping in his way. 'A terrible mistake. It, more than anything the druchii have done to us, has tortured her mind and driven her to despair.'

'She deserves it,' grunted Gotrek.

'She does deserve it,' said Max. 'For it is part of the charter of her college that its students shall not use their powers for personal gain, or allow someone to come to harm by failing to warn them of danger. If we escape this nightmare and return to Altdorf, I will see to it that she is punished by the Celestial Order, and she has agreed to accept that punishment without complaint.'

'That's all well and good,' said Felix, not at all satisfied. 'But–'

'Did you not tell me once that you killed a man in a duel, Felix?' asked Max evenly.

'Yes, but…'

'Youth is a terrible time, Felix,' Max continued, 'as you may remember. A time when our strength and prowess often outstrip our ability to use them wisely. We may do a thing out of petulance or quick anger that we then regret for the rest of our lives – you your duel, Aethenir his Belryeth, Claudia her silence. But, given a chance, given the gift of forgiveness and a second chance by older, wiser heads, we may live long enough to learn from those mistakes, and make amends for them.'

Felix turned away, unable to let go of his anger. He had certainly done things in his youth that he regretted, but this... this was criminally irresponsible. The girl deserved more than just punishment. He should give her to the skaven. He...

'Come on, manling,' said Gotrek. 'A long way to go yet.'

Felix grunted, angry, but faced the stairs and started up them again, helping Claudia up as before, though he felt like leaving her to drown.

As THEY REACHED the seventh flight, there came a deep, muffled crack from the depths of the ark. It was followed by ominous thunderings and crashes that echoed from above and below and all around. Then the stairwell tilted, sending them all slamming into the left wall, and the stone around them groaned and splintered. Everyone froze and looked around, waiting for death to strike.

The howling reverberations that had been shaking the ark lessened slightly, as if some great pressure had been released, and in the relative silence they heard a noise coming from below them that turned Felix's spine into a column of ice – the gurgling and slapping of swiftly rising water.

Gotrek stood. 'The cracks have gone through to the bottom of the ark,' he said. 'Hurry.'

He started up the stairs with Max again, practically carrying the magister. Felix pulled Claudia up and they all fled up the stairwell as the water whispered and giggled at their backs, closer and closer with every step.

The water was faster. At the top of the flight, Felix turned and looked back. The dim light of Max's globe of light reflected on the ripples of black water at the bottom of the flight. He could see it moving, inching up the dust-powdered walls.

They ran on. The water closed the gap. At the eighth landing it was half a flight back. Ten steps later it was licking at their heels. At the ninth landing they were wading through it. Halfway to the tenth, it was up to their waists, and bitterly cold. It dragged at Felix's legs, slowing him and numbing his body.

As they rounded onto the eleventh flight, Felix had to keep his chin up, and was lifting Claudia out of the water so she could breathe. Gotrek was paddling as much as walking and Max was floundering weakly.

'We're not going to make it,' said Claudia.

Felix hoped it wasn't a prophecy.

He was on tiptoes as they came around the last landing and saw to his great relief the gate at the top, flung wide and abandoned by its guards. He felt with his toes for the submerged steps and pushed on. They reached the top neck and neck – quite literally – with the water, and slogged up out of it as it crested the top step and spilled through the open gate into the barracks corridor beyond.

Felix set Claudia on her feet and Gotrek helped Max to his.

'Keep moving,' said the Slayer. 'This will fill slower than the stairs, but it'll still fill.'

He strode through the gate and down the sharply tilted corridor towards the barracks like he was walking along the side of a peaked roof. Felix, Max and Claudia shambled after him, moaning with weariness. The rising water chased them as they went, running along the base of the left wall like it was a mill race.

The barracks area was deserted and destroyed, a chalky mist of rock dust still settling as they hurried through. Great portions of the roof had come down, and most of the barracks, cut into the solid rock, had caved in, their fronts fallen away to reveal collapsed floors and ceilings with bunks and chairs all fallen and smashed, the mangled bodies of slaves jumbled into the mess. But the truly terrifying damage was to the parade ground, which slanted away before them like they were walking down a hill. There was a jagged gaping crack running at a diagonal across it, the ground on the near side of the crack a foot higher than the ground on the far side. Out of the crack gurgled more water, racing away down the slanted ground. Felix looked up and saw that there was a corresponding crack running across the roof.

'It's going to split in half,' he murmured, swallowing nervously.

'Might sink first,' said Gotrek.

The Slayer picked up his pace, splashing quickly through the knee-deep water to the front gate – the gate that had cost him two gold bracelets to pass through only hours before. It had collapsed. The massive wooden doors lay shattered and askew between the ruins of the guard towers and gate house, with the cave roof fallen in on top of the lot – a solid mountain of rock. All the water from the crack in the floor was pooling here, rapidly hiding the doors and the bottom-most rubble.

'Trapped again,' said Max dully.

'Bah!' said Gotrek and started towards the right-hand guard tower, which was still semi-whole. There was a wooden door in its base, half-submerged in the water. He tried the handle, but the door was stuck in its frame, twisted from the pressure pushing down on it from above.

'Stay back,' said Gotrek, then slammed his axe into the door. The curved blade bit deep, and he kept chopping, ripping long chunks out of the door near the frame. Felix kept an eye on the tower above, afraid that the door was the only thing holding it up. Finally, Gotrek hacked a hole through it, then reached in and pulled. The door wrenched open with a splintering shriek.

Felix closed his eyes, expecting the whole structure to crash down and bury the Slayer. He should have known better.

'Come on,' said the Slayer, and waded into the tower.

Felix, Max and Claudia followed. The water at the door was up to Felix's waist, and got deeper within. Gotrek was up to his neck in it. Felix looked around. There was no other door in the small room. What was the Slayer doing?

'Up,' said the Slayer, and started up an iron-runged ladder set in the wall. Felix followed him warily up through a hole in the ceiling into another tiny room – this one studded with narrow arrow slots and completely crushed on the left side by the fallen cave roof. The walls that still stood did so only barely, the stones sitting precariously one atop the other with all the mortar turned to powder between them.

As Max and Claudia crawled up through the trap, Gotrek crossed to one of the arrow slots and kicked at the frame. Felix flinched back, expecting the ceiling to come down as the narrow window shifted and the wall around it crumbled, but once again the Slayer seemed to know what he was doing. A few more kicks and the stone frame fell out of the wall in one piece. An avalanche of mortared stone tumbled out after it, but to Felix's great relief, the roof stayed where it was. Gotrek stepped to the V-shaped hole he created and looked out. After a slight hesitation, Felix joined him.

The tower looked out over a lake where the wide plaza that fronted the barracks area had once been. On the far side was a broad arch that opened into the huge central stairwell that led both up and down to the other levels. The plaza was tilted at the same angle as the parade ground, and it was flooded with rapidly rising water – shallow at Gotrek and Felix's end, and deep near the stairwell, and filled with floating corpses. As Felix watched, the two witchlights that flanked the archway to the stairs were swallowed up, and glowed strangely from beneath the waves.

'Throw the seeress down to me, then jump,' said Gotrek. He stepped up into the gap and leapt down into the water with a big splash.

Felix turned to Claudia and motioned her forwards. Max led her to him, and Felix helped her up into the gap. She groped weakly at the edges, trembling and looking down. Felix shoved her. She squeaked and dropped out of sight, and there was a splash.

Felix looked guiltily at Max. 'Sorry,' he said.

Max shrugged. 'It had to be done.'

The magister stepped up into the gap and jumped of his own accord. Felix jumped a second later. Gotrek was already dog-paddling for the stairs. Felix then put Claudia's arms around his shoulders, and he and Max struck out after him.

Only a foot of the archway to the stairs was still above water as they began, and it was being swallowed up more quickly than they were swimming. Gotrek was a slow, awkward swimmer, Max was breathing like a bellows, and Felix, with chainmail on and Claudia clinging to his back, could barely keep his nose up. They had got no more than two-thirds of the way across, shouldering floating corpses out of the way all the while, when the arch vanished under the water.

'We'll have to swim down and back up,' said Felix.

When they reached the wall, Gotrek inhaled and dived. Felix pulled Claudia's arms tight and made her lock her hands around his neck.

'Take a breath and hold on,' he said over his shoulder.

He waited until he heard her suck in air, then plunged down beneath the waves. The glow of witchlights gave the scene a strange beauty. Even the bedraggled corpses that drifted half-submerged in the current looked graceful. Felix kicked down hard towards the submerged arch, and remembered just in time to kick down a little further so that he wouldn't scrape Claudia off his back when he went under it. With a final kick he was through and paddling for the surface again. Instead he cracked his head on a ceiling. He nearly yelped in surprise and terror, and he heard Claudia do just that. She started thrashing and kicking in terror.

He turned his head up and saw what had happened. He had come up in the landing. The ceiling was flat above him. The stairs up were to his left. He clamped down on Claudia's thrashing arms and kicked left as hard as he could, and at last they got out from under the roof and broke the surface, both retching and gasping for air. Gotrek was bobbing beside them.

Felix wiped the water from his eyes and looked around. 'Where's Max?'

Without a word Gotrek ducked back under the water and pushed back towards the submerged landing. He was no swimmer, but he had no fear of being under water either.

Felix paddled for the stairs where they rose up out of the water and helped Claudia out. She sat wearily on a step, her bald head bleeding from a dozen long scrapes.

'I'm sorry, fraulein,' he said. 'It wasn't intentional.'

She huddled over her knees, not looking up. 'You've done more than you should,' she said. 'More than I deserve.'

A moment later, Gotrek reappeared, spitting water and hauling Max to the surface. The wizard came up choking and coughing, and could barely drag himself up the steps when Gotrek pulled him over.

Gotrek climbed out and whipped his crest out of his eyes. 'Come on. Can't stop.'

Felix rose wearily and helped Claudia to her feet. Already the place they had been sitting was two feet under water. Max pushed himself up, swaying like a drunk. Gotrek stepped beside him and put the magister's around his shoulder again.

'On,' he said.

THE CENTRAL STAIR was broader than the barracks stair, and with higher ceilings, but the water seemed to rise just as fast. Again they were limping and cursing and stumbling with the water coming up behind them like some vast, silent snake, ready to swallow them, while the ark groaned and shuddered around them. At the harbour level they looked towards the docks, wondering if there might be an escape that way, but the corridor tilted down in that direction, and was filling rapidly with black water. Slaves and dark elves clambered up the slope towards them like they were running up a hill.

Gotrek snorted. 'Only elves would build a harbour inside a floating rock.'

They hurried on, joined in their flight by the slaves and the druchii alike – none, in their terror, paying them the slightest attention. More fleeing ark-dwellers poured out of the next level and the stairs were soon filled with a scrambling, surging mob.

Two flights later, as they rounded a landing in the middle of the panicked throng, Felix saw a sight he had never expected to see again – daylight. It shone through a great, columned archway – a warm, golden radiance that made even the cruel faces of the druchii and the gaunt faces of their slaves beautiful as they turned towards it. Felix thought he had never seen anything so wonderful in his life.

The crowd raced towards it like lost children running towards their mother, and Felix, Gotrek, Max and Claudia were borne along with it. At the top, they spilled into a square plaza, dominated by a black statue of a robed and hooded woman, and hemmed in by tall, sharp-roofed buildings. Beyond these Felix could see houses and temples and fortified walls climbing up a central hill towards the massive black keep that perched at the top of the ark – all of it tilted dizzyingly to the left. Streets radiated from the plaza at odd angles, but the druchii and the slaves were all running towards one that rose towards the upper reaches of the city, heading for high ground.

'Follow them!' said Gotrek.

He and Felix helped Max and Claudia to run with the crowd as the water bubbled out of the stairwell behind them and began to spread across the square.

But after only a few uphill turnings, Felix's earlier fears were realised as they came to a locked gate. This appeared to be a barrier between the merchant quarters and the enclaves of the highborn. A huge mob of druchii and slaves pushed at the sturdy iron gates, roaring for entry, while on the far side, guards with repeating crossbows fired into them and shouted at them to fall back. Even nobles and officers were being shot down in the guards' panic.

Felix and Gotrek paused and looked around as Max and Claudia leaned against them, gasping and catching their breath. There had to be another way. Perhaps they could climb to the roofs. As he turned, searching for an escape, he looked down over the lower quarters, spread out below them, and saw something that stopped him dead. Waves were slopping over the city's outer wall, and water was running down the inside. Felix stared. He hadn't thought the ark had sunk so far, but the ocean was spilling into it like water filling a ladle dipped into a bucket.

'Gotrek!' he said, and pointed.

Just as the Slayer looked around, the pressure from the water outside the wall became too much and it buckled exploding inward in a shower of stones and a towering avalanche of foam. The first breach quickly triggered others, and towers and curtain walls came down all along the west-facing side of the city.

The slaves and druchii in the square shrieked as the ground shook and tilted under their feet, then the shrieks became wails of despair as they turned and saw the ocean water surging through the city below them, levelling houses and toppling temples, and rising fast.

The crowd redoubled its efforts at the gates, and they bent inwards, but Gotrek turned away from them.

'Too late for that,' he said, starting down a side street. 'Come on.'

Felix followed after him dumbly. What could the Slayer do now? The water would rise and swallow them no matter where they went. There was no escape. Any high ground they could find would be under water in a matter of minutes. Again the mad plans of High Sorceress Heshor had left them to be drowned in a sunken city.

But the Slayer trotted down the tilted street regardless, looking around, as the thunder of the approaching water got louder and louder and the ground slanted more and more under their feet.

'Ha!' Gotrek said suddenly.

Felix looked up and saw a sturdy wooden cart filled with large casks dragging two terrified dray horses backwards across the sloping street as they bucked and kicked. The cart slid sideways into a house and came to rest as Gotrek ran to it.

'Here,' he shouted.

Gotrek wrenched down the cart's tailgate then climbed up. The casks were nearly as tall as he was. He glared when he saw dwarf runes branded into the wood.

'Filthy thieving elves.'

He stove in the top of one of the casks then tipped it on its side. The heady brew spilled down the street in a golden tide.

'In,' he said, rolling the cask off the cart and setting it on its end. 'Two of you.'

'Are you sure this will work?' asked Felix, hesitating.

'Just get in!' roared the Slayer.

Felix lifted Claudia into the cask, then climbed in awkwardly after her as Gotrek chopped through the top of a second cask and emptied it, then dropped it to the cobbles.

He jumped down into it. 'In, magister!' The sound of the approaching water was so loud now he had to bellow. Felix looked down the street. He could see it coming up the hill faster than a man could run, swallowing houses and carrying dark elves and slaves and tumbling debris with it as it rose.

Max started climbing feebly into the giant barrel.

Gotrek grabbed him by the scruff of the neck and pulled him in head-first. 'Get down!'

'It won't work,' cried Felix. 'We'll be smashed to pieces.' The black tide reached them.

Felix dropped down into the bottom of the barrel next to Claudia as he felt the water lift them and shove them down the street. The cart horses screamed as they and the cart were carried away. Felix's teeth snapped shut as the barrel smashed into something and rushed on. Another impact, and another. The barrel splintered. Water slopped into it. Claudia's knee cracked him in the jaw. He caught her and held her tight, as much to protect himself as to shelter her as they bounced around like dice in a cup. From all sides he heard shrieks and wails and juddering collisions, and always the water was lifting and throwing them around.

Felix looked up through the opening of the barrel and saw one of the massive walls of the highborn quarter rising above them and coming closer. They were being carried towards it by the water. Then a hand gripped the lip of the barrel. A dark elf face appeared, eyes round with fright. He tried to climb in. He was going to capsize them!

Felix let go of Claudia and punched the druchii in the face. He snarled and caught Felix's wrist. Felix rose up and punched with his other hand. The dark elf wouldn't let go.

Then suddenly the black wall filled his vision and they slammed into it. Felix fell back as the dark elf was mashed flat, his ribs snapping like sticks. He fell away screaming as the great wave receded and the barrel was swept back from the wall again.

Felix peeked over the lip as currents began to pull them this way and that, and saw the rooftops and chimneys of the merchant quarter disappearing below the crashing, spuming waves. Eddies and whirlpools whipped the refuse of the city around in a chaos of clutter. The barrel swirled around nauseatingly. Felix thought he saw the cask with Max and Gotrek in it, but then he was spun around and lost it again.

There was a crack like thunder above him and Felix turned and looked up. A massive castle-sized section of the retaining wall sheered off from the rest and slid down into the water, houses and people and furniture tumbling after it. A huge rolling swell rose up as the black cliff vanished in a towering splash, and Felix and Claudia's barrel was pushed even further away from the city.

Felix couldn't take his eyes off the demise of the ark. It sank more slowly than he expected, as if the dark elf magic that had kept it afloat for four thousand years was still fighting to support it, but it sank all the same, coming to pieces as it did. Knife-sharp towers crumbled and toppled, walls collapsed. Cracks ran up through the once-solid ground, ripping the mansions and palaces built upon it asunder with a sound like an endless cannon barrage. Dark elves and slaves were crushed by falling masonry or were swallowed by chasms that opened beneath their feet or fell screaming into the water. Felix felt the barrel being pulled back towards the ark by a powerful undertow as more of it was sucked under the waves and his heart raced. They were going to be pulled into the cataclysm and swallowed, and there was nothing he could do.

The temple level disappeared as they swirled closer, explosions of black fire erupting all over it, and great crackling arcs of purple energy leaping from building to building, shivering stone to dust wherever they touched. Felix swore he saw a river of blood pouring from the imploded ruins of a brass-walled temple and staining the water as it sank. An unearthly howling that sounded like neither man nor beast rose up to a hair-raising shriek, and then was cut off as if a door had shut.

The barrel was hit from behind as it rushed towards the sinking ark, then again from the left and the right. All the floating debris from the sinking city was converging towards the sucking centre, crowding the sea with bobbing, bumping junk and knocking Felix and Claudia this way and that.

They were close enough to see the eyes of the black stone dragons that were carved into the eaves of the roof, when waves finally reached the massive black keep, its proud, jutting towers still miraculously whole, but smoke rising in billowing columns from every window. Then, with a crack that Felix felt more than heard, the castle cleaved in half, jagged orange fissures appearing in its basalt flanks as the fire that raged within it was revealed.

The half closer to Felix sank more quickly, its towers toppling as it slid down into the sea to show blazing rooms and corridors and frantic silhouetted figures burning like paper dolls as they leapt into the water. The other half followed immediately, and suddenly Felix and Claudia's barrel was tilting down a surging hill of water as the tallest tower of the keep slipped down into the sea and disappeared into the centre of a swirling whirlpool. Felix saw a glossy black carriage heave up beside them and topple towards them as the vortex sucked them down, and he dropped back down into the barrel and clung to Claudia for dear life.

'Hold on, fraulein!' he shouted.

Then everything became a terrifying jumble of sound, motion and jarring impacts. Water swallowed the cask, whirling and slamming it around like a cork beneath a waterfall. Felix was upside down, then right-side up, crashing into Claudia, then mashed by her, all in the space of a second, unable to see anything but swirling bubbles, crashing water and flashes of waves, refuse and sky, as the cask was sucked under the pummelling waves. Bodies flew past in the water – men, women, druchii, horses, rats. Things slammed into the barrel, knocking it up, down and sideways. A human child caught the edge of it, looking pleadingly into his eyes, then was gone again before he could react.

The barrel filled with water as it went down and down. His lungs screamed for air and the world began to turn black and blurry at the edges. He wondered if they would be pulled all the way to the bottom of the sea, or smashed out of the barrel and crushed to death by whirling debris. He felt himself floating and pressed against the sides to keep himself in.

Then, long after it seemed possible that it could continue, the water began to calm, and he felt the cask slowly rising through the silt-clouded water. They broke the surface miraculously face-up, the top of the barrel almost level with the water. Felix pushed up and sucked air greedily, then realised that Claudia was still in the barrel, under the water. He reached down and hauled her up and she clung to him, choking and puking water down his chest and shivering.

He looked around at the mad scene around them, hoping to see the Slayer and Max. The sea in all directions was cluttered with ships and floating junk – barrels, boxes, planks, carts, wooden spoons, bits of clothing, papers, trash, what appeared to be a wig, and corpses of all races floated everywhere. To his left, three small druchii sloops were entangled, thrown together by the mad whirlpool of the ark's sinking. Further away, more black ships pulled swimming druchii out of the water, or fired crossbows into floating masses of pleading slaves while sea serpents, both mounted and unmounted, breasted through the rubbish and fed indiscriminately upon all.

Felix heard a splash and a familiar cough. He turned. Another barrel floated not far away, upside down! Was it the one?

'Gotrek!' called Felix. 'Max!'

Gotrek's head bobbed up next to the barrel, and he hauled Max up beside him and helped him cling to the cask. The magister was barely conscious, but he was alive. Felix shook his head in wonder. They had made it. They had survived. As impossible as it had seemed, they had escaped the black ark.

Then Felix heard a noise behind the moans, screams and shouts of the survivors and the 'hoog' of the serpents that sent a chill up his spine – the clamouring wail of the Harp of Ruin.

TWENTY

FELIX AND GOTREK looked around, searching for the hellish instrument amid the chaos of ships and trash and fighting. Then Felix found it. He blinked, confused, for it seemed to be floating about a yard above the water, as if it were somehow levitating. He looked closer and saw that the harp was hooked to a halberd, and that the halberd was strapped to the back of a dog-paddling skaven, who was heading right for them at the head of a cluster of swimming skaven. The water around them frothed with the thing's vibrations.

Gotrek pulled his axe from his back and shook it over his head. 'Come on, you vermin!' He roared.

But it seemed he might not be the first to reach the rat-men. Bearing down on them from behind was a phalanx of sea dragon knights, with High Sorceress Heshor mounted behind Commander Tarlkhir on the first. Heshor looked entirely healed from the wound the daemon had inflicted upon her. Tarlkhir spurred his mount and the serpent scooped a skaven out of the water and choked it down with a single gulp.

'Hoog!'

'Foul serpents!' cried Felix, drawing his sword.

Karaghul's runes were glowing brightly in the presence of so many sea dragons, and Felix could feel the urge to swim towards them welling up in him. His muscles twitched and tingled with barely controlled violence. He fought down his fury with difficulty. He had already fought a sea dragon while bobbing helplessly in the middle of the sea and hadn't cared for it much. Doing so floating precariously in a flooded beer keg with a half-conscious girl beside him was unlikely to be an improvement. Maybe the damned serpent would choke to death on the barrel, he thought.

But then, without warning, the cask rose up under him as if lifted by a hand. He swayed and clutched the lip of the cask. All around them the sea was mounding up into a hill of water.

'What in Sigmar's name?' he said.

Gotrek and Max and their barrel tumbled down the hill of water as it continued to grow, and Felix and Claudia's cask toppled with them, spinning end over end and plunging them under the sea again. Felix pushed and kicked out of the barrel, then took Claudia's arms and pulled her after him. Was the ark rising again? Did they have to do it all over again?

They came gasping to the surface and clung to a raft of debris beside Max and Gotrek as a massive rusted tower burst out of the mounded water, bristling with pipes, tanks and brass guns. Then, below the tower, a great bulk breached the waves – a verdigrised monstrosity like a scrap-metal whale, longer than a druchii galley, with a corroded metal deck and strange weapons jutting from a prow like a rat's snout. It loomed more than a storey above them, a barnacle-covered brass cliff, shedding water and hissing and blowing like a living thing.

The serpents reared back fearfully at the sight of it, fighting their riders' spurs, and in the distance, the cries of the druchii echoed from their ships, alarmed at the appearance of this massive threat in their midst. Felix could see galleys turning towards it, their ranked oars raising and pulling as one.

'What kind of machine is this?' asked Max.

'It is the thing that ate Felix and Herr Gurnisson,' said Claudia miserably. 'The thing that I allowed to take them.'

'A skaven submersible,' said Gotrek, spitting contemptuously.

Max grimaced. 'It reeks of warpstone.'

The swimming skaven clambered up the submersible's tall side as Tarlkhir's sea dragon snapped at them, ripping two away and chewing them in half. The other serpents lunged in behind the first, their heads snaking after the fleeing thieves. Skaven armed with rust-grimed swords poured out of a hatch and raced forwards to defend their brothers, then shied as the submersible began to vibrate like a gong when the black-clad skaven who carried the howling harp set foot on the deck. The water around the edges of the craft simmered and splashed as if it was on the boil.

'The harp is going to shake it apart,' Max said.

'Good,' said Gotrek.

Next out of the hatch was the ancient skaven sorcerer, hobbling forwards with the aid of its staff, and surrounded by a retinue of black-armoured vermin and followed by its albino rat ogre and its tottering tailless minion.

Felix found himself growling in his throat as he watched the black-clad thief hurry the grey seer. He was free, he had his sword, and the vermin that had hurt his father was before him.

'Him,' rumbled Gotrek. 'Come, manling. I owe him much.'

'Not if I get him first,' said Felix, and kicked for the side of the skaven submersible. Gotrek followed. Max did too.

Felix looked back. 'Maybe you should stay behind, Max.'

'There is too much magic there,' said Max. 'You will not prevail without me.'

Felix was more worried about Max prevailing. The magister looked more dead than alive.

'I will come too,' said Claudia, paddling after them.

'Claudia–' said Felix, but she shook her head.

'I must make recompense for my crime,' she said.

Felix was going to protest more, but then he shrugged. Was she really any safer clinging to a barrel in the middle of a sea full of sea dragons?

The black-clad skaven went down on one knee before the grey seer, the halberd strapped to its back extending forwards over its head to put the harp within the sorcerer's reach. Its fellow thieves knelt behind it.

'We did exactly what he wanted,' said Felix angrily as they reached the side of the submersible near its stern. 'We stirred up trouble with the dark elves and allowed his thieves to snatch the harp in the confusion. He's been pulling our strings since he freed us.'

'I am no one's puppet,' growled Gotrek, and began to climb the side of the submersible.

'Nor am I,' said Felix, as he, Max and Claudia followed, pulling themselves up the strange pipes, flanges and poorly fitted plates that made up the behemoth's skin. The metal was vibrating so much that holding it stung the hands.

The ancient skaven stared at the screaming harp, seemingly caught between horror and desire, as his minions edged away from it. The rat ogre moaned unhappily and covered its ears. The seer reached out a tentative claw towards it, but before it could touch it, a cloud of black fire exploded around it, staggering it. The skaven thieves dived away from the black flames with uncanny quickness, while the tailless minion fell back clumsily and the rat ogre howled, but many of the warrior skaven around the seer shrieked and died in the ebony fire, shrinking to charred skeletons within their armour. The seer squealed in agony and rage, but seemed to absorb the fire without damage. It turned towards the front of the submersible, where Heshor and Tarlkhir rode high on their sea dragon, surrounded by the other serpent riders.

The skaven sorcerer swept its staff in a circle and the air rippled before it, travelling out in a spreading arc towards the druchii. The sea dragons went mad, roaring and thrashing as if beset by wasps. They threw their riders and attacked themselves and each other, ripping their scaly hides with dagger teeth. Heshor and Tarlkhir were tossed into the sea as their knights screamed and tried to regain control of their mounts.

Karaghul howled for Felix to run and dive and slaughter them all. He ground his teeth, forcing himself to ignore the insistent call, and instead stepped with Gotrek, Claudia and Max onto the rattling deck of the submersible. There would be a time to unleash the sword's fury, but now wasn't it, and they weren't the targets. It was the ratman sorcerer he wanted to kill.

They crept towards the central tower as the loose plates of the submersible clanged and clattered in deafening harmony to the harp's howl.

The skaven seer returned its attention to the harp, which the thief again held before it at the end of the halberd. It threw its arms wide, shrilling a harsh incantation, and the air around the harp began to thicken, warping light and muffling its whine. Then the old skaven slowly brought its arms closer together, squeaking all the while, and the air between its paws grew thicker still, gelling like aspic, and the harp quietened even more. The seer trembled with the effort.

The rattling metal plate around Felix and the others calmed, and the deck under their feet grew still.

'Such power,' said Max, in wonder, as they watched from the shadow of the central tower. 'To quell so powerful a thing.'

'I'll still kill him,' snarled Felix.

The grey seer brought its paws together and the harp stopped ringing entirely. It reached out and took it from the halberd as easily as if it picked up a book.

The sudden silence was eerie. It felt as if Felix had been hearing the sound of the harp all his life and, with it gone, a weight he had carried since childhood was lifted off his shoulders. The cries of the dying, the slap of the waves, the rumblings from within the submersible, the roars of the sea dragons, all were clear and close, the chittering of the skaven and the shouting of the druchii knights loud in Felix's ears.

There were more distant cries too, and Felix saw that two dark elf galleys were sailing their way, their prows cleaving paths through the floating debris as their sweeps rose and fell.

The grey seer hurried back towards the hatch from which it had emerged, triumphant, surrounded by its remaining guards and followed by the shambling rat ogre and its scampering servant. Gotrek drew his axe and prepared to charge. Felix, enflamed by Karaghul's hate for the sea dragons and his own for the skaven sorcerer, fought the urge to run out ahead of the Slayer.

'Now?' he asked eagerly.

Just then the hatch cover trembled and slammed shut by itself with a loud clang, cutting in half a skaven who was just climbing out.

The other skaven fell back, frightened. The grey seer whipped around. Behind it, at the prow of the sub-mersible, Heshor floated up out of the sea, arms still extended from casting the spell that had closed the hatch, while Tarlkhir and his sea dragon knights clambered out more prosaically and surrounded her.

Still clutching the harp in its right paw, the skaven sorcerer snarled and shot spears of green light towards Heshor with its left. She threw up her hands and a shield of dark air flared into being in front of her and the green spears glanced away. She shot curling snakes of smoke back towards the seer and the battle was joined. Leather-clad sword-rats charged Tarlkhir and his knights. The albino rat ogre and the black-armoured skaven warriors remained at the seer's side.

'Now, manling!' roared Gotrek.

'Wait,' said Max, 'Let me provide you with some pro-tection...'

But Gotrek and Felix were already charging straight at the skaven sorcerer's back, roaring jubilant battle cries. Felix let Karaghul take full control and a red rage con-sumed him.

The armoured skaven turned at their roar, but not quickly enough. Gotrek's axe took the head of one, carved a trench through the chest of a second and hacked through the legs of a third. Felix cut down two more. The Slayer bellowed for the hulking rat ogre to face him. It obliged, roaring and raising battering-ram fists as it rushed to meet him. Felix leapt at three black-armoured skaven, trying to smash through them towards the grey seer.

The old skaven spun in mid-spell and shrieked at the sight of the carnage behind it. It raised a hand and began a new spell, this time directed at them. Felix felt a tingle and for a moment thought the worst, but then a sphere of golden light enveloped them and he realised that Max had completed his spell.

As Gotrek hacked at the albino monstrosity and Felix fought the armoured skaven, a flash of blinding un-light shot from Heshor and the skaven sorcerer hissed and twitched, blackness crawling over its body and invading every orifice. The seer stumbled, trying to force a counter-spell through grinding teeth.

Felix cut down two of the big skaven. To his left, Gotrek was in the grip of the rat ogre, which lifted him high over its head. Felix ducked a slash and parried another. When he looked back, the rat ogre was toppling backwards, Gotrek's axe blade deep in its skull. It hit the metal deck with a hollow boom and Gotrek wrenched his axe free, then bulled on towards the seer, who was still fighting Heshor's web of power. As Gotrek slashed at the ancient skaven, it shrieked and threw itself backwards. Gotrek's axe chopped through its wrist, severing it in a spray of black blood.

The grey seer screamed as the harp clanged away across the deck towards the dark elves, its right claw still gripping it. It fell to the deck, squeaking and clutching the bloody stump of its scrawny wrist as it turned terrified black eyes on Gotrek.

'Your head is next, vermin!' roared the Slayer.

A knot of skaven swarmed in to defend the grey seer. Gotrek charged into them.

'No, Gotrek!' shouted Felix. 'He's mine. He hurt my father!'

Felix hacked through the armour-clad skaven, trying to reach the fallen seer, but just then the black-clad skaven assassin leapt at him, stabbing with gauntlets from which jutted long metal claws.

Felix gutted the assassin as it crashed into him, its claws ripping red grooves in his back and chest. He threw it aside and joined Gotrek just as he decapitated the seer's last guard and loomed over the figure that writhed at the edge of the submersible.

'I would have to kill you a dozen times to cancel my debt with you, vermin,' said Felix.

'Once will have to do,' growled Gotrek.

Together they raised their weapons over the cowering grey seer, but suddenly, with a shrill squeak, its little lop-tailed servant leapt forwards and tackled its master over the side of the submersible and into the sea.

'Come back here!' shouted Felix.

Gotrek roared angrily. 'Face your death, coward!'

'Gotrek! Felix!' shouted Max, from cover. 'The harp! The druchii! The ships are getting closer!'

Gotrek and Felix turned reluctantly. The harp, with the old skaven's severed paw still clutching it, had awoken again, and was dancing and jittering in the middle of a crazed melee as the submersible began to shake anew with its resonance. Tarlkhir and his knights fought a horde of sword-wielding skaven over it, while to port and starboard, the two druchii warships ploughed ever closer. Felix swallowed. If they didn't get the harp now, it would be too late.

He and Gotrek started towards the harp, hewing their way through skaven and dark elves as they went, but Heshor wasn't about to let them close to it. She cried a foul phrase and beams of un-light shot at them. Max's golden sphere absorbed some of their power before popping like a soap bubble. The beams came on.

The Slayer cursed and threw up his axe. The beams parted around him, glancing off the blade and impaling the skaven around them, sending them squealing to the deck with blood pouring from their mouths, noses and eyes. Felix crouched behind the Slayer, but even so, horrible scything pains shot through his lungs and joints and nearly brought him to his knees.

Then a bright bolt of lightning shot past from behind him and struck Heshor. The high sorceress snarled and turned, shooting her black beams towards the tower where Max and Claudia hid.

Felix sent a silent thanks to the seeress as his pain eased slightly. He stumbled on with Gotrek, hacking through the mad scrum of fighting dark elves and skaven after the harp. It was a terrible thing to try to catch, for its vibrations made it impossible to pick up. The skaven that grabbed for it snatched their paws back in pain, only to be cut down by druchii who also could not hold it, and it skittered and slid back and forth across the deck as each side tried to grab it.

At last Gotrek and Felix hacked through a swarm of skaven and found the harp before them. Gotrek strode towards it as Felix defended his sides.

'No, dwarf,' snarled a voice.

Gotrek and Felix looked up. Tarlkhir and a handful of his sea dragon knights were advancing towards them.

'You have sunk our city,' Tarlkhir shouted over the noise of the harp. 'Vengeance demands that we bury yours.'

'You sank your own damned city,' said Gotrek. 'Calling daemons and playing with magic.'

The Slayer charged the druchii commander, axe held out to his side. Felix howled and raced in behind him, as Karaghul sang to him sweet songs of slaughter. He knew the knights were druchii elite. He knew they would kill him. But Karaghul didn't care, and so neither did he.

Fortunately, the sword seemed to lend him some of its arcane fury, and he found himself fighting with an unnatural vigour and speed. Even so, he could not break through the perfect guard of the two hard-eyed dark elves he faced, but neither could they break through his. Gotrek was facing the same difficulty. One on one with Tarlkhir he would undoubtedly have triumphed, but three other druchii knights fought him as well, and his flashing axe could only block as the druchii blades thrust in at him from all sides.

'Damned tricksy elves,' Gotrek rasped.

Felix could barely hear him over the harp's hellish wail. It was tearing the submersible apart. Hot steam was whistling up through ruptured metal plates. Felix fell back from one, scalded. He felt himself faltering. The energy flowing from Karaghul did not flag, but his body was so battered and worn out that it was having difficulty keeping up. His muscles screamed for rest and his lungs felt filled with hot sand.

Behind the knights, Heshor was preparing another spell. That would be the end, Felix knew – at least for him. He was not behind Gotrek's axe now, and Max's protective spells had collapsed. The black energy would rip through him undiluted this time and tear his insides to pieces.

At least, he thought, it was a good ending. At least he and the Slayer were going to die as they should – knee-deep in the slain, surrounded by enemies, fighting for the fate of the world after sending to the bottom of the sea a floating hell of depravity and oppression. At least this was as grand and epic as the Slayer could have wished. The Slayer had done everything Claudia had spoken of in her prophecy. He had fought in the bowels of a black mountain, he had fought foes without number, he had fought a towering abomination, and now he was going to die. It was right. It was fitting. He was content. If only he could have found out what had happened to his father before he died.

A juddering impact knocked him and everyone on the deck to the right. Then another crash threw them to the left. The combatants staggered and looked around. The druchii ships had arrived. On the left, a black galley was scraping against the side of the submersible, tearing up corroded metal plates as it ground to a halt. On the right another galley had crashed nose-first into the skaven craft, beaching itself on its deck and crashing into the tower in the centre. The submersible groaned and shuddered like a dying elephant.

Gangplanks slammed down from the galleys and scores of druchii corsairs poured onto the deck towards the combat.

Tarlkhir roared an order at them as he staggered to his feet, and the corsairs stopped reluctantly.

Tarlkhir faced Gotrek, his eyes blazing, while the Harp of Ruin jigged madly on the deck between them. 'This is not for the likes of them,' he said. 'Your death shall be mine alone.'

Gotrek shrugged. 'Suit yourself.'

The Slayer ran at Tarlkhir, swinging high. The druchii commander whipped his sword into a parry and Gotrek's axe scraped down it in a shower of sparks.

Gotrek slashed again, and Tarlkhir circled to the Slayer's left, his blind side. Gotrek had to turn quickly to keep his good right eye on him.

Tarlkhir lunged when Gotrek was on his off foot, and the Slayer had to duck out the way. One of Tarlkhir's knights raised his sword, but the commander shouted him back. Felix rose and went on guard, ready in case any of the other knights got ideas.

Gotrek charged again, his axe a steel blur as he drove Tarlkhir back. The ferocity of the attack stunned the dark elf and he began to lose his composure, parrying desperately and stumbling as he gave ground.

All around, the corsairs and the knights edged in. Felix swallowed, terrified.

'Even now you have failed, dwarf,' sneered Tarlkhir, as he fell back before Gotrek's assault. 'Kill me or no, we will still get the harp.'

'At least there will be one less elf in the world,' said Gotrek, and leapt forwards again, roaring.

Tarlkhir raised his sword to block, but Gotrek's axe sheared right through the black metal and swept on, splitting the commander's breastplate down the middle and burying itself deep in his chest. Blood welled up through the blued armour as Tarlkhir's eyes rolled up in his head.

Heshor wailed from the prow of the submersible. The corsairs cried out as well, then surged forwards to avenge their commander's death. Felix was so weary he almost welcomed the end.

Gotrek didn't even look at them. Instead he laughed and raised his axe above the howling harp. 'Now they all die!' he roared.

Heshor's wail turned into a terrified shriek. 'No!' she cried.

Gotrek slammed the heavy blade down on the hellish instrument with a deafening clang. The harp cracked and danced away, the ancient skaven's hand still gripping it, and weird purple light spilled from hairline fissures in its frame. Gotrek staggered back, covering his single eye, and Felix and the dark elves and the skaven were knocked off their feet. The discordant ringing quickly rose to a daemonic scream. The corsairs and knights scrambled back in fear. Behind them, Heshor shrieked, her face a white mask of terror, then turned and leapt into the sea.

'Felix! Gotrek!' called Max from the submersible's tower. 'Away! Into the water!' Then, following his own suggestion, he turned and ran, dragging Claudia with him.

'Come on, Gotrek!' called Felix, then sprinted after the magister and the seeress. He was joined in his flight by terrified corsairs and skaven, all running for cover from the spinning, spitting harp.

Felix ran towards the submersible's stern, then jumped into the water behind the galley and came up near Max and Claudia and the floating casks. He shook the water out of his eyes and glanced around. Gotrek wasn't with them.

'Gotrek?'

Felix looked back towards the submersible. The Slayer stood alone in the centre of the deck, lit from below by a terrible purple light, his axe raised, his feet braced wide on either side of the dancing harp as druchii and skaven dived away from him in all directions. Then, with a roar, Gotrek swung down again and chopped the harp in half.

'Down!' shouted Max, and shoved Claudia's head under the water as he dived down himself.

Felix ducked, the image of Gotrek vanishing in a flash of blazing purple light that was burned into his retinas as the water closed over his head. He felt a wave of heat and pressure pass through the water, and heard a deafening concussion like a clap of thunder directly overhead.

Seconds later he came gasping back to the surface and looked towards the deck. It was empty but for a raging purple fire where the harp had been, and crackling arcs of purple energy that crawled and leapt across the rupturing, steam-shot metal. Gotrek was nowhere to be seen.

'Did… did he escape?' said Felix, stunned. 'He can't have died.'

'He died,' said Max, looking in terror at the dancing purple energy. 'He has to have done. And killed us as well. The blast has agitated the warpstone on the skaven craft.'

'The aetheric winds are building,' said Claudia staring as well. 'It will not hold.'

Then, from above them, came a familiar groan.

Felix looked up. 'Gotrek?'

The druchii galley loomed over their heads. Gotrek's groan had come from somewhere upon it.

'Gotrek!' Relief flooded Felix's heart, and he began swimming towards the aft gangplank of the druchii ship.

'Felix!' called Max after him. 'We must get away! The submersible will explode!'

Felix swam on, ignoring him. How were they to get away anyway? Fly? There was nothing they could do, but if the Slayer was still alive, Felix knew he should be with him at the end. It was the fitting thing to do. He grabbed the gangplank and pulled himself up onto it, not daring to touch the surface of the glowing, shuddering submersible.

He ran up it onto the broad deck of the black galley, sword out, fully expecting to die fighting a crowd of corsairs as he tried to reach Gotrek, but the few druchii who had clambered back on board lay writhing and clutching themselves obscenely, their eyes mad and blind and their white skins burned pink.

Felix picked his way through them to the sterncastle as the rumbling and hissing from the submersible got louder and more violent, and found Gotrek at last by the aft rail, lying motionless on his side, both hands still holding his axe in a death grip. The Slayer looked ghastly. His one eye was rolled up in his head, his beard, crest and eyebrows were blackened and smoking, and the front of him was as red as a lobster, and steamed slightly. But the most extraordinary thing about him was his axe. It glowed a bright red from blade to pommel, and was as hot as if it had been pulled seconds ago from a forge. Smoke curled from the haft where Gotrek's hands clenched it, and it hissed and popped like fat on a fire. Felix smelled cooked meat.

'Gotrek? Do you still live? Can you stand?'

He looked back towards the skaven craft, then knelt beside the Slayer, to listen for his breathing. He paused when he heard footsteps coming up the steps to the stern deck, then stood. A powerfully built druchii with a short sailor's cutlass and a whip appeared, looking around cautiously.

Felix ran at him, hoping to kill him before he reached the deck, but the druchii lashed out with his whip and cut Felix across the thighs. His chainmail took the brunt of the blow, but it still stung, and he stumbled, nearly impaling himself on the dark elf's cutlass. Felix parried, and what had been a charge quickly became a retreat as the druchii gained the deck and forced him back.

Then a cry and a sudden burst of light made them both cringe. Felix dived away and looked towards the skaven craft, expecting to see it erupting, but it was not the submersible, it was Max, staggering up the gangplank with Claudia and shooting a stream of light at the druchii sailor. He shielded his eyes and swiped blindly at Felix, dazzled by the magical light.

Felix charged in and dispatched him in two quick strokes while he was still defenceless, then collapsed from exhaustion on top of him.

'Get below!' gasped Max. 'It's going to blow.'

'Will that save us?' asked Felix.

'I doubt it,' said Max as he led Claudia across the deck. 'But it's our only chance.'

The seeress trailed behind him, mumbling up towards the sky and pawing at the air.

She's gone truly mad this time, thought Felix, as he hurried back to Gotrek. Heshor's counter-spells must have crushed her mind. He hooked his hands under the Slayer's arms and pulled, but it was like trying to shift a bull. He was so weak, and the Slayer was so heavy. He hauled again, and moved Gotrek perhaps a foot, the glowing rune axe branding a smouldering black line in the deck. It would take him an hour to get him to the door to the lower decks.

He ran back to the rail that looked down to the deck. 'Max!' he called. 'Help me move the Slayer.'

His voice was drowned out by a wrenching crash and once again he flinched and looked towards the skaven craft, expecting the worst. Instead he saw the gangplanks twisting and tearing away from the galley as the submersible slid past, still glowing and shaking and crawling with purple lightning.

Max stared too, stepping towards the rail.

'They're sailing off!' Felix shouted, elated.

'No,' said Max. 'We are.'

The magister turned towards Claudia. Felix followed his gaze. The seeress was still mumbling at the sky, but now her arms were outstretched towards the galley's lateen sail, which was bellied out and straining full of a wind that existed nowhere else. They *were* moving, slowly still, but picking up speed, thumping through the clutter of debris that floated all around them as they went.

Felix ran back to the Slayer and hauled at him again. A moment later Max joined him, though in his weakened state he wasn't much help. Still they had to try. Every yard they sailed gave them a little more hope for survival. And if he could get the Slayer below the decks, his chances might be better still.

At last they got him to the top of the stairs. Max looked down them, then back to the skaven ship. 'There's no way,' he said, panting.

With a curse, Felix heaved Gotrek up and over, and pushed him down the stairs. The Slayer bounced down loosely and sprawled at the bottom, unmoving. Felix hurried down after him with Max close behind, and started dragging him towards the door.

The galley was beyond the swamp of floating garbage now and sailing past other druchii ships, which still circled the mess. There was nothing but open sea before them, and Felix began to hope that they might make it after all, when suddenly, with Gotrek's body still two yards away from the underdecks door, an enormous 'whump' of sound buffeted Felix's ears and a blinding green light blazed off the aft rail.

Max cursed and tackled Claudia to the deck as Felix threw himself down next to Gotrek. The magister shouted a terse incantation and a fragile bubble of golden light sprang into being around them. And just in time, for with an impact like a hammer, a hot wind slammed into the ship, spinning it around and heeling it over on its side.

Felix looked back and saw a huge cloud of glittering smoke racing towards them faster than a cannon ball. Then it was over them, as thick as mud, and pushed by a howling, oven-hot wind, filled with spinning bits of metal, wood and flesh. Bodies and spars and twisted metal plates smashed into the deck and punched holes in the sails and tore away the rigging.

Max's golden bubble kept out the smoke and the rain of glittering powder that skirled across the deck, but heavier things came through. A severed druchii hand slapped Felix in the face and nearly dislocated his jaw. A decorative silver candlestick flew past and smashed into the bulkhead behind them.

'Inside!' cried Max. 'Hurry!' He crawled for the door, the bubble of pure air moving with him.

Claudia dragged herself after him. Felix grabbed Gotrek's body under the arms again and hauled at it.

Max reached the door and threw it open, then shoved Claudia through. With strength born of desperation, Felix dragged the Slayer over the threshold, then collapsed in a heap behind him. Max shouldered the door closed again against the horrible hot wind, turned the latch and slumped against it.

'Are we safe?' asked Felix, raising his head.

Before Max could answer the ship rose beneath them as if it were the *Spirit of Grungni*, and for a moment Felix felt almost weightless. Then they crashed down again with a colossal impact and Felix and the others were thrown about the little corridor like rag dolls. Felix crashed head-first into a cabin door, them slammed back down to the deck as water poured in under the deck door and dripped down from the ceiling.

The last thing he saw before he lost consciousness was Gotrek's massive chest rising and falling. Ah, he thought. So that's all right.

Then all went black.

WHEN HE WOKE again, Felix was still in the cramped, ebony-panelled corridor of the dark elf war galley, and the others were still lying around him as they had been when he had passed out, but some things had changed. The ship was still. Water was no longer coming under the door, and no wind howled around them. In fact, there was hardly any noise at all.

Felix tried to sit up. His body refused, every muscle screaming with agony and his head throbbing and spinning. After several more tries, he finally managed it, then went about the even more complicated process of getting to his feet.

A minute later, with the assistance of the walls, he had done it, and he tottered slowly and painfully to the door, stepping over Max and Claudia's unconscious bodies as he went. He pulled it open and stepped cautiously onto the deck. It was a sight to behold, blackened and shattered and strewn with bodies and wreckage flung there by the submersible's explosion. The mast was snapped off halfway up its length, and the broken end hung over the port rail, the sail drooping into the water.

He stepped past it and looked out over the sea. Except for the climbing pall of smoke blotting out much of the northern horizon, it was a beautiful late autumn afternoon. The sun was setting in the west. There was a light breeze from the south east and the ocean was blue and empty in every direction for as far as he could see.

He shook his head in disbelief. Somehow, incredibly, they had survived – a thing that had seemed impossible almost since they had left Marienburg a thousand years ago. And not only had they survived; through luck, strategy and Gotrek's single-minded determination to die well, they had succeeded in averting the disaster that Claudia had foretold. The Harp of Ruin was destroyed, and the plans that the druchii and the skaven had had for it were foiled. Marienburg would not be swept away. Altdorf would not be flooded. The Empire and the Old World would not fall – at least not from this cause.

Of course, though they had survived and succeeded, many had died too. Around him on the deck, amidst the twisted wreckage, lay dozens of twisted corpses – the remains of the corsairs, their slaves, and the scrawny, furred bodies of skaven – all with their flesh half-eaten away by the glittering poison that had rained down from the smoke of the submersible's explosion.

And these were only a few of the dead. Aethenir, Rion and his house guards, Max's Reiksguard escort, Farnir, his father Birgi, and thousands more. A whole city had died – and not just wicked druchii, but human, dwarf and elf slaves and prisoners, not all of whom had given their lives willingly for the cause. Felix tried not to feel guilty for this horde of ghosts. It certainly hadn't been him who had enslaved them, or who had woken the deadly instrument that had shaken the floating island to pieces, but once again, had he and Gotrek not been present, they would not have died. On the other hand, had he and Gotrek not been present Marienburg *would* have died, and Altdorf drowned – hundreds of thousands dead instead of a few.

And there might be one more dead.

The moment he thought it, his heart thudded in his chest and he wanted instantly to be home. His father. He had to learn what the vile skaven had done to his father. He had to discover if the old man were alive or dead.

The thought brought him out of his reverie and he looked around. The galley drifted quietly, its mast broken, its sails slack and torn. Much of the rigging was hanging in tangled ruins. He stepped to the rail. He could see no land in any direction. They had survived, yes, but how were they to get home? How could two men, a dwarf and a not particularly handy young woman sail a dark elf galley back to the Old World? Even if any of them knew how to sail it would be impossible. There were too many things to do at once. They would need a whole crew.

The thought brought him up short. Perhaps they had one. He turned and climbed painfully to the sterncastle. There he found the druchii with the whip and the cutlass, or what was left of him. He pulled the ring of iron keys from his belt – the corroded leather tore like tissue – then hurried as fast as his battered body would take him back down the stairs and into the bowels of the ship.

He found them in the dank, sweat-grimed hell of the rowers' deck, and for a wonder, most of them were still alive – the only dead being those closest to the oar holes where the poison cloud must have blown in. Those that still lived looked up from their oars as he unlocked the latticed iron door that imprisoned them, and stared when they saw that he was human. They were a gaunt, haggard lot – men and dwarfs with dirt-blackened, whip-scarred skin and dreadlocked hair and beards, all chained at the ankle to the hard wooden benches that rose in tiers along the length of the galley.

'Greetings, friends,' said Felix as he stepped to the first iron padlock and opened it with the key, 'Do any of you know how to sail a ship?'

* * *

GREY SEER THANQUOL sat chest deep in water in the bottom of a leaky ale cask in the middle of the Sea of Chaos, contemplating the follies of ambition as his servant, Issfet Loptail, bailed water using a druchii helmet for a bucket.

For almost twenty years Thanquol had longed for only one thing, vengeance on the tall yellow-furred human and the mad red-furred dwarf. For almost twenty years he had nursed his hatred for the pair and dreamed of new and more creative ways of dismantling them body and soul. And after twenty years he had had them at last. They had been at his mercy. He might have done anything he pleased with them.

But then the words of that vainglorious prick-ear, the tale of the Harp of Ruin and what it could do, had set his mind to thoughts of position and power and the rightful return to his former rank and privilege. And like a human in a maze who drops one piece of meat for a bigger piece of meat and in the process loses both, he had let go of his nemeses, used them to confound the druchii and steal from them the harp, and just when everything seemed to have gone according to plan, he had lost it all.

The human and the dwarf had escaped him, the harp had been destroyed, the submersible, surely the most glorious invention in the long history of skaven innovation, and which he had hired at great expense and with many promises of political favours from Riskin of Clan Skryre, had been blown to dust, and... and...

He looked at his tied-off right wrist, the ragged stump already healing due to his sorcerous ministrations. The dwarf would pay for this painful, humiliating maiming. He would never stop paying. Though Thanquol had nothing now, having squandered all his coin and influence hiring the submersible and Shadowfang's night runners, he would rise again. He would amass wealth and power and influence, and when he had it, he would reach out his remaining claw and crush the vicious, black-hearted dwarf to a pulp, but not before tearing off his disgusting pink limbs one by one, as if he were a fly.

'What now, oh most bereft of masters?' asked Issfet as he dumped the last of the water out of the cask and leaned, panting, against its rim.

'What now?' snapped Thanquol querulously. 'What else, fool? Start paddling, quick-quick!'

THE COMPLETE GOTREK

ISBN 978-1-84416-374-8

Buy all these titles or
read free extracts at
www.blacklibrary.com

ISBN 978-1-84416-417-2

& FELIX SERIES

ISBN 978-1-84416-261-1

ISBN 978-1-84416-391-5

ISBN 978-1-84416-509-4

Have you read
them all?

WARHAMMER

OATHBREAKER

NICK KYME

ISBN 978-1-84416-543-6